THE STAG WEEKEND

THE STAG WEEKEND

MIKE GAYLE

HODDER &
STOUGHTON

First published in Great Britain in 2012 by Hodder & Stoughton
An Hachette UK company

2

Copyright © 2012 Mike Gayle

Hardback ISBN 978 1 444 74282 4
Trade Paperback ISBN 978 1 444 70859 2

Typeset in Benguiat by Hewer Text UK Ltd, Edinburgh

Printed and bound by Clays Ltd, St Ives plc

Hodder & Stoughton policy is to use papers that are natural, renewable
and recyclable products and made from wood grown in sustainable forests.
The logging and manufacturing processes are expected to conform
to the environmental regulations of the country of origin.

Hodder & Stoughton Ltd
338 Euston Road
London NW1 3BH

www.hodder.co.uk

For the girls

Acknowledgements

Thanks to Simon Trewin and all at United Agents, Steve Brayford (for research duties), Chris McCabe, Merel van Beeren (for the Dutch lessons), and above all, to C, for pretty much everything.

Friday

1.

'Shouldn't you be packing?'

Phil Hudson furtively covered the open notepad in which he had been scribbling at the kitchen counter with a nearby tea towel and swivelled around on his stool to face his fiancée.

'When did you come in?' he asked as she stared intently at him from the doorway, two carrier bags of shopping in her hands.

'Just now.'

'I didn't hear you.'

Helen eyed Phil suspiciously. 'You weren't meant to. And just so you know, once we're married be prepared to see more of me popping up in places you aren't expecting me to be. I'll be everywhere. I promise you.' Having clearly amused herself, she chuckled and set down the bags on the table. 'What were you doing anyway? Isn't the boy Simon meant to be picking you up at ten?'

'That's what he said.'

'So you're all packed?'

'I made a start but couldn't find half the stuff I needed. I think we need a system.'

3

'A system?'

'Yeah, a system, you know, so that we both know where stuff is without having to ask.'

'We already have a system you big goon!' snapped Helen. 'How do you think I find the things we need every day? What you actually mean is that *you* don't understand the system because whenever I try and explain it, you do that thing that I hate where you make out you're listening but are in fact doing the opposite.'

'Like when?'

'Like when what?'

'Like when wasn't I listening?'

'Er . . . let me think . . . perhaps it was the last time you told me that we needed a system! Or the time before that, oh and the time before that too!'

Fun though it was, Phil reasoned that he had probably wound Helen up enough for the day and so applying his best cheeky chap grin, he walked over, put his arms around her waist and kissed her. 'But you love me really don't you? he said, approximating a suitably coquettish eyelash flutter.

'You know I do,' she smiled, 'but don't think for a minute that it's a get-out-of-jail-free card, okay?'

'Wouldn't dream of it.'

'Good.'

Phil started to rummage through the carrier bags. 'What have you bought? Anything nice?'

Helen shrugged. 'Nothing much. Just a few bits and bobs to make sandwiches.'

Phil plucked out a packet of pre-sliced Gouda cheese. 'Sandwiches for what?'

Clearly embarrassed Helen snatched the cheese from Phil leaving him to answer his own question. The penny dropped. 'You're planning to make sandwiches for me aren't you?'

Helen glowered.

'You do realise,' began Phil, 'that making sandwiches for me to take on my stag do is adorable, don't you? I mean it's something a Disney character might do, if, say, Disney characters' fiancés were the type to go on stag dos to Amsterdam. Right now you should have cartoon bluebirds flying around your head and animated squirrels at your feet.'

Helen scowled. 'You don't have to have them if you don't want them,' she said narrowing her eyes at him. 'I could just as easily put it all in the bin if you're going to be all smart-arsey about it!'

Phil once again took Helen in his arms and kissed the top of her head in a manner he hoped she would interpret as playfully patronising rather than, as it was, a demonstration of his deepest and most true affection for her. He loved this woman, and the idea that she was going to be his wife thrilled him to his core. 'Smart-arsey? Me? Never. Of course I'll take them. I'll take them and proudly eat them on the plane and when all the boys are mocking me mercilessly I will ignore their abuse secure in the knowledge that while their other halves – if they have them – have sent them to Amsterdam without so much as a KitKat, mine has kitted me out with . . .' Phil paused while he checked the contents of the carrier bags, 'Wagon Wheels, satsumas, ham, a large packet of Starburst and . . .' he paused glancing over at the confiscated cheese, 'let's not forget Gouda sandwiches. You are undoubtedly a nutter, my sweet, but I honestly would not – for a single second – want you any other way.'

Helen reluctantly kissed Phil and then set about unpacking the bags. As she turned her back in order to put some of the shopping in the fridge, Phil retrieved the notebook from under the tea towel and tossed it casually on top of a pile of magazines on the counter next to the microwave.

'So,' said Helen returning from her trip to the fridge. 'What were you doing in here?'

'Doing?'

'Yes,' she replied as though Phil was hard of hearing, 'doing. As in "What were you doing in here when I came in?" '

'I wasn't *doing* anything,' said Phil. 'I came in for a glass of water and stayed a moment or two to ponder the nature of my own mortality.'

'Where's the glass?'

Phil stared at the counter as if expecting to see the glass that he knew full well wasn't there. 'Oh, that, I washed it up.'

'You're telling me you came into the kitchen, poured yourself a glass of water, drank the water and *then* washed up the glass?'

Phil maintained an air of innocence even though it was apparent that he had been well and truly caught out.

'Now I know you're lying. You've never used a glass and washed it up straight away in the entire time we've been together. What's going on?'

Any excuse Phil might have offered would be torn apart by Helen in a matter of seconds, but he was saved by the sound of his mobile phone's ringtone – one more suited to signalling to the crew of a World War Two battleship to man battle stations.

'Hey you,' said a female voice. 'I'm at work. Got a full day ahead but I just thought I'd check in before you get off.'

Helen silently mouthed: 'Who is it?' in his direction and he mouthed 'Caitlin' in reply. Helen's response was to go cross-eyed, stick her tongue out and mime self-strangulation.

For reasons that Phil had never been one hundred per cent sure of, Helen and his younger sister Caitlin had never got on. Yes, maybe in the vague realms of the past there had been some hard feelings over him choosing to go out with Helen instead of reuniting with his sister's friend Beth, but that had been a long time ago. Even with insider knowledge of the women with whom he had shared his life, Phil couldn't believe a regular human being could hold a grudge that long. There must be something more to their antagonism, something on one level to do with him but on another nothing to do with him at all, and everything to do with some kind of mysterious feminine primeval power play.

7

'Hey, sis! How's it going?' said Phil seizing the opportunity to take both himself and his conversation out of the kitchen and into the hallway. 'All ready and packed for your weekend of luxury in Ashbourne?'

'Did it all last night but I'm actually not due to arrive until Saturday morning.'

'How come?'

'Too much on at work.'

'But aren't all the other girls arriving tonight?'

Caitlin sighed. 'Come on Phil, you know what Friday night traffic is like. Plus, I've got a hair appointment, sort of a pre-wedding job. Got to look good for those photos!'

Phil didn't laugh.

'What?'

'You know.'

Caitlin tutted loudly. 'Not this again! I've promised that I'll try harder with her. Isn't that enough?'

'Well actually, no,' snapped Phil glancing over at the kitchen door, 'not unless you follow through with it.' He lowered his voice. 'Look, Helen inviting you on her hen weekend is her way of saying that she wants to make a fresh start. Surely the least you could do is meet her halfway by not turning up late for her hen weekend?'

'Listen to yourself!' snapped Caitlin. 'She's got you so wrapped around her little finger that you don't even know it! Less than a couple of minutes into what was supposed to be a pleasant phone call to wish you well for the weekend it's an argument with you taking her side over mine!'

The Stag Weekend

Phil had heard this accusation many times before and he was having none of it. 'Oh come off it Cait, what are you, six? It's not a question of me taking sides. I just want the two of you to get along, that's all. This time next week, whether you like it or not, she'll be family and I want you both to make the effort.'

'So you'll be giving her a stern talking to as well I hope?'

Exhausted at the prospect of this war between Caitlin and Helen carrying on throughout his married life Phil sat down on the stairs and rubbed his eyes. He didn't want to be having this conversation so early in the morning and certainly not at the beginning of a weekend that would see his fiancée and his sister spending the weekend together without him present to act as referee. He needed to make peace with Caitlin if only because it fell to him as her older brother to lead by example. 'Look, I'm sorry, okay? You're right. I shouldn't have doubted you. You turn up when you can and I'll keep my big nose out of it. So are we good?'

'Of course we are,' reassured Caitlin. 'We're always good. So come on then, tell me more about your plans for the weekend. How raucous is it going to be? Bit different from Helen's weekend.'

'It's a stag do in Amsterdam,' sighed Phil, 'How good can it be?'

'You're not looking forward to it?'

'It's not that. It's just I'd rather stay at home.'

'But I thought it was going to be a no strip clubs, no coffee houses, strictly classy affair.'

'That's how it was sold to me. But you know what the

9

boys are like. On their own they're fine but together they're experts at whipping each other into a frenzy. Put them in a place like Amsterdam and well . . . pretty much anything could happen.'

They talked for a while longer about arrangements for the wedding but Phil's heart wasn't in it. Ending the call with one last plea to Caitlin to be on her best behaviour, Phil returned to the kitchen where Helen was standing over a chopping board making the very sandwiches for which he had earlier mocked her.

'What's up with the little princess now?'

'Nothing,' said Phil leaning on the granite counter top, 'she was ringing to wish me well for the weekend. She sends her love by the way.'

Helen rolled her eyes. 'I bet she does,' she said sarcastically. 'Is it too late to beg you to take her with you? I'm sure the boys won't mind having someone as glamorous as your sister about.'

'I couldn't think of anything worse. It's all I can do to stop them drooling over her whenever they see her.'

'Well, she's coming with me so you're safe on that score. Not that any of your mates would be up to her usual standard anyway. What was it the last one did for a living?'

'I don't think he actually *did* anything,' replied Phil. 'He was always whisking her off somewhere exotic in a bid to impress her, seemingly oblivious that when it comes to blokes my sister takes being unimpressed to such a high level that it's practically an art form.'

Helen sliced through the sandwiches she had just

made and looked up at Phil. 'Do you think she'll ever settle down?'

'Who knows?' said Phil helping himself to a sliver of pre-sliced Gouda. 'Maybe if she bags herself a minor royal. But until then I think it'll strictly be the handsome and the unattainably rich that do it for her.' He took a huge bite from the cheese, chewed and then folded up the remains and dropped it into his mouth.

'You'll give yourself indigestion,' said Helen moving the cheese out of reach.

'Maybe,' said Phil, 'but the thought of you and Caitlin carrying on the way you do is absolutely guaranteed to do so.'

'So that was what the call was about? Her complaining about me? What am I supposed to have done now? Dared to breathe while in her presence?'

Phil walked over to Helen and put his arms around her. 'Come on you, I know she's a pain in the arse sometimes, I know you haven't exactly got much in common but will you find a way to make this weekend work? Just for me? I don't know whether it's that I won't be there to pull the two of you apart if it comes to blows, but I've got a horrible feeling that this weekend is going to be make or break for you.'

'It'll be fine,' said Helen. She kissed his neck. 'I promise, I'll be on my best behaviour and no matter what she says or does I won't let her get to me.'

Chuckling to himself, Phil sneaked a final slice of cheese and retreated to the bedroom to recommence packing for the weekend.

2.

Phil dropped three pairs of Calvin Klein briefs into the bag and hovered over it staring at them. Were three pairs of pants enough to cover all manner of potential underwear emergencies? Deciding to err on the side of caution he added an extra pair and then picked up his trainers from the floor and dropped them in too. A couple of pairs of socks were next, then he walked over to the wardrobe and picked out three white shirts, three casual tops and his favourite jeans. Placing them on the left-hand side of the bag, he picked up the sheet of paper that had been lying on the opposite side and began to read.

The print-out in his hand was an email Simon, his best man, had sent to everyone listing everything needed for the weekend. Phil had received the list earlier in the week and had scrutinised it carefully in an attempt to deduce what its contents might reveal about the secret plans his friend had organised for the weekend. The list included: 'clothes suitable for an outdoor sporting activity', 'a valid UK driver's licence', 'enough Euros to cover two days of solid drinking', and a demand that everyone should sort out some form of

12

insurance because 'A guaranteed way to put a dampener on the whole weekend is to have to fork out for a medical helicopter out of the beer kitty when one of us knocks himself unconscious.' The stand out item on the list, however, (written in bold with certain sections highlighted with capitals for added emphasis) was the mention of a black suit, black tie and at least three white shirts. Phil had emailed Simon to find out the reasoning behind these items and was rebuffed with the not altogether reassuring response of: 'All will become clear.'

Phil tossed the list back on to the bed and continued packing. He grabbed a final pair of briefs before making his way to the bathroom for a shower.

While he waited for the water to warm up he looked at his watch. A week and a day from this exact moment he would be getting ready for his wedding. He swallowed hard at the thought but when he looked up at the mirror in front of him, he had a huge grin on his face.

Half an hour later, showered, shaved and dressed, Phil, feeling not unlike a secret agent and/or contract killer in his black suit and tie, descended the stairs carrying his weekend suitcase to the sound of raucous laughter from his best man.

'And here he is! The man of the hour!' trumpeted Simon as the two men exchanged man hugs. 'Are you all ready fella?'

'As I'll ever be.'

Helen looked Phil and Simon up and down. 'What do

you two look like in those suits? Are you going to tell me what the whole get up thing is all about?'

Phil shrugged. 'You're asking the wrong man.'

'My attempt to set the right tone for the weekend,' explained Simon. 'Amsterdam is going to be full of boys doing the stag weekend thing. But we'll be the only ones working the *Reservoir Dogs* look the whole time.'

Phil laughed. 'And the only ones arguing about who's not going to be Mr Pink – which given it's my stag do is most certainly not going to be me.'

'Si was just telling me the story of the stag night you organised for him back in the day,' said Helen. 'Apparently you didn't need themes back then. Just beer money and an evil imagination. I can't believe how awful you lot were to him.'

'We were young and over excited,' explained Phil. 'He was the first of our lot to get married. To be fair I actually think he got off quite lightly.'

'It's true,' said Simon. 'My middle brother got hitched the year after me and his mates practically tortured him for the whole of his stag do. At one point they were threatening to strip him naked and abandon him in the middle of Brighton and it was only when I intervened that they settled for shaving off one of his eyebrows instead. You should see his wedding photos – they are the funniest things ever – I think some of them are on YouTube if you can be bothered to look for them. One of his mates uploaded them as an anniversary present a few years ago and put them on a video set to the music of Johnny Cash. Even now whenever I hear the opening bars of "I Walk the Line" I'm practically doubled over with laughter just thinking about his face with a drawn-on eyebrow. He looked like one of the missing Marx Brothers! His missus went mental and didn't talk to any of us for a good half year after the big day.'

Helen threw Simon a wary glance. 'I take it you've got all that out of your system now? It's not like you're in your twenties any more.'

'True,' sighed Simon. 'More's the shame. I could do with a laugh.'

Phil raised an eyebrow. 'Everything okay?'

Simon shrugged. 'Got a lot on at work. It'll all get sorted but it's just a bit of a pain in the arse when you're stuck in the middle of it. Anyway, nothing could put a dampener on this weekend. And I do mean nothing. I don't want to oversell it, mate, but if this weekend doesn't make it into your all-time top ten great times I will happily resign as your best man and let Degsy take the lead role.'

'Well,' Helen butted in, 'it better had be the weekend of your life because I promise there is no way that I'm going to let Degsy have anything to do with the main ceremony. He's not all there, that boy.'

Phil protested. 'That's a bit harsh, babe. He's just a bit special that's all.'

'The last time I saw him he licked the inside of an ash tray because one of you lot bet him that he wouldn't.'

15

'And that makes him not all there? He's just a man who likes a challenge.'

'Well, challenge or not, he's not going to be your best man. There's no knowing what he'd do.'

Phil looked at Simon. 'She's right you know. A lot of family and friends would have to die before I'd even consider him and even then I'd still pick a total stranger over him much as I love the guy.'

'Cool,' said Simon, 'then it looks like I'm going to have to stick to my word and pull off the single most amazing weekend of your life.'

'No pressure there then.'

'None at all.'

Phil and Simon first met each other back when they were teenagers working as Saturday sales assistants in Sharper Sounds, a Hi-Fi shop in the middle of Derby city centre. Phil hadn't been all that keen on Simon to begin with mainly because Simon had seemed so much more different from himself than most people he knew. Simon spoke with what to Phil sounded like a posh accent, lived in a big house over in Strutts Park and went to a nearby grammar school while Phil spoke with a Derby accent, attended a local comprehensive and lived on the Brandswood estate where pretty much every shop bar the local chip shop had grilles over their windows. And although they had shared many things from music through to the kinds of girls they found attractive Phil couldn't imagine how they might ever become friends who saw each other out of the shop, but that's exactly what they did.

Years later when Carl, the owner of Sharper Sounds announced that he was putting the shop up for sale the two men went to the pub to discuss the news.

'You should buy the lease and take over,' suggested the recently graduated Simon. 'I'll help you put together a business plan. It'll be a doddle.'

'Thanks but no thanks,' replied Phil who in the intervening years had worked his way up to assistant manager of the shop. 'It's too big a risk. I've seen the books, you have no idea how close the shop has come to closing in the past.'

Knowing that owning the shop had always been Phil's dream, Simon refused to take no for an answer and Phil finally caved in, funnelling all his savings and those of his mum into a year-long lease. Within six months of signing the paperwork he produced the most profitable financial quarter in the shop's twenty-two-year history.

Phil in return had over the years been equally as good a friend to him, not only bailing finance manager Simon out of his innumerable scrapes and situations brought on by his own recklessness, but he was also responsible for introducing him to Yaz, the woman who would one day become his wife.

At the time in question Phil and Simon had both been single and desperate for a holiday, and so when Simon had suggested that they should both book a week off work and fly off somewhere warm Phil had leaped at the chance, and within a short space of time they found themselves heading off for a last-minute break to Crete.

On their first night out at the resort while sitting in a bar near their hotel that overlooked the beach Simon spotted two girls walk in, one of whom he claimed to be the most beautiful girl he had ever seen.

'You should talk to her,' encouraged Phil. 'What's the worst that could happen?'

'I could find out that she's going to start work at my place and have to sit opposite her in meetings all day,' replied Simon who had recently had his confidence knocked after after being turned down by someone he fancied at work.

With no other option available Phil did the only thing he could think of and downed the remains of his beer glass, walked over to the girls and making it clear to Yaz that he was interested in her friend, talked the girls into joining him and Simon for a drink at a different bar further along the strip.

Three bars and a visit to a nightclub called the Frisky Palace later and Simon was getting on like a house on fire with Yaz, and things continued in that vein on their return home to England. After five years and a move for Phil from Derby to Nottingham they were getting engaged and throwing a party to celebrate, an event which in itself would change Phil's life because it was there that he met Helen for the first time.

'Right,' said Simon setting his empty mug down in the sink. 'I think we should probably be getting off. I know it doesn't take that long to get to the airport but I got caught out a few weeks ago trying to catch a flight to

Düsseldorf because of a pile-up two junctions before the motorway exit. Missed the flight, the next one wasn't until early afternoon and that was fully booked so I ended up having to travel the following day and staying twice as long to reschedule all the meetings I'd missed.'

Phil laughed. 'To be fair, mate, the way you've been talking up this weekend I'd be more than a bit relieved to miss the flight. Right now the idea of being stuck in Nottingham for the weekend is looking pretty attractive.'

Simon shook his head in dismay. 'You, my friend, are the queen of old ladies. I promise you, sunshine, this'll be the last time I'm lowering my standards to be your best man.'

'I should hope so,' said Helen. She hugged Phil tightly. 'I mean it Simon,' she said looking stern. 'I will hunt you down like a dog if anything . . . and I do mean anything *at all* untoward happens to Phil. He might not look like it on the outside but he's a sensitive soul so just go easy on him, okay?'

Simon was about to hug Helen goodbye when Phil's phone rang.

'Probably work,' said Phil reaching for his phone.

'More likely Degsy calling from the wrong airport wondering where we all are.'

Phil glanced down at the screen. 'Looks like we're both wrong. It's my dad.'

It had been weeks since Phil had last spoken to Patrick Hudson, and even that was only because he had dialled the wrong number. It wasn't so much that Phil and his dad didn't get on. They got on well enough given that in Phil's twenties they'd gone the best part of four years without talking. It was more that Phil had long since grown tired of waiting for his sixty-six-year-old frequently absent, philandering, former rock-band roadie of a father to grow up.

'Dad,' said Phil making his way into the hallway and sitting on the exact same stair where he had earlier spoken to his sister. 'What's up?'

'All right, son? Just thought I'd check in and see how you are.'

'I'm fine, Dad. You?'

'Never better. How's that fiancée of yours? She good?'

'She's great, Dad.'

'You've got a special one there, you know that don't you? Don't cock it all up by being Jack the lad now will you?'

It was too good a line to pass up. 'You mean like you did with Mum?'

'That was different, son. And you know it.'

Phil sighed and looked at his watch. He didn't want to have this argument again, especially as the last half dozen times it had ended with one or other of them putting the phone down mid-conversation.

'Fine,' said Phil. 'Look, Dad, I was actually just heading out the door. I got your reply to the wedding invite the other day so I'm assuming you're still all right to come.'

'Wouldn't miss it for the world!'

'I'm pleased to hear it.'

'So where are you off to in such a rush?'

'Amsterdam, Dad, it's my stag do.'

'Amsterdam! Now there's a city that knows how to party. I remember being there back in the early seventies for a European tour with this American rock band who were tipped to be the next Iron Butterfly. The night after their first gig I fell asleep in a hotel room and woke up in a tree in a park! A tree! No idea how I'd got there and even less of an idea how I'd managed to sleep. Nearly missed the coach taking us on to Belgium too!' He chuckled, a deep throaty laugh of the variety that sounded more insincere than heart-warming. 'Those were the days, I tell you. What I wouldn't give to be twenty-five again.'

'Yeah well,' said Phil, who had heard the story many times before, 'when you find a way of doing that, let me know and I'll do the marketing for you.'

'And we'll make a fortune,' said Patrick wistfully.

Phil ran out of patience. 'And so the thing that you called me up for was . . .'

'Do you have to be so brutal?'

'I'm not, Dad, I just want you to get to the point that's all. I've got a plane to catch.'

'Fine,' snapped Patrick. 'I could do with a little extra help this month.'

'Don't tell me you've got through it already?'

'I was a bit short last month – couple of unexpected bills – and it's had a knock-on effect that's all. I'll pay you back, every last cent, on that you have my word. Haven't checked last week's lottery numbers yet but I've got a good feeling about them.'

'How much?'

'Five hundred would take the edge off.'

'Fine.'

'But if you could make it six that would be even better. And you'll get it back. Scout's honours and all that.'

'Fine,' said Phil. 'I'll get the money moved to your account first thing Monday, okay?'

'That's brilliant son,' said Patrick. 'You're a good boy, you know that?'

'Yeah,' sighed Phil. 'I'm pretty sure I'm the best.'

Phil returned his phone to his pocket and picked up his bag from the floor in the hallway. 'Come on then, Si,' he called into the kitchen. 'Let's go if we're going.'

'You seem annoyed,' said Helen as they made their way to the front door. 'What did your dad want?'

'The usual.'

Helen squeezed his hand. 'I'm sorry, sweetheart. I know he can be a pain sometimes but you shouldn't let him get you down. This is your weekend and you need to make the most of it.'

'And I will,' said Phil. He kissed her one last time. 'You take care, okay? Have a great time and I'll see you back here on Sunday night.'

3.

It was quarter to eleven as Phil and Simon disembarked from the airport shuttle bus in front of the large revolving doors at the entrance to East Midlands Airport. The last time Phil had been here, he and Helen had flown to Madrid for a long weekend over the May Day bank holiday and getting Helen to marry him seemed about as unlikely as him learning to speak Spanish. Some three years later he was back, about to fly to Amsterdam for his own stag do.

Once through the revolving doors, the boys looked up at the screens above their heads for flight information.

'That's us,' said Simon pointing. 'Flight 368 to Amsterdam checking in at desks 16 to 18.'

Phil nodded but didn't say anything, which was no great change since he'd barely spoken since Helen had waved them off from the house. Reasoning that whatever was bothering him would come out sooner or later, Simon had left his friend to his brooding, content to allow the radio to keep him company.

Taking the lead Simon scanned their surroundings and parked Phil at the end of the queue for the check-in desk. Simon checked the queue and then double-checked the surrounding areas for the boys in case (though this would be a highly unlikely scenario) any of them had arrived on time. No sign.

'You okay?' asked Simon as a trendy looking couple joined the queue behind them. 'You hardly said a word on the way over.'

Suddenly conscious of his own reticence, Phil sighed, rubbing his eyes as though he'd just woken from a deep sleep. 'Yeah, I'm fine, mate, really. It's just I've got a few things on my mind that's all.'

'Your dad?'

'He's one of them.'

'What's he up to now?'

'Nothing new. I just wish . . . I don't know . . . I just wish he was like other dads, that's all. Why couldn't he be more like your old man?'

'You wouldn't want my old man for a father believe me,' said Simon warily. 'Never had a decent conversation with him in my life. At least your old man's lived a little and you can have a laugh with him. I'm not even sure I've seen my dad smile.'

Phil wasn't convinced. 'He's not that bad. A bit reserved maybe but at least he was always around.'

'A bit too much if you ask me,' replied Simon, 'but I get what you're saying. Still, for all his faults no one can tell a story like your old man, can they? Only last week I was telling a couple of guys from work that story about him going to bed in a hotel in Amsterdam and waking up in a tree in a park. Don't you think he'd be great to have on the stag weekend?'

'My dad? Are you mental? He'd be a nightmare.'

Simon looked crestfallen. 'Really?'

'Yes, really' replied Phil. 'You'd never know what hare-brained scheme he'd be working on. I'd never relax. And as for that ridiculous anecdote – which I'm pretty sure he made up – he told it to me again less than an hour ago.' Exhausted at the very thought of his dad Phil rubbed his eyes with his fists. 'I'm just sick of bailing him out that's all. If he hadn't been waking up in trees or running off to the Far East with whichever band he was working for at the time then maybe he wouldn't have to come to me for handouts every five minutes.'

Simon placed a reassuring hand on his friend's shoulder. 'It must be tough mate but I'm sure he appreciates it.'

Yeah,' said Phil, 'I'm sure he does in his own way.' He looked at Simon. 'This weekend: it's not going to be just drinking and dodgy clubs is it?'

Simon laughed. 'You make it sound so sordid when you say it like that.'

'You know what I mean,' said Phil. 'I'm as up for a laugh as the next man but it seems a bit of a waste coming all the way out here just to drink beer and watch bored couples have soulless sex for public consumption.' Phil laughed. 'If that's what you're after we could save ourselves the airfare, nip into town at throwing out time and stand outside the Ritzy.'

Simon eyed his friend suspiciously. 'Are you saying you want to visit an art gallery or two while we're out there? It's a stag do, not a school trip!'

25

'And don't I know it! All I'm saying is, given that I've never been there before, I wouldn't mind actually seeing some of it if the opportunity comes up.'

'Well if it does I'll let you know, okay?' said Simon, 'But I'm pretty sure there won't be enough time. Anyway, to be honest mate you're not missing much. I went there when I was a student and it wasn't all that. Okay, so there's Van Gogh and his Sunflowers, Anne Frank's house, tulips, clogs, Edam and a bunch of canals. But let's face it, even back when pretending to be "into" culture might have got you the girl, the best thing about the place was getting off your face and checking out the red-light area. Say what you like about Amsterdam as a city of culture, but any place where you can smoke pot *and* drink world class beer has got to be the number one destination for a stag do. It's the Las Vegas of Europe, only without any annoying Yanks to take the edge off things.'

Phil laughed. 'I've known you way too long to think for a minute that you're that ignorant.'

'People change,' said Simon shrugging. 'You might not like it. They might not like it. But it happens all the time.'

The queue surged forward as a large extended family featuring at least four different generations was beckoned to the check-in desk. Phil and Simon picked up their bags and moved forwards to take up the slack and yet another silence descended.

Simon nudged his friend in the overly jocular fashion that a schoolboy might try to coax another schoolboy out of a black mood. 'So, come on then, what else is on your mind?'

Phil frowned. He was sure that he'd snap out of his mood soon but all this attention really wasn't helping matters. 'How do you mean?'

'You said you had a few things on your mind. Unless I've miscounted your dad is only one.'

'Well, the other is my kid sister.'

'Caitlin? What's she done?'

'Nothing *yet*,' replied Phil, 'but that could have changed by Monday morning. Helen invited her to the hen weekend.'

'Oh that,' said Simon. 'I thought she was winding you up with something new. That spat with Helen's been going on for ages hasn't it? Why are you suddenly worried about it now?'

'Because this is different,' said Phil. 'Normally I'm around to referee before the claws come out but who knows what'll happen without me there? I can feel it in my gut. Trouble is brewing. Caitlin can be pretty bitchy when she wants to be and Helen . . . well once she gets her back up . . .'

Simon laughed. 'Remember that time when the four of us went to V festival and that drunk bird kept deliberately bumping into her?' Simon winced comically. 'Now that was a tongue-lashing and a half! I bet that girl gets flashbacks even now!'

'Exactly,' said Phil, 'so imagine what it would be like being at the receiving end of a tongue-lashing that's been eight years in the making.' Simon did his comedy wince again and this time it provoked the beginnings of a smile. 'See what I mean? It's too much to even contemplate.'

'Still,' he continued, 'I can't imagine Caitlin getting into anything with Helen the week before the wedding. It's too important.'

Phil grudgingly conceded his friend's point. 'I suppose not. If they did my mum would have a right go at the pair of them.'

'How's Caitlin doing anyway?' asked Simon. 'Haven't seen her for a while.'

'You know her,' said Phil, 'she's always fine. Whether it's being the only girl from our school to get into grammar school or the first member of the family to go to university, that girl always lands on her feet.'

'She seeing any one?'

Phil studied his friend. 'Why the interest? You're not trying to palm that idiot brother of yours off on her again are you?'

'Have you any idea how much that "idiot" is making these days as a fully qualified barrister? Only last week he was telling me how he was test driving a Ferrari!'

'And you think that would impress Caitlin? Honestly, mate, you have no idea of the kind of guy she goes for. I wouldn't be surprised if she turned up with a proper "A" list celebrity the next time we go to Mum and Brian's for Sunday lunch. She's done the rich thing, now she wants them rich *and* famous.'

Before Simon could reply there was a sharp tug on his trousers and they were halfway down his thighs exposing his expensive designer underwear to the world. Frantically pulling up his trousers he spun around angrily to see Reuben, Deano, Spencer and Degsy (all dressed in black suits and ties) bent double in hysterics.

'Do that again and I'll knock you out,' threatened Simon in a doomed attempt to wrest back his dignity.

'Mate,' sniggered Deano, 'it was just too good an opportunity to pass up. You know we love you really.'

'Yeah, I bet,' replied Simon peering over Deano's shoulder. 'And right now there's a copper with a high-vis vest coming this way who looks like he wants in on the joke.'

A look of horror spread across their faces, all the more amusing for the lack of an actual policeman. Suitably chastened Deano and the boys immediately shed their adolescent skin and acting more like grown men who had jobs, mortgages and responsibilities, joined Phil and Simon in the queue.

Phil had known them all in one capacity or another for years. Reuben had been one of Simon's oldest friends from school and as such had inevitably become one of Phil's closest friends too. Spencer was the former assistant manager of Phil's Nottingham store who now worked as a rep for an electronic goods distribution company and had recently separated from his long-term girlfriend. Deano was an old friend from the cricket team Phil used to play with back in his early twenties who along with his ex-wife ran the Horses, an up-market pub and bistro that the six friends often frequented. And finally Degsy was Phil's oldest school friend who, having followed many different career paths over the years, was currently trying his hand at painting and decorating while trying to win back the mother of his two kids. All six were part of an irregular five-a-side (it was a rare week if all six of them turned up at the same time) team called the Beeston Wanderers who played once a week at the local sports centre.

After what felt like a lifetime they finally reached the front of the queue and one by one checked on to the flight. En route to the departure gate they were all casually engaged in separate conversations with Phil and Spencer chatting about work, Deano and Simon talking about a couple of films Simon had watched and Degsy and Reuben talking football, but before they reached the escalator that would take them up through to security Simon called them all to one side.

'This is like school trips used to be back in the day!' whined Degsy. 'What's up now headmaster?'

Simon pulled out a Tesco carrier bag from his rucksack and theatrically dropped his phone in it. 'This is what's up.'

Reuben laughed. 'Are you going to do a trick?'

'Nope,' said Phil reading his friend's mind. 'I think he wants us all to hand over our phones.'

Reuben made it clear that he wasn't going to comply. 'No, can do,' he said firmly. 'I told the missus she'd be able to call me any time.'

'Which is exactly why I want us all to leave them behind,' said Simon. 'I know it's a pain in the arse, but

30

this weekend won't be the same if we're all tied to our phones for the whole of it.'

'You just don't want us uploading pictures of your hairy backside to Facebook!' retorted Reuben.

'No mate,' replied Simon, 'what I actually don't want is to spend the whole weekend watching you yakking to your missus on the phone.'

'Like that would happen.'

'I've seen it with my own eyes! The last time we went to see County play. You spent more time looking at your phone than you did watching the game!'

'We just like to keep in touch that's all.'

'More she just likes to keep a track of where you are and what you're doing. Why don't you go the full hog and get yourself a GPS device fitted?'

'Si's right,' said Deano dropping his phone into the bag. 'I went on a stag do last summer and it was a real drag. You'd be there trying to have a laugh and every five minutes some guy would be taking a call, sending a text or wandering around the pub looking for a signal.'

'Cool,' said Simon, 'so that's two down.' He jiggled the bag in Phil's direction. 'Come on mate, you know it makes sense.'

Phil looked at the bag blankly. While he didn't normally feel the need to text home as often as it appeared Reuben did, he did during the normal course of a day like to send Helen at least one or two just to say hello, even more so when he had to go away overnight on business. The idea of not communicating with Helen for the best part of three whole days was disconcerting and if it had been any other group of people in any other situation he wouldn't even have contemplated it. But these were his closest friends who, even though some, like Degsy, weren't exactly flush with cash, hadn't so much as raised an eyebrow at the expense involved simply because it was his stag do.

'Okay, I'm in,' said Phil dropping his mobile into the bag. 'Let's keep it old school.'

'Me too,' said Degsy.

'A pre-Nokia world it is then,' said Spencer with a stoic raise of the eyebrow before adding his to the bag.

'You guys don't get it,' implored Reuben, 'my missus will do her nut if she can't get hold of me all weekend. She once couldn't get hold of me for a day because I'd left my charger at home and by the time I got back from work she'd practically packed her bags.'

'Mate,' said Simon holding out his hand, 'you're embarrassing yourself. Just give me the phone.'

'Just know this,' said Reuben looking at Phil as he dropped his phone in the bag, 'you owe me big time.'

Clutching the bag of phones Simon disappeared in search of a left luggage locker and returned some twenty minutes later just as a message came over the tannoy: "Could passengers Dean, Corrbridge, Collins, Hudson, McDonald and Brayford please come to gate 11 immediately where flight 368 to Amsterdam is ready to depart."

Not needing to be told twice the boys ran full pelt along the corridor to security while Simon went into a long explanation of why it had taken him the best part of half an hour to leave the bag of phones at the left luggage counter which involved staffing problems and a malfunctioning credit card reader. Once they were through to the other side, they were conscious of the curious looks they were getting from their fellow passengers because of their matching attire.

'Do you think the whole weekend's going to be this frantic?' panted Phil as he handed in his ticket to the flight staff.

'Nah, mate,' replied Simon, 'Take it from me, my son, this is the easy part.'

4.

Having gratefully consumed (after much mockery) the packed lunch Helen had made within half an hour of taking off, the group spent the remainder of the journey trading drinking stories. They'd landed at Schipol Airport, caught the express train into Amsterdam Centraal and were now standing in the square outside the station enjoying what Deano claimed to be the best sight so far: six beautiful twentysomething girls, all wavy hair, summer tops and short shorts, making the most of the early afternoon sun.

'Wherever they go tonight,' drooled Deano, 'is where I am going to be.'

'Mate,' said Simon, as the girls passed by oblivious of the boys' appreciative gaze, 'if they've got any sense they'll be spending the weekend in a different country not hanging around bars here waiting for you to pester them.'

Deano grinned. 'This kind of bitterness really doesn't become you, fella.'

'Bitter? Why should I be bitter?'

'Because you're married, mate. So tonight while I'm giving it the chat with some young Dutch filly, you will have no choice but to look and bite your fist in – that's right, I said it – *bitterness*.'

'Mate.' Simon put his arm around Deano and planted a patronising kiss on his friend's head. 'If I'm biting my fist while you're talking to some young Dutch filly it'll be for one reason only: to stop myself laughing as she kicks you to the kerb. Don't forget, I've seen you in action. Watching you on the pull is like watching a car crash in slo-mo. You want to look away but you just can't.'

The boys burst into raucous belly laughter, momentarily drawing the attention of the girls. Phil looked up at the perfect blue sky, closed his eyes and soaked up the sensation of the sun on his face. It was going to be a good weekend, a really good weekend.

'Fun though this is,' he said, 'we should get to the hotel, check in and start enjoying ourselves. This weather is too good to waste.'

'Phil's right,' said Spencer, 'the sooner we get to the hotel the sooner we can get the beers in.'

'And what about the suits?' asked Degsy tugging on the lapel of his jacket. He looked like an overgrown schoolboy on his way to a funeral. 'I don't know about you lot but I'm baking in this thing. Are we ditching them?'

'It's up to Phil,' said Simon. 'What do you reckon? Suits on or suits off?'

Phil reflected. However corny Simon's idea had been, as Spencer had put it when they had queued up to go through immigration, they 'looked the business'.

'Suits on,' said Phil. 'After all it's not every day you get to look like you're in a movie.'

'What my boy wants, my boy gets,' nodded Degsy. 'But if we are going to look like a bunch of tarts for the rest of the day then at least let's get a group shot while we still look half decent.'

Rooting around in his bag Degsy pulled out a digital camera, and catching the eye of a young woman passing by called her over and asked her to take a couple of pictures of the boys. Embarrassed but game for a laugh the woman agreed and so the boys mugged for the camera while she snapped away.

Leaning over Degsy's shoulders the boys reviewed the woman's handiwork and while comments ranged from 'We look like bank managers,' to 'this picture's so cool I'm going to get it blown up and hang it in my living room,' Phil opted to keep his thoughts to himself because the only thing he could think of as he took in the boys' grinning faces was how lucky he was to have such a great bunch of mates by his side.

The Royal Standard, was, as Spencer put it, 'a hotel with a two-star upstairs and four-star downstairs'. So while the lobby looked like London's Bloomsbury the rooms were more like Blackpool's Golden Mile. Disappointed though they were by the threadbare carpets and dated decor, this only served to reinforce their resolve to spend as much time out of the hotel as possible, so once they had dumped their bags they were back downstairs in the lobby ready to investigate all that Amsterdam had to offer.

Much as Phil hoped that there might be the

opportunity at some point of seeing Amsterdam's more cultural sights, he knew they wouldn't be going anywhere or doing anything before sinking the first pint of the weekend. With this in mind they headed to Leidesplein.

When Phil had told the guys at work where he was going for his stag weekend, Leidesplein had been the place they had all agreed that he should visit and as the boys finally reached their destination, having passed all manner of interesting bars and cafés on the way, Phil could see exactly why: it was a stag weekend paradise. A large square, surrounded on all sides by bars, cafés, restaurants and pubs and with more of the same on every street that radiated out from each corner, it was as if a team of Dutch town planners had consulted with a broad range of young British men in order to come up with their perfect weekend destination. Ticking all the boxes from all-you-can-eat curry houses within staggering distance of Irish theme pubs right through to industrial sized coffee houses with menus featuring twenty-two different kinds of hash, it was a veritable cornucopia of manly distractions and as such, pretty much the perfect location for the boys to have their first pint of the weekend.

Choosing a pub with outdoor seating overlooking the busy square, the boys sat down at an empty table, rearranged the chairs to accommodate their group and donned their sunglasses, certain, if only for this particular moment, that this was indeed the life.

A waitress approached. She was young and pretty

and it was a forgone conclusion that Deano would try and chat her up.

'Good afternoon, gentlemen,' she began with a smile. 'You look very hot in those suits.'

'We're working a look,' explained Deano, before anyone else could respond, 'you know, *Reservoir Dogs*. Quentin Tarantino. You must have seen it.'

She nodded and smiled knowingly. 'So you and your friends are on a British stag party? No?'

'We are as it happens,' he replied, 'but I have been here on business before now.'

'Which business is that, mate?' teased Phil. 'Banking? Finance? Novelty rubber chickens?'

'I'll have you know I have business dealings that might surprise you, thank you very much,' retorted Deano in a bid to save face. 'It's not just Si and Reuben who know a thing or two about the Footsie one hundred.'

'Mate,' laughed Simon. 'You know nothing about the Footsie one hundred. Don't forget I do your accounts. I've seen your way with a calculator and it's not nice.'

Confused, the waitress continued with her patter. 'So, are you liking Amsterdam so far?'

'We're liking it a lot more now you're here,' leered Deano,

As embarrassed for Deano as he was for the waitress, Phil stepped in. 'Any chance we could order a couple of lagers?'

'Yes, yes of course.' She took their orders and returned inside the bar.

Reuben groaned at Deano. 'Could you have been any more obvious about trying to get into her knickers?'

'I was doing no such thing!' protested Deano. 'I was merely making conversation. That's what human beings do.'

'She was barely eighteen! You dirty old perv!' chuckled Degsy. 'You're old enough to be her geography teacher!'

'Are you lot going to be like this the whole weekend?' sulked Deano. 'You're seriously cramping my style.'

'If this is you in action I can safely say that you won't need us to cramp your style, you're killing it as it is.'

Deano and Reuben's bickering seemed to set the tone for the rest of the afternoon, and as the ice-cold lagers arrived and the light-hearted banter continued, Phil thought their afternoon together was one of the best they had enjoyed for months. Everybody seemed on good form, the conversation as always veered between vaguely intelligent political debate and downright silliness, and the heat of the sun made everything perfect.

Some hours later as the afternoon gave way to early evening Phil made his way back to the table from what felt like his hundredth trip to the loo when it occurred to him that if he hadn't handed his phone over to Simon, about now would have been when he would have paused to send Helen a text telling her how well things were going. It felt odd not being able to undertake this small but important act and even more odd that he'd only now realised how important these daily interactions with Helen were to him. Some of his friends might interpret such a desire as an indication that he was

39

under the thumb, but he wasn't all that bothered. Whether he was just about to be awarded the Nobel Peace Prize or had snagged a fingernail on his favourite jumper, there was one person in the world to whom the news would be equally important as it was to him.

As Phil approached the boys he sensed that something was wrong. When he had left they had been swapping anecdotes about their best holidays but now they were oddly muted, as though for his benefit they had hastily arranged a change of topic for which none of them could muster much enthusiasm.

His curiosity piqued, Phil determined to monitor the situation and so picked up his half empty beer glass while the conversation limped on around him like the work of a bunch of bad actors in an improv class.

'No, I can't stand them,' said Reuben.

'Me neither,' said Spencer.

'They're all right,' said Degsy. 'Mind, I have to be in the right mood for them like.'

There was a long silence then Deano looked at Simon. 'What about you mate?'

'They're not bad, I suppose,' shrugged Simon. 'But I can't say they'd make my top five.'

Phil could torture them no more. 'What's wrong with you lot?'

'What are you talking about?' said Degsy, delivering his outrage like a second-rate soap star. 'There's nothing wrong with us.'

'No? So why when I left you were you all having a laugh and now I'm back you're talking about . . . let me

guess . . . how you feel about cheese and onion crisps?'
Degsy widened his eyes as though convinced his best
mate had learned how to read minds. 'Mate, how long
have I know you? Thirty-odd years? Do you really think I
don't know that under pressure to drum up a change of
conversation your stock question is: what's your least
favourite crisp flavour? You've been asking people that
since we were at primary school. What are you hiding?'

'Nothing.'

Phil rolled his eyes as Deano cast a withering glance
in Degsy's direction.

'I told you not to do the crisp thing,' snapped Deano.

'Don't try and drop me in it,' protested Degsy. 'It's
not like anyone else was saying anything.'

Deano set his glass down on the table and addressed
Phil. 'Look, mate, we didn't mean anything by it but
you're right, we were sort of talking about you.'

'Only because you brought it up,' replied Spencer.

'Doesn't really matter who said what,' said Phil. 'All I
want to know is what you were saying.'

'We were debating why you're getting married,'
revealed Deano reluctantly, 'because, come on mate,
it's not like you need to, is it? You and your missus
have been together ages. Why would you want to
change things for no good reason?'

'I've got my own good reasons, thank you very much.'

'Of course you have,' said Deano. 'And we shouldn't
have brought it up. We were out of order.'

'You're right,' said Phil. 'But now the topic's up for
grabs why don't you tell us why you married Sheena.'

Deano and Sheena had met at a pound a shot night at a bar in the centre of Nottingham back when Deano had been in his mid-twenties. A fiery relationship from its consummation, it wasn't expected to last beyond a few months, let alone the four years that they managed to rack up together as cohabitees, then husband and wife.

'Because it was what she wanted,' said Deano.

'So you just went along with the idea?'

'Pretty much.'

'Not exactly the greatest endorsement for marriage I've ever heard,' said Phil stifling a grin.

Deano mulled the comment over. 'We weren't that sort of couple,' he said swirling the remains of his lager in his glass. 'Things were fun before, but if we're being truthful it was signing on the dotted line that did for us in the end.'

Phil raised an eyebrow. 'And you carrying on with one of the barmaids had nothing to do with it?'

'I've told you before: that was a symptom, not the cause. If she hadn't caught me I would have caught her if I'd tried hard enough.'

Phil turned to Reuben. Reuben and Alena had been together nearly eight years having met through old university friends of Reuben. The first time Reuben introduced Alena to the boys he warned them up front that she wasn't just beautiful but actually *'stunningly beautiful'* and not to give into the temptation to stare at her like a colony of rabbits caught in her headlights. Phil assumed that Reuben was exaggerating for effect and so when he finally did meet Alena he was mentally so ill prepared for a woman so stunning that all he could do for the entire conversation was mumble.

'What about you Reub?' asked Phil. 'You're married. You must have had a good reason.'

Reuben shrugged. 'You'd think so, given that the whole thing cost the best part of eighteen grand wouldn't you?'

'But I know you proposed because Alena told Helen the whole story the week after you told everyone. Or was that her idea too?'

'Look,' sighed Reuben, 'I don't regret it but if we're all being honest here then I have to say it wasn't my idea. Alena started going on about it after we'd been together two years and although I probably would have done it under my own steam at some point, the truth is she forced the issue.'

'Gun to head style?'

'More veiled threats. She's a drop dead gorgeous half-Russian girl with a degree in Economics who likes football and tiny underwear. If I hadn't proposed she would've moved to London and snagged the nearest millionaire banker the second she got off the train at King's Cross.'

Phil turned to Spencer. 'Come on mate, what about you? You and Emma were together ages. Surely you must have at least thought about giving the marriage thing a go?'

'Why do you think she's not around any more?'

'I thought it was because you didn't want kids?'

'It was . . . in part. But the whole thing was wrapped up in a lot of other stuff too: marriage, kids, where we were going to live. The more she went on about her vision of the future the more I realised it didn't look anything like mine.'

Reuben laughed. 'You have a vision of the future? You must be joking! How many times have you missed out on stuff because you never make up your mind until the last minute? Last year's Party in the Park, that holiday we all took in Ibiza, the last time the Rams played Forest . . . the list goes on and on.'

'I don't like to be hemmed in that's all. I like my freedom.'

'And now you've got all the freedom you could ever wish for.'

Degsy took a sip from his glass and then spoke up: 'I would have married my Leah like a shot,' he said, unprompted, of the woman who was the mother of his two kids. He and Leah had met at secondary school and been off and back on again more times than a light switch. Right now they were going through an off stage that would soon be celebrating its second anniversary.

'So why didn't you?'

'I asked tons of times but she wouldn't have me. Said I was too much of a liability.'

'Should have proved her wrong, mate,' said Spencer. 'Birds love that sort of thing.'

'I tried.'

'And what? You proved her right instead?'

Everyone around the table did the bloke wince – that

universally accepted visual shorthand for: 'That was a bit below the belt, mate.' Chastened, Spencer held his hands aloft in admission of his overstepping the line. 'You're right, sorry about that Degs, okay mate?'

Degsy nodded half-heartedly and drained his glass.

There was only Simon left to speak now. Phil thought briefly about Simon and Yaz's wedding day and the inside view that he had got of their relationship through his role as best man. If anyone had anything positive to say about marriage it would be Simon.

'So come on then, Si,' said Phil, 'Only you left to reveal all. Why did you and Yaz decide to get hitched?'

'Love,' said Simon after a long, ponderous silence.

Phil had had enough individual heart-to-heart conversations with the boys over the years to know that despite their bluster the boys were far from being emotional cripples but even he was a little shocked by his friend's frankness and unsure what to do to relieve the resulting tension. Phil could see his friends mulling over the various options available from a well timed fart gag through to the suggestion that they should all check out the arse on the waitress who was currently bending over to pick up a teaspoon that had fallen on the floor. In the end Phil himself provided the six friends with the best way out of the conversational cul-de-sac in which they found themselves.

'I'm starving,' said Phil. 'Who's hungry?'

'I am,' said Simon getting to his feet. Then he added, almost as if the news had only just occurred to him, 'Oh, and by the way I've left Yaz.'

5.

Phil knew Simon wanted everyone around the table to carry on as if nothing had happened because that was the way the friends had always chosen to deal with big news. Like the time Degsy told everyone that his girlfriend wouldn't let him see his kids any more. The time Reuben revealed that he and his wife were struggling to get pregnant. The time Deano confessed that his dad was dying of liver cancer. Each of these moments had been met with silence. A silence that acknowledged the scale and magnitude of the problem in question while recognising the pointlessness of any words the English language might offer in such a situation. The silence said without actually vocalising: 'I feel your pain, mate, feel free to fill in the blanks.'

Perhaps if this had been any other friend, Phil might have let him get away with dropping such a bombshell without cause for a soap opera style reaction and immediate dissection. But this wasn't any other friend, this was one of his oldest and closest friends. His best man. And they weren't in a dark corner of some shabby Beeston pub on a Tuesday night. They were sitting outside a bar in central Amsterdam, with the specific

46

intention of celebrating Phil's last weekend as an unmarried man. Regardless of any accusations that might come his way following his failure to observe the rules of The Great Book of Bloke, Phil *was* going to ask questions. And lots of them. He just couldn't see any way around it.

'You've done what?'

Simon closed his eyes, making clear the extreme nature of his disappointment. A number of moments passed by then he opened them again and said: 'Look, I know it's a shock mate, but there's a time and place and this isn't it. I just thought you all ought to know.'

Still refusing to obey the rules of the game, Phil continued with his line of enquiry: 'How long?'

'A while,' replied Simon. 'Now let it go.'

Phil attempted to process this information but needed some kind of explanation.

'Why?'

Simon's half-embarrassed shrug appeared to acknowledge its own woeful inadequacy.

Phil felt like shaking some sense into his friend. He thought about Yaz and what might be going through her mind, because after all the years he had known her she was as much his friend as Helen's.

'How's Yaz taken it?'

'She's fine.' He looked down at the table and added: 'She'll probably tell Helen this weekend.'

Phil swallowed hard. He didn't like the idea of Helen getting this news so close to the wedding. He'd lost count of the number of times in the past that problems in the relationships of people *he didn't even know*

47

had ruined his evenings by replacing an evening's DVD viewing with a three-hour debate about 'feelings'. If Yaz told Helen about her bust-up with Simon then it stood to reason the debate about 'feelings' would be longer than three hours. Much longer.

'What about the kids?'

'They're fine too.'

'Really?'

The muscles in Simon's jaw tensed. 'You need to stop now,' he said leaving out the words: 'or you and I are going to fall out', mainly because they were clearly implied. Simon had never been one for making empty threats. The others were slack-jawed watching the conversation unfold. No one knew what to do. No one said a word. A group of young Spaniards with designs on their table hovered in the corner of Phil's eye line.

Phil signalled to all the terms of his peace accord with Simon – unconditional surrender – and adopted his best non-judgemental face to look back at his friend. 'Still hungry?'

'Starving.'

'Right,' said Phil. 'Then let's go and get something to eat.'

In a bid to lighten the mood as they walked across the square and down a side street packed with restaurants, Degsy started a conversation about a documentary on the Discovery channel about the science behind how swords are forged. It focused on a guy in America who had honed the art to such a degree that he was now able to produce broadswords that could near enough slice a small tree in two.

Under normal circumstances Degsy would have been lucky to get so much as a grunt out of a conversational gambit of that calibre but there was little choice but to make the most of it.

As his friends, with the exception of Simon, began offering up a hitherto unsuspected depth of knowledge about broadsword production, Phil scanned the road ahead for a suitable restaurant while his mind was firmly on Simon.

It didn't make sense, Simon leaving Yaz like that. Simon and Yaz were one of the best-matched couples that he knew, with Yaz's stridency being tempered by Simon's own laid-back nature. There were half a dozen couples of his and Helen's acquaintance that he would have guessed more likely to split up than these friends. This really was a bolt from the blue.

His automatic assumption was that Simon had met somebody else possibly through work. But having met a number of his female colleagues Phil couldn't imagine which it might be. Maybe Yaz was at fault and not Simon at all, but although she frequently talked of running off with Jude Law, you only had to be around her when she'd had a glass of wine or two to see just how much she still fancied Simon after all these years.

Whatever the reason, it sounded as if it had been Simon's decision not Yaz's and, while he hoped that there was no one else involved, experience told him that this was unlikely. As Helen had said to him the evening that their friend Lou had announced that Hamish had walked out after eleven years together insisting that no one else was involved: 'When it comes to men leaving women there's always someone else. Always. Men don't leave wives and girlfriends to be on their own. It's just not how they work.'

So who was this woman? Phil considered his friend, his head bowed, and his face fixed in a surly demeanour, walking in silence just behind Spencer and Reuben. There was no clue to be had.

Having dismissed countless eateries for the flimsiest of reasons the boys found themselves at a junction and took a left while dodging past crowds of after-work drinkers, groups of exchange students and rival stag parties.

On a hunch, Phil had begun following a group of young revellers who looked like they knew where they were going when Degsy tugged his arm.

'What about this place?' he asked.

'You joking?' Phil eyed the Union Jack in the window of the Britannia Chippy.

'Never been more serious,' replied Degsy. 'I'm starving, mate, if we eat here we could be in and out and back on the beer in no time.'

'He's got a point,' said Reuben. 'I'm not really in the mood for anything too fancy.'

Phil looked at the rest of his friends. 'Anyone not want chips?' The boys' hands remained resolutely at their sides. Phil's spirits fell. At best he'd have settled for a Dutch restaurant so they could sample some typical local food and at worst he'd have settled for a curry in a restaurant that they had never been to before, but chips from a chip shop that could easily have been found on any high street back home disappointed him more than he wanted to let on.

Degsy ordered six portions of fish and chips and six cans of Coke and Simon paid for them out of a hastily arranged kitty while the rest of the boys spread themselves across two Formica tables.

The food was ready within minutes and to Phil's surprise was actually quite good, given that Degsy had discovered during the course of a long and involved conversation that the proprietor, a small, hirsute man who may or may not have been Greek, had never so much as set foot in England.

By the time they'd finished eating all thoughts of divorce and indeed broadswords had long since disappeared, and although they would have all scoffed at the idea there did seem to be a new enthusiasm, as though they had all decided that the evening needed rescuing and it was up to them to do it.

'We need to start drinking again,' said Reuben. 'This food has sobered me up no end.'

As one they all stood up and thanking the chip shop owner politely as they left, stepped out into the street.

'How about over there?' said Deano.

They followed his pointing finger across the road to a fashionable looking bar where a huge queue waited to go inside.

'Now you're talking,' said Degsy. 'Where there's a queue there's action!'

51

They joined the queue behind an impossibly handsome couple dressed in black who appeared to be more interested in the contents of their BlackBerries than they did in each other.

After ten minutes in the queue, and still feeling some residual distress at Simon's news, Phil was about to suggest to the boys that maybe they should try somewhere else, when the impossibly handsome couple simultaneously looked up from their phones, took in the number of people currently ahead of them and after murmuring to each other in Dutch, cast a withering glance in the boys' direction and left the queue.

'Maybe we should join them,' said Reuben closing the gap so that they were now behind a group of well dressed women. 'By the looks of the trendy types in this queue there's every chance we won't get in even if we do make it to the front before midnight and to top it all we don't even know what we're queuing for. It could be Amsterdam's top gay bar for all we know.'

'And even then you wouldn't be able to pull!' said Deano dodging past Phil and tapping one of the women in front of them on the shoulder.

The woman turned round and Phil was surprised at how attractive she was. She had black shoulder-length hair and a luminous complexion that made her look fresh and youthful. She looked like she was an actress or a model or even a singer and because of this Phil began to imagine that he recognised her.

'Can I help you?' she asked in English. Her accent although clearly European, was very MTV American.

'Yes, you can,' said Deano ditching his Derby accent for his best Hugh Grant 'yes-I-am-that-unbelievably-English' impression. Phil could barely keep a straight face. 'My friends and I were wondering if there was any chance you could tell us what this place is. It's just that we haven't a clue but thought it might be fun.' He looked up at the sign above their heads. 'The Lab. What is it?'

Phil cringed. This poor woman had done nothing to deserve the full Deano onslaught but now that his friend had started there was little chance that he would stop until expressly told to do so. Possibly by the police.

'It's just a bar,' said the beautiful woman. 'It opened a week or two ago and you know how it is when something's cool . . . everyone has to be there. It's my first time. I'm here for my friend's birthday.'

'But it'll be worth the wait?'

The beautiful woman laughed. 'Well, I'm hoping it'll beat sitting in front of the TV.' She turned back to her friends, leaving Deano staring lasciviously at her bare shoulders. Phil tapped him on the arm thereby ending what was clearly a sordid reverie.

'We should go,' said Phil, keen to stay as far away as possible from women who weren't his fiancée.

'Can't,' said Deano. 'First, Simon doesn't want to leave, do you Si?' Simon laughed and rolled his eyes. 'And second, I think I may possibly be in love.'

'This *is* still my stag do isn't it?' said Phil exasperatedly. 'I do still get some say in what we do?'

'Of course you do,' said Deano. 'Just not yet. You know how it is mate.' He lowered his voice. 'I have to talk to this woman again. She was well into me. And her mates are hot too!'

There wasn't enough alcohol in the entire world to make either this woman or her friends remotely interested in Deano but this made not one jot of difference to his friend.

'Fine, we'll stay,' said Phil reasoning that Deano's antics would offer some much needed light relief. 'But I'm nobody's wingman all right? I don't want to talk to, look at, or stand next to any of these women okay?'

'Ha!' scoffed Deano. 'Like they'd even be looking in your direction!'

Before Phil could reply to Deano's insult with a few of his own, his attention was caught by a group of four lads swaggering down the street towards them. From their accents, demeanour and general lack of sobriety it was obvious that they were part of a British stag party.

They came to a halt next to the beautiful woman and her friends. 'All right girls?' said the tallest of the men in a rough Essex accent. 'What's this queue for then?'

In an attempt to humour them, the beautiful woman explained very carefully what the queue was for but if they hoped that this would be enough to make the stag party go away they couldn't have been more wrong. Without any encouragement the men attempted to join the women in the queue and when they made it clear that they didn't want to be joined things began to get ugly.

'Stuck up bitches aren't interested, boys!' said the tall man to his friends. 'British blokes not good enough for you lot?'

'Not in this case,' said the beautiful woman. 'So why don't you just leave us alone?'

'You heard her,' said Phil, embarrassed by his fellow countrymen. He stepped in front of the beautiful woman so that he was facing the tall guy head on. 'They're not interested.'

Tall Guy glared at Phil. 'And you are?'

'Someone who's sick and tired of brain-dead morons like you giving us all a bad name.'

Tall Guy laughed. 'Boys, this cock in a suit thinks he can tells us what to do!'

'He does because he can,' said Simon positioning himself next to Phil, flanked by the rest of the boys. 'You, my friend, need to go, and you need to go now.'

Phil could see Tall Guy's friends weighing up the odds, but drunk as they were, they could see they were outnumbered – and thanks to Reuben and in particular Spencer – out-bulked too.

'Come on lads,' said Tall Guy fixing Phil with a menacing stare. 'One way or another I'm sure we'll see these guys around later.'

Wary of being caught off guard, the boys stood their ground as the Essex stag party sauntered into the mid-distance, and only once they were sure they had gone did they relax.

'He's right you know,' said Phil. 'Chances are we will see them later. It's not like Amsterdam is a huge place.'

'And when we do,' replied Simon, 'we'll sort them out just like we did this time.'

Phil turned to the beautiful woman. 'You all right?'

She nodded. 'Thank you for that. You were really kind to help out.'

'It was nothing,' replied Phil, suddenly self-conscious. 'I hope that it doesn't spoil your evening.'

Content to relive every nanosecond of their altercation (an event that quickly became known as The Time We Kicked Arse While Wearing Reservoir Dogs Suits) the next twenty minutes passed by in a blur of posing and posturing. Just as even Deano was beginning to murmur that maybe they had spent too long in the queue, a large group left the bar and the door staff began letting people in again and in no time at all the boys were second in the queue.

Readying themselves for their first encounter with Dutch door staff the boys tried to make themselves as presentable as they could fixing ties and sorting out collars. One of the bouncers, a tall wide-neck manmountain lifted the rope at the front of the entrance and then addressed the women: *'Horen deze heren bij u?'*

Phil breathed a sigh of relief. Despite their suits the doorman had seen the boys for exactly what they were: six British blokes on a stag do – the very epitome of the kind of customer any half-decent Dutch drinking establishment would not want to entertain for the evening. Soon they would be turned away and left with no choice but to find themselves a proper pub where they could drink, argue and talk nonsense without cause to contemplate the opposite sex.

But then the beautiful woman turned, winked at Phil and without missing a beat said in English: 'Yes, they are.'

6.

Phil had no idea what to think but as the doorman ushered the boys inside he reasoned that at the very least they would soon be getting a drink. A combination of the chips, the queuing and their near fight had sobered him up and he was now desperate to get back to that easy-going state of mind that he'd enjoyed earlier in the evening.

Inside, Phil made sure not to be too close to the women ahead in case they feared that he was going to spend all night following them and making a nuisance of himself following his good deed. Once they were past the second set of doors, however, the women peeled off to the right and joined a group at a table opposite the huge plate glass windows that looked out on to the street and Phil made sure to go the opposite way.

As the boys gathered Phil glanced over at the woman and she looked up at him and smiled. Phil smiled back and to show his appreciation of her kindness in a non-threatening manner devoid of all sexual connotations gave her the thumbs-up and immediately regretted it.

'I just gave that girl who got us in here the thumbs-up,'

57

shouted Phil over the bar's club music, as the woman looked on confused.

'We know,' yelled Deano, lines of laughter apparent at the corner of his eyes. 'We saw. After that public display of eighties-style sign language I think you've pretty much ruined all our chances. You gave her the wacky thumbs-up, fella! Even with the best will in the world there's no coming back from that mate. Beer?'

Phil nodded. 'I'll have whatever they've got. Just make sure it's cold and strong.'

Led by Simon, the boys headed off to get the drinks leaving Phil alone with Deano. Phil had been to many bars like The Lab in his time and he had loathed every aspect of them from their pretentious decor through to their even more pretentious clientele. These weren't so much places to have a drink and a catch up with mates but rather places that people went to in order to see and be seen, as though the very act of having made it past the door staff made you something special.

Phil did not feel special. In fact having compromised his beliefs by coming here he felt sort of dirty and soiled and wished he could be in their usual corner in Deano's pub back in Beeston, sipping Carlsberg while cracking jokes about Degsy's love life.

'What are we doing here?' asked Phil as a couple of attractive women passed by looking straight through them. 'This isn't us. After this beer we should go, find ourselves a proper pub and bed in for the night.' He scanned the bar. All the seats had long since been taken and even standing room was at a premium. 'There isn't even anywhere to sit.'

'Mate,' said Deano, 'are you ever going to stop bloody moaning? All you've done all evening is whinge. Look around you, fella, this place is crawling with top class talent of every description!' He pointed to a tall girl with shoulder-length blonde hair. 'She's gorgeous!' He moved his finger across to the right by several degrees to a beautiful girl wearing a silver metallic barely there minidress. 'What I wouldn't do to be able to lick her armpits!' And finally he moved his finger to a beautiful brunette who was now looking right at him. 'Look at her! She's lovely! And because she's seen me pointing at her I'm on her radar!'

'As a potential stalker!' said Phil marvelling at his friend's brazenness. 'She's probably calling the police as we speak.'

A group of people at a table a few feet away stood up and left but before Phil could make a grab for their seats they were leapt upon by a group of young guys in tight tops sporting inordinate amounts of gel in their hair.

Thwarted, Phil turned to Deano and tried to make conversation to distract himself from the pain in his knees. 'So what's your take on this business with Si? It doesn't sound right does it?'

'Not even a little bit. It's got to be another bird though.'

'Any ideas who?'

Deano shrugged. 'I've seen him chat to a few women

in the pub but no more than a quick hello. But that's Si, isn't it? He'll talk to anyone about anything when he's on form. I didn't even notice he'd stopped wearing his wedding ring.'

'Has he? I didn't even think to look.'

'I clocked it when he told us in the bar.' Deano paused. 'You're not going to let it bother you though? You know, let it get under you skin, and convince you that all marriages are doomed and blah, blah, blah.'

Phil laughed. 'I hadn't been thinking that but cheers for putting it out there fella.'

'I'm just saying . . .'

'What?'

'Nothing.'

'What?'

'Nothing.'

'Are we going to carry on like this all night?'

Deano sighed. 'All I was going to say is that I've seen you and Helen together and I can tell – just from looking at you guys – that you're going to work.'

There was an awkward pause then Phil said: 'Was that as hard to say as it was to listen to?'

'Mate,' replied Deano, 'it was excruciating.'

'Let's agree to never do that again, okay?'

'On that,' said Deano, 'you have my absolute word.'

Although The Lab turned out to be more fun than he expected (even as a happily engaged man it was hard to not be impressed by the high concentration of gorgeous girls in the bar), after an hour or so there was no getting away from the fact that the lager was too expensive, there still weren't any seats and although Deano had toned down his dog on heat routine there was still every chance that the evening would end with the boyfriend of one of his victims punching his lights out.

Returning from a trip to The Lab's toilets (not so much your common or garden toilet as state of the art unisex space pod featuring toilets, male and female urinals) Phil began working his way back to the boys trying to work out exactly how best to pitch his plan without getting into an hour long debate about the pros and cons of moving on. To his immediate discomfort he saw the woman from the queue standing in front of him.

'Ah, Mr Thumbs-up!' she grinned. 'We meet again.'

Phil cringed but as he tried compose himself he was once again struck by the familiarity of her face. He couldn't possibly know her, could he? Surely she was far too attractive for him to have met her in person and forgotten.

'Look,' said Phil. 'I am very much aware how uncool that thumbs-up thing was.'

'I thought it was funny. Quite sweet actually. Sometimes I miss the English and their funny ways.'

'You know England then?'

'A bit. I'm actually half English. My dad was a Londoner but I was raised here in Amsterdam, then moved to London in my twenties. I haven't been to the UK for a while but if there's one thing I miss about the English, it's the way that you moan. No one, not even the Danes, can moan like you Brits. It's your nation's most endearing feature.'

Mike Gayle

'Yeah, well,' said Phil. 'We do begrudgingly aim to please.'

Phil thought this had better be the end of the conversation. 'Well,' he said. 'It was nice to meet you.'

'You too,' she replied. 'And I really want to thank you for your assistance outside. I hope the rest of your stag weekend goes well. Congratulations. I hope marriage suits you better than it did me.'

Phil eyed the woman suspiciously. 'How did you know I was the one getting married? Do I look engaged?'

'It's in your eyes, I think,' she said. 'But it's not a bad thing. It's nice. Believe me you don't want to be like that friend of yours.'

'Deano? He's not that bad. You know what they say about barks being worse than bites? Well that's him all over.'

'Maybe. But I stand by what I said. You don't want to be like him.'

'I'll try not to be.'

'So what's planned for the rest of your boys' weekend? Anything good? No fights I hope.'

'Oh, no . . .' said Phil. 'We'll probably just be doing the usual stuff.'

'Visiting the red-light area, getting stoned and drinking 'til you throw up?'

'I thought you said you liked the Brits?' protested Phil. 'We're not all clichés.'

'So tomorrow you and the guys will be hitting Amsterdam's top cultural spots? Stedelijk followed by the Van Gogh Museum then after lunch heading to

62

Oude Kerk and maybe finishing the day off at the Begijnhof?'

'We might be.'

The woman clearly wasn't convinced. 'Now that,' she said, 'I'd love to see.'

'Does it get you down?' asked Phil moving out of the way of a couple trying to get around him. 'Having your country invaded every weekend by hordes of Brits?'

She shook her head. 'Not really. I don't go out that often. I just sometimes wish you lot would recognise there's more to Amsterdam than clogs, hash and working girls.'

'In that case,' said Phil raising his right hand. 'In return for getting us in here tonight – thanks for that by the way – I hereby promise to go somewhere cultural tomorrow. You name it and I'll go there.'

'Seriously?'

Phil grinned. 'I never joke about culture.'

'Then in that case you should go to the Van Gogh Museum. It's nice there. Plenty to see. You'll love it.'

Phil smiled as if to say, 'Well I suppose that's that,' and she offered him a smile in return. Carefully wrapping his thumbs inside his fist in case they got ideas of their own he headed back to his friends.

'Where have you been?' said Reuben. 'We were about to send out a search party!'

'Nowhere,' said Phil rolling over the encounter in his mind. 'I just got a bit lost that's all. This place is bigger than you think.' He took his glass from Degsy and

63

drained it in one. 'I was thinking that maybe we should get off?'

'No can do, mate,' said Deano.

'Why not?'

Deano looked over Phil's shoulder. 'Because I think the woman of my dreams has finally come to her senses.'

Phil turned around to see the woman from the queue walking over to them. 'For you,' she said, handing him a torn piece of paper, 'to thank you for your help earlier and in case you use not having anyone to go with as an excuse to chicken out.'

Phil looked at the paper in his hand. A name and mobile number written in the same gloriously feminine handwriting.

'Cheers . . .' he looked down again, 'Sanne . . . that's really nice of you.'

'You're welcome,' she replied, nodded a brief acknowledgement to the boys and headed back to her friends leaving him with five pairs of eyes staring at him.

'What was that about?' asked Deano.

'Nothing,' said Phil. 'I bumped into her a few minutes ago. We were just talking, that's all.'

'And now she's giving you her phone number?'

Phil nodded.

'And you think this is normal?'

He hesitated. 'Maybe not normal exactly but . . .' His voice trailed off. 'Look, I just bumped into her, that's all. We started talking about museums and stuff and

I'd said I'd check one of them out and that's why she gave me her number, okay? Nothing sinister . . . she's simply offering to go with me if I want her to.'

'And do you?'

'No, of course not.'

'Then give it to me,' said Deano making a grab for the paper.

'It wasn't like that, okay?' said Phil snatching it away. 'She knows I'm getting married.'

'You told her?'

'She guessed and I saw no reason to deny it.'

Deano shrugged as though this made no difference to his overall judgement of the situation. 'So are you going to call her or not?'

'What with? My phone's in England.'

Deano rolled his eyes. 'Mate, guess what? It's just like home. They have payphones.'

Phil shook his head. 'No,' he said firmly. 'I will not be calling her. Even though she was simply being nice and I'm sure there was nothing in it I think it's probably best if I don't.'

The boys jeered.

'She wasn't being nice,' said Spencer. 'She was after a slice of Hud pie! Girls used to go mental for your sensitive guy schtick back in the day. Do you remember that one with the legs up to her armpits at that campsite in the south of France? How long did she write to you for?'

Phil groaned. Sometimes he wished he'd never taken that holiday. 'Nearly a year.'

'And you wouldn't let her come over!'

'She had a boyfriend.'

'Once again you miss the point. Who cares? She was loads hotter than the girls we were knocking around with back then.'

'Can we stop this?'

'We're only just getting started!'

Phil gave Deano a threatening look not altogether dissimilar from the one Simon had given him when he too had overstepped the mark.

'Fine,' said Deano relenting. 'Have it your way. We should probably get going anyway. I read on the web about some bar near the red-light district staffed completely by eastern European girls wearing nothing but thongs.'

Phil didn't even comment. He just threw Deano a glance that said: 'Over my dead body.'

'A mate of mine told me about a place off Dam Square that does speciality beers,' said Spencer. 'You know the type, high alcohol, knock your head off stuff. What do you reckon?'

'Sounds a bit tame if you ask me,' said Deano.

Simon laughed. 'What are you after? A dwarf only bondage bar? Mate, it's not even midnight, yet. Calm down.'

The boys finished their drinks and proceeded towards the exit of the bar. Phil threw a last glance back in the direction of Sanne and her friends. Completely oblivious to him she was deep in conversation.

'Are you coming or what?'

Reuben was holding the door open for him.

Shaking his head free of thoughts he didn't want there Phil nodded and left the bar.

It was still just light outside. Spencer got out the map from the hotel, checked their position and pointed in the direction that they needed to go.

They had only been walking a few minutes when Phil turned to Spencer and asked: 'Did she look familiar to you? You know the girl that gave me her number.'

'Not really. Why should she have done?'

'Now you mention it,' said Simon overhearing the conversation. 'You might have a point. Her face . . . it is sort of familiar. What was her name again?'

'Sanne.'

Simon shook his head. 'You'd remember a name like that wouldn't you? I don't know any Sannes do you?'

'That's the thing,' said Phil. 'Even the name sounds familiar.'

'What do you think she is?' asked Spencer. 'An actress or a model? She's good-looking enough to be both.'

'I'm pretty sure it's something like that,' said Phil, dodging past a couple of drunken English guys sitting on the kerb. 'If I had my phone with me I could have Googled her.'

'If you'd had your phone with you, Deano would have nicked it and spent the night posting libellous status updates on your Facebook page,' chipped in Reuben.

'Hang on,' said Degsy, clearly not wanting to be left out of the conversation, 'wasn't there a girl called Sanne in that girl band that had a couple of hits a few years back? I only know that because my eldest was mad about them for a while. What was their name again? Misty something or other . . .'

'Misty Mondays!' shouted Phil. 'That was it! She was the—' Phil stopped. He knew exactly who she was and why he recognised her. 'This is absolutely the weirdest thing,' he began, 'but I've remembered how I know her and it's not just the band thing either.' He looked at Degsy. 'She used to be married to . . . Aiden Reid.'

'The radio DJ?'

Phil nodded.

'Really?' mused Degsy, 'I know a lot of people think he's a tosser because he's loaded and always copping off with top models but I have to say I love his show. Funniest thing in the world. That thing he does with his co-host Crazy Dave cracks me up every time.' He stopped and looked at Phil. 'I suppose it is a bit weird that you've been chatted up by Aiden Reid's ex-missus. Maybe you could sell the story to the tabloids: "Radio Star's Ex Gives Bloke From Nottingham Her Number".'

'You're not getting it,' said Phil. 'That's not even the weird part. The weird part is that Aiden Reid is the last bloke that Helen went out with before she met me.'

'Really?'

'Yeah, really.' What Phil neglected to add was that Aiden Reid was also the reason why after nine years together he and Helen had finally decided to get married.

Saturday

7.

As Phil made the transition from oblivion to consciousness he became aware that all was not well with his world. His temples throbbed as if his brain was trapped in a cycle of inflation and deflation: one moment taut and hard, pressing on to the outreaches of his skull and the next soft and saggy and barely taking up space in the cavernous void in which it was housed. The one constant in this situation was the pain, the deep, dull ache that in tempo and persistence seemed perfectly to echo the pace of his slow, dull pulse.

He was never going to drink again. Never. He would never go to the pub, visit a bar or even walk down the booze aisle of his local Morrison's. Drink was evil. He knew that now. After twenty-odd years of being legally able to indulge in the demon drink the lesson had finally been learned, the hard way. Now, all he needed to do was to survive the war of attrition between his body and the alcohol he had so willingly imbibed, and the booze free vision of the future that he had so keenly constructed would be his.

Lying very still, not even daring to move so much as a single muscle Phil built up the courage to open his

71

---

eyes. Beginning a countdown from ten he fought against his instinct to preserve his cerebral cortex from yet more needless pain, and reaching zero prepared to open his eyes when something happened that made him squeeze his eyes shut tighter than ever: a foot of which he had no ownership grazed his lower calf. Phil's eyes shot open and he found himself looking directly into a face.

'Degsy!'

Degsy woke with a shock, mumbling incoherently. 'What are you shouting for?' he asked, mole-like eyes blinking.

'What do you mean what am I shouting for?' barked Phil. 'You're in my bed!'

'What's with all the bloody yelling?' called a voice from the other side of the room.

Phil looked at Degsy in confusion and flicked the switch on the wall by the bed. A dim pool of light illuminated a corner of the room. Phil could just about make out the outline of a body lying on the floor. Degsy picked up his pillow, crawled to the end of the bed and brought the pillow down sharply on the figure below. It yelled in surprise.

'That'll be Reuben,' said Degsy. 'I'd recognise that girly scream anywhere.'

Reuben, looking like death warmed up, sat up and scowled. 'Have you any idea what kind of headache I've got?'

'No,' said Degsy. 'But I promise you it's not a patch on mine.'

Phil looked from Reuben to Degsy and back again and noted that they were still wearing their suits and ties. He looked underneath the duvet and noted that he too was fully clothed.

Phil reached for the main light switch and as he flicked it on, the rest of the room came to life: Deano began unfurling from the foetal position from his place by the door, Spencer, still half asleep, twitched on Degsy's side of the bed, and scratching his head, Simon emerged from the darkness of the bathroom.

Speechless, Phil was fumbling for an explanation of the situation when out of the corner of his eye he noticed a red cement-splattered pneumatic drill leaning against the wall and a bright yellow hard hat crowning the TV.

Phil nudged Degsy with his elbow and silently pointed at them.

'Building site next to the hotel,' he said, through helpless laughter.

'You nicked them?' gasped Phil. 'Why?'

Degsy shrugged, 'I dunno, mate, why do men do anything? My memory's blitzed when it comes to motivation.'

'And where was I when all this was happening?'

'Asleep,' said Degsy. 'On a bench. You were out like a light, mate. We practically had to carry you back here. What was up with you last night? One minute you were you and the next it was like a night out with your old man.'

73

'It's true,' said Reuben, sitting down on the edge of the bed. 'Once we reached that place that sold the oddball beers you were like a man possessed. Honestly mate, by the end of the night you were so off your face we nearly got chucked out of the lap dancing club.'

Phil blinked hard. 'We went to a lap dancing club?'

'Not one,' explained Degsy. 'Two, one after the other. And then a strip bar and before you start complaining we didn't drag you anywhere. You dragged us. You said it was your stag do so you should get to choose.' Degsy squinted in Phil's direction. 'Don't you remember any of it?'

Phil shook his head and regretted it instantly. 'Not a second.'

'So what's the last thing that you actually do remember?'

Lying down on his pillow Phil closed his eyes as the major turning point of the evening – the woman from the queue being Aiden Reid's ex-wife – came back to him.

Unlike most boyfriends who for reasons of self-preservation jettison such information as soon as it's handed to them, Phil could recall perfectly both the exact moment that Aiden Reid's name was first mentioned to him. It had been eight years earlier, he and Helen had been dating for about a year and they had been sitting in their local Thai takeaway waiting for a set meal for two when Phil had picked up a

74

two-day-old copy of the *Sun* and begun reading an article entitled: 'Who will get top DJ job?'

The story was a follow-on from the biggest story of the previous week: the news that BBC breakfast radio DJ Xan Collins had been caught on film by the *News of the World* snorting cocaine in a hotel bedroom in Mayfair with two underage models. Despite Collins' record-breaking audience figures the BBC had had no option at all but to sack him on the spot, thereby creating a vacancy for the single most coveted job in the whole of UK radio, and the article was all about who should replace him.

Phil had been about to turn the page when Helen had pointed to the picture of one of the three DJs vying for the job, a ridiculously good-looking stubbly chinned type who he recognised from TV. 'That's my ex,' she said succinctly.

Phil was momentarily speechless. 'The one you were going to marry?'

Helen nodded and Phil stared at the paper. 'Your ex is Aiden Reid? Why didn't I know this before?'

'Why would you?' replied Helen. 'It's not like I know the names of all your exes, do I? I just thought I ought to say, that's all. Chances are, he's going to get that job, and if he does it's a guarantee that the tabloids will come sniffing around looking for a story on him. If they do, say nothing, not a single word. Not even in my defence.'

Helen was right. Not only about Aiden getting the BBC Radio breakfast job but also the tabloid hacks making contact, looking for a story about 'Aiden Reid's first love.' They called Helen constantly both at home and at work and when that failed to give them what they wanted they concentrated their efforts on Phil. 'How does it feel to be dating the ex of one of the country's most famous celebs, Mr Hudson? Anything you'd like to tell us about the way he went about wrecking your partner's life when they were engaged? We've got someone on record claiming that Aidan was the love of her life and that she's never got over him: would you care to comment?' Just as Helen had told him, Phil made no comment, but it was difficult, especially the lies about her never having got over him.

Running parallel to these events was Phil and Helen's relationship, which in a short space of time progressed from its tentative initial stages into something neither party had expected at all. Phil had never before experienced anything close to what he felt for Helen with anyone else and on the day that this had first dawned on him (a Sunday evening a year or so after the Aiden Reid furore) as she was loading her car in order to drive back to Liverpool.

'We should get married,' said Phil as the thought occurred to him. Confused, Helen had stared at him blankly. 'I mean it,' he continued. 'I think we should get hitched.'

Helen didn't drive back to Liverpool that night. Instead she and Phil had stayed up until late with her explaining why although she felt as strongly for him as he did for her it was too soon to talk of marriage. Despite his enthusiasm Phil eventually came around to Helen's point of view, which is why he waited another year (by which time they were living together in Nottingham) to ask her for a second time as they celebrated their third anniversary of their first official date.

'I want you to marry me,' he said as they stood underneath the awning outside their favourite Italian restaurant on Weekday Cross sheltering from the rain as they waited for a cab home. 'I mean it, Helen, I'm absolutely convinced you're the one.'

Again Helen turned him down, citing a million and one reasons, from the fact that they were both very busy at work right through to the fact that they were looking to move to a bigger house soon and could do without the stress. Though clearly disappointed not to have received the yes he had been hoping for, Phil had eventually agreed, and so, having put the idea on the proverbial back burner, they both got on with the business of carving out a life for themselves.

But when Phil popped the question once again some two years later only to be met once again by the most logical of excuses, he made the decision that his days of proposing marriage were over for good. After all, enough was enough wasn't it? But then a few years later, a date to the cinema and the finding of a child's toy plastic ring, not only was he back to proposing but after all these years and all these rejections he finally said out loud the one thing he hadn't dared to say all these years: that the reason Helen wouldn't marry him had nothing to do with him and everything to do with Aiden Reid.

The accusation not only hit home, but it hit home hard, so hard in fact that once he'd delivered a heartfelt declaration never to propose to Helen again, without missing a beat she actually proposed to him. And they were happy, really happy, or at least he'd thought so at the time. But now, as he lay in bed fighting through his raging hangover and reviewing his reaction to the news that Helen's ex had reared up in his life again, he began to wonder not only whether he was happy, but also if Helen, whom he had effectively bullied into saying yes, was happy too.

Leaving Phil to his thoughts the boys gathered themselves together and came up with a plan for the morning ahead.

'Well,' said Simon, 'I did have us down for something later in the day but that was before we got trashed, rolled in at five in the morning and kipped on the floor. Perhaps I'd better cancel it.'

Phil sat up. 'Don't,' he said firmly. 'Whatever it is let's do it anyway. Keep ourselves busy.'

Surprised by Phil's response, Simon shrugged: 'Fine, I'll leave it. But first off we've got to eat. How about we meet downstairs in half an hour, then nip out and find somewhere to get a decent breakfast.'

The boys began trooping out when a question occurred to Phil. 'I get the fact that things went a bit mental last night but what I don't understand is how you all came to be sleeping in my room.'

Degsy laughed. 'Who knows? I'm just glad that we didn't end up kipping in the hotel corridor like we did for my thirtieth. My back's never been the same.'

Alone in his room Phil yawned and ran a hand over his scalp hoping to calm the raging chaos inside his skull and then, summoning every last particle of his energy reserves, he made his way to the bathroom, turned on the light and as the extractor fan began whirring in the background stood looking at his reflection in the mirror above the sink.

Phil was perversely pleased to see that he looked as awful as he felt because he knew it would help make the case that he ought to stay sober for the rest of the weekend. Simon and Degsy were expert at drinking their way through the pain of even the worst hangovers and he knew that they would encourage the others to do the same. The prospect made Phil's stomach churn. He didn't want to get in that state ever again, even more so, having made the connection between his readiness to drink and the appearance (albeit in an abstract manner) of the man who had been a constant bone of contention in his relationship with Helen.

Reaching into his trouser pocket Phil pulled out Sanne's phone number. There was no way he would use it. Even though he had made it clear that he was getting married, she was an attractive woman and he, being a man, was programmed to find attractive women

79

attractive. It really was a complication he could do without. He put it back in his pocket.

On the other hand, Sanne was Aiden Reid's ex-wife and having never met the man who had blighted his girlfriend's life to such an extent that she wouldn't even contemplate marriage the best part of a decade later, Phil was sorely tempted to meet her again, if only to find out what about Aiden (apart from his fame, good looks and bags of money) made him so special.

Phil knew it was a stupid, petty and childish way for a grown man to think, and that it was beneath him even momentarily to indulge these feelings of inadequacy. But in this instance at least what he felt in his heart carried more weight than what he thought in his rational mind.

Phil shed his suit, climbed into the bath, pulled back the curtain and turned on the shower, cowering away from the cool spray until steam began to rise from the lower reaches of the bath. Stepping under the hot water Phil's skin tingled as the water blasted through the dirt and grime that had plastered itself to him over the past twenty-four hours leaving him if not entirely like a different person, then at least the next best thing.

Stepping out of the bath he stood in front of the mirror, picked up his towel and wiped a patch of the glass free of condensation to reconsider his image. He looked better. Not great, but better. The eyes were less bloodshot, the sheen had returned to his skin and although his teeth were in need of a good sandblasting, it was nothing that a burst of Colgate and a good scrub couldn't handle.

In the bedroom Phil pulled out underwear and fresh clothes and then recalled his instruction that they should wear the suits for the entire weekend. He picked up his from the floor and hoped the worst of the creases would fall out during the day. The white shirt however was beyond redemption, so he pulled out another one and began dressing.

He put on his jacket and again fished out the piece of paper with Sanne's number on it. He stared at it a moment before screwing it up and tossing it on the table next to the TV. Congratulating himself on doing the right thing he picked up his room key and left the room, only to return, walk over to the pneumatic drill and hide it carefully in the wardrobe.

Reaching the ground floor Phil stepped out of the lift feeling more centred than he had any right to be given his hangover. And as he made his way to the lobby to meet the boys he promised himself that no matter what problems came his way during the day he would remain positive. There was no need to keep blowing up over the smallest thing, what he needed to do was to remain calm. As he scanned the lobby he spotted a scruffy denim-clad figure with a rucksack standing with friends. In an instant all notions of peace and goodwill to the universe vanished.

The man turned around and opened his arms to greet Phil. 'How's this for a surprise?' he said in a rich, deep voice like an old delta blues singer. He flashed Phil a dirty great grin that revealed a set of teeth that had seen better days. 'I bet you weren't expecting to see me here, were you, kid?'

'No, Dad,' said Phil flatly. 'You've pretty much hit the nail on the head with that one.'

8.

'Someone needs to explain!' barked Phil loudly enough for a number of the Royal Standard's guests to glance over at him. 'And they need to do it now!'

Simon stepped forward wearing a look of weary resignation. 'Well in that case I think it probably ought to be me.'

'You?' questioned Phil. 'You're supposed to be my best man not a cut-price Jeremy Kyle!'

Simon pulled Phil to one side and lowering his voice to a whisper said: 'Look, mate. Don't do this.'

'Do what?' boomed Phil, refusing to comply with the volume established by Simon. 'You're the one who invited my dad, of all people, on my stag do. What were you thinking?'

'He asked to come. What could I say?'

'I think no would have sufficed. That's the word you use when you don't want things to happen isn't it?' Fizzing with frustration Phil snarled: 'You didn't even bother to warn me!'

'Would you have still come if I had?'

'Of course I wouldn't! Why would I go on a stag do with my dad?'

'Because he's a laugh. He always has been.'

'He's only a laugh if you're not related to him. If you share DNA with the old scrote I think you'll find that the word "laugh" is better translated "embarrassment".'

'So what do you want me to do? Send him back?'

'Could you?' retorted Phil. 'That would be great! And while you're at it you could get him to pop round to my mum's and apologise to her for being an arsehole for the best part of forty years!' Phil glared at Simon. 'Did you pay his plane fair?'

Simon winced. 'He promised he'd pay me back.'

'What with,' snorted Phil, 'fresh air?'

They both turned to look at Patrick who already appeared to have the boys in stitches.

'So can he stay or what?' asked Simon.

'Doesn't look like I've got much choice, have I?' replied Phil bitterly. 'I'll tell you what though . . . next time you've got a big Saturday night blow-out planned I'm definitely bringing your mum along.'

Leaving Simon to contemplate the error of his ways Phil strode over to his dad and considered giving him a hug but thought better of it. He looked older, more worn than Phil remembered and it occurred to Phil that Patrick Hudson would not always be around to be angry at.

'So, all sorted then?' said Patrick raising his bushy eyebrows expectantly.

Phil nodded. 'It's done. You're staying.'

'Excellent, son!' he said genuinely pleased. 'I promise you, you won't regret it! So what's the plan? Bit too

84

early to start drinking, eh? Especially after last night!' He nudged Phil in the ribs and ran one of his big calloused hands over his son's scalp. 'A right chip off the old block!'

'Cheers, Dad,' said Phil envisaging the long day ahead. 'You have no idea how proud that makes me feel.'

'We're going to get some breakfast, Mr Hudson,' said Simon.

Patrick eyed Simon sternly. 'It's Patrick, son. I'm only Mr Hudson when I'm in court or being grilled by the filth.'

Phil reluctantly found himself warming to his dad's infectious charm. 'Let it go Pop, it's not like you're the Godfather is it?' he said. 'The only criminal record you've got is for refusing to pay your council tax until they reinstate the old-style wheelie bins.'

Patrick let out a rasping chuckle. 'And every time I take out the rubbish I still think those bins are just too damn small!'

Phil noted his father's rucksack. 'Do you want a few minutes to nip up to your room and drop that off, Dad? You don't want to be carrying it around all day.'

'I'm fine thanks, son,' replied his dad, squeezing the strap of his bag. 'It's got my angina medicine in it, so I'll keep it with me to be on the safe side.'

Following Simon's lead Phil, Patrick and the boys made their way outside the hotel. It was another bright, sunny day – classic T-shirt weather – and although Phil still felt like death warmed up his spirits couldn't fail to be lifted by the vividness of the cloudless blue sky above their heads as he slipped on his sunglasses.

The good weather had drawn the inhabitants of Amsterdam into the city centre as well as those there for the weekend. There was a buzz about the city as people got on and off tram cars, stood in crowds watching English-speaking outdoor theatre performers or simply sat watching the world go by outside numerous cafés and restaurants.

The boys having dismissed several possible breakfast venues on the basis that they 'didn't look right', finally came to a halt outside a pub off Dam Square. It was called the Shamrock Inn and had two faded Guinness posters blu-tacked to the glass doors at the entrance. Phil tried to keep his mouth shut but he just couldn't help himself. 'You come all the way to Amsterdam and this is the place you want to eat your first meal of the day?'

'It does English breakfasts,' said Degsy. 'We can't come on a stag weekend and not have a full English breakfast. It'd be criminal.'

'The lad's right,' said Patrick. 'I've had breakfasts all round the world from Bangkok to Wilmington Ohio and I haven't had one better than the Great British breakfast. It's one of the few things we do well.'

Reuben, Spencer and Deano nodded in agreement.

Phil hoped that at least Simon might be the voice of reason. 'Come on Si,' he encouraged, 'You know this is wrong.'

Simon shrugged. 'Mate,' he said wearily, 'I'm starving

and my head feels like it got hit by a truck. I don't care what we eat or where we eat it as long as we eat it now.'

The debate concluded, they took a table between a scruffy-looking British couple sipping tea from large mugs that said 'I love London', and five lads in their late teens tucking into a plate of sausage sandwiches while broadcasting in braying public school accents the highlights of the sex show they had been to the night before.

Clearly working on the basis that targeting people with hangovers would keep the people who cared about the provenance of their sausages far away, the Shamrock Inn's English breakfast was as disappointing as it was overpriced. The eggs were pale and undercooked, the bacon hopelessly chewy, the toast cold, the bright orange baked beans congealed and the sausages little more than cereal rusk and mechanically recovered meat stuffed into a flimsy casing.

Phil ate no more than three mouthfuls of his breakfast before abandoning it in favour of a mug of tepid sugary tea, which he drained in three gulps.

'Not hungry?' asked Spencer spying Phil's full plate.

'Nah,' said Phil. 'I think I've lost my appetite.'

'So can I . . . ?' Spencer nodded towards the food. 'Shame to see it go to waste.'

'Help yourself, mate.'

Not needing to be told twice, Spencer shared out the leftovers among the grateful boys.

Phil stood up and stretched. The thought of spending

the next ten minutes watching the others eat breakfast was about as appealing as eating the breakfast himself. 'I'm going to go for a walk,' he said. 'Clear my head a bit. Are you guys going to be here for a while or shall we just meet up later?'

'Hang on a sec and I'll come with you,' said Simon as the boys murmured that they wouldn't be going anywhere soon. 'I'm not ready to start drinking but I could do with getting hold of some fags.'

Donning their sunglasses the two friends headed towards Dam Square in silence, content, it seemed, to allow the sights and sounds around them to be their entertainment.

'You're hating this, aren't you?' said Simon as they passed a group of kids splashing each other in one of the square's fountains. 'I can see it on your face.'

'I'm not hating it, exactly,' replied Phil.

'But you're not loving it either?'

Phil shook his head. 'No,' he said, 'not if I'm honest.'

'So what can I do to make it right?' They passed an elderly couple throwing bread to a flock of increasingly aggressive pigeons. 'I don't want to ruin things for you, mate. It's supposed to be your weekend after all.'

'Well the boys seem to be having a laugh. I'm just being a bit of a misery that's all.'

'And I'm guessing from the way you were knocking back the hard stuff last night that you were a bit freaked out by that girl turning out to be Aiden Reid's ex-missus.'

'Just a bit. It's not her so much as him. I've never

even met the guy, but sometimes it seems like he's everywhere I go.'

'You've said in the past that you thought Helen might still—'

'That was ages ago,' said Phil cutting him off. 'And I don't think that any more. Me and Helen couldn't be any more rock solid if we tried.'

'So what's the problem then?'

'There isn't one.'

Simon laughed. 'You'll have to do better than that. Remember I've known you a long time.'

They passed a middle-aged man wearing a Manchester United top fast asleep against one of the lion statues. 'Fine,' said Phil as the man stirred. 'The thing is I'm thinking about seeing Sanne. The girl from last night.'

'Why would you do that? Because you want to know about him? Then read a paper, mate. He's in there every other day.'

Phil came to a halt next to a bench but didn't sit down. 'I knew you wouldn't get it.'

'Of course I don't get it,' said Simon, 'there's nothing to get. Why would you want to go winding yourself up over your missus's ex a week before you're getting married? Makes no sense.'

'And leaving your wife and kids does?'

'You don't know all the facts.'

'Then why don't you tell me them?' said Phil, with more than a hint of anger in his voice. 'I'm your mate, aren't I? You're my best man. What proof do you need that I'm on your side?'

'It's not that easy.'

'That doesn't mean you can't try.'

'I can't, mate.'

'Can't or won't?'

'Does it matter?'

'To me it does, yeah. I know you think this isn't any of my business and maybe you're right, but if the tables were turned you'd be having a go at me. I know you would.'

Simon bit his lip in frustration and then in a sudden burst of resignation, said: 'You want the truth? Well here it is: I've fallen in love with someone else.'

'Fallen in love? Who with?'

Simon shook his head. 'Believe me when I say mate, that you do not want to know.'

'Well maybe I do.'

'No,' said Simon firmly, 'you don't.'

'At this point we should agree to disagree but that's just not going to happen is it,' said Phil. 'I'm not going to let this go, Si, I'm not. So just tell me, okay? It's not Reuben's missus is it?'

'No, no of course not.'

'Then who?'

'I can't.'

'Yes, you can. All you've got to do is say the name and it's done.'

A group of teenage girls passed by singing in Dutch at the top of their voices.

'It's Caitlin,' said Simon. He looked Phil in the eyes. 'I'm sorry mate,' he continued, 'I'm really sorry. I didn't mean for it to happen, it was just one of those things.'

'One of what things?' exploded Phil. 'You haven't actually told me anything yet!'

'Look, mate,' said Simon backing away, 'we don't need to talk about this. You know now and that's all that matters.'

Phil stepped towards Simon. 'You think you can get away with leaving it like that?

'I don't want to talk about it now, that's all,' said Simon. 'This is *your* weekend.'

'And Caitlin's *my* sister,' said Phil, advancing so far into Simon's personal space that he could smell the tea on his friend's breath. 'How long has this been going on? Months? Weeks?' Simon shrugged and took a step back. Phil repeated his question: 'How long?'

Simon cast his eyes down to the cobblestones. 'Since before Easter.'

Phil cast his mind back to the time in question. 'Deano's birthday?' Simon nodded. 'You were talking to her loads that night I remember.' Phil shook his head in disbelief. 'That's my kid sister!'

'I know,' said Simon. 'I feel awful about it. I really do.'

'But not awful enough to keep your hands off her!'

'It wasn't like that.'

'No,' said Phil. 'It never is, is it? When were you going to tell me? When you moved in with her? Was I supposed to drop in to see her, see your shoes in the hallway and put two and two together?'

'You know it wasn't like that,' stammered Simon, 'I just couldn't find the right time to tell you.'

Phil's face was the picture of disbelief. 'And you've been carrying on like this ever since Deano's do?'

'Sort of.'

'Sort of? What does that mean? Whatever it is you have to say, just spit it out.'

'It's complicated.'

'Complicated how?'

'She ended it about a month ago.'

Phil breathed a sigh of relief. 'So it's over?'

'Not for me.'

'And what's that supposed to mean?'

'It means,' said Simon solemnly, 'that I love her. I really love her.'

'And that's why you've left Yaz and the kids, is it?' scoffed Phil. 'Because you think you're in love with Caitlin? You do know what sort of girl Caitlin is, don't you? You do know that there are half a dozen blokes around the country who all think that they can't live without her. Come on Si, I love her to bits but even I know that she's a total bitch when it comes to men. She uses them. She always has done and probably always will. She likes their money and their attention but the second she's bored she's off and – be under no illusions about this – she won't come back.'

'You don't know that,' said Simon. 'Her and me together, it was special. Really special.'

'So what? You're leaving Yaz and your kids to prove your commitment to Cait in the hope that she'll take you back?' Phil felt genuine pity for his friend but also like he might throw a punch at any moment. 'I need to get out of here.'

Simon shrugged. 'What do you want me to tell the others?'

'Tell 'em what you told me,' snapped Phil, 'and see where that gets you.'

9.

Back at the hotel, Phil headed straight up to his room. The door was open and the chambermaid's cart was parked directly outside. He shuddered at the thought of her reaction to the chaos within, and again at what she would have seen had he not had the foresight to hide the stolen penumatic drill.

Apologising for disturbing her, Phil began searching for the piece of paper with Sanne's number that he'd screwed up and left on the table next to the TV. It wasn't there. The chambermaid must have dumped it. He spotted a large bin bag on the floor and began frantically rooting through it. Used tissues. Plastic bags. Sandwich wrappers. Half-empty water bottles. The rotting remains of a fruit salad. On the point of giving up Phil delved one last time and there, still screwed up in a ball was Sanne's number.

Phil held it open with one hand while he reached for the phone with the other and then tried to work out what exactly to say to Sanne. The essence of which was that having endured the triple whammy of a raging hangover, having his sixty-six-year-old dad join his stag weekend and discovering that his married best man had been sleeping with his sister, he now wanted to spend time in the company of someone who couldn't surprise him with any more revelations. And while he appreciated that Sanne by virtue of her association with Aiden Reid had already knocked him sideways with a revelation of her own, the fact remained that he needed to get away from both friends and family, and as Sanne was neither, she was his safest bet.

'Hello?'

The line wasn't great and neither was his recall of her voice hidden as it had been for most of the night under the constant thump of the blandest of club music.

'Hi, Sanne, it's me,' said Phil. 'The English guy from last night.'

Sanne laughed. 'You say that like you imagine I gave out my number to so many people last night that I might have forgotten! How are you? I hope you didn't run into those guys again. Did you have a good night?'

Phil's head throbbed at the very thought of it. 'It was fine, thanks. And no, we didn't see those guys again. How about yours?'

'It was good fun. It's always nice to catch up with friends that you haven't seen in a long while. So, I take it you're calling because you want to take up my offer?'

'Definitely, if it's still there.'

There was a short pause and then she said: 'I can probably spare you an hour if you'd like. I thought I was going to have longer but a friend called this morning with a boyfriend crisis. You know how it is,

95

she needs me to do the whole shoulder to cry on thing.'

'An hour's fine,' said Phil. 'Do you still think the Van Gogh Museum is the place to go?'

'Absolutely. It'll take me a little while to get ready and cycle over there so how does an hour from now sound?'

'Perfect.'

'Meet me at the entrance. Do you need directions?'

'No,' said Phil making a mental note to get hold of a guidebook. 'I'm sure I'll be fine.'

It was a little after one in the afternoon as Phil, having got lost several times along the way, finally reached his destination. Pulling his jacket and shirt, damp with perspiration, away from his back, Phil scanned the crowds milling outside the entrance to the museum but couldn't see Sanne anywhere. Deciding to find a shop and buy a bottle of water he was about to cross the road when he felt a tap on the shoulder, and turned around to see Sanne.

She was wheeling a bike which, unlike the thousands he had seen so far this weekend was a bright metallic pink, rather than black, and had a basket on the front decorated with plastic roses.

She was once again looking head-turningly attractive, wearing sunglasses, a light blue floral dress and gold sandals and he wondered how could he have not realised that she was famous when standing next to her now it was impossible to imagine that she could be anything but.

'So, you found your way here without too much trouble?' she asked, taking in his suit without comment.

'I have a killer sense of direction,' joked Phil. 'I should have been a boy scout.'

'But you weren't?'

'What?'

'A boy scout?'

Phil shook his head. Why had he even mentioned boy scouts in the first place? 'I was a sea cadet for a while when I was fourteen,' he explained, 'but after six weeks without seeing so much as the inside of a canoe I reasoned that it wasn't for me.'

'I was what we call in the Netherlands a *Padvindster*,' she explained as they walked towards the museum entrance. 'It's like your Girl Guides in the UK. At the end of each meeting we'd have to say: ' "I am a link in the golden chain of world friendship, and I will keep my link strong and bright." '

'And did you?'

Sanne laughed. 'I most certainly did!'

The queue for the museum seemed to be moving quite briskly. At a loss about what to talk about Phil opted to fall back on the weather.

'The weather this weekend has been amazing hasn't it?'

Sanne smiled and looked at her watch. 'I bet myself that you'd mention the weather within five minutes of us meeting and I was right!'

Only a little embarrassed by his poor conversational

skills Phil attempted to make a defence. 'Well, it is a nice day!'

'The Dutch aren't like this,' continued Sanne. 'We notice the weather but never feel the need to go on and on about it like the English. That's one of the things I actually miss about not living in UK any more. In England there's always a way of making conversation with anyone no matter who they are or what they do.'

'Well, since we're on the subject of national stereotypes,' grinned Phil, 'when exactly did they make it obligatory for Dutch people to ride bikes? Do you get given one at birth?'

'So, you'd rather we went everywhere by car like you do in the UK?' countered Sanne. 'I'd never seen people drive such short distances until I lived in your country. Need a pack of fags . . . jump in the car. Need a stamp . . . jump in a car. One day the English will grow wheels.'

'It's because in the old days an Englishman's home was his castle,' explained Phil. 'These days his castle is more likely to be his Ford Mondeo. So,' he said leaping on the first subject that came to mind, 'is Van Gogh a particular favourite of yours?'

Sanne nodded. 'Everybody in Holland loves Van Gogh,' she replied. 'He is our country's favourite son. Why? Do you not like him?'

Phil shrugged. 'I don't know much about him beyond him lopping off his ear, having Don McLean write a song about him and that Kirk Douglas once played him in a film.'

Sanne was scandalised. 'You don't study art in UK schools?'

Phil recalled the level of artistic debate that had existed at his local comprehensive. 'Not the one I went to.'

'Was yours a special school of some kind?'

'That would be one word for it,' joked Phil. 'Put it this way, it was a bit rough. Not the kind of school where there was a lot of talk about art.'

'And since then?'

'What?'

'You've done no learning about art?'

'Not really,' he replied. 'I've been to the art gallery in Nottingham a few times and watched the odd documentary on TV but I wouldn't really say I've learned about it. I'd like to though. I've always felt like – much like with music and film – the world would be a poorer place without it.'

'Do you have any pictures on your walls at home?'

'A few, but they're mainly things that my girlfriend bought.'

'So she's the artistic one in your relationship?'

'Yeah,' said Phil, wondering what Helen would say if she could see him standing in the queue outside the Van Gogh Museum with a beautiful, famous Dutch girl who just happened to be Aiden Reid's ex-wife. 'I suppose you could say she is.'

They reached the ticket desk and Phil paid for two tickets. They went inside, checked in their bags and passed through the security scanners into the first gallery, which Sanne explained was dedicated to paintings by artists who were friends, contemporaries or were considered an inspiration to the young Van Gogh.

As they worked their way around the room studying each painting Phil read a few of the names on the wall beside the paintings. Being here with an actual art lover made him feel more keenly what he always felt whenever he went to museums or art galleries: that he was on the outside looking in at people who spoke a language no one had taken the time to teach him.

Sanne, he observed, understood the language of art perfectly. Every now and again she would stand in front of a picture over which Phil had passed a cursory glance and would tilt her head slightly to one side and bite her lip absentmindedly as though she was lost deep inside the painting. He had seen Helen do the same thing and although he had tried with her help to make that connection with a work of art, most of the time he had felt nothing.

As they wandered through the galleries on the upper floors which divided Van Gogh's work chronologically, somewhere around 1880 Phil's mind began to drift. Chief amongst the thoughts that sought to occupy him was what his friends were up to and what excuse Simon dreamed up for his absence. Knowing Simon, the excuse would be sufficiently vague not to cause alarm and with his father present to act as the entertainment, they would hardly miss him. Phil had no idea what that afternoon's activity might be but even though he didn't seem to be getting very much from seeing the work of one of the world's greatest artists first-hand it had to be better than getting stoned or gawping at the girls in the windows of the brothels in De Wallen.

'You don't seem to be enjoying yourself,' said Sanne as they entered the final gallery, Auvers – 1890. 'You look a bit bored.'

'Not bored,' replied Phil. 'Just disappointed I suppose. In myself, not him. Given that this is the year he tops himself and I've yet to be moved by any of the paintings I've got a horrible feeling that art isn't for me at all.'

'I used to have a friend just like you,' said Sanne. 'He was a really dynamic guy, and he loved all sort of culture but he never got art. And when I brought him here he said exactly the same thing right until the very end.'

'And then what happened?'

'I showed him my favourite picture.'

Phil's curiosity knew no bounds, convinced as he was that the 'friend' was Aiden Reid.

The painting depicted a bright yellow wheat field with three paths in it underneath a dark foreboding sky. Phil stared at it long and hard imagining himself standing next to the painter, seeing what he was seeing and feeling what he was feeling.

'What do you think?' asked Sanne.

Phil thought hard. He felt lots of things but nothing he cared to put into words. 'I think your friend was right,' he said quietly as he imagined Aiden Reid standing in front of this very picture. 'One single picture really can change your mind about everything.'

'I really want to thank you for that,' said Phil as they stood in the shade of the museum. Most of the hour she had promised him had gone by now. 'I never expected to enjoy looking around here as much as I did.'

'My pleasure,' said Sanne. 'Always glad to add another convert to the Van Gogh army.'

'Well, should you find yourself in Nottingham I'll gladly return the favour,' replied Phil, 'although the best we can do is a statue of Robin Hood who might not even have existed.'

Sanne laughed. 'Or we could get a drink if you've got time.'

'But I thought you needed to—' Sanne looked guilty and the penny dropped. 'There was no friend in urgent need of a shoulder, was there?'

'Oh, come on,' protested Sanne, 'don't look at me like that! I met you in a queue outside a bar! I didn't know anything about you!'

They walked across a wide, open area which Sanne informed him was known as Museumplein towards a large paddling pool crammed full of parents and young children splashing in the water. To the right of the pool was their destination, a café with a large terrace: and ducking inside out of the glare of the sun they re-emerged, carrying an iced coffee and a Coke and sat down at a table in the shade of a huge awning.

Phil tried to coax out more of Sanne's personal

history even though he was already aware of the salient parts of it. She was, he learned, currently working part-time as a dance teacher specialising in modern, tap and ballet but prior to that had worked in the music business over in the UK. These days as far as the singing went she gigged at clubs in and around Amsterdam doing what she described as 'a kind of acoustic, twenty-first century Joni Mitchell thing'. Curious to see how reluctant she might be to tell him about her previous fame Phil attempted to get her to be more specific but all she would say was that the work had involved 'music videos, backing vocals and the like', and that although it had been fun at the time she had no regrets that this period of her life was over.

'So what brought you back to Amsterdam?' he asked. 'Or is that too personal a question?'

'No, it's fine,' she replied. 'My marriage ended and I felt the only place I might be able to heal would be back home.'

'I'm sorry to hear that,' replied Phil, meaning it. 'He must be an idiot, your ex-husband.'

Sanne smiled. 'That's kind of you to say so,' she said. 'But it was a bit more complicated than that.'

Phil just couldn't help himself. 'How so?'

'You can't really be interested.'

'You'd be surprised,' replied Phil. 'Despite what you saw last night, I'm a lover not a fighter. So come on then, what was the reason?'

'All the time he was with me he was in love with someone else . . . someone from his past.'

'An ex?'

She nodded. 'Yes, an ex.'

Phil's chest tightened. 'I know this is going to sound weird,' he began, 'but does this woman have a name? I'm just curious I suppose, I'm just trying to picture the kind of woman that would have that sort of effect on a guy.'

'Helen,' said Sanne quietly, 'her name was Helen.'

10.

Phil was standing in front of the sink in the café's gents' toilets frantically splashing water on his face, like people do in films when trying to regain their composure after a shock. If this had been a film, maybe the water-splashing would have done the trick and allowed him to return to the table outside and act like a normal human being but as it wasn't a film, but real life in all its Technicolor glory, he just managed to drench the front of his shirt and part of his tie, earning himself a number of odd looks.

Aiden Reid's marriage had collapsed because of Helen. That had been the long and the short of what Sanne had said, hadn't it? After all those years, after all that time, Helen's ex's feelings for her had remained so strong that they had overcome what he felt for Sanne, his wife. Did Helen know that Aiden felt this way? Had he tried to contact her after his marriage ended or even while they were still together? Phil tried to recall when he had read in the papers about Sanne and Aiden Reid separating. Last year? The year before? He recalled past occasions when Helen had seemed out of sorts. Like the period when for weeks on end

105

she would get up in the middle of the night and watch TV claiming that the stress of working under a new station manager was affecting her sleep patterns or the time before that when he would find her in tears in the darkness of their bedroom. She'd claimed it was because she was worried about her dad's struggle with Alzheimer's or her mother's upcoming operation. There were more such incidents and although each came with a perfectly plausible explanation Phil wondered if at least one of them had been due to Aiden Reid.

Phil suddenly felt tired and hungover again. He was too old to be plagued by this kind of insecurity. He didn't need thoughts of some oily celebrity stalking his girlfriend a week before his own wedding. Whether Aiden had contacted Helen or not, he knew Helen would never let him down. He did know that, didn't he? In all the years they had been together, making a home together, she had never given him any cause to doubt her loyalty. Helen had chosen him as the man that she wanted to be with for all time. They were getting married. This time next week he would be putting a ring on her finger.

Feeling more positive after his internal pep talk Phil wiped his face on a paper towel, made his way outside and stood for a moment observing Sanne watching two small children taking turns to chase each other around the children's playground a few feet from their table. It was a shame. Her beauty, former fame and connection to Aiden Reid aside, she was actually really easy to get on with and perhaps in a different life they could have been friends.

'I'd better be getting off,' said Phil as he reached the table.

'Oh,' said Sanne rising to her feet, 'are you sure? I was just thinking that if you really wanted to see Amsterdam I could show you around Vondelpark. It's not far at all.'

'That's really kind of you,' replied Phil, 'but I've got to go. The boys . . . well you know, I'm supposed to be on a stag weekend . . .'

Sanne smiled. 'Yes, of course. You should go.' She kissed his cheek. 'It was lovely to meet you Philip Hudson, it really was and I wish you and your wife all the happiness in the world.' She handed Phil a club flyer from her bag. 'A parting gift from me to you! It's a gig I'm doing tonight at the Yellow Robot, it's an acoustic thing. I'm pretty sure it won't be to your friends' liking but if you do get a chance to drop in you should say hi.'

He felt relieved and guilty as he walked away. Pleasant though she was, she was the gateway to a very special kind of madness that he could do without. For the rest of the weekend at least he would forget all about art, culture and the pursuit of deeper meaning for his time in Amsterdam and join his friends in the things that really mattered on a stag weekend: having a laugh and getting trashed.

Keen to get out of the sun for a while, Phil caught a tram to get him closer to the hotel, alighting at

Amsterdam Centraal. The city centre was crawling with a heady mixture of locals and tourists. Outside the station Phil spotted a crowd being entertained by a mime artist duo whose skin, clothes and hair were covered in silver paint and he felt a sudden pang for Helen. If she had been with him they would have stopped to enjoy the spectacle before heading off somewhere nice for a canalside drink.

Right now Phil needed to hear Helen's voice more than anything in the world. He missed her and wanted, if only for the duration of a three-minute call to be connected to her in some meaningful way. He scanned the square for a public phone and eventually found one back in the station next to a bank of ticket machines.

Phil pulled out some loose change and dropped the coins in the slot. He was about to tap the first digit of Helen's number into the keypad when the fatal flaw in his plan dawned on him. Although he could remember all manner of phone numbers from his Nan's before she moved into a home, to the office fax which hadn't been used in a decade, the one number he couldn't recall was Helen's.

It wasn't just that he only ever called Helen's mobile from his own, it was also that Helen had lost her phone or changed providers so many times that he couldn't even begin to guess what it might be. Was there a double seven in there somewhere? He felt sure there was, and of course it would start with a zero, but other than that, he just kept drawing a blank.

Returning the receiver to its cradle, Phil scooped the

coins out of the tray and headed back outside into the sunshine. One of the silver-painted mime artists, waved at him robotically, and Phil dug into his trouser pockets for the very same coins he had hoped to use talking to his fiancée, and dropped them into the silver hat at their feet.

Phil stepped through the revolving doors of the hotel into the air-conditioned cool of the lobby. He was boiling in his suit, and his head still ached and all he wanted was to go to bed for a couple of hours but as he came around the corner he walked straight into the boys and his father coming in the opposite direction.

'Big man!' bellowed Deano. 'Where you been?'

'I . . . er . . . I,' Phil's voice trailed off as he noticed that the boys were no longer in their suits but dressed in tracksuits and trainers. 'What's with the gear? Are we playing footie or something?'

'Better than footie mate!' chipped in Spencer. 'Paintball.'

'Paintball?'

Phil looked at Simon. He was lurking at the back next to Patrick and Reuben looking down at the floor but clearly paying attention to what was being said. 'Is that really what we're doing, Si?'

Obviously still smarting from their earlier encounter Simon nodded once but didn't utter a syllable.

'Mate,' said Spencer excitedly. 'We looked up the place at an internet café after we finished breakfast and it looks ace!'

'He's not wrong either!' added Reuben. 'This place is

the business. Loads of different scenarios, a big full-on battle at the end and one hundred paintballs included in the price. It's like everything you ever wanted back when you were a kid.'

Spencer did a little dance. 'It's true, fella,' he said cheerfully. 'I can't wait! It'll be like *Black Hawk Down* mashed with *Saving Private Ryan*. But don't worry bro' I've got your back! No man left behind!'

Phil thought hard even though Spencer hadn't actually asked a question. Did he really want to spend a sweltering afternoon in a tracksuit running around some abandoned farm in some unknown location in Amsterdam with the mother of all hangovers? Phil had been paintballing many times and had always hated it on the grounds that, for reasons he could never quite fathom, he somehow managed to get shot in the first five minutes of the game. The thought of adding an unspecified number of assailants (many of whom would be suffering from raging hangovers), to what was already a pretty dangerous game, made him feel ill.

He looked at his dad. 'You're not doing it too, are you?'

His father let out an emphysemic chuckle. 'I'd like to see the man who would be able to stop me!'

'Fine,' said Phil, 'give me five and I'll be right with you.'

The BattleZone Paintball Centre was everything Phil feared and more. Located on the outskirts of Amsterdam on several acres of wood and farmland, it was staffed by needlessly muscular English-speaking Dutch guys dressed like extras from a Chuck Norris film. There were life-sized posters of soldiers from every major Special Forces unit in the world on the walls in the main reception and painted on its front door were the words: 'No guts, no glory.' It was a solitary beacon in what passed for the Dutch countryside to British stag parties city wide to come, shoot and be merry, and could only have been more successful with this demographic had it actually been situated in Leidesplein or in De Wallen.

Once they had registered Phil, the boys and his dad were ushered into a large, empty hanger with about fifteen stag parties, all of them British. The instructors explained the dos and don'ts of paintball but Phil was distracted by the fact that a number of his fellow combatants were paying the instructors no attention at all, grinning inanely at the cache of weapons about to be distributed. This, thought Phil, did not bode well for the afternoon ahead.

Because of the numbers involved (and presumably to cut down on the risk of anyone actually being killed) all the individual stag parties were divided in two, to form two new teams, Delta Black and Cobra Red, and given their first mission 'Operation Relic' in which they had to rescue an ancient statue from a recently crashed plane on an abandoned airfield. It was, Phil noted wearily, essentially a 'grab the flag and get it back to your own base without getting killed' type scenario that he had played dozens of times before.

Mike Gayle

With orders in place all the men were handed overalls, kneepads, facemasks, coloured armbands and fully loaded paintball guns. They were instructed to meet at their respective command centres at opposite ends of the playing field (which for the purposes of authenticity had been made to look like an abandoned airfield).

Phil watched as members of Delta Black including Simon, Deano and Spencer exited the hanger with the rest of their team leaving Phil with his dad, Reuben, Degsy and a bunch of blokes he had never met before to make their way to their own base camp.

On the way a man in his mid-twenties with a crew cut and a partially visible neck tattoo struck up conversation with Phil.

'You done this before, mate?' he asked with a Bristol accent so strong Phil thought for a moment that he might be putting it on.

'Nah, mate,' said Phil. It occurred to him that he ought to return the question if only out of politeness. 'You?'

'Me and my mates back home do it every weekend.'

'Really?' replied Phil, relieved at not having to face this tattooed weekend warrior on the battlefield. 'So, how would you advise me to stay alive as long as possible then?'

The young man grinned, lowered the mask that had been sitting on his head and with a muffled voice said: 'Kick arse, mate, it always seems to work for me!'

With the profundity of his comrade's advice still echoing around his head Phil reached base camp where a Scouser called Jason appeared to have elected himself commanding officer.

'You lot over there take the right side,' he said pointing at one group, 'you lot over there take the left side,' he said pointing to another, 'and me and these guys,' he said gesturing to Phil's party and the few who remained, 'will cover you both and advance at the same time.'

It seemed no one had either the will or the desire to argue with Jason, so once the whistle was blown for the commencement of the battle his orders were followed to the letter.

For a while Phil couldn't tell what was happening. He could hear a lot of shouting and the sound of paintball pellets whistling overhead but as for how many people had been shot and who was closest to getting to the statue from the aeroplane he had no idea.

Phil would have been content to remain hidden in their sandbag dugout firing the odd paintball bullet in the air for the rest of the game but after about five minutes in Jason nudged Phil sharply in the ribs and whispered hoarsely, 'Let's go for it!' and before he knew what was happening he was being dragged over the top through the middle of the battlefield in the direction of the plane.

It seemed as though every last member of Delta Black was firing in their direction and Phil was convinced that it was only a miracle that neither of them had been hit before they reached a sandbag dug-out a few metres from the tail of the plane. Relieved, they stopped to take a breather but then the shots stopped and through a gap in the sandbags Phil made out a figure that was unmistakably Simon making a break for the door of the plane.

For reasons that Phil didn't want to analyse the thought that Simon might be about to win the game for his team filled him with rage. Who was this guy who felt that everything was his for the taking? Who was this guy who thought that it was okay to take up with his best mate's sister when there was a world full of unrelated women? Whoever this guy was he needed taking down, and he needed taking down now. Without a second thought Phil leapt over the sandbags screaming, 'Not on my watch!!!' at the top of his voice and ran full pelt across the open space to the plane without getting hit.

Spying Simon about to make a grab for the statue Phil released an extensive volley of paintballs in his friend's direction so that in mere moments his face and body were splattered with bright luminous yellow paint.

'I'm dead!' screamed Simon thrusting his hands in the air in defeat. 'You've got me! I'm dead!'

'I don't care!' screamed Phil, as he continued to unload paintball after paintball into Simon's head far closer than the regulation five-metre minimum distance they had been advised, 'I just want you to grow a pair, go back to your wife and stop poking my sodding sister!'

11.

The conversation in the minibus on the way back into central Amsterdam was muted to say the least. Simon sat up front with the driver glowering at any passerby who had the misfortune to catch his eye, while Phil was at the back doing pretty much the same. Between them sat the boys and Phil's dad, who while not being fully conversant with everything that had brought 'Operation Relic' to its abrupt conclusion were aware that *something* had gone on and that there was a very good chance that the 'something' in question was connected with Phil's earlier disappearance.

Phil was busy examining his own behaviour. The news that Simon had left Yaz for Caitlin had obviously upset him more than he had initially thought and the unacknowledged aggression that he felt towards his friend had manifested itself during the paintball game. As a result, his best man had not only suffered severe bruising around the chest area but also the beginnings of a black eye.

But was that all there was to it? Yes, Simon had felt the force of Phil's anger, but had he been the only source? Wasn't at least some of the anger directed at Aiden Reid, who, despite Phil's attempt to keep him under lock and key, had somehow managed to escape and was now wreaking havoc in the darker reaches of his mind? Phil just wanted to live in a world free of stress. A place where his best mate hadn't left his wife in order to sleep with his sister and his fiancée's ex wasn't so in love with her that he had allowed his marriage to fall apart because of it. None of this would have come to light if they had stuck to his original plan and gone go-karting followed by a pint and curry in Beeston.

The tension between Phil and Simon showed no sign of waning as the boys alighted from the minibus. Because it was clear that Simon (who usually acted as leader/tour organiser) wouldn't be doing a great deal of leading/tour organising any time soon Deano stepped into the power vacuum that had been created and as they all hovered in the lobby, set out his plan for the evening.

'Here's what we're going to do,' he announced. 'We're going to take an hour to clean up, wash, get a bit of kip and get ready, then it's back down here at seven on the dot to grab a tram to Leidesplein. Agreed?'

Although the closest Deano got to a verbal agreement was a grunt from Simon it was implicit from the absence of any alternative that his plan had been passed unanimously and so one by one the boys dispersed leaving Phil standing alone.

Keen to avoid further confrontation with his best man, Phil took the stairs to his room and quickly stepped inside. Leaning against the door he gradually allowed his feet to slip from underneath him until he'd completely collapsed on the carpet.

Phil had no idea how long he sat scrunched up at the base of the door but it was certainly long enough for his legs to become so numb that that he had to crawl to the bathroom for his second shower of the day.

He threw on some underwear and lay down on the bed, going over events in increasing amounts of detail. He felt his eyelids become heavier and his breathing shallower until he was just a few breaths away from unconsciousness when, completely unbidden, a partial mobile phone number popped up in his mind's eye and even though parts of it were indistinct he knew it was Helen's.

Bolt upright now Phil grabbed the phone by the side of the bed and tapped in the few numbers he could recall before they faded from memory. The first six numbers came as easily as if he had been reading them but the next three felt glued to the inside of his skull and needing to be forcibly ripped out with his fingertips. The last two remained complete mysteries. He stared at the keypad hoping the digits might leap out at him. He eventually pressed a four and then a two and waited.

'Hello?'

A man's voice, a Midlands accent, yet even so he didn't want to give up hope.

'Is Helen there?'

'Don't know any Helen mate,' said the man. 'You must have the wrong number.'

The line went dead. With a heavy heart Phil put down the receiver and manoeuvred himself under the bed covers. It had been a long day, and a lot had happened, maybe everything would look better after a good sleep. As he closed his eyes and waited for sleep there was a sharp knock at the door.

Phil ignored the knock and put a pillow over his head but then a second knock came, this time even louder. Rubbing his eyes, and feeling heavy of limb Phil crawled out of bed, grabbed the door handle and twisted it open. The door was barely more than a fraction ajar when there was a loud grunt from the other side and the door burst open, sending Phil flying to the floor.

Bewildered, Phil saw Simon's huge form descending on him as if they were in the opening bout of a WWE wrestling tournament. There was no time to move out of the way so he braced himself for the impact and hoped that his friend wouldn't do too much damage.

Phil didn't waste valuable energy trying to work out why his best man had kicked opened his door and was trying to pummel him into submission. Simon was wrestling with him for one reason and one reason only: he had grown tired of the energy required to sulk and had made up his mind that they should sort out the situation man to man.

It was, to be truthful, far from the most gainly of altercations by anybody's standards and had more in common with a documentary Phil had once seen on the mating rituals of otters than it did with Hollywood style punch-ups with their over the top sound effects and dynamic kung-fu poses. This was simply two men, in their late thirties, who knew that they had work on Monday, pretending to fight when all they were really doing was minimising each other's attempts to deliver a blow that might actually cause lasting damage.

It didn't take long for them to realise that now Simon had lost the element of surprise, they were so equally matched that it was pointless for them to continue wrestling. Both were regulars at the gym and while Simon was taller, Phil was more muscular so, much like two equally matched tug o' war teams, they cancelled each other out.

'Truce?' called Simon from inside Phil's headlock.

'Thought you'd never ask,' replied Phil as Simon released his crushing grip from around Phil's waist.

The two men lay on their backs panting as if they had both run a marathon. Simon grinned at his friend. 'That was pathetic wasn't it?'

'Too embarrassing for words,' said Phil rubbing his rib cage. 'We should keep this just between the two of us.'

'I've already locked it in the vault,' said Simon. He held out his hand. 'Mates?'

Phil knocked Simon's hand away and stood up. 'Don't think for a second that this makes things right between us. You've been banging my sister you tosspot. I'll never forgive you for that.'

'And you shot me in the head with a paintball at point blank range!' defended Simon. 'Have you seen my face? I look like I've gone twelve rounds with Mike Tyson!'

Phil looked at the bruising on Simon's face and smiled. 'I did get you good and proper, didn't I?'

'You think that's bad you should see my back. It's like I've been trampled by a rhino.'

Phil sat down on the bed. He wasn't sure he had the energy to stay annoyed with Simon for the whole weekend. 'If it's any consolation,' he conceded, 'I'd say a good seventy-five per cent of the aggression I unleashed at you was actually meant for someone else.'

Simon closed the bedroom door and sat down on the bed. 'Who? Your dad? What's he done now?'

Phil shook his head. 'Not dad, though that's not to say he couldn't do with shooting. I'm talking about Aiden Reid.'

'What about him? He's a twat, let it go, move on.'

'I would do,' began Phil, 'but . . . well . . . after I left you and the guys this morning I met up with that Sanne girl from last night.'

'And did what?'

'Walked around the Van Gogh Museum for the most part. Did you know he shot himself in the chest because he was depressed but it still took two days for him to die?'

'Do you fancy her?'

'Who?'

'Who do you think? She's bloody gorgeous!'

'Honest mate,' replied Phil. 'It's not like that.'

'So enlighten me.'

'I needed to get away – from you mainly – and so like

I said we went to the museum and then afterwards to a café and talked.'

'And what did she say that got you riled up enough to want to shoot me in the head?'

'She told me the reason that she and Aiden Reid split up,' said Phil looking down at the floor, 'was because he was in still love with someone from his past. I asked her this woman's name and she told me there on the spot: Helen.'

'So what did she say when you told her who you were? She must have been well freaked out.'

'I didn't. Like you said it would be too weird. I mean what are the chances of me chatting to some random woman in a queue outside a bar only to discover that she's my fiancée's ex's ex-wife.'

'But that's what actually happened!'

'I know,' replied Phil, 'but she'd never believe it would she? Anyway, she's playing a gig tonight and I'm thinking about seeing her again. I need to know the full story. I need to know if he's been in contact with Helen or even if he's capable of doing something reckless like turning up at the wedding next week. He's a proper full-on celebrity, Si, he drives Ferraris and interviews Hollywood stars and hangs out with footballers and to top it all he's Helen's first love. How am I going to compete with all that unless I arm myself with as much info as I can?'

There was a silence and then Simon stood up. 'Mate . . . I'm going to tell you something and I want you to listen hard, okay?'

Phil nodded. 'Okay.'

Simon put a hand on each of Phil's shoulders and stared into his eyes. 'Stop being an idiot.'

'But—'

Simon held his hand up in the air. 'No ifs, no buts, just stop it and stop it now. Helen's mad about you, any fool can see that, and all that's going to happen if you go down this road is that you'll drive yourself mental and ruin a perfectly good weekend away for no reason. Stay clear of Sanne, don't give Aiden Reid airspace in your head, and stop being an idiot, okay?'

Even though the problems between them were far from resolved Phil felt relieved to have his best man back on side. He looked at his watch and then at Simon. 'Hungry?'

'Starving,' said Simon.

'Chinese or Indian?'

'It's your weekend, mate,' said Simon. 'You choose.'

It was just after nine as the Bombay Garden's headwaiter brought over the bill to Phil's table.

'I'll take that,' said Phil, snatching it up. 'It'll be my way of apologising to you lot for ruining the day.'

'No you won't,' said Simon plucking the bill from between his friend's fingers. 'It's mine and let that be the end of it.'

Calling the waiter to one side Simon handled the bill while the rest of the table made ready to leave.

'So what's the plan?' asked Reuben pushing in his chair. 'More beer, different location?'

'There was a place we passed last night that looked quite good,' suggested Spencer. 'It was a couple of doors down from the bar where his Lordship started binge drinking, can't remember the name but I'm sure we'll be able to find it if we keep our eyes open.'

The boys piled out of the curry house into the street, searching for Spencer's mystery pub.

'Are you sure you have to take that bag with you everywhere?' asked Phil as the others broke off leaving him free to talk properly with his dad for the first time that evening. 'Can't you just jam a bottle of tablets into your pockets or something?'

'I can't son,' replied Patrick. 'There's too much of it.'

'You're all right though?' asked Phil. 'You're not sick are you?'

'I'm fine, son,' said Patrick. 'No need to worry about me. I'm indestructible!'

'Even so,' replied Phil. 'Promise me that you'll take it easy tonight, okay?' We've had no major mishaps so far and I'd like to keep it that way.'

'Of course I will,' said Patrick rolling his eyes in dismay. 'Not that I need you telling me what to do. I'm a grown man!'

'I know you are,' said Phil. 'I'm not trying to tell you what to do, Dad, I just want you to look after yourself.'

'Well, if we're all doling out the advice,' countered Patrick, 'might I suggest that you do the same? Getting into rows with your mates, getting us thrown out of paintballing . . . drinking so much you can barely remember the night before . . . I'd have to go

123

a long way to beat what you've been up to this last twenty-fours hours.'

'That's different, and you know it.'

'Different how, because it's you and not me? What's going on with you exactly? I've heard bits and pieces but it would be nice if I could hear what the problem is from my own son.'

'Look, Dad,' said Phil trying and failing to remain patient, 'can we just drop it? It's all sorted now, so there's no point in going over it again is there?'

'So this bloke off the radio isn't sniffing round your Helen after all?'

Phil sighed. The boys had obviously been talking and figured out more of the story than he had hoped. 'No,' replied Phil, 'he isn't . . . well he is sort of but it's more complicated than that . . .'

'Complicated?' questioned Patrick. 'What's that supposed to mean? Is he after your Helen or not? Because if he is, I don't care who he is, I'll sort him out myself.'

'Cheers Dad. That's good to know.' Phil wondered if there was any point confiding in his dad. 'Look, it's like this: I met a girl last night who it turns out used to be married to Aiden Reid. Anyway, she seemed to think the reason they split up was because he still had a thing for Helen and I had sort of planned to see her tonight to find out more, but Si talked me out of it.'

'Talked you out of it?' said Patrick indignantly. 'Why would you want to be talked out of it? If this woman knows more than you, you should hear what she's got to say because at least then you'll be able to make up your own mind.'

'I don't need my mind to be made up,' protested Phil. 'It is made up. Helen's marrying me next weekend. That's all there is to it.'

'If that really is all there is to it then why don't you find out anyway?' suggested Patrick. 'Honestly, son, sometimes I think your sister was born with more testosterone than you. Just get in there, find out what you want to know and then act accordingly. That's the trouble with your generation. Too much thinking and not enough action.'

Phil wasn't about to let that comment go unchallenged. 'Says the man who spent the last two decades of his working life on the dole.'

'But at least I lived the life!' boasted Patrick. 'At least I've got stories to tell! At least when I'm lying on my deathbed I'll have no regrets.'

'Well you should have if you've got anything close to a conscience,' retorted Phil.

'Oh, you know I don't mean all of that,' said Patrick dismissively. 'I mean the other stuff. The life stuff. You shouldn't get trapped in your own head son. If your gut is telling you to talk to this woman and put your mind at rest then that's what you should do. What have you got to lose?'

12.

Armed with the knowledge gleaned from the folded flyer in his pocket that Sanne wouldn't be coming on stage until ten thirty, Phil continued with the evening as planned. This meant that over the next hour he and the boys roamed Leidesplein drifting from theme bars to real ale pubs in search of good times. Now, they were holed up a bit further out of the neon glare of Leidesplein in a tiny bar sandwiched between a bakery and a travel agent's.

'You want another?' asked Simon noticing Phil's empty glass.

'I can't,' Phil replied. 'I'm off in a sec. Where do you reckon you'll be around midnight?'

Simon shook his head and sighed. 'Are you going where I think you're going?' he asked. 'I thought we agreed it was a bad idea.'

Phil glanced over at his father who was deep into an anecdote about the time he roadied for Pink Floyd during the first leg of their 1972 European tour. 'I just changed my mind, that's all.'

Simon raised an eyebrow in resignation. 'Do you want me to come with?' he asked. 'Bit of moral support?'

'I'll be fine,' he replied. 'Just tell me where you'll be at midnight and I'll meet you there.'

Simon looked over at the boys and asked the question. Deano and Patrick answered simultaneously. Deano's suggestion involved a visit to De Wallen while Patrick seemed entirely focused on getting stoned.

'I'm too old to get stoned,' said Simon, 'and I don't want to watch some miserable economic migrant taking off her kit while her dead eyes scream how much she hates me.' He picked up Reuben's guidebook and made a decision on behalf of the group. 'We'll be in a bar called Hoppe near Spuistraat,' said Simon. 'The Dutch drink there apparently so it can't be that bad.'

Outside Phil took a moment to get his bearings. Although he had been in Amsterdam for less than thirty-six hours, he was beginning to get a feel for the city and without even referring to the map in his back pocket he took a left and headed towards the bright lights at the end of the road, confident that he would know exactly where to go once he reached it.

The Yellow Robot, as Phil discovered, was a small subterranean club less than a hundred metres away from Amsterdam's infamous Milkweg club and housed in what according to a sign outside the venue used to be a coffee merchant's back in the 1800s. Relieved to have found the place with relative ease Phil descended the stairs, paid the entrance fee, and then entered the room where a young man on stage armed only with an acoustic guitar was in the middle of what Phil assumed was an ironic cover of a Kanye West song.

The song finished, the crowd clapped and Phil looked around. Although there were plenty of tables dotted about, they were all taken and even standing room at the back of the room appeared to be at something of a premium. Phil made his way to the bar and ordered a beer while the Kanye West cover guy announced in English that he was about to play his final song of the night, a ballad, about a girl he'd once spent the night with during the year that he was living in Barcelona. The audience clearly loved both him and his tragic demeanour and applauded him frantically and later (at his encouragement) even joined in with the song's heartbreaking refrain.

Although Phil loved talking about hi-fi and hi-fi related equipment because of what he did for a living, he had pretty much given up on modern music only stooping to purchase the occasional must-have CD which he would play for a week before abandoning it in favour of stuff that had long since proved its worth and stood the test of time like early Dylan, the Rolling Stones, Etta James, early Don Cherry or even mid-period Beastie Boys. Hearing the Kanye West cover guy, and more importantly seeing the way the audience reacted to him, made Phil resolve that first thing Monday morning he was going to trawl Amazon in a bid to catch up on everything he'd been missing out on since he'd unofficially decided to allow himself to get old.

The house lights came up signalling an interval and Phil sipped on a bottled Amstel while a technician came on stage and began setting up for Sanne, carrying off the previous act's microphone and returning with a new microphone, a stool and a small table on which he placed a bottle of water.

A short while later the house lights went down for a second time and the stage was plunged into darkness as over the PA came the opening bars to Stevie Wonder's 'Isn't She Lovely?' One by one the audience got the joke and a wave of anticipation spread over the crowd. They broke into applause as a single spotlight picked out the chair at the centre of the stage and moments later Sanne, wearing a silky blue dress and green shoes walked on to the stage carrying an acoustic guitar.

Revealing a hitherto unseen sense of comic timing Sanne whispered into the microphone, 'I am, aren't I?' As the Motown soul legend's vocals began the music faded, she strapped on her guitar and plugged it into the amp at her feet, and sitting down on the stool began her opening song, a passionate ballad sung in English, called (if the song's chorus was anything to go by) 'What chance did we have?'

Some three songs into Sanne's set, at least three quarters of the men in the room currently captivated by her every sound or movement had fallen in love with her. Sanne had that kind of face, and she sang those kinds of songs and the killer combination stirred something so instinctive within the masculine frame that had there been any princess-abducting dragons or fair maidens in need of rescuing from the clutches of their evil stepmothers, neither the dragons nor stepmothers would have stood a chance.

Mike Gayle

Phil wasn't totally immune from this sensation. While he had appreciated Sanne's attractiveness from the moment they met, he had persuaded himself it was a theoretical admiration only. He admired her beauty in the same way that some of his customers admired the new stock in the shop even though they had functioning audio kit at home. A thing of beauty, they would reason, was a thing of beauty whether you actually needed it or not. But here on the stage, singing song after song about love and heartbreak, her intense vulnerability added a depth to Sanne that made her beauty far less abstract because her songs revealed a truth that most in the room could never know first-hand: pretty girls got their hearts broken too.

By the end of her set Phil felt he knew Sanne better than he had previously and as she concluded with a cover of Prince's 'Condition of the Heart' followed by an acoustic rendition of her former band's biggest hit, 'Love Times Two', Phil felt almost as angry with Aiden Reid on her behalf as he did on his own.

When the house lights rose for the final time, Cat Stevens' *Peace Train* began playing over the PA. As he stood staring at the empty stage Phil realised that he hadn't given much thought to how exactly he was going to get to talk to Sanne. Although it was a small club she hadn't been in the audience before the gig and there was every chance that she would leave through some unseen side entrance without him knowing. And while it was true he still had her phone number, the

130

conversation he needed to have would be much more likely face to face.

Finishing off his beer Phil walked up to the technician and asked him if he would mind passing on a message to Sanne. Replying in English the guy refused, informing Phil that he was the fourth guy to have asked in the last ten minutes. He added that even though he personally didn't think she was 'all that' he was pretty sure she wouldn't be interested.

Phil tried to explained that he actually knew Sanne, and that all he wanted was to say hello, but the guy still refused, so then Phil pulled out a fifty Euro note and said, 'Look, just tell her that English Phil from the Van Gogh Museum is here and wants to talk and the money's yours.'

Shrugging, the guy held out his hand for the money up front. Reasoning he wasn't in much of a position to bargain Phil handed over the cash.

'English Phil from the museum?' said the technician, swiftly tucking the money into the front pocket of his jeans.

'No,' corrected Phil. 'English Phil from the *Van Gogh* Museum.'

Offering Phil a 'whatever' shrug the technician jumped on stage and disappeared behind the curtains at the wings. A number of moments passed and just as he was giving up all hope the technician returned with Sanne in tow and from his position at the side of the stage pointed out Phil. Phil waved and she waved back and began walking over to him.

'What are you doing here?' she asked, crouching down. 'I never imagined that you'd really come when you had so much of that oh-so-important drinking to do!'

'Yeah . . . well . . .' he said, trying to pluck up the courage he needed. 'Some things are important.' He took a deep breath and just came out with it: 'I need to talk to you. Quite urgently, actually.'

'Urgently?' Sanne looked confused and understandably so, thought Phil, considering that they barely knew each other. 'Why urgently?'

'Maybe urgent is the wrong word,' corrected Phil. 'Maybe complicated would be better. I promise it shouldn't take more than a few minutes.'

'I'm not sure I can spare the time,' she replied. 'I promised some friends I'd catch up with them later tonight.' She remembered her earlier white lie. 'And this time these friends are real.'

'Look,' replied Phil, 'I can see I'm making you nervous and that's the last thing I want. Let's just have a quick drink here, I'll explain and you can be off with your friends before you know it.'

Sanne considered his proposition carefully. 'You're not a weirdo are you? You didn't seem like one when I first met you but it's hard to tell sometimes!'

'Listen,' he replied, 'by the time I've told you what I need to say you'll definitely think I'm odd but not weird, I promise you.'

Sanne nodded as if to say she had concluded her extensive 'weirdo' detection tests and was analysing the results. 'I can't imagine that you're any weirder than some of the guys who used to follow the band back in the day. Just wait there while I get the promoter to look after my things and we'll go somewhere quieter.'

Sanne turned to walk off stage but then a couple of guys who had been lingering behind Phil clearly trying to overhear their conversation called her over, waving their pens in the air. The look of reverence on their faces as Sanne scribbled her name on the CD covers they had brought along with them was striking, and as soon as she was done they tried to engage her in conversation and when that failed they pulled out their digital cameras and practically begged for a photo session.

When Sanne finally got away Phil was left trading stares with Sanne's fans who were clearly wondering who was the guy in the black suit and tie. Keen to make himself less conspicuous, Phil's eyes fell on Sanne's merchandise stall, which had previously been hidden from view by the audience.

There were a number of CDs, badges, three T-shirts with different designs and a DVD of a recent live show. Phil picked up two CDs one of which was an official looking release called *Late night lullabies* and another that had a deliberately amateurish cover that was entitled *Home Demos 2*. Phil pulled out some money and handed it to the girl who was manning the stall. She carefully wrapped the CDs in a brown paper bag and handed them back as though acknowledging how fastidious Sanne's fans could be about packaging. Phil dropped them into his jacket pocket and returned to the stage to wait for Sanne.

He didn't have to wait long. Within a few minutes she appeared at the side of the stage wearing a denim jacket and, much to the annoyance of the small group of fans who had been staring daggers at him, beckoned him over. Phil followed her as she led him through the semi-darkness of the backstage area down some stairs, along a corridor and out through a fire door into the bustling side street.

Sanne walked as if she had a destination in mind and Phil offered no opposition.

'You were amazing tonight,' said Phil as they walked past a couple of shops selling everything from books to designer chairs. 'Really impressive.'

'Thank you,' she replied. 'They were a good crowd. Amsterdam crowds can sometimes be a little stiff but these guys were great. They were really into it.'

'It was hard not to notice,' said Phil. 'Are your fans always that keen?'

Sanne grinned. 'You mean the guys that wanted the autographs? They're a little intense but they're harmless enough.'

'Were they fans of your old band?'

Sanne shook her head. 'So you know about my old band?' she said. 'How did you guess?'

Phil laughed. 'You played one of their songs.'

'I wouldn't have had you down as a Misty Mondays fan.'

'I wasn't,' replied Phil. 'I just put two and two together, that's all. Don't you like people knowing?'

Sanne shook her head. 'I don't like people thinking they know me just because they've seen things in the papers. That period of my life is over, it was fun while it lasted but it's definitely over.' Sanne came to a halt in front of a dimly lit pub that didn't appear to have a name and was so small it looked more like someone's living room.

'It's not the coolest place in the world,' said Sanne reading Phil's face, 'but I think you'll like it. It's homely . . . like you.'

The barman waved at Sanne the moment she entered the room as did a number of the regulars. As they looked around for a table, a couple at a table in the window stood up and left and Sanne immediately took their table while Phil ordered a white wine and a beer at the bar.

'So,' began Sanne as they clinked glasses, 'what exactly is on your mind?'

'Everything,' replied Phil, though to his ears it sounded more than a little cheesy.

'Everything how?'

Phil struggled to find the right words. 'You and me . . . we're . . . connected.'

Sanne's brow furrowed. 'Is this to do with my old band?'

Phil shook his head. 'That's not the connection. Aiden's the connection,' he swallowed hard. 'Aiden Reid.'

13.

'What's going on?' demanded Sanne, her face lined in fury. 'Are you a journalist?'

'Of course not,' protested Phil. 'I'm just a bloke on his stag weekend!'

'Then why the talk about my ex-husband?' she snapped. 'What's he done now that's made him so newsworthy all of a sudden? I'm sick and tired of you guys following me around and hassling me about him, always taking pictures and poking your noses in where they're not wanted! That's the main reason I left the UK. I don't like you guys in my life!' She picked up her glass and tossed the contents in Phil's face. 'Just leave me alone! Just leave me be or I swear you'll regret it!'

She grabbed her jacket and turned to leave. Desperate to persuade her to stay, Phil made a grab for Sanne's arm. Of all the wrong moves he could have made this was undoubtedly the worst. Not only did it thoroughly enrage Sanne, but every man in the bar too and before he knew it he was being pinned against the wall.

'You've got it all wrong!' yelled Phil over the fracas even though he could no longer see if Sanne was still

136

in the room. 'You've got it all wrong! I'm not a journalist! I'm Helen Richards' boyfriend! You know, Helen Richards as in Aiden's—' Phil stopped as Sanne's face appeared among those already crowded around his own. She shouted something in Dutch to the men and gradually the less aggressive of the pack released their grip on Phil until only one, a young guy wearing a baseball cap and logoed sportswear, remained. Sanne placed her hand on the man's forearm and calmly repeated the phrase that she had told the others until he released Phil's shirt, offering a barely perceptible nod in her direction before returning to the bar where he had been standing with his friends.

Sanne slipped on her jacket, dug deep inside her bag and withdrew her purse. She spoke to the barman in Dutch and gave him a handful of notes. The barman took the cash; Sanne grabbed Phil's hand and dragged him outside.

'Are you all right?' she asked, checking his face for signs of injury. 'They didn't hit you did they?'

'I'm fine,' said Phil, wiping the remnants of Sanne's wine from his face. 'It was nothing.'

Sanne smiled. 'Not even a flesh wound?'

'No.' Phil noticed that he was still holding her hand and pulled it away. 'Not even a flesh wound.'

Sanne began walking. 'I'm sorry about what happened back there. When you mentioned Aiden's name I just saw red and assumed you were a journalist.'

Phil smiled. 'I take it you're not a fan?'

'Hardly,' she replied. 'It was bad enough when I was

137

in the band, we'd check into hotels and find them waiting outside our bedrooms or one time actually in our bedrooms hiding inside a wardrobe but the minute I started seeing Aiden it went insane. The paparazzi were camped outside the entrance to my apartment morning, noon and night. I couldn't even go to my grandfather's grave in Golders Green without at least one of them following me and taking a snap that would end up under some horrible intrusive headline. It was a living nightmare and not one I'll ever go back to.'

'Helen had that too for a while,' said Phil as Sanne took a sharp left off the main road down a long narrow street, 'obviously nowhere near as bad as you but bad enough. It started when Aiden first got famous so the tabloids started trawling through his friends and family to see if they could get any dirt on him, then when you guys got engaged it took off big time and they offered Helen silly money if she'd agree to dish the dirt in an exclusive. They got so desperate they even tried to drag me into it a couple of times, door-stepping me at work and trying to rile me so that they could get some kind of quote from the bloke going out with Aiden Reid's first love.' Phil winced as a look of hurt flashed across Sanne's features. He would have apologised but thought that it would make things worse. They continued in silence across canal bridges and along tiny cobbled streets until they came to a halt outside a bustling canalside café and took a seat at one of the outdoor tables.

A waitress handed them both menus. Phil looked at

his watch. It was only ten minutes to midnight. If he jumped on a tram now he could be with the boys before they moved on. But even as he constructed his getaway in his head Phil knew that he wouldn't be going anywhere too soon. There was too much to say, too much to talk about.

Tired of lager and desperate to counter the fatigue currently leeching away at his bones Phil ordered an Americano for himself and a cappuccino for Sanne and for good luck added a slice of cheesecake to the order.

As they waited Sanne, obviously keen to avoid any real conversation while they were still in danger of being interrupted by the waitress, told him the history of the area in which they were sitting, how in the seventeenth and eighteenth centuries the city's richest families had built homes there resulting in some of the unique style of architecture throughout the city. As Sanne spoke Phil gazed up at the illuminated three-storey buildings around them and marvelled at one in particular with a turreted roof and stone cornicing elaborately carved into the shape of herds of wild horses. It was truly spectacular and increased his sense of wonderment at the city that for two days had been his home.

The drinks and cheesecake arrived. Phil offered Sanne the first taste of his dessert but she declined. A long silence fell.

'When did you realise who I was?' asked Sanne eventually. 'In the queue when we met or later?'

Phil swallowed down a mouthful of cheesecake. 'I thought you looked familiar the minute I saw you,' he replied, 'but it was when I left the bar that it hit me.'

Sanne picked up Phil's fork and dipped it into the cheesecake. 'So why didn't you say anything when we met at the museum?' She manoeuvred the fork to her lips. 'Were you trying to catch me out or something?'

'It would've been too weird,' replied Phil as she set the fork down on his plate. 'I mean what are the chances? Me meeting you, and us having this huge thing in common?'

'You'd be surprised,' said Sanne. 'My mum once flew out to see me in LA and on the way back who should she sit next to but a woman she used to be best friends with in kleuterschool. They hadn't seen each other since they were six! Weird stuff happens all the time.'

'Maybe,' said Phil. He sighed and took a sip of his Americano. 'But it still felt too odd for my liking.'

'So what changed your mind?' she asked. 'Or is that a silly question?'

Phil's whole frame filled with embarrassment. What exactly had he hoped to learn by talking to Sanne about her ex-husband? Was he simply looking for a way to torture himself for no good reason? 'I was fine until you told me why your marriage broke down . . . and I guess . . . well I guess it sort of freaked me out. I mean your ex is a rich guy and I know from the papers that your divorce cost him big time and the idea that a guy like him would give up half his fortune because he thought he was still in love with my girlfriend was . . .'

'Unsettling?'

'That's it exactly,' said Phil. 'I know it's been a while since you guys split up but do you know if he ever tried to get back in contact with Helen?'

Sanne frowned. 'Don't you think she would tell you if he had?'

Phil shrugged. 'I don't know. Would you have done if you were in her shoes? He's Aiden Reid, if anyone's going to make a bloke feel a bit emasculated it would be someone like him with all his money and fame. Why would you put someone you loved through that? I know Helen inside out. I know what makes her laugh and I know what makes her cry. And if she did hold back the fact that he had been in touch it would be for a good reason.'

Sanne nodded thoughtfully. 'She sounds like a good woman.'

'She is,' replied Phil. 'The best.'

Sanne blinked several times and then rubbed her eyes and Phil knew that he had inadvertently hit a nerve. 'I used to hate her you know.' She looked at Phil, gauging his reaction. 'I used to hate her with every fibre of my being. When I moved in with Aiden I came across some photographs of her tucked away in a box in his wardrobe and I knew that she was someone special. Men like Aiden don't keep photos of women they've been with, at least not these kinds of photos – happy photos, full of warmth and love. I asked him who she was and he just took the photos and told me to mind my own business.'

141

Phil was confused. 'So he never told you about her?'

'Oh, he told me all right,' said Sanne, 'but it was months later and he was drunk and distraught because his mum was ill at the time and he wasn't coping very well.'

'And what did he say exactly?'

'He told me she was his ex, and that they'd planned to marry but he had been unfaithful to her.'

'And that's all?'

'No,' said Sanne, 'he also told me that he had never stopped loving her.'

Phil felt a rush of blood to his head. 'He actually said that?'

Sanne nodded. 'It's typical Aiden, always wanting what he can't have. It's how he's built.'

'So how did you end up getting married if you knew he felt this way?'

Sanne shrugged philosophically. 'How does anything happen in these situations? You simply become blind to what you don't want to see. By this time I was so in love with him he could have told me anything and it wouldn't have made the slightest difference to how I felt. I adored him. He made me feel like I'd never felt before. That he had these feelings for someone in the past was hurtful, yes, but it was by no means a deal-breaker. I was convinced that if I loved him enough, one day he'd feel that same way about me.'

'And did it work?' he asked, before the full implication of his question reached his brain.

Sanne didn't reply. She pulled a handful of notes from

her purse, tucked them underneath her cappuccino cup and stood up. 'I need to walk,' she said. 'You can come or you can go, it's up to you.'

Berating himself for not having kept his big mouth shut, Phil ran after her and caught her halfway down the cobbled street.

'Listen, Sanne I'm sorry,' he said quickly. 'That question has got to be the stupidest thing I've ever said. I'm an idiot. Just ignore me.'

Sanne wiped her eyes but even without a street light Phil could see her lashes glistening in the moonlight. 'I just find . . . I don't know . . . even now it still hurts a little.' Reaching into her bag she took out her phone, dialled a number, turned to Phil and said: 'How do you feel about—?' but then stopped as her call was answered and she began talking animatedly in her mother tongue. 'That was my friend Janneke,' she explained as she ended the call, 'the friend who I was meeting tonight. She's at her place now with a few of our friends. It's not far from here if you fancy it for a while. They're good people. You'll like them.'

Sanne's friends' small gathering turned out to be a party on the top floors of an old four-storey house with huge windows that looked out across the Amstel. Armed with a can of lager Phil spent the first half-hour touring the house and the second being introduced to Sanne's friends the names of whom had all pretty much eluded him the moment he shook their hands.

Unlike his friends back home in Nottingham (most of

whom worked in ordinary occupations with needlessly complicated job titles) virtually all of Sanne's friends appeared to be 'creative' in some way. Phil had never met so many people who claimed to work in the field of performance poetry, and after the fifth he longed to talk to someone ordinary about something ordinary, if only for a short while.

A tall skinny girl with bright red bobbed hair came over to the performance poet Phil had been stuck with for the last ten minutes, and seizing his opportunity to flee Phil made his way over to Sanne who was on the fringes of a large group standing by the window.

'Are you okay?' she asked as Phil appeared by her side. 'Still enjoying yourself?'

'I'm fine,' said Phil, 'I think the fatigue's just kicking in, that's all.'

'Do you want to get off? I don't mind.'

'No,' said Phil. 'But I tell you what I could do with though . . . your phone, just for a minute, if that's okay.'

'Yeah, of course,' replied Sanne. 'If you want to call your friends and invite them over they'd be more than welcome.'

'I couldn't even if I wanted to,' explained Phil. 'For reasons that I won't go into we all left our phones back in the UK and I've been wanting to call Helen but can't remember her number.'

'So you're going to call a friend and get it?'

Phil shook his head. 'The only person I can think of is my sister who's actually with Helen this weekend and I can't remember her number either.'

'So what are you going to do?'

'Well, if it's okay with you I'll check my voicemail and see if she's called me. I just want to know if she's okay, does that make any sense?'

'Of course,' said Sanne, 'I think it's sweet.'

Sanne explained how to use the phone and then excused herself to go to the kitchen to get them a couple of fresh lagers. Phil, desperate to get away from the noise, headed out into the hallway and began dialling.

The message had been left Friday evening:

Hey you, it's just me saying a quick hello. Arrived safely, the hotel is amazing, and the girls are all here now and we're having a lot of fun. Obviously I'm not looking to cramp your style in front of the boys but I thought you might like to know that I love you madly! No need to ring me back, okay? Love you, bye.

It was so good just to hear her voice and Phil felt comforted. Everything was all right. All of that worrying was for nothing. Aiden Reid was nowhere to be seen. Relieved, he pushed on to hear the second and final message left only an hour earlier:

Phil, it's me. I'm not looking to cause trouble, I promise you, but you know that Aiden Reid guy off the radio? Well he's here at the hotel and Helen knows him – they used to work together or something – and well I don't know how to say this nicely because I know it'll be painful so I'll just come out with it: I've got a horrible feeling that something's going on between the two of them. Ring me when you get this and let me know what you want me to do. Take care and I'll speak to you soon.

14.

Phil had been halfway to the front door when Sanne, carrying the two bottles of lager, had called his name.

'Where are you going?'

'I've left your phone with one of your friends,' explained Phil urgently. 'I have to go.'

Sanne's brow furrowed. 'Go?' she asked, stunned. 'Why? Has someone upset you? Who was it? Let me at least try and sort it out. Please, let me at least try. I'd hate you to just go like this.'

'It's Aiden,' explained Phil. 'When I was checking my messages I found one from my sister. She thinks that something is going on between Helen and Aiden.'

'Why would she say that?' questioned Sanne. 'How would she even know something like that?'

'The girls – Helen and her mates – they've gone to some posh hotel in the Peak District,' replied Phil. 'Caitlin says that Aiden's there too.' He looked at Sanne. 'Now how's that for the king of coincidences?'

Sanne bit her lip. 'Nothing about this sounds right,' she said putting a reassuring hand on Phil's arm. 'I'm not calling your sister a liar but are you sure that she couldn't be mistaken?'

147

'Mistaken?' replied Phil. 'Mistaken how? I've never even mentioned to Caitlin that Helen knew Aiden so why would she bring his name up now?'

'I don't know . . .' said Sanne. 'Maybe she Googled Helen's name one time and Aiden's name came up?'

'And so she thought she'd ruin my stag weekend with a practical joke?'

'No, of course I'm not saying that but maybe . . . I don't know . . . maybe Aiden was there by accident – he used to take me to those kinds of places all the time when we were together – maybe they spoke and your sister's got a bit freaked out that her sister-in-law to be is on such good terms with someone as famous as Aiden.'

'I'm not naïve,' said Phil, trying his best to stay calm, 'One thing my sister isn't, is stupid. If she's called me at what . . . one in the morning UK time? To tell me she thinks there's something going on between Helen and Aiden it's because she genuinely thinks there is.'

'So what's your plan?'

'Go back to the hotel to get my stuff and then the first flight back home to sort this out face to face.'

'Why don't you just call her first? I'm sure with a bit of detective work you could find out the number of the hotel, call her room and speak to her.'

Phil was aware that Sanne was trying to calm him down but he didn't want to be calmed down. He wanted to take action. Action was the only thing that made sense to him right now. 'What if she's not there?' he said urgently. 'What if he picks up the phone? Look, this is driving me crazy and I haven't even spoken to her. I need to be able to see her, I need her to tell me whatever it is she's got to tell me face to face. Once I see her face, once I look into her eyes, I'll know everything I need to know.' Sanne took Phil by the arm, led him to the stairs and sat him down.

She gripped his hands tightly. 'Listen, before you do anything rash let me just try one thing. I'm still not convinced Aiden is there. Like you say, it would be too much of a coincidence for him to be there by accident, so why don't you let me make a few calls to some people I know back in England who might be able to shed some light on this and then we'll take it from there. What do you say?'

As unsettling as Caitlin's call had been, it did seem a bit far-fetched that Aiden should just happen to be at the same hotel as Helen. And despite the shadow that Aiden had cast over his own relationship did he really believe that Helen would give up on the life they had built together after a single weekend? Like Sanne said, maybe it made sense to see what light she could shed on the matter before he jumped on a plane and headed back to England all guns blazing.

Sanne disappeared back to the party to get her phone while Phil headed downstairs and waited outside staring across the shifting surface of the Amstel as it scattered the moon's reflection into a million tiny fragments. It was hard not to appreciate the city's beauty. And as he stood watching a passing boat filled with revellers he imagined how if Helen had been here

149

to share the view it might have become one of those moments that they would always remember, like the time they had driven through the night to Southwold to watch the sunrise over the north sea, or the time a few years later when they had got snowed in at Helen's mum's cottage and had spent a morning lying in bed watching the snow fall past the bedroom window. Without her by his side, it was just another one of the stream of passing minutes that made up the hours of his waking day.

The sound of footsteps alerted Phil to Sanne's descent. He studied Sanne's face and knew immediately that his fears had been confirmed.

Sanne made her way out of the front door with Phil following close behind.

'The Royal Park Hotel is not too far from here,' she explained keeping her eyes focused on the road ahead. 'We can get a cab from there to your hotel, pick up your things and drive . . .' Her voice choked. '. . . drive to the airport.'

Phil put a hand on her shoulder. 'Are you okay?'

Sanne shook her head and wiped away tears. 'My mother is a staunch dyed in the wool Catholic and when my sister and I were kids we were always screaming how much we hated each other and whenever we did this she would always take us to one side and tell us how wrong it was to hate another human being. But right now, I don't think there's any other word for how I feel about Aiden.' Phil felt the muscles in his stomach tighten as he braced himself for the blow. 'Your sister was right.'

'About Aiden being at Helen's hotel?'

Sanne nodded. 'Have you heard of Ally Fallon?' Phil nodded. She was the flame-haired former kids' TV presenter, a real party girl who was always in the tabloids, falling out of some bar on the arm of some long-haired tattooed musician. 'Well Ally and I go way back to when we were at stage school together, and now she's engaged to Karl Peters.' Phil nodded again: Karl Peters was the Five Live guy notorious for shouting at the guests on his show to get his point across. 'So I called Ally because Karl is one of Aiden's closest friends and I asked her if she knew where Aiden was this weekend and the moment I said his name, I just sensed that something was up, and well, after that she told me everything. Apparently Aiden turned up at their house in the early hours last weekend and he was drunk and maudlin but wouldn't say why, and eventually Karl managed to coax out of him what the problem was: he'd just heard from a friend of a friend that you and Helen were getting married the weekend after next and it had sent him over the edge. So anyway, Karl sits up with Aiden all night and by the morning they've come up with a plan for him to get Helen back.'

'Which was?'

'To find out where Helen was having her hen night, crash it by inventing a good reason to be at the venue and then somehow talk her into taking him back. By the Monday morning they had found out the hotel, by the Tuesday they had roped in a few of Aiden's celebrity mates to come along in the hope that they

151

might impress either Helen or her friends and by the Wednesday it had been decided the cover story would be that Aiden and his friends were there for Karl's stag weekend.'

Phil felt as if his head was about to explode and rubbed it frantically trying to calm down his overactive synapses. Was this really happening? Had some bloke off the telly really recruited a bunch of his celebrity mates in a bid to try and seduce Phil's fiancée? None of it seemed real. He needed more information.

'And that's it? That's everything?'

Sanne nodded. 'That's it.'

'And your friend didn't say anything about Helen or whether Aiden's plan was working?'

'No. She hasn't spoken to Karl since Friday night.'

'So why did you look so horrified when you came to tell me? I get that this guy has gone to a lot of effort but there's something else you're not telling me, I can feel it. It's almost as if you think I don't stand a chance.'

'Of course, it's not like that. That was just me over-reacting. It was a shock, that's all.'

Phil remained unconvinced. 'I'm not taking another step until you tell me exactly why you were so worried. I need to know.'

Sanne took a deep breath. 'Because I know what he's like. Aiden is a man who spends all day every day charming hundreds of thousands of people of all ages and races, rich or poor into listening to him day, after day, after day. People love him. People love him because they think he's warm and funny and honest and all the things they know they'll never be. But most of all people love him because even though they know it's not true, when they hear his voice coming to them through the airwaves, they feel like he's actually talking to them and them alone. Now imagine how it must feel when he really is talking to you and you alone. I don't know Helen, but I do know Aiden and I know that when he wants something – whether it's the most coveted job in UK radio or one of thirty-six super rare classic Italian sports cars that he knows he'll get bored of within a week – there's nothing he won't do to get it. Because for men like Aiden it's the getting, not the having, that makes them feel alive.'

The taxi pulled up in front of the hotel. Phil climbed out of the car and Sanne instructed the driver to wait.

Sanne said she'd wait in the lobby and took a seat next to a fake potted palm as Phil made his way up to the second floor. Phil barely registered the state of his room as he frantically packed his case. Whether it was his mud-sodden tracksuit or his dirty underwear, or the CDs of Sanne that he had bought earlier in the night, it all got shoved in until all his belongings were packed away, and his passport placed carefully in the inside pocket of his jacket.

As he made his way downstairs he wondered if the boys were back and whether he should check to see if they were in their rooms but even as this thought occurred to him he dismissed it. This was the last night of probably one of the last stag dos any of them would be going on for quite a long time; none of his friends (still less his father) would be getting in any time soon.

He handed over his key card to the girl in reception, gave her his room number and crossed his fingers that room service hadn't come across the pneumatic drill hidden in the wardrobe.

The girl tapped away on the keyboard in front of her and stared at the screen. 'I've got a note here that we've taken a message for you.'

She walked over to a bank of drawers, opened one and began flicking through the drop files in front of her. Phil willed her to find it quickly. It was from Helen. It had to be. She must have called his room and when he hadn't answered thought it best to leave a message on reception. She must want to tell him about Aiden, he reasoned, she must want to tell him that everything was going to be fine.

The girl stood up, holding the piece of paper aloft. 'Finally!' She handed him the note. On it was written the date and the time (some two hours earlier) and a message requesting that he call the number that had been written down below. Phil didn't recognise the number. It wasn't Helen's mobile number, in fact it didn't even look like an English number.

Phil settled the bill and returned to the lobby. Sanne was playing with her phone.

'I was just texting Ally thanking her for being so nice to me on the phone. I didn't appreciate how late it was when I called her. She was probably still up partying with her friends, but even so, I feel a bit bad. All done?'

Phil shook his head. 'Not quite. I was just checking out when I got this.' He handed the note to Sanne. 'It looks like a Dutch number to me.'

'It is,' said Sanne. 'Do you want me to call it?'

Phil shook his head. 'I'm sure it's nothing.'

Sanne smiled. 'Then use my phone and I'll go check on the driver.'

Phil dialled the number and waited. It rang three times and a voice, clearly a recording, started speaking to him in Dutch. He could tell he was being offered options of the 'press 1 for Yes, press 2 for No' variety, but had no idea what exactly those options were. He ended the call. Someone must have made a mistake.

He walked through the lobby to the front entrance and found Sanne arguing with the cab driver. The cab driver seemed more amused than annoyed by Sanne's tirade but once she had finished he simply shrugged, gave her the middle finger and drove off.

'What was the problem there?'

'The man was a pig! We don't need him, there are plenty of taxis in Amsterdam at this time of night.' She exhaled heavily and ran her fingers through her hair. 'Did you find out who the message was from?'

'No, it was a recorded voice speaking in Dutch. Didn't make any sense. I think maybe the hotel made a mistake.'

Sanne took her phone from Phil's hand, pressed redial and put the phone up to her ear. Phil watched intrigued as she followed the instructions, punched in the correct numbers before finally getting to speak to a real live person.

The conversation took place in Dutch. Several times Phil saw her looking over at him until finally she ended the call.

'So, what's the deal? Wrong number?'

Sanne's brow furrowed. 'Is your father here with you on your stag do?'

Phil nodded. 'What's that got to do with the call?'

'Well that was the police,' she replied, 'apparently he's managed to get himself arrested.'

15.

It was a quarter past two as a tired and weary Phil, together with Sanne entered Bureau Beursstraat in De Wallen in the heart of the red-light district. A sole police officer manned the front desk hidden behind a plexiglass screen and was taking details in English from a young Spanish woman and her boyfriend. The woman had apparently just had her bag stolen by two youths on a motor scooter and was particularly upset because the bag contained her passport.

Phil felt sorry for the young woman but even more sorry for himself. He should have been on his way to the airport and this diversion was turning what was already a terrible situation into a catastrophe. Every minute that passed was another minute that Aiden Reid would be using to change Helen's mind. Phil had seriously considered leaving his father where he was and letting him sort out his own problem but he would never forgive himself if anything bad happened.

It took twenty minutes for the duty officer to deal with the Spanish couple but then as Phil stepped forward he muttered in Dutch that Sanne translated saying he would be back in a minute.

Phil's irritation at the delay was obvious, and picking up on this Sanne gently nudged him aside as the officer returned. She spoke in Dutch and they talked for ages, occasionally breaking into laughter. Even without a rudimentary knowledge of the language Phil could tell that she was flirting and that somewhere during the course of the conversation the officer had recognised her and had been flattered that she was being so nice to him.

Finally, the officer grinned and pointed to a row of grey plastic chairs.

'We should take a seat,' said Sanne as the police officer disappeared out of view. She sat down on one of the chairs. Phil didn't want to sit, he was too wired with nervous energy to find any comfort from taking the weight off his feet but Sanne had asked to and he felt he couldn't say no when she was doing so much for him.

'Well, the good news is that he should be out by first thing in the morning,' said Sanne.

'And the bad?'

'He's been arrested for dealing drugs.'

'Dealing drugs!' Phil couldn't believe what he was hearing. 'My dad's a bit of a liability but I'm pretty sure he's not a drug dealer. This makes no sense at all! And while I'm at it where were the boys? Why weren't they looking out for him?'

'According to the officer they were doing a sweep in De Wallen after some complaints about dealers hassling tourists when they caught your father in the act of selling a hash cake to an American tourist. On

158

arresting him they discovered that he had a further twenty-nine carefully tucked away in his rucksack.'

'He told me that bag of his was for his heart medication! I wondered why he'd been carrying that damn thing round with him all weekend.'

'But where did he get them from? No coffee shop would sell them in bulk like that.'

Phil shook his head as an answer slowly dawned on him. 'He made them.'

'Who? Your father?'

Phil nodded. 'That's my dad all over. He's the only man in the world who would buy cannabis in the UK, take it through customs and then try and sell it in one of the few places in the world where it's freely available.' Phil stood up, every muscle riddled with fatigue. 'Well now that little mystery is cleared up at least we can go.'

'Not yet, I talked the duty officer into asking his boss if it might be okay for you to see him.'

Phil checked his watch. 'I don't want to see him and I certainly don't want to see him now when I should be at the airport. He's okay, and while the daft old sod might not appreciate being locked up I can't imagine that it will do him any harm.'

'Fine,' said Sanne flatly, 'we'll go if that's what you want.'

She rose to her feet and Phil bent down to pick up his bag but then the sound of the duty officer returning to his desk made them both turn around.

'You can come now,' the officer called out to them in English. 'He's in interview room two.'

The officer pressed a buzzer and a reinforced metal door to the left of them clicked open. Phil followed Sanne through the door, along a corridor and into the interview room where Patrick was sitting on a chair behind a plain grey table.

As annoyed as Phil was, he couldn't help but feel sympathy for his father. With an officer standing behind him he looked small and old.

'You okay, Dad?'

'Never better, son. I've been in a few nicks in my time but I must say the Dutch ones are easily in my top three.' He looked over at Sanne. 'Who's your friend?' Phil made the introductions. 'Pleased to meet you, Sanne, although it would have been much nicer under different circumstances.'

'Look, Dad, Sanne's had a word with the duty officer and he says you'll be free to go first thing in the morning. There may be a fine but I'll sort that out now.'

'And you'll pick me up in the morning?'

Phil shook his head. 'No Dad, I can't. I'm heading back home now. There's sort of an emergency – a work thing – it needs my attention straight away. I'll leave a message at the hotel for the boys to come and get you. Where are they by the way? Did you lose them?'

Phil's dad winked. 'I'll tell you later son, you take care and I hope you get things sorted.' He looked at Sanne. 'Oh, and nice to meet you love, sorry it's been so short but maybe I'll see you at the wedding next weekend. In my experience someone always drops out at the last minute so there'll be plenty of room for you if you want to pop over.'

Sanne grinned to cover her embarrassment and then they said their goodbyes and left the room.

'I'm going to go and pay the fine,' said Phil quickly in the hope that they might be able to skip any awkward silence.

'I'll wait for you outside.'

Although the fine was large enough to have covered Phil's share of a very nice holiday for two somewhere posh in the Caribbean, he was glad that for the moment at least his dad was out of trouble.

Stepping outside Phil spotted Sanne hailing another cab. She waved to him to join her and they set off to the airport.

Within minutes of leaving the confines of central Amsterdam Sanne had closed her eyes and as the driver seemed absorbed by the phone-in show on his radio Phil was free to let his thoughts roam unchecked.

He was surprised to discover that the main topic on his mind was the woman whose head now rested on his shoulder. Forty-eight hours ago she had been little more than a name in a newspaper and now later they were . . . what exactly? He thought back to the moment in the queue outside the bar when she had smiled at him and told the bouncer that he and the boys were with her and her friends. Then there had been that moment after the Van Gogh Museum when she had wanted to show him Vondlepark; was it his imagination or had there been real disappointment in her eyes when he'd had to go? And tonight at the party she had put her hand on his arm and he had felt as if every nerve ending had been alerted by a single contact. Was this all in his mind? Was he reading too much into it? And what did this mean for the way he felt about Helen?

Phil rubbed his eyes. He didn't want to live in a dream world where beautiful women he barely knew fell in love with him over the course of a manic weekend. He belonged in the real world, the one in which his mates drank pints, his mum cooked Sunday roasts and he fell asleep on the sofa in the arms of the woman that he loved after a long day at work. A momentary fantasy versus a lifetime's reality? It wasn't even a fair fight. Helen was the girl he wanted, he was sure of that. She would always be the one for him.

Phil filled the rest of the journey imagining in great detail the punch he would throw in Aiden Reid's direction the moment he laid eyes on him. One fist jabbed through the air at lightning speed and making such a perfect connection with his nose that Reid would know he'd messed with the wrong man.

Phil didn't care whether it ended with the police being called or pictures of him across every tabloid in the country, all he cared about was kicking seven bells out of Aiden Reid.

Reaching the airport Phil gently roused Sanne and paid the driver before climbing out of the car. He felt oddly calm. Everything was going to be okay. Everything was going to turn out for the best.

The first sign that his initial feelings of well-being might be premature came when he looked at the departure board and saw that that there were no flights in or out of the airport until 5.05 a.m. The second sign came when he realised that there was no one manning any of the low budget airline desks and the KLM desk said the first available flight to the UK that wasn't already fully booked wasn't leaving until seven in the evening, a whole hour after he would have been flying home with the boys anyway.

'And there's no way you can get me there any earlier?'

'Without taking a transfer somewhere else? No, and even then I couldn't guarantee you'd get there any earlier. It's the middle of summer, Mr . . .' she glanced down at his passport that he had handed over during the course of the conversation, . . . Hudson . . . the height of the holiday season, many airports are already at maximum capacity. I'm afraid it's just one of those things.'

Phil barely spoke a word in the cab on the way back into Amsterdam. There wasn't a great deal to be said. If even half of Sanne's claims about Aiden were true, the chances were he would have been too late anyway.

'Do you think she always loved him?'

The question was as much a surprise to Phil as it was to Sanne. She looped her arm through Phil's pulling him closer to her.

'Don't do this to yourself, Phil. It's not worth it.'

'I'm not sure she did,' continued Phil quietly. 'I think . . . I think she really did try her hardest to get

163

over him. You would, wouldn't you, if someone had hurt you like that? You'd make all kinds of promises to yourself not to let them do something like that again. But wouldn't a small part of you always be wondering "what if?" Wouldn't some part of you – a part that you might not want to exist – still be holding out for that happy ending? It's how we're built isn't it? No matter how many times you get slapped in the face you have to believe that next time will be different. And then in comes the guy who hurt you all those years ago, and he wants to make things better and to prove he's not all talk – this time it will be different.' Phil looked out of the window at the bright lights of the passing buildings. 'How could she not fall for that? How could she not think that if she chose him it would finally lift the shadow that he'd cast over her life? All that hurt, all that suffering wouldn't have been for nothing then, would it?' He looked at Sanne. 'If he'd have come back to you like that, would you have taken him back?'

Sanne couldn't meet his eyes.

'It's fine,' he said, reaching across to take her hand, 'it really is, I wouldn't have expected you to answer any other way. Everybody's got an Aiden in their life and I'm pretty sure that in time Helen will become mine.'

The traffic on Herenstraat had been stationary for the best part of twenty minutes. Tired of watching the blue lights of police cars and an ambulance, Sanne paid the driver and climbed out of the car. Unsure of his exact plans Phil climbed out of the car too and joined her on the pavement.

'What are you going to do?'

Sanne yawned. 'I'll walk home from here. My place is the other side of town but it shouldn't take too long.'

'You can't walk on your own at this time of night. Let me take you home. I'm pretty sure that I've got the hang of this place so I won't get lost when I head back to the hotel.'

'Have you forgotten?' grinned Sanne. 'You've already checked out.'

'Then I'll check back in again, or if the worst comes to the worst I'll wake up one of the boys and kip in his room.'

They turned left along Herenstraat heading in the direction of Prisengracht. Apart from the odd cyclist and occasional car, these streets were empty, making it seem like he and Sanne were the last two people on earth.

They were too exhausted to talk and as if to counter the silence at some point their hands reached out for one another in the darkness and formed a union of fingers.

Skilled as he was at avoiding such issues, Phil couldn't manage more than a few moments without wondering exactly where the end of this evening might take him.

They took a left into Egelantiersgracht, a pretty tree-lined street with houses on either side overlooking the central canal, stopping a little way before the first bridge.

'This is my place,' said Sanne, and she reached into her bag for keys.

Mike Gayle

Phil looked up at the five-storey house, wondering which of the flats belonged to her.

'I'm guessing your place is the top one.'

Sanne shook her head.

'Okay, the next one down.'

She shook her head again.

'The next one?'

She shook her head one last time.

'You own the whole bloody lot?'

Sanne shrugged. 'What can I say? I had a good divorce lawyer.' She pointed to the top of the house. 'The top floor is a sound-proofed studio and I use the bottom floor for my yoga classes or the odd dance class, and I'm always having friends and their kids over to stay but yeah, basically, it's just me and a big old house.'

'I should go,' said Phil quickly. Now that the moment he had been trying not to think about was here it was disconcertingly unreal. 'I'm sure I'll be able to find my way back.'

Sanne held his gaze.

'You don't have to.'

'Maybe not,' he replied, and looked down at his hands that were still entwined with Sanne's, 'but can you think of any way this might be a good idea?'

Sanne shook her head, and still holding his hand she opened up the heavy front door and they stepped inside.

Sunday

16.

Something as simple as a person entering a room can be enough to break the spell between two potential lovers; a new dawn can have a similar effect.

With his arms still wrapped tightly around Sanne's waist Phil had been thinking about this phenomenon as he watched the tiny shards of light breaking through the wooden shutters across Sanne's bedroom illuminating the dust particles in the air and making them appear to dance.

Sanne gently squeezed the hand that had been resting on her belly.

'Are you awake?'

Phil yawned. 'Yeah.'

'Did you sleep well?'

'Okay. You?'

'Not bad, though I can't imagine I'll be good for much today.'

There was a silence. Phil wondered what might be going through Sanne's head. 'I've been thinking,' he began. 'Maybe I will go and pick up my dad. Make sure he's okay and everything.'

'Yeah sure, of course, you should do that.'

'But once I've got him, maybe the three of us could go out for breakfast.'

'That would be great. There are a couple of nice places in Waterlooplein overlooking the Amstel, they aren't too far from where your dad's being held.'

'Sounds great. How long do you think it should take me?'

Sanne shrugged. 'Not long. If I meet you in an hour by the Spinoza statue you should have more than enough time.' Phil swallowed as Sanne wearing nothing but a T-shirt and her underwear, crossed the room and disappeared into the hallway. She really was stunning.

Returning a few moments later with a towel and a toothbrush still in its packet Sanne handed them to him and sat down on the edge of the bed.

'You can use the en-suite to take a shower or there's another bathroom down the hallway.'

Phil picked up the towel. 'I'll use the bathroom down the hallway and leave you in peace for a while.' He looked guiltily at his suit trousers lying on the floor.

'I'm going to make myself a coffee, do you want one?' said Sanne.

Phil interpreted this as code for 'I'm going to give you five minutes to put your trousers on,' and said yes in relief.

Sanne left and he slipped them on. Feeling a sudden heaviness in his heart, Phil lay back on the bed and began to wonder if he wasn't in danger of making the biggest mistake of his life.

Nothing had happened.

Although if he was being totally honest it wasn't for want of trying on his part. It had been Sanne who had saved him from himself. Ready to abandon nine years of loyalty Phil had made every effort to let her know how he felt. After all, he wasn't cheating when he'd already been cheated on was he? But Sanne would have none of it. She wanted to be close to him, but she made it clear that she didn't want to be anyone's cause for regret. And so while certain lines had been crossed, others hadn't even come close to being traversed and, while not even a single kiss had passed between them, the fact that they had awoken partially dressed and wrapped in each other's arms spoke volumes about what they had felt.

Had Phil fallen for Sanne? He considered the question carefully on his way to the bathroom and felt sure that the correct answer must lie somewhere in his head. What he did know for sure was that he had never met anyone like Sanne. She was different, and that difference spoke to Phil in a way that he had never thought possible. Last night had taught him that he could be a completely different person living a completely different life. Did a person exist who had never been tempted by that prospect? He thought about his childhood and the embarrassment he'd felt at having free school dinner tickets, he thought about the tiny house that he had grown up in and the graffiti and the litter that had plagued his estate, he thought about his education and exams he had failed and the opportunities he had missed. With a single action all

171

the worries of his past could belong to another life and another time, and he could concentrate on being someone new somewhere new. It was a pipe dream of course, a holiday state of mind brought on by being free of the day-to-day routine, but what a pipe dream and what a state of mind.

He appeared fully dressed at the kitchen door. The room was modern, tasteful and obviously expensive. Sanne was sitting at a dining table underneath a window looking down at the canal beneath. A mug of coffee was by her hands, a second sat on the table beside her.

'I think I'd better get off.'

'What about the coffee?'

'I'll have to leave it. So, I'll see you later?'

'Eleven, by the Spinoza statue, Waterlooplein.'

'Promise?'

'Promise.'

They hugged goodbye but the embrace felt different, awkward. Phil thought about the shards of light that he had watched coming through the bedroom shutters. Everything looks different in the daytime, her embrace seemed to say, even love.

Beursstraat politiebureau in the daytime was a considerably more hospitable place than it had been in the early hours of Sunday morning. There were two officers manning the duty desk and a much shorter queue, which resulted in Phil's dad arriving more quickly than he had expected.

Patrick still looked old and weary, just as on their

last visit but there was a brightness about his eyes that had been missing before. 'Son, what are you doing here? I thought you had a work emergency?'

'It's fine,' said Phil. 'It's sorted. You all right, Dad?'

'Of course I am,' he turned to the officer who had escorted him into the waiting room. 'Son, this is Peter, he's been looking after me this morning.'

The officer was a tall blond man who couldn't have looked more Dutch if he had been wearing clogs and a PSV Eindhoven top. Phil gave him a nod and raised an eyebrow in sympathy.

'Your father, he's a bit of a character, isn't he?'

'You could say that.'

'He's been regaling us all with stories of his past touring with bands. Did you know, back in 1972 he fell asleep in a hotel room in Amsterdam and woke up in a tree in Vondelpark?'

'I may have heard that story once or twice.'

'Right then, Pat,' said the officer holding out his hand, 'it has been nice meeting you but let's hope that we don't meet again, at least not under these particular circumstances.'

Patrick raised his hands in surrender. 'On that, young Peter, you have my word! My days in the drug trade are over for good.'

The two men shook hands while Phil looked on with a look of bewilderment.

'So where to now?'

Phil looked at his dad. 'This hasn't even slowed you down has it?'

'Not for a second. They haven't built a jail that can keep hold of Patrick Hudson.'

'What were you even doing bringing hash cakes into the country?'

'So you know?'

'Well I couldn't think of any other reason why you'd insist on carrying that stupid rucksack wherever you went. Are you mad? One: if the border police had picked you up with that lot in the UK I can guarantee that they would have been a lot less friendly than Peter here, and two: why would you bring hash cakes into Amsterdam of all places? There's a shop on virtually every street corner selling the stuff!'

'Yeah, but it's the commercial stuff, no one likes that, it's far too strong. My stuff was guaranteed all organic and pesticide free.'

The penny dropped.

'You're growing it?'

Patrick let out a schoolboyish chuckle that managed to be at once charming and annoying. 'I got the basics from the internet in the local library and then filled in the gaps from some books I borrowed off Little Stevie from the pub. I've turned over part of the greenhouse on my allotment to full-time cultivation.'

'You're growing it on the allotment?'

Patrick nodded sheepishly. 'And a bit on the windowsill at home. But I promise you it was for a good cause.'

'And what cause would that be, Dad, the keep Patrick Hudson in beer, fags and horses fund?'

'No,' said Patrick. 'It was for a wedding present for you and Helen. I know you don't think much of me, and it's not like I've been the greatest dad in the world, but I did want to do something to show that I wished you both all the luck in the world.'

'What were you going to get?'

'I don't know, son, do I? A tea set . . . some cutlery . . . something or other from John Lewis in the Victoria Centre if I could scrape together enough cash.'

Phil and never felt guiltier.

'You know you don't have to do any of that. Helen and I have got everything we need.'

'I just wanted to give you something nice, something that might make you think that you old man's not a total dead loss.'

Phil laughed, 'You would've had to sell a lot of hash cakes to get the cash together for a private jet, Dad.'

'Doesn't mean that I couldn't try though, does it?'

Had they been any other father and son, this might have resulted in a man-hug, but as it was they simply exchanged grins, shoved their hands deep into their pockets and kept their eyes fixed on the road ahead.

It was five to eleven by the time Phil reached the Spinoza statue on Waterlooplein, and as he had suspected there was no sign of Sanne. She wouldn't come, he knew that. Last night had been last night and this morning was a whole different story.

Patrick sat down at the base of the statue. 'Who is it we're meeting again?'

'Sanne,' replied Phil, 'you know, the woman you met last night. The one that used to be married to Aidan Reid.'

Patrick considered this. 'So did you get your answer? You know, find out what it was you wanted to know? You were worried about her ex-husband or something.'

Phil shrugged. 'It's hard to say. We talked but I'm not sure I'm any the wiser.'

'But you're not worried about Helen any more, are you? This Aiden Reid guy, he's out of the picture?'

'I don't know, Dad,' said Phil, 'I really don't.'

They waited by the statue for the best part of twenty minutes, talking about the past, making comments about the people they saw and the buildings around them, and it was only when Patrick began to moan that he could murder a cup of tea, that Phil finally accepted that Sanne wasn't going to turn up.

There was a café opposite the statue and although it seemed busy, they headed towards the entrance.

They had barely taken more than a few steps when Phil heard someone calling out his name and turned around to see Sanne, cycling furiously and waving at him as she crossed the bridge. Leaving his father outside the café he ran over to the bridge to meet her.

Sanne came to a halt right in front of him and dismounted. She was wearing a cream T-shirt, a denim skirt and flip-flops and despite having only slept for a handful of hours still managed to look amazing. Phil wished that he had at least changed his shirt, let alone his underwear, and was aware that facially speaking he

176

looked like a man who had had a very rough weekend in Amsterdam.

Phil was glad that he had been wrong about her. He was glad that there was still hope. 'I was beginning to think you weren't going to come.'

Sanne looked directly at him. 'I wasn't.'

Phil nodded, it made sense of course. 'But you're still hungry?'

Sanne grinned. 'Starving.' She glanced back over the bridge. 'There's a little place I go to a lot with friends. It's a bit further down but I think you'll like it. It's a nice Dutch place, no luke-warm tea in chipped mugs, no tomato ketchup in a squeezy bottle and definitely no English breakfasts!'

The café was just as Sanne had described. They found a table outside for three, sat down and perused the menus.

Patrick, being Patrick, opted to stick with what he knew and asked Sanne to order him bacon and eggs but Phil, wanting to both impress Sanne and distance himself from his father's limited outlook on Dutch cuisine selected a dish at random from the Dutch menu called *ontbijtkoek* and seemed thoroughly pleased with himself when he had done so.

Sanne, who had ordered an egg-white omelette on brown toast, looked at him and smiled as the waitress left the table.

'Do you even know what you've ordered?' she asked, clearly amused by his choice.

Phil hoped to bluff his way through. 'Is it some kind of Dutch sausage?'

'It's a cake made from rye flour and spice that comes with butter. I quite like it, and my mother adores it, but I'm pretty sure after the night you've had you'd be better off having something like *Uitsmijter*. It's still Dutch, you'll love it and best of all you still get your "I love the Netherlands Brownie points".'

Sanne called the waitress back and reordered Phil's breakfast for him and once that was done she set about charming Patrick which, with Sanne looking the way she did, took all of ten seconds. It took Patrick approximately three and a half minutes to return the compliment by telling her, without a single deviation in the detail, about how the last time he'd been in Amsterdam he'd gone to sleep in a hotel bedroom and woken up in a tree in Vondelpark.

With the sunshine, the canalside setting and the laughter, it was, thought Phil as he finished the last of his Uitsmijter (fried eggs, ham and aged Gouda on white bread), one of the tastiest meals he had ever eaten and one of the most memorable. But as the waitress appeared to clear away their plates, and his gaze briefly met Sanne's he realised that it was all about to come to an end.

Phil paid the bill, and Sanne suggested that as it was such a beautiful day they should take a stroll along the back up to the edge of De Wallen before she would take her leave.

Pushing Sanne's bike for her, Phil tried to prolong the

journey, eking out precious minutes by asking Sanne about the various buildings that they passed along the way. Finally Sanne came to a halt and explained to Patrick that it was time for her to say goodbye.

Patrick hugged her tightly, 'You're the second Dutch person today that I've really got on with and I'm quickly coming to the conclusion that I like your lot more than I like my own.'

Sanne kissed his cheek. 'What can I say? The feeling's mutual.'

Instructing his father to sit on a nearby bench, Phil walked with Sanne until they were out of his father's eyeline to say his goodbyes but when he opened his mouth he couldn't think of what to say.

'This is ridiculous,' he said eventually. 'It's like my whole mind's gone blank.'

Sanne put her arms around him and held him tightly. 'I should go,' she said finally. She looked up at him, quickly pressed her lips against his own and hugged him tightly. 'I'm not very good at goodbyes.'

Phil kissed the top of her head. 'Look,' he said, 'I am coming back.'

'Don't say that, please, don't say that if you don't absolutely mean it.'

'Why wouldn't I mean it? It's all I've been thinking about since last night.'

'Because you haven't seen Helen. Because you haven't worked things through. Because you don't know anything for sure. And you need to be sure about this, Phil. There's still a chance for you and Helen, all the Aiden stuff might not be as it seems, and then this time next week your life could be as exactly as you've always wanted it to be.'

'But it won't, I just feel it.'

'You need to know for sure.'

'And you'll wait?'

'This isn't about me, it's about Helen. You have to have faith in her. You have to believe the best of her until you know the truth. Despite everything she just might have what it takes to amaze you, and prove you wrong. But you need to fight for her, don't give up until you've explored every possible avenue, proved to her that she's the one for you.'

17.

It was after one as Phil and Patrick reached the hotel lobby and began searching for the boys. On the basis that they would have long since had to check out of their rooms Phil reasoned that even with the good weather there was every chance after the night of drinking they had no doubt indulged in that they wouldn't have gone too far. But when after half an hour of searching the bar, the restaurant and even the hotel toilets proved fruitless, he began to think he would simply have to meet them at the airport.

Frustrated he wondered aloud where could they be, only to have Patrick answer back: 'Any one of a million places. It's not like Amsterdam's Derby city centre is it?'

Phil wasn't convinced. 'Dad, with the best will in the world the boys would be easy to find even if we'd all gone to New York. They're creatures of habit, plus they'll have massive hangovers and be desperate to get rid of them and finally, they probably won't have eaten anything since . . .' Phil stopped as it dawned on him exactly where his friends would be. 'I'm an idiot! I know exactly where they are, right. That place we went to yesterday. They'll be at the Shamrock Inn off Dam

Square knocking back a full English breakfast and wishing for the most part that they were dead.'

Phil was right about everything. Not only were the boys at exactly the same bar, they were even at the same table and when they spotted Phil and Patrick crossing the square they let out a mighty cheer followed by a round of applause.

'Like father like son!' called out Degsy as the two men approached the table. 'Where have you two been all night? Living it up without us? We've been looking for you everywhere.'

'And you thought you'd find us by parking your arses outside an Irish pub and tucking into a double heart-attack on a plate?'

'So where were you then?' asked Simon. 'We stayed in Café Hoppe until gone one waiting for you to turn up.'

Phil shrugged. 'Long story, I'll explain it all later.'

Simon looked at Patrick. 'And what happened to you? One minute we were all in that bar in De Wallen and the next it was like you'd just vanished.'

Phil and his dad exchanged glances. 'I don't know what to say boys. I can only apologise for any trouble that I caused.'

'But where were you? We looked for you for ages.'

Phil knew the boys wouldn't give up until they got their answer. 'He got nicked.'

'Nicked?' said Spencer spitting a mouthful of tea back into his mug, 'What for?'

Phil looked at his dad. 'Do you want to tell them or shall I?'

'It was a bit of a misunderstanding with the local constabulary lads. Nothing to be proud of.'

'He got caught selling hashcakes to tourists.'

This time it was Reuben's turn to spit out his tea. 'He got caught doing what?'

Phil decided to jump in before the questions got out of hand. 'Look, it's all done and dusted and I'm sure, once he's had time to digest it all, he'll bore you to tears next time you see him, but for now, let's just say it's a lesson learned.' Phil checked out the self-inflicted damage that the boys had wreaked about their own person. Degsy's skin looked grey, Reuben had dark shadows under his eyes and Simon's eyes were so bloodshot that they almost looked like they would crack if he blinked too hard. 'I don't need to ask how the rest of your night went, do I? Your faces say it all. What time did you get in?'

Simon shook his head mournfully. 'We didn't. After we lost your dad we went to some club near Leidesplein and when we got bored of that we went to another and then around six some girls that Deano got talking to told us about some bar that they were going to, so then we went there and had a few drinks and Deano didn't get anywhere with the girls, so we pretty much fell asleep on the sofa and by the time we woke up it was gone ten. We staggered out, jumped on a tram to the hotel, had to jump off it because it was going the wrong way, jumped on a different one, made it to the hotel, grabbed our stuff, got the concierge to put it in storage and then rocked up here to try and recover.'

183

'And you think a bit of fried bread and a couple of bangers is going to help you do that? You look like extras from *Dawn of the Dead*.'

Simon chuckled. 'You can talk, fella, have you looked in the mirror lately? Bit of a late one was it?'

'You could say that,' replied Phil. 'So what's the plan? Wait out hangovers and the like here and then hop on the plane?'

'Funny you should ask,' said Simon, 'we were just talking about that when you arrived.'

'And?'

'Well, given that this is your stag weekend the conclusion we came to is that it should be up to you. Anything at all, you name it and we'll go there.'

'Anything?'

'Yeah, anything.'

'Fine,' said Phil, 'then I want to go to Vondelpark.'

'To see your dad's tree?' asked Degsy. 'I wouldn't have thought you'd be interested.'

'I'm not,' replied Phil enigmatically. 'It's just something I want to do.'

The boys responded with a variety of groans making it clear that they had in fact been hoping that Phil would be as keen to sit outside the Shamrock Inn doing as little moving as possible as they were, but when Phil said that he was happy to go on his own, they reluctantly rose as one to their feet, donned their sunglasses and followed Phil to the tram stop.

There was only one reason Phil wanted to go to Vondelpark and that was because of Sanne. She had wanted to take him there after their visit to the Van Gogh Museum and he had declined; now he wished that he could just go back in time, stop being such an idiot, and make the most of hanging out with someone like Sanne. But without a time machine to hand his only option was to take himself off to see the things she might have wanted to show him.

Vondelpark was much like any other urban green space, but just as parks in England come alive in a heat wave the same was true here. It seemed like everybody in Amsterdam from teenage boys larking about by the edge of the lake through to multi-generational families preparing barbecue lunches was out enjoying the sunshine.

The boys made a lap of the park and bought ice creams from a nearby stand and, while the majority went off with Patrick to see if they could find the very tree he claimed to have woken up in all those years ago, Phil and Simon lay down in the shade of a plane tree watching them.

Simon shook his head. 'They've got no chance have they?'

'Of finding a tree that Dad claims to have woken up in some time in the seventies?' replied Phil. 'Nah, mate. No chance.'

'And yet still they search.'

'Well, if it makes them happy.'

Simon looked up at the leaf canopy above his head. 'I've been a bit of an idiot haven't I?'

Phil joined his friend looking up at the tree. 'Yeah.'

'You were right about Caitlin, she'd never want to get back with me. It's not like she didn't make it clear enough the half a dozen times I asked her. I suppose I just didn't want to hear it.'

'So what now?'

Simon laughed. 'Now, I've screwed up my life? Not a clue.'

'Couldn't you talk to Yaz, try and maybe patch things up?'

'You think it's patchable? I screwed her over and left her and the kids to chase after Caitlin of all people! I'll be lucky if she doesn't kill me on the spot the second she hears the full story.'

'Still,' said Phil, 'what other option is there?'

'None,' replied Simon.

Phil sighed. 'Don't you sometimes wish that life was just a little less complicated?'

'Meaning yours is up the spout too?' grinned Simon. 'Last time we spoke you were minutes away from flying back to the UK, hunting down Aiden Reid and stringing him up good and proper.'

'And I nearly did,' replied Phil. 'Among the many mental things that happened to me last night I tried to get a flight back home.' Phil told Simon everything that he had learned about Aiden Reid's weekend.

Simon sat bolt upright. 'And he's there now? We should hire a plane and kill the tosser right now! What have you done about it? Have you called Helen? Tried to warn her at least?'

'And say what exactly? He's been there since Friday

night – chances are anything that he wanted to say to her has already been said. She'll already have made her decision.'

'Mate,' exclaimed Simon, 'just listen to yourself. You're giving up without a fight! Just because he's famous and loaded doesn't mean you have to roll over and admit defeat. Don't sit there feeling sorry for yourself, get up and do something!'

'Like what?'

'Like anything!'

'I've told you there's nothing I *can* do. Plus, last night it sort of got really—' Phil stopped suddenly and leapt to his feet.

Confused, Simon stood up too. 'Are you going to finish that sentence? What happened? Are you saying something happened with Sanne?'

'Forget all that for a minute!' replied Phil. 'I've got it! I've finally got it!'

'Got what?'

'One minute: nothing and then the next it was like – bam! – and it was there in my head! Helen's mobile number,' said Phil breaking into a run.

With Simon by his side Phil ran to the entrance to the park and then stopped as he remembered he and the boys had no way of contacting each other should he lose them again. He ran back to his friends, who were all standing at the base of a beech tree looking up at its branches.

'We've got to go,' panted Phil, 'I need to get something and we all have to go.'

187

'But we've only just found your dad's tree!' said Deano. 'It's a pretty cool one too, and look right up there in the branches: a couple of parrots! How cool is that?'

Phil shook his head in disbelief and looked. He couldn't see any parrots but this was the least of his objections. 'How can you even tell if it's the same tree? Don't you think it might have changed a little bit in the last forty-odd years?'

'It's definitely the one!' said Patrick. 'When you go to bed in a hotel and wake up in a tree my friend, believe me you remember the tree!'

'Fine! Take a snap of the tree *and* the bloody parrots if it makes you so happy and then let's go!'

Deano whipped out his digital camera and handed it to Phil while the boys and Patrick (who was beaming like he'd just won the lottery) stood with their arms around each other in front of the tree. Just as Phil pressed down on the shutter release three pale green parrots swooped down from inside the tree, rested on a branch next to his father's head as though desperate to be in the shot and then, alarmed by Patrick's yell of surprise, soared up into the safety of a nearby oak tree.

'Can we go now?'

'Go where?'

'A phone shop,' said Phil. 'I need to buy myself a phone.'

Phil ran as fast as he could back out on to the street and then stopped as he realised that he had no idea where to find a mobile phone shop.

Determined not to fall at this first hurdle Phil stopped an elderly man wearing a yellow sun hat.

'Excuse me, do you know where I can find a mobile phone shop?'

The man spoke in a flurry of dissociated consonants that Phil assumed was Dutch.

Phil explained that he didn't speak Dutch but the man just shrugged and continued on his way, so Phil ran to a group of teenage girls standing at a tram stop and asked the same question. Their immediate reaction was to giggle amongst themselves for a frustratingly long time because they were teenage girls and that's what teenage girls did whether they were from Nottingham or the Netherlands, but then one of them composed herself long enough to screech: 'There is a GSM shop, maybe three hundred metres that way!' and so Phil thanked her profusely and then ran full pelt in the direction in which she had pointed.

He almost had the shop in his sights when he came to a sudden halt. Coming down the street towards him were the guys from Essex who they'd had words with on Friday night. He counted them up; there were at least twelve to his seven if he included his dad, which he wasn't sure he should in the circumstances.

This is it, thought Phil, this is how my life is going to end: at the hands of a bunch of soft southern bricklayers.

'Look who it ain't,' called Tall Guy who had done most of the talking on the Friday night. 'It's Mr Suited and Booted and his friends. Told you we'd meet them again sooner or later.' He walked over to Phil.

189

'Not so hard now are you?' he spat as he pushed him in the chest.

Phil pushed him back and a scuffle of sorts ensued with both groups edging closer. Wrenching the guy's arm away from his jacket Phil managed to break free of his grip but only at the expense of his clothing. There was a loud rip as the sleeve of his jacket came loose.

'Wait!' yelled Phil as the boys rushed to his side. The last thing he needed was a fight. Phil looked at the Essex stag boys as if seeing them for the first time. Were they really all bricklayers? Were they even all from Essex? Somehow Phil doubted it. By and large they looked just like the boys, thirtysomething husbands, fathers and boyfriends all of whom no doubt had work first thing Monday morning. So okay, some of them were arseholes when they had had a skinfull, but at the end of the day these guys could easily have been people he'd call friend.

'Which one if you is getting married?' asked Phil, addressing the Essex stag boys.

'What's it to you?' barked Tall Guy.

'Listen,' said Phil, 'before this kicks off I just want to speak to him, man to man.'

'It's me,' piped up a young guy at the back of the group, 'what is it you want to say?'

Phil held up his hands in peace and walked over to the young guy, holding out his hand. 'My name's Phil. What's yours?'

'Jim,' replied the young guy, reluctantly shaking Phil's hand.

'Nice to met you, Jim. Where you from?'

'Chelmsford.'

'Cool,' said Phil. 'I hear it's nice down there, is it?'

'It's okay.'

'Well, Jim,' said Phil, 'I'm from Nottingham. I don't know if you've ever been but if you haven't you should go some time. You'll love it.'

Jim looked confused.

'Listen, Jim,' continued Phil, 'when are you getting married? Next Saturday?'

Jim nodded.

'Well that's great news,' said Phil, 'because, guess what, so am I.'

Jim said nothing.

'Now listen, Jim,' said Phil, 'I'm going to ask you a question, man to man, like, and I want you to think about it really carefully before you reply: What is your missus going to say when you come home tonight with a black eye and split lip? If she's anything like mine she is going to do her nut, isn't she? It'll be all: you've ruined what's supposed to be the best day of my life! How am I supposed to show my photos to Aunt Fanny in Australia when you look like you've just stepped out of a boxing ring! She is going to be livid isn't she?'

Jim smiled reluctantly. 'She'll blow her top, mate. My life won't be worth living.'

'Exactly,' said Phil, 'and neither will mine and given that once she gets wind of half the stuff that's happened over the weekend she'll already be borderline nuclear, winding her up any more than necessary isn't something

191

that I'm keen to do. So why don't you tell your mate or brother or whoever it is who's got the mouth to back down and I'll back down too and we'll go our separate ways, and neither of our missuses need give us a hard time. But you if don't, I promise you as one groom to another no matter what happens to me in the process, I will make sure that come next Saturday, there won't be a single photo of your wedding day that won't remind your missus of just how much she hates you.' Phil paused. 'So what do you say? Truce?'

'Sod it,' said the young guy, holding out his hand, 'I never wanted to fight you guys in the first place.'

He called out to Tall Guy. 'Gav, yeah? Let's just leave it, okay? Straight up, the guy's cool, okay?'

Phil could barely breathe as the tall guy nodded to his friends and they left without incident. Once they were gone the boys rushed over to Phil's side.

'I thought we were goners there,' gasped Degsy. 'My whole life flashed before my eyes! What did you say to make him back down like that?'

'Nothing much,' replied Phil, 'I just appealed to his better half.' Phil fingered the gaping hole at the shoulder of his jacket, 'I'm just glad it's all over and done with because I've got a phone to buy.'

The GSM shop was pretty much like every mobile phone shop that Phil had ever been in: needlessly oversupplied with choices. A young sales assistant, with bad skin and a ridiculous haircut, sensing Phil's urgency approached him and said something in Dutch.

'Do you speak English?'

The man nodded as if Phil was an idiot. 'Yes, yes of course. My name is Mart, how can I help you today?'

'I need a phone.'

'Well that's good because we have many phones here. What sort of features were you hoping for?'

'I don't care! I really don't care. I just need a phone, any phone, that can be up and ready as soon as possible, by which I pretty much mean now.' Phil pulled out his wallet and handed the young man his credit card. 'Any pay as you go phone, I don't care which or how much as long as you can make it happen now.'

The young man walked over to his boss and began talking to him, occasionally pointing in Phil's direction. Phil worried that having quite clearly shown himself to be a nutter in a dishevelled black suit and tie on a ludicrously hot day there was every chance he might not get a phone at all but then the young man disappeared into a back office only to reappear five minutes later with a phone in his hand.

'We had this pay-as-you-go-phone up and ready in the back office with nearly ten Euros on it and can do you a deal on it if you like?'

'I'll take it,' said Phil. 'Don't bother wrapping it because I'm going to use it right now.'

Phil paid for the phone and joined the boys outside the shop. It was clear from their faces that Simon had filled in the salient information for them.

'So what are you going to say to her?' asked Deano. 'Are you going to give her what for?'

'He doesn't need to give her what for,' said Reuben. 'She hasn't done anything.'

'Yeah but, you know,' said Spencer. 'He's Aiden Reid, isn't he?'

'And Phil,' said Simon, 'is Phil Hudson, the one and only if you don't mind, and he's got something up his sleeve haven't you mate? What are you going to say to her?'

'Nothing,' said Phil. 'I'm not going to say a single word.' Phil then switched on the phone, eventually worked out how to set up text messaging, typed in Helen's number and stared at the blank screen waiting for inspiration to strike. He thought about what Simon had said earlier, he thought about the advice Sanne had given him and finally he thought about all the years he and Helen had had together. In that instant the message seemed to write itself. He pressed send and looked up at the boys with the widest of grins.

Simon spoke first.

'You done?'

Phil nodded.

'And now?'

Phil tucked the phone away in his pocket. 'Now, we go home.'

18.

The boys entered the hotel lobby for the last time. Pooling their ticket stubs together they handed them to the concierge then sat down in the reception area joking and larking about while waiting for their bags to arrive.

With all the seats taken Phil stood leaning against the wall content to watch his friends enjoying themselves. Putting the big question of everything that had happened to him personally aside for a moment, for the boys at least the past two days had been exactly what they had all needed: a break from the norm, combined with laughter on tap and plenty of opportunities to seek out trouble. It had been like the old days, back before they had wives, mortgages and kids, when every weekend had the potential to be the best weekend of their lives. And while there was no way that Phil wanted to revert to his old lifestyle, their escapades in Amsterdam had proved that the occasional relapse was no bad thing. Regardless of whether or not he would be married this time next week, he resolved that he and the boys would get another weekend together, and always take the time to remember why exactly they were all friends.

With their bags safely retrieved, there was nothing

for the boys to do but leave the hotel. Phil looked up the street in the direction of the station at various groups of young men, much like themselves, who were now making their way back home to their wives and girlfriends and to the lives they had left. For a few days the city that had briefly been their home would return to normal and its citizens would go back to work. Then come the weekend, when the first budget flights of the day hit the tarmac at Schipol Airport, the international occupation of Amsterdam would begin all over again.

The journey to the airport was uneventful. A general lack of sleep over the weekend had rendered not just the boys but pretty much the entire carriage silent, and most occupants seemed content to rest back in their seats, close their eyes and doze for the twenty-minute journey out of the city centre.

Groggy from their naps, the boys followed their fellow passengers up the escalator to the main station concourse. Reuben took charge and, once he had discovered the check-in desk, corralled the boys to the appropriate location. Much to their collective disappointment, it wasn't a case of simply handing over passports and printed e-tickets to an overly made up check-in clerk; the airline had switched to a self-service check-in area that would require the boys to use their brains.

Spencer stepped forward to the machine and began following the onscreen instructions for the inputting of his ticket number and the scanning of his passport details and while it took him two attempts to get it right, in the end he agreed it was a great deal less frustrating than he had initially thought. As a self-appointed expert he assisted each of the boys to input their details until only Phil was left.

'Right then,' said Spencer, adopting a comedy female voice straight out of Monty Python, 'would sir like to hand me his e-ticket print-out and passport?'

Amused Phil reached into his pocket and pulled out his e-ticket but his passport wasn't there.

Determined not to make a scene Phil quickly checked the pockets of his bag but when that search too proved fruitless he began to panic.

'What's up?' asked Reuben. 'You've not lost it have you?'

'Of course I haven't. It's in here somewhere I just can't lay my hands on it.'

The rest of the boys gathered around and began searching through Phil's case in a bid to help him, but it quickly became clear that the passport wasn't in the case at all.

'When did you last have it?' asked Patrick. 'Just think back to when you last saw it and work backwards from there.'

'The last time I saw it was last night wasn't it? After seeing you at the station I came here to try and get an early flight home and I definitely had it because I remember showing it to the girl on the desk.'

'So where did you go after that?'

'I took a taxi back to Amsterdam and when we reached the city centre there was some sort of traffic jam so we got out and I remember checking the back of the cab like I always do since I left my phone in a cab one time and then I'm pretty sure that I double-checked that I had the passport because I was worried about losing it and then I—' Phil stopped. He'd slept at Sanne's hadn't he? The passport could've slipped out of his jacket pocket when he'd taken it off to sleep, when he'd picked it up off the floor in the morning or even when he'd undressed to take a shower in Sanne's bathroom.

He looked at his watch. There was no way he could go all the way back to Sanne's, pick up his passport and still make the flight and he had to make the flight. He just had to. There was too much to lose if he didn't.

'I'm screwed,' said Phil. 'I'm really screwed.' Deciding that this was neither the time nor the place for a mental meltdown, Phil forced himself to consider his options and concluded that there really only was one. He pulled out his new phone hoping that he could find the piece of paper with Sanne's number, but then Simon jabbed him in the ribs. Sanne was standing straight ahead of him holding his passport in the air.

'You have no idea how glad I am to see you.'

'I think I can guess,' said Sanne and they hugged tightly. 'After I left you I cycled to Rembrandtpark to clear my head a little so by the time I got home I was so exhausted all I wanted to do was sleep the afternoon away. I was getting into bed when my foot hit something on the floor and there was your passport. I knew there was no way I'd find you unless I came to the airport.'

'I don't know what to say,' said Phil. 'I'm completely in your debt. I should give you something in return . . . I don't suppose you're in the market for some hi-fi equipment?'

Sanne laughed. 'Look, just book yourself on to your flight before they close! Once you've done that maybe I'll let you buy me a coffee.'

Phil rushed back to the check-in area, logged on to one of the terminals, booked on to the flight and, job complete, walked over to the boys.

'So?' said Deano, his voice oozing suggestively, 'the hottie from Holland had your passport? How did that happen then? Slip out somewhere did it?'

'Doesn't matter,' said Phil, 'I've got it now, that's the main thing. Listen, you guys, I need to say a proper thank you so rather than having you lot hanging around watching my every move like a bunch of overgrown school kids why don't you check in my bag for me, go through security and I'll see you on the other side.'

'If that's what you want,' said Simon, 'that's what we'll do.' He grabbed Deano by the arm. 'Come on you, show over.'

As the boys began walking away, Phil called out to his father.

'What's up?' said Patrick.

'You haven't got any more on you have you? Like I said, if they catch you again it won't just be a fine.'

Patrick sighed, pulled out a joint from his pocket and handed it to his son. 'I bought some when you disappeared earlier today to say goodbye to your friend. I had to really, fella told me it was a strain he'd come up with himself.'

Phil dropped the joint in a nearby bin and then looked over at Simon. 'Just give him the once over before you hit security will you, otherwise they really will lock him up and throw away the key.'

Once they were out of sight he walked over to Sanne.

'So how about that coffee then?'

Sanne shook her head. 'I don't think we should, do you?'

Phil grinned. 'It's just coffee.'

'No,' said Sanne, 'it's not, when it's the middle of the afternoon in a busy international airport.' They both sat down. 'Have you decided what you're going to do?'

Phil shrugged and looked over at a couple pushing a trolley piled high with suitcases. 'I know I still love her, and that's about all I know for sure. I suppose at the end of the day the rest – whether we stay together, whether we get married or not, it's up to her – I'm not the one who's changed my mind. I'm still the guy who wants to spend the rest of my life with her.'

'That's good, that's exactly the kind of thing she'll need to hear.'

'If it's so good then why do I feel so bad? I know something happened between them. I can feel it right at the centre of my gut. And part of me wants to punish her and part of me wants to beg her to stay and I just don't get what the right thing is to do here.' He stopped and looked directly at Sanne. 'I mean last night . . . I could have ruined everything.'

'But you didn't and that's the important thing, if I'd thought, even for a moment that you didn't really love her . . .'

Phil grinned. 'You mean I could have been in with a shot with Sanne from Misty Mondays? How cool would that have been?'

Sanne threw her arms around him for what he was sure would be their final embrace. 'I don't get it,' said Phil. 'I'm not a singer, or a DJ or even an actor, I'm just an ordinary bloke from Nottingham who runs a hi-fi shop and you're . . . well you're you. How could I have ever stood a chance with you?'

'What can I say?' replied Sanne, with a grin, 'I'm just a sucker for a man in a suit.'

Phil looked into her eyes. In a few moments he would never see her again and Sanne must have had the same thought because she tilted her head up and placed her lips firmly against Phil's. It was all over in a matter of seconds, and although the line that Phil had fought so hard not to cross had been transgressed, this time he felt no guilt at all.

Sanne tapped Phil lightly on the chest with the palm of her hands. 'You should go,' she said quietly, 'or you'll miss the plane.'

He didn't move.

THE HEN WEEKEND

THE HEN WEEKEND

MIKE GAYLE

HODDER &
STOUGHTON

First published in Great Britain in 2012 by Hodder & Stoughton
An Hachette UK company

1

Copyright © 2012 Mike Gayle

A CIP catalogue record for this title is available from the British Library

Hardback ISBN 978 1 444 74282 4
Trade Paperback ISBN 978 1 444 70859 2

Typeset in Benguiat by Hewer Text UK Ltd, Edinburgh

Printed and bound by Clays Ltd, St Ives plc

Hodder & Stoughton policy is to use papers that are natural, renewable
and recyclable products and made from wood grown in sustainable forests.
The logging and manufacturing processes are expected to conform
to the environmental regulations of the country of origin.

Hodder & Stoughton Ltd
338 Euston Road
London NW1 3BH

www.hodder.co.uk

For C.

Acknowledgements

Thanks to Sue Fletcher, Swati Gamble, and all at Hodder, Phil Gayle, the Sunday Night Pub Club, Jackie Behan, the Board and above all, to C, for pretty much everything.

Friday

1.

It had been three hours since Phil had left for Amsterdam, an hour since she had dropped Samson off at the kennels and Helen Richards was now staring, in a bewildered fashion, down at her open weekend suitcase. In one hand she held a Braun hairdryer and in the other a brand new pair of GHD hair-straighteners. Her ability to get maximum enjoyment from the coming weekend was contingent on both items making the journey to Ashbourne with her, but as the case was already full of belongings deemed so essential that she had opted to pack them *before* her hairdryer and straighteners it was clear that the only options open to her were upgrading to a larger case (something which Yaz, who had agreed to drive half of the party to their weekend destination, had specifically forbidden) or to spend the last weekend of her unmarried existence in a state of abject frizzy-haired misery.

Paralysed by indecision, she was saved by the ringing of her mobile. She dropped the items in her hands on top of the case, picked up her phone from the bed and glanced at the screen, convinced it would be Phil

calling to update her on his journey. It wasn't Phil, however, it was Yaz.

Helen and the forthright Turkish-born, Cleethorpes-raised Yaz had been friends for many years. Starting out their careers in radio as broadcast assistants at the same local station in Nottingham, they had bonded over a shared sense of humour and love of red wine. Over the weeks that followed, their friendship continued to grow, and driven by a desperate need to find an affordable place to live so that they could stop sleeping on friends' sofas, they had scoured the lower end of the accommodation food chain until they came across 111 Jevonbrook Road, a large, dilapidated terraced house without any form of central heating situated in the Lenton area of the city. Despite the cold, the mould and the guy no one seemed to know who took up residence in their kitchen, Helen loved those days, reminiscing fondly about how they would party until dawn, crawl into bed for a few hours, work a full day and then start the partying all over again. With Yaz even the dullest day ended up with them having a giggle or some weird encounter which would entertain them for months.

All these years later, having moved homes and changed jobs several times, they were both back in the city in which they had met. Yaz was now a full-time mum to two small children living the suburban dream in a modern four-bedroom semi as close as humanly possible to the best primary school in the area and Helen, following a bad break-up, had devoted herself

to her career and was now the presenter of her own pre-drivetime afternoon show, *The Chat* with Helen Richards, on BBC Radio Sherwood.

'All packed?' enquired Yaz.

Helen looked down at the suitcase in front of her. 'Nearly. A few last minute issues but nothing I can't handle. How about you?'

'Did it last night while the kids were asleep. I knew I'd never have the time today because mornings are always so mental around here. Plus I'm entertaining Simon's mum as she's babysitting for the weekend. I'm sure I'll get to the hotel and find out that I've forgotten half the things I need but I can always buy what's missing. After all, that's why they invented shopping.'

'You'll be fine,' said Helen. 'How many times have we been away together and I've never once seen you forget a single thing? Who was it who pulled out a tube of superglue when Katie's heel broke off while we were out for her birthday? You're the living embodiment of "Be Prepared!" '

'Was Simon on time to pick up Phil? I bet he wasn't. I told him last night to fill up the car and go to the cash point and he was like "Yeah, yeah, yeah," and then what's the last thing he said to me this morning after sloping out of bed at half nine when I'd been up since six getting the kids ready for school, making their sandwiches, doing the school run *and* tidying up the spare bedroom for his Mum's arrival? "Oh, I think I'm going to need to fill up the car and get some

money out." ' Yaz sighed. 'They'd be lost without us wouldn't they?'

'Hopelessly so.'

'Anyway, I was just calling to let you know that I got a text from Dee to say that she's got this work thing she's got to do and could we leave half an hour later than arranged. I was going to do a whole group text thing to let the rest of the girls know but I honestly couldn't be bothered with all that typing.'

Even though they would be seeing each other in an hour Helen and Yaz continued chatting because that was the relationship they had. They were friends who spoke about anything and everything, often two or three times a day, with no excuse needed and although on the surface Yaz appeared to be the more dominant of the two, scratch below the façade and it became apparent that theirs was a relationship of equals.

They talked about the weekend and how much they were looking forward to it and Yaz confessed that she had even dreamt about it and was about to give Helen the full details when the conversation was cut short by the howling of a small boy, who had just banged his head on the table while playing armies with his older brother.

Helen tossed the phone on the bed and returned to her suitcase dilemma before recalling that she was now in possession of an extra half-hour which might be put to best use by the drinking of a cup of tea and the eating of a consolatory milk chocolate Hobnob.

As the kettle boiled and she hunted in the cupboard

6

for her favourite mug she pondered the dirty jokes, filthy laughter, luminous cocktails and dancing on tables of past hen dos. How long since she had been on one? Years, surely. And there had been some good ones too. Yaz's infamous weekend in Blackpool, Helen's cousin Esme's one in London that had ended with two girls being arrested for indecent exposure and not forgetting her first ever hen do when an old school friend had invited her to her last hurrah at the local Yates's Wine Lodge in Doncaster when they were both nineteen. Good times each and every one. But perhaps unsurprisingly the one that she dwelt on longest was the worst one of her life: her own, some ten years earlier, for the wedding that never was.

Helen and her former fiancé Aiden Reid had met at work. Although she had been attracted to him from the very first moment she had spotted him in the canteen at BBC Radio Merseyside, Helen never considered, even for a fleeting second, that any relationship that might result from their dating might end in a marriage proposal, because while Aiden was undoubtedly driven, charming and utterly beguiling, one thing of which she and even the most deluded of women would agree upon was that he was not exactly marriage material. A fact to which he attested.

'Last night was a laugh wasn't it?' he told her on the doorstep as he prepared to leave after their first night together. 'But you know I'm not looking for anything serious, don't you?'

Helen laughed. 'Believe me Mr Deluded if I was in

the market for something serious yours would be the last door that I would come knocking on.'

'Because you don't think I can do serious?'

'No,' said Helen, 'because I know so.'

And so even as they graduated from casual fun-filled fling to a state of existence where Aiden spent more nights at her home than he did in his own, Helen remained resolutely indifferent to any talk of the future. What they had was fun and light-hearted, which proved a great relief from their stressful day-to-day jobs as overworked production assistants regularly putting in thirteen-hour days, often six days a week in order to prove themselves and climb a little further up the career ladder.

But, as is often the case in these situations, somewhere between Aiden's increasingly playful daydreams ('It's such a shame you're on the pill because you and me would make some right proper beautiful babies,') and Helen's emotional detachment ('I don't care if you're here all the time I don't want you leaving your stuff here,') a compromise was struck, and the daydreams became less abstract, the emotions more engaged until finally they both realised that they had managed to somehow fall in love.

The proposal came a month after they had officially moved in together. Helen and Aiden had spent a rare free weekend at a music festival in the Midlands with mutual friends and had been travelling in the car back to Liverpool. Without any sort of build up (they had just finished talking about how much they both hated

having to leave the festival so much earlier than their friends) Aiden said: 'You know what, Richards? You make me really happy. I think we should get hitched.'

Without a single moment's hesitation Helen surprised herself by saying: 'You know what, Reid? I've been sort of thinking the same thing myself.'

The plans for the wedding took on a life of their own and it seemed like every spare moment was taken up with making decisions about the logistics of various wedding venues and caterers and above all how best to curb the number of invitees without causing huge swathes of distant family and long lost friends irreparable offence. For Helen at the end of a long day at work, all this planning was exhausting and exasperating but she did it because she knew it would be worth it in order to create the perfect happy ending.

The first sign that things weren't quite going to plan came some six months after the proposal when Aiden came home from work one evening and informed her that he had been offered a job hosting an early evening music show for a BBC station in London.

'How could you do this?' yelled Helen who hadn't even been aware that he had put together a showreel let alone that he had been actively auditioning for jobs outside of Liverpool. 'We both agreed that we'd only ever look for jobs in the north-west.'

'I know,' replied Aiden. 'Which is exactly the reason why I didn't tell you. I never thought for a minute that I'd get the gig, but they loved me, Helen, they really loved me.'

Aiden explained his actions away in the same manner that he always explained everything away when people didn't agree with his methods, utilising a heady mixture of charm and bombast that enticed the listener into believing that to stand in his way was in effect to stand in the way of progress. 'It'll be the best thing that's ever happened to us,' he assured her. 'I've got a feeling, Helen, a really good feeling that this will be the making of both our careers.'

'And what about the wedding?' asked Helen. 'Do you want to call it off?'

'Of course I don't,' he replied. 'It's only a six-month contract. And I promise I'll be home every weekend and we can do all the wedding stuff you like. But this is a chance of a lifetime! My own show! Who knows what it might lead to. It's just too good to turn down.'

Although she wasn't entirely sure what Aiden's move would mean for them (after all her job, home and the majority of her close friends were in Liverpool), Helen knew that she couldn't stand in his way and so, despite her reservations, gave her blessing reciting to all who questioned her judgement the very arguments Aiden had used to convince her.

For the first few months while Aiden was away Helen kept herself busy with work and the wedding, choosing to live only for the weekends when Aiden would return from London. But when his show began to take off and his initial six-month contract was extended indefinitely Helen found herself becoming less patient and more enraged until finally one evening during a telephone

call he told her that he wouldn't be able to make it up at the weekend because he was too tired.

'Too tired?' repeated Helen indignantly. 'Have you any idea how tired I am? I work too! And I run this home and I'm planning this whole wedding by myself! How dare you tell me you're too tired to see me!'

Following the argument that ensued they didn't speak for two whole weeks but even through the worst of it Helen continued to work on the wedding plans convinced that all would be fine. And it was, inasmuch as, unable to cope without him, she travelled to London, apologised for the part she had played in the argument and promised to be more supportive of his career in the future. Everything returned to normal, which is to say that for Aiden at least not a single thing changed.

A week before the wedding Helen gathered together a group of her oldest, closest friends that had of course included Yaz, who was then working in marketing for a media company in Manchester, to a bar in Liverpool where they sipped cocktails and exchanged horror stories from their dating pasts, before moving on to a trendy restaurant near the quayside where well presented food was consumed and more cocktails imbibed before heading off to a nearby nightclub to dance until the early hours.

As daylight broke across Merseyside and Helen along with Yaz and a couple of other friends who were staying with her for the weekend returned to her apartment, Helen's phone rang.

'Is this Helen?' It was a female voice, young,

undeniably sexy even though currently laced with stress. Helen confirmed her identity. 'I think you should know that Aiden's been cheating on you.' Helen couldn't speak. The woman carried on regardless. 'He's a bastard, an absolute bastard and he doesn't deserve to be happy.'

Any doubts as to the veracity of this life-shattering statement evaporated when Aiden called her less than a minute later. He lied of course, claiming she was the deranged ex-girlfriend of a mate and was trying to get back at her ex by being a right royal pain in the arse to all around her, but Helen didn't buy it for a second. It wasn't the words so much as the guilt in Aiden's voice, which he seemed unable to hide almost as if on some unconscious level he actually wanted her to know the truth that he was too cowardly to say to her face.

Eventually forced to confess, Aiden blamed everything from the pressure of work to Helen's desire to stay in Liverpool for leading him astray, While Helen only blamed herself. As she contemplated the misery and embarrassment that lay before her she made two promises to herself: that she would never let her career backslide again for the sake of a man, and that if she fell in love again (which she couldn't imagine) she would never, absolutely never, agree to get married.

Leaving the indignities involved in having to cancel the wedding a week before it was due to her mum and Yaz, Helen managed to talk the travel agents where she had booked her honeymoon into allowing her to exchange it for eight nights at a spa hotel in Paxos,

where she embarked on a daily routine of beauty treatments, sunbathing, swimming and drinking bottle after bottle of local wine to the point of unconsciousness.

Returning home she cleared out anything that reminded her of Aiden, gave up alcohol, took up running and buried herself in her job, thinking nothing of working weekends and double shifts. Helen soon attracted the attention of upper management and received a promotion to producer of the mid-morning current affairs show, a post which she'd had her eye on since joining the station. Although thrilled to have reached her goal within weeks of starting the job, she found it still wasn't quite enough. She wanted a bigger, better challenge, something that could completely absorb her and which she could mould as her own. It was only when she made these comments to Yaz late one Saturday evening when her friend had come to visit for the weekend that she finally realised what she wanted to be. 'I want to be on air,' she told Yaz, 'I want to be a presenter on my own show.'

Determined to make a point to whomever might care to observe it Helen devoted all her spare time to putting together an amazing showreel that highlighted both her natural skills as a broadcaster and those she had picked up working with the brightest and best at the various stations across the nation. On a sunny spring morning a few weeks later she crossed her fingers and sent the CDs she had prepared out to the ten best radio stations in the country.

Within six months every one of them had rejected her.

Refusing to give up, she continued sending out showreels until she had exhausted every option bar one.

Disheartened, she knocked on the office door of her own station manager and after a brief conversation outlining her desires had handed him the CD convinced that as well as marking the end of her dreams it would also result in the erosion of any credibility that she had. Management were suspicious of production people who wanted to become on-air talent: they felt it showed a lack of commitment while revealing the full extent of their bloated egos.

The following afternoon Helen got a call from the station manager's PA asking her to come and see him. Prepared for the worst Helen found herself nervously reviewing the job ads at the back of *Broadcast* as she waited to be called in to his office. When he told her that he had liked her showreel so much that he was offering her a try out covering Kit Emmerly's weekend overnight show the following month Helen convinced herself it was all an elaborate joke. It was only when she found herself covering Matthew Hutcherson's early-evening phone-in the month after, and Jane Edwards' mid-morning talkback show the month after that, that she finally accepted her dream was coming true right before her eyes. The day that they told her she had finally landed her own show, *Call-back, with Helen Richards*, an overnight show covering Monday to Thursday, she was on such a high that she didn't come down for days.

It was around this time, with a new job and the

worst of what had been a monstrously unhappy year behind her, that Yaz chose to announce that she and Simon were getting married. And it was at her friend's hastily thrown together engagement party that Helen encountered Phil Hudson for the first time and came to realise that the second of her vows made after splitting up with Aiden, might not be quite so easy to keep as the first.

2.

Meeting a potential life partner hadn't even been on Helen's agenda as she entered Simon and Yaz's crowded living room clutching a plastic cup of red wine. She hoped to chew over old times with a few good friends and at worst she thought she might drink too much, talk about work a little too loudly and around midnight end up dancing and singing to *I'm Every Woman*. It was, then, very much to her surprise, when after three glasses of wine and an hour of room circulating she found herself being introduced to Phil, one of Simon's friends, and thinking as his hand touched hers: "Hmm, he's nice."

Phil was tall but not too tall. He had short black hair, dark brown eyes that seemed to radiate warmth and peeking out from underneath his hairline by his right temple was a tiny scar. He was wearing jeans and a long-sleeved black t-shirt, which was so tight across the shoulders that Helen was tempted to reach out and give the outline of each deltoid a prod with her index finger.

'Are you okay?'

Helen blinked, aware that she had been away in her

16

own private daydream. 'Yes, yes. Sorry about that. I was away with the fairies.'

'No problem,' said Phil. 'I just wanted to make sure that you weren't drifting off into a diabetic coma. That would have been terrible.'

'For me or for you?'

Phil was horrified. 'You're not actually diabetic are you?'

Helen shook her head and Phil wiped imaginary sweat from his brow.

'I thought I'd really put my foot in it there.'

'Don't worry, there's still plenty of time.'

They continued talking, mainly about Simon and Yaz. Phil thought Yaz was the best thing that had ever happened to Simon and liked the way that she seemed to have calmed down the excesses of his youth. He usually saw them two or three times a year but wished he could see them more because although he had friends where he lived, none were as good as Simon.

Phil revealed that he was the owner of Sharper Sounds, a high end TV and hi-fi shop in Derby. Helen deliberately played down her job's glamorous side and focused on the hard work that she had to put in every day but she couldn't help feeling a flush of pride when he appeared genuinely impressed, even asking her to send him a CD of her show to listen to in the car on his way to work. She took his address and promised that she would send him the disc first thing Monday morning, but even as she kissed him on the cheek as

17

they parted, she knew it wasn't going to happen. Nice as he seemed she wasn't anywhere near ready to start dating again.

The next time they met was the following New Year's Eve when Simon and Yaz had a small get-together at their house. Phil and several of Simon's other friends arrived just after seven and the first thing Phil did on seeing Helen was to ask her what happened to the recording she had promised to send. Helen had lied and blamed the post, but Phil said that it didn't matter anyway as he had offered one of his regular mail-order customers a ten per cent discount if they sent him a recording of her show. He claimed to have listened to it so many times that he had inadvertently committed parts to memory and proceeded to recite a minute's worth of on-air banter about women's underwear that she had exchanged with Sandy, the weather girl following the three o'clock news. Phil's teasing had Helen in stitches and for the rest of the evening all they did was talk and laugh.

'Call me and we'll meet up,' she said as she hurriedly tapped her home number into his phone.

'Promise?'

'On my life.'

Two days later, as she sat on her sofa watching TV Phil did indeed call but she didn't pick up. Instead she stood next to the machine while he left a long and rambling message in the style of Sandy, the weather girl. The message made her laugh out loud but it also had the effect of making her think about the past, and

she shed more tears in a single evening than she had in the previous six months.

Finally, some six months later, they met for a third time, on Simon and Yaz's wedding day, in their roles as best man and maid of honour. At the reception, as Simon and Yaz took to the floor for the first dance of the evening Phil turned to Helen and asked her what exactly she was afraid of and without missing a beat she said: 'Getting hurt, again.'

He gave her words careful consideration then reached for her hand and squeezed it, as if he was confident that this small action was all the reassurance she could need. In any other man, Helen would have found this response remarkable in its inadequacy but from Phil it felt like a beautifully eloquent gesture. He made her feel safe, he made her feel cherished and right there and then she knew he was all that she wanted.

Nine years, two house moves, three job changes, a large mortgage and a red setter called Samson later and Helen felt exactly the same way. Phil made her feel safe and secure and they were happy, really happy, until one evening out in the centre of Nottingham enjoying a post-cinema visit to Nando's, Phil went and spoilt it all.

'Look what I've found,' he said reaching down beneath their table. He held out his hand and showed Helen a bright pink plastic ring with a red plastic jewel in the middle.

'Somewhere out there is an under-accessorised

four-year-old who is ruining her poor mum's evening because she's lost her favourite ring,' joked Helen. 'You should hand it in to the staff, there might even be a reward.'

'Or,' mused Phil, 'I could just give it to you.'

Helen stared at the ring, saying nothing.

She was obviously in need of greater encouragement. He rolled the ring between his thumb and forefinger. 'So come on then. How about it?'

She pushed his hand away. 'Very funny, Hudson, you've had your fun, that's enough.'

Defiantly, Phil placed the ring on the table in front of his plate. 'Plenty of men would be more than a little bit crushed by a comment like that.'

'Well given that you're not one of them the point is, as they say, moot. Now, eat up and tell me what you thought of the film. If you're lucky I might even pass off a few of your more perceptive comments as my own in tomorrow's show when Carol-the-film-critic comes in for her slot.'

Phil began sawing at the chicken leg in front of him in a petulant fashion while Helen breathed a sigh of relief. She took a bite of her chicken burger and looked at Phil expecting to see him chewing. His lips were set in a grim line.

Helen calmly set down her knife and fork.

'What now?'

'Is there any need to use that voice?'

'What voice?'

'Your annoyed voice.'

20

'I am annoyed, Phil! I just wanted us to have a nice night out and now you're being all weird and sulky for no reason.'

'No reason?' Phil snorted loudly. 'Of course there's a reason! I can't believe that you still don't get it!'

'Get what?'

'How insulting it is.'

'How insulting what is? I have no idea what you're talking about!'

Phil's eyes widened in disbelief. 'Are you kidding? I've just asked you to marry me!'

'Using a kid's toy ring that you found on the floor! Am I supposed to be flattered?'

'You know that's not the point! I'm always asking you to marry me, and you're always saying the same thing. How many times do I have to ask before you say yes?'

Hearing the genuine hurt in his voice amongst the anger and indignation made Helen feel terrible. He was right, of course. She had lost count of the number of times he had proposed. There had been several formal proposals in their first three years (one in a Michelin-starred restaurant on their first anniversary, another, in Venice during a private gondola ride as they passed under the Rialto Bridge) followed by countless informal ones over the next seven years when he was bored, drunk, sober, amorous, sentimental and, on at least one occasion, angry. No matter the context or the manner in which the question was posed Helen's response had always been the same.

21

'What do we need to get married for when things are working just fine as they are?' asked Helen wearily.

'Do you have that on a recording?' Phil said bitterly. 'Because you really ought to. Could you imagine? With a single press of a button on your iPhone your response – downloaded directly from completecliches.com – would be played back to any unsuspecting man who dared to suggest spending the rest of his life with you.'

'But I do want to spend the rest of my life with you, you must know that by now. I'm not going anywhere, Phil. I've got a mortgage with you, I've got Samson with you, in fact I've pretty much built my life around you. Isn't that enough?'

'If it was I wouldn't be asking you, would I?'

'And that's it is it? You want so you get? I just don't want to get married and I don't understand why you won't respect that.'

'You know why.'

Helen sighed. 'What would you say if I told you I didn't?'

'I'd tell you that – deliberately or otherwise – you were lying. You know as well as I do that this is all about him. It always has been and it always will be.' He stood up, his face revealing the same blend of hurt and anger as his voice. 'I'll see you at home. For some reason I've completely lost my appetite.'

Phil was wrong. She was sure of this. Not wanting to get married had nothing to do with Aiden. Aiden was just an ex. A part of her history that she would have willingly erased from her brain years ago. As it was, he

was a part of her history that few would let her forget because rather than disappearing without a trace after his initial success in London as Helen had hoped, professionally Aiden had gone the opposite way, rocketing to the top of the radio and TV talent pool. The man who had been so broke when they first met that he'd had to borrow money from her to take her out on their first date was now a multi-millionaire radio and TV presenter, with (if the tabloids were to be believed) a pop star for an ex-wife and a string of glamorous model girlfriends to help ease the pain of life at the top.

Since Aiden's rise to fame Helen had lost count of the times tabloid hacks looking for an angle on a story about Aiden had dug up her name from his cuttings file and either doorstepped her in the hope of getting a reaction to whatever newsworthy antics he had been up to or offered her hard cash for an exclusive, private photos of the two of them together, plus studio shots of her wearing 'something sexy' to illustrate the story. Helen ignored the offers and the journalists themselves, in the hope that they would go away but she had naïvely believed that her former fiancé's fame and fortune hadn't impacted at all on her relationship with Phil.

It was some time after ten when Helen got home to the three-storey Victorian terrace in Beeston which she shared with Phil.

She hung up her jacket, kicked off her shoes and called out to Phil over the sound of the TV coming

from the living room. He didn't respond, which Helen thought was stupid and childish but also possibly an indicator of just how strongly he felt about this issue.

Phil was sitting in the leather armchair in the corner of the room staring grimly at the TV. He looked over, his face as unfamiliar and unyielding as it had been in the restaurant, picked up the remote and switched off the set, a sign that he was attempting to meet her halfway.

She sat down on the sofa opposite.

'Did you really mean what you said earlier?'

'Forget it. I was blowing off steam that's all. I'm sorry, okay.'

'I can't forget it though, can I? You know I love you, I love you more than anything or anyone. And what you said really hurt.'

He looked down at the stripped oak floor. 'Then I'm sorry. I was out of line. Look, just forget I said anything.' He pointed to the TV with the remote. 'I was just watching the tail end of that Denzel Washington film you like. Why don't you make yourself a cup of tea and come and sit with me for a while?'

Helen didn't move. 'It's not because of him you know. It's got nothing to do with him at all.'

Phil smiled wryly. 'Who? Denzel? I'm glad to hear it because I don't think I'd stand a chance against a guy like that.'

Relieved that Phil was back to making stupid jokes rather than being angry with her, Helen went to sit at his feet and rested her head on his knees.

He stroked her hair. 'I shouldn't have rocked the boat like that. You're right, we don't need to make any changes.'

'But that's not true, is it?' said Helen looking up at him. 'This keeps coming up and it's not fair on you. I need you to believe that it was never about him. It was always – absolutely always – about me thinking that good things go bad when you try and change them.'

'Look, you've got to remember that I'm this ordinary guy with a rubbish education who happens to have got lucky with you. Meanwhile the bloke who broke your heart just happens to be a ridiculously good-looking, well-educated millionaire TV presenter who can snap his fingers and have any woman he wants. How am I supposed to compete with that?'

Helen took both his hands in hers and kissed them. 'You have no idea how amazing you are, do you? You're twice the man he'll ever be.'

'Look,' said Phil, 'the point is I've always felt like the whole marriage thing is off the cards because of him. He hurt you, I get it, he let you down, but I'm not him.'

'I never said you were.'

'You didn't need to. He's been hanging around us since day one.'

'That's not true.'

Phil raised an eyebrow. 'So the reason you never called me when we first met was nothing to do with him?' Helen didn't reply. 'Look,' continued Phil, 'I'm not having a go, I promise you. All I'm saying is that I

25

want the mistakes I get blamed for to be mine and mine alone. That's not too much to ask, is it?'

Tears began to roll down Helen's cheeks. 'I'm sorry, Phil, I'm really sorry.'

'It's fine. I just wanted to get that off my chest and now I promise I'll never ask you to marry me again.'

'Good,' said Helen, 'because it's about time I took my turn.'

3.

Helen was struggling on the stairs with the 'slightly larger' suitcase she had eventually chosen when her phone rang. Being in danger of being crushed to death if she attempted to leave it precariously propped up against the banisters while she took the call she soldiered on and after a great deal of time, low volume expletives and exertion she succeeded in her task. She looked at the screen and saw that the missed call was from her mum. Closing her eyes she drew a deep breath and pressed the call button.

'Hi, Mum how are you?'

'I'm ever so good thank you, sweetie. You're not on the motorway are you? You know you shouldn't take calls and drive don't you?'

Helen laughed. 'No, I'm not driving – I haven't even left yet! Yaz is coming for me any minute.'

'Are you excited? That picture you showed me of the hotel the other day looked ever so lovely.'

'I can't wait, Mum. It's easily the poshest place I'll ever stay in.'

'Well you deserve it. You work so hard it's a wonder you haven't keeled over with exhaustion. Is Phil still there?'

'He went this morning. Yaz's husband picked him up.'

'Where have they gone again?'

'Amsterdam.'

'I hope he's not doing anything bad while he's there. You do read such stories about the things young men get up to on these stag weekends. There was a programme on cable the other day – I only saw it as I was flicking through – there was a group of lads sitting outside a bar and one of them kept dropping his trousers and the camera had to go all funny so that you couldn't see his backside.'

Helen just managed to stop herself laughing. 'I promise you, Mum, Phil will definitely not be dropping his trousers in public. He's not that kind of guy. In fact my weekend will probably end up more raucous than his.'

'I don't know why you young people need to have these stag and hen things. Your father and I didn't and we were none the worse for it.'

Helen swallowed. 'How is Dad?'

'Exactly the same. Nothing changes.'

'He seemed brighter last time I visited him. Much more like his old self.'

'I doubt that.'

'You have to keep positive, Mum.'

'And keep lying to myself like you do? He's not going to be well enough to walk you down the aisle, Helen, it's just not going to happen. Your dad's ill and that's all there is to it, and he'll get worse and worse until one day if we're lucky his body will give way just like

his mind did and put him out of his misery. It's a terrible thing to see a proud man like your father in this state.'

They continued talking out of mutual feelings of guilt rather than the desire to communicate and once their time was served they prepared to exchange civil goodbyes.

'Okay, Mum,' said Helen. 'I'd better go as Yaz will be here soon. I'll see you later.'

'Yes of course,' replied her mum. 'But just a quickie before you go . . . about the wedding dress.'

'Mum, I've already said that I'm not talking about it.'

'I know you did and I still don't know why. Your auntie Caron was asking about it only last night. Have you any idea how embarrassing it is for me to have to say that I haven't seen a picture of it!'

'No one has, Mum, I told you, this is something I want to do on my own. I don't understand why you won't respect that.'

There was a click and the line went dead. Helen filled with rage. Why did her mum always insist on winding her up like this? Why did she always insist on getting her own way?

Much as they loved each other (and they did, quite fiercely) their outlook on life differed too much for them to have any common ground when it came to how Helen should live her life.

Despite Helen having explained her desire to do things differently this time around her mum seemed incapable of accepting this fact but it was the topic of

Helen's father that caused the most upset between them. (Her mum, a practitioner of the school of thought that called a spade a spade, viewed her husband's rapid descent into the advanced stages of Alzheimer's almost as if he had already died while Helen, an eternal optimist at least in terms of her father's health, refused to even consider that a day might come when her father would be permanently absent from her life.)

Helen headed upstairs to get the rest of her bags and, when the doorbell rang, she checked her reflection in the mirror and opened the door to an impatient-looking Yaz, holding a carrier bag.

Helen opened the door wider for Yaz to step in. 'Before you start, I know what you said about not going overboard with the luggage . . .' Her voice trailed off as she pointed to the bulging case and numerous bags standing in the middle of the hallway. 'I tried to keep it to a minimum but I failed, okay? So, don't give me a hard time about it.'

Yaz stared in disbelief. 'How long do you think we're going for? Is there anything you haven't packed? If I open up that case will I find you've brought the kitchen sink?'

'Look, do you want me to have a good time or not?'

'Of course I do! But I was sort of hoping that you'd be able to do it without bringing your entire wardrobe. Is everything in there absolutely necessary?'

Helen shrugged. 'I don't know, but it's too late to try editing it now. It took me the best part of ten minutes

to get it closed so I'm not risking opening it again until we get there.'

Yaz rolled her eyes theatrically. 'Okay, fine, you take the case. It's not like the rest of the girls will need to sit down or anything. But you have to do something for me.' She reached into the carrier bag and pulled out a bright pink T-shirt with a photo of Helen taken on her last birthday wearing a three-cocktail grin and a pink glittery cowboy hat with the words 'Bride in training' emblazoned across it. Helen had never seen anything quite so ugly in her life.

'No!'

'But you have to!'

'Why?'

'Because it'll be fun.'

'But you promised we weren't going to do this kind of stuff. You said – and I quote: "The weekend will be tasteful," which means no male strippers, no inflatable willies and no tacky T-shirts!'

'And it will be tasteful. Just not this bit. Come on, mate, indulge me this once.'

Feeling guilty about the suitcase, Helen reluctantly accepted the offending items. She slipped the T-shirt gingerly over her top, placed the hat on her head and stared at her reflection in the hallway mirror.

'I look like an idiot.'

'True,' said Yaz practically speechless with laughter, 'but you won't be alone.' She put on her own T-shirt and hat, pulled a camera out of her bag and took a photo of Helen. 'There,' she said, checking the photo

31

on her camera's tiny screen, 'if that isn't one for your Facebook page I don't know what is!'

Helen wondered how she might have spent this weekend had she not succumbed to the pressure to have a hen do. Although she was looking forward to The Manor, with a week to go before the wedding and so many unchecked items on her to-do list, the thought of it all made her feel as though she was drowning in a sea of uncompleted tasks.

From the moment Helen confessed to her friends and co-workers that she and Phil were finally getting married, the question of the hen night became paramount. Given the disaster of her previous hen night, Helen had been keen to forgo the tradition completely, but every time she attempted to explain her stance to those around her she received the same 'I don't get it' blank stare. 'It's because most of us are in our late thirties and haven't been to a hen party for years,' explained Yaz, when Helen commented on her friends' reaction, 'and if anyone's in need of an excuse to let down their hair and blow off some steam it's got to be our demographic all the way. This isn't just about you H, it's about them. Your friends need a hen do.'

Although Yaz's tongue was lodged firmly in her cheek throughout much of this speech, Helen conceded she had a point. Lots of her friends who were married – with or without kids – would love to have some time to themselves without having to feel guilty. Relenting, Helen handed Yaz a list of the people she wanted to invite and gave the go ahead for what she hoped might

be a modest get-together at a local posh pizza place in West Bridgford, followed by an evening of cocktails and dancing. One week and several phone calls later those plans had morphed into a two-night stay at a five-star luxury hotel on the edge of the Peak District.

'I know I'm being a right bossy old cow,' said Yaz as the two friends made their way into the kitchen, 'but it's only because I want you to have the most amazing weekend, babe.'

'I know it is,' said Helen hugging her friend, 'And while I might not always look like I appreciate all the effort you've put in I really do. It can't have been easy sorting all this out while juggling the kids.'

Helen sat down at the kitchen counter idly flicking through a magazine while Yaz went to the loo. Then she washed up a dirty plate and mug, turned on the burglar alarm and locked the front door. With great effort the two women managed to drag Helen's luggage to Yaz's dark blue people carrier aka The Mum-mobile and loaded it in the rear of the vehicle.

'Right,' said Yaz starting up the engine as Helen buckled her seatbelt, 'I've got the bride to be and her extensive luggage now all I need to do is pick up the girls and this weekend has officially begun!'

'The girls', to be accurate, were three women, Lorna, Dee and Kerry, who formed the inner core of Helen's friends. Helen had known Scottish-born-and-raised Lorna since first moving to Nottingham when she had been an overworked and underpaid stylist at one of the city's coolest hair salons and the only woman who

Helen would let within an inch of her hair. Back then Lorna was constantly broke and had a serious unsuitable boyfriend addiction. Now she was still the only woman Helen would allow to cut her hair but she was also solvent and happily co-habiting with Dez, her boyfriend of three years. She was also the owner/ manager of Revival, an up-market salon in the centre of Beeston catering to the great and the good of its well-heeled constituency.

Next there was Dee, a previous next-door neighbour, a big-hearted, plus-sized, Abba-loving ball of energy and English teacher. Dee and her husband Johnny had been the couple that Helen and Phil socialised with most after Yaz and Simon. Then Johnny left and everything changed. Now single, Dee worked for a Nottingham-based adult education outreach agency and when not going on teeth-grindingly awful internet dates her favourite thing was to regale Helen with tales of teeth-grindingly awful internet dates.

Finally, there was twenty-six-year-old Kerry, the baby of the group, whom Helen had known since Kerry's first day at Radio Sherwood as a single, timid, fresh out of university trainee broadcast assistant. Seeing more of herself in Kerry than she liked to admit, Helen had taken her under her nurturing wing. Five years on and recently engaged, Kerry had worked her way up the ranks to become the producer of Helen's revamped afternoon show and had done such a brilliant job that the show had been nominated for its first ever Sony Award.

Although Helen saw the girls individually, they also met

up every couple of months for a seemingly innocent meal which would inevitably morph – several drinks in – into the kind of evening that required a frenzied exchange of phone calls the following day to piece together exactly what had happened.

'What's taken you so long?' exclaimed Dee wrenching open Kerry's front door before Helen had finished making her way up the path. 'Somewhere out there is a swanky room with my name on it that's going to waste while we sit watching daytime TV!'

Helen hugged her friend tightly with one hand while holding on to her hat with the other. 'Rest assured Yaz will have her foot to the floor the whole way. No one wants to be at that hotel faster than she does. That's why she refused to let me drive.'

Dee wrinkled her nose. 'That's because you drive like my Nan! In fact scrap that, you actually drive worse than her because bless her, while she's convinced that if she goes over forty she'll end up in outer space, at least I have seen her do thirty-one in a thirty-zone on a couple of occasions.'

'I'm a law-abiding citizen!' protested Helen.

'More like a law-abiding *senior* citizen!'

Realising that it was highly unlikely that she would ever win this argument, Helen changed the subject.

'Yaz is going to go bonkers when she sees that lot!' said Helen pointing at the mass of weekend bags, miniature suitcases and designer logoed carrier bags at her friends' feet. 'She gave me a hard time and it's my hen-do!'

35

'What's your hen do?'

Yaz, who had been making room for the girls' luggage in the car, was standing in the doorway wearing a quizzical expression on her face and holding the carrier bag containing the pink hats and T-shirts.

'Nothing,' said Helen. She shuffled next to Kerry and Lorna in the hope of hiding the bags from view. 'We were just chatting.'

'Why are you all yakking instead of getting the weekend started? Is this how it's going to be? Me organising and you lot goofing off all the time?'

'You love it really.'

'Well,' said Yaz, 'That's as maybe but it doesn't mean you have to take advantage of my good nature.' She handed out the hats and T-shirts. 'Before you start moaning like this one did, you don't have to wear them all weekend but they are compulsory in the car *at all times.*'

'She's not joking,' said Helen, 'my hat fell off on the way over and she pulled over and waited until I'd put it back on.'

'I know it all sounds a bit draconian,' said Yaz, 'but you'll thank me once the weekend's over and all you have is memories.'

Lorna laughed, 'Is that an actual command or are we allowed to thank you of our own free will?'

'She doesn't care as long as we do,' said Kerry fluttering her eyelashes sweetly.

The girls put on the T-shirts and hats while Yaz, as predicted, told them off for over-packing. It took the

best part of half an hour to pack all the luggage into Yaz's people carrier and even then there were multiple handbags and carrier bags left which in the end Dee, Kerry and Lorna had to have on their laps as punishment.

Soon after loading up they were slipping *Never Forget: The Ultimate Take That Collection* into the CD player and journeying their way towards the A52, belting out the lyrics to *A Million Love Songs* at the tops of their voices and feeling like they didn't have a care in the world.

4.

The blazing summer sun was high in the sky as Yaz slowed the car and pulled in between the grand limestone pillars at the entrance to The Manor. Reaching the dashboard she turned down the volume of the music that had accompanied them for the entire journey to a bare minimum and wound down her window to take in the unmistakable sounds and smells of the English countryside – Beeston, this was not.

'Hey, Yaz!' called Helen as she too wound down her window, 'this place is so up-market that even the Mum-mobile crunching on the gravel sounds classy. If I close my eyes I can almost imagine we're in a Rolls-Royce heading up to our country pile for the weekend.'

The driveway was long and winding, not only to make the most of the surrounding countryside but also to heighten the anticipation of arrival and it did both extremely well. Straining to get the first peek at the place that would soon be home, Helen and the girls were literally on the edge of their seats until round a sharp bend there it was: a beautifully constructed, architecturally imposing, white stone country house looking out over a wide shimmering reed-lined river.

'Now *that*,' said Yaz, 'is what I call a hotel!' She turned to Helen. 'What do you think then? Still wishing we'd stayed at home?'

'It's amazing,' said Helen as the drive swept over a bridge and up towards the house. 'Come check-out time on Sunday they are literally going to have to prise me kicking and screaming from my room.'

'This is going to be one of the best weekends of my life,' said Helen as they came to a halt at the main entrance and a young man, in a dark grey shirt and trousers, handsome enough to be a model, descended the stairs. 'It's too perfect for words.'

The porter greeted Helen and her friends warmly and pointed them in the direction of reception while he began unloading the luggage. Not needing to be told twice, the girls made their way to the reception desk where they were welcomed by a pretty French girl, also dressed in the hotel's dark grey uniform. She allocated their rooms, handing out slim, black key cards inside stiff white card wallets. None of the rooms had numbers, instead they were all named after the different types of trees that could be found in the hotel grounds. Yaz's was called Bird Cherry, Lorna's was Larch, Dee's Chestnut, Kerry's Bay Willow and Helen's the Sycamore room.

'Right then,' said Yaz, after the receptionist had given them directions to all the rooms, 'according to my schedule it's free time from now until seven thirty when we'll meet in the Silver Lounge, for cocktails.' Stifling her competing desires to both mock and hug

Yaz for having made a schedule, Helen made her way to the lift.

Despite having spent many idle moments in her studio poring over the artfully fashioned photos on the hotel website, Helen was astonished by how much better the reality was than its two-dimensional counterpart. As she stood in the doorway to her new home for the next two nights she could hardly believe her eyes. There were glossy magazines on the Danish coffee table in the lounge area, a beautifully presented bouquet of freshly cut flowers on the dressing table, and a small box of handcrafted Belgian chocolates on the bed. And as for the room itself, everything from the antique French chandelier to the vintage satin cream duvet cover resplendent across the super-king-sized bed, from the state of the art Bang and Olufsen TV through to the Ligne Roset floor lamp screamed luxury to such an extent that Helen wondered if she had slipped into the pages of *Elle Decoration*.

As a rule Helen's favourite part of any posh hotel experience was the bathroom. Yes, she appreciated tastefully chosen furnishings, and attention-grabbing colour palettes but nothing quite got her going like an exquisitely decorated bathroom and so it was with no small degree of trepidation that she approached the only door in the room she had yet to open.

She was not disappointed. It was perfect, absolutely perfect. Four times the size of her own bathroom, presented in a classic dove white and decked out with

a twin sink, a zinc-floored walk-in shower with a huge rainfall showerhead, and a roll-top bath to die for. It was beyond her wildest bathroom imaginings.

But even so, as she unwrapped one of the individual rose petal soaps she observed that without the sound of Phil in the other room, flicking through the TV channels and bemoaning the price of a bottled beer from the mini-bar, she might as well have been in a fifty-pound-a-night Novotel. *Maybe that's what love means*, she thought as she began drawing herself a bath. *You can only be happy in paradise if the person you love is there with you to share it.'*

It was a little after six when a wet-haired Helen, encased in one of the hotel's super fluffy towelling robes and matching slippers emerged from the bathroom and opened up her case. Her excitement at the prospect of getting ready for the evening ahead was tempered by a slight feeling of stress. Having had barely any time to plan her outfits during the week, she had spent a frantic afternoon in Nottingham city centre purchasing half a dozen tops, two pairs of trousers and four different hair accessories, most of which she knew she would be returning unused first thing on Monday morning. In her work life Helen was the very definition of decisive but standing alone and faced with so many sartorial options she felt the complete opposite.

Deciding to leave her choice of clothes until later Helen picked up her hairdryer and as she did so there was a sharp knock at her door.

Helen's immediate thought revealed much about the negative nature of her psychology, for she assumed that the knock heralded the arrival of a member of the hotel's staff to tell her there had been a hideous mix-up and that she would have to leave her room immediately and stay in a nearby bed and breakfast. When she opened the door to see Yaz, Lorna, Dee and Kerry brandishing a condensation-covered bottle of Cava, and carrying piles of clothes, shoes, and make-up bags, she was both relieved and cheered.

'It was all her idea,' said Yaz pointing at Dee.

'And I'm not ashamed of it either!' grinned Dee, as unbidden the girls all made their way into Helen's room and closed the door behind them. 'Getting ready for a big night out is the best part of an evening!' Her face fell. 'You don't mind, do you?'

'Mind?' said Helen, 'I've never been so bloody grateful to see you lot in my life! Dee you open the Cava, Lorna you find some glasses, Kerry, put some music on, Yaz, well . . . you can just make yourself at home and I am going to blow-dry my hair into submission, then with your help throw together a killer outfit, paint my face to within an inch of its life and leave this room for dinner tonight looking like a million dollars!'

The hour and a half that followed was like a montage from a chick flick. Not just any chick flick montage. The ultimate chick flick montage with the best bits from *Dirty Dancing*, *Thelma and Louise*, *Beaches* and *Mamma Mia* with all the associated tears, laughter, lip-syncing dance sequences and gratuitous displays of

female bonding that such a description implies. And at the end of it all as Helen admired herself in the mirrored wardrobe in her new sleeveless embroidered black top, skinny leg trousers and black heels, standing next to her impeccably dressed and beautifully made-up friends as the final chorus of *Relight My Fire* played loudly from the wall mounted stereo system, she knew it would be a night to remember.

The five friends were still laughing and joking with each other when they emerged from the lift and clicked their way across the marble tiled lobby until they reached the Silver Lounge.

Again the Manor website photographs didn't do justice to the true opulence and sophistication of the Silver Lounge. Perfectly air-conditioned, with walls alternately painted in a gun-metal grey and brilliant white, furnished with sumptuous velvet sofas arranged around low gloss white tables and with lighting so subdued that even seven thirty on a summer's evening could have passed for three in the morning, it was every inch the perfect place for the five friends to start their evening.

Spreading themselves across two of the huge velvet sofas the girls pored over the cocktail menu before jointly making the decision that they would each order something different. Drinks orders were taken and then taken again because half the group had changed their minds before the waiter had even left their table and then the girls settled into a quarter of an hour of

gentle banter before their drinks and several small platters of olives and nuts were presented to them.

'We should have a toast,' said Kerry raising her glass. 'Here's to our girl Helen, one of the best friends a girl could have!'

Clinking glasses, the girls ploughed headlong into more laughter and conversation while exchanging sips of cocktails with each other along the way. This resulted with almost indecent haste in a table full of empty glasses and a call to the waiter for the return of the drinks menu. He arrived to the eruption of a cacophony of screaming and laughter that could only mean one thing: more of Helen's weekend hen party guests had arrived.

The three new arrivals were friends who for one reason or another (most often a clash of schedules) Helen rarely got to see. There was Dublin-born Ros, a tall and elegant Cambridge-based former magazine journalist turned web-developer who was currently in the middle of a divorce. Then there was Heather, a Bournemouth-based former paediatric nurse now a happily married full-time mum of four who Helen knew from her sixth-form days. Finally there was Carla, a part-time social worker and single mum of two who she'd known since they both started Brownies together at the age of eight and with whom she had recently reconnected via Facebook after a fifteen-year gap.

Helen raced over to the girls, hugged them and ushered them over to the sofas to be introduced to the rest of the party.

'Everyone,' said Helen eagerly, 'this is Ros, Heather and Carla.' The girls all waved their hellos. 'Ros, Heather and Carla, meet the girls!'

As she caught up with everyone's news Helen remembered the reservations she had had about the weekend. Surrounded by some of her oldest and closest friends, watching them all laughing and joking together, it seemed impossible that she had entertained such thoughts. This weekend couldn't be more different from that raucous night in Liverpool all those years ago. More importantly, this time she wasn't marrying an egocentric idiot who would break her heart.

Tapping her engagement ring (a platinum four-claw mount with a single carat diamond ring that Phil had surprised her with the weekend after she proposed) on the side of her glass, Helen rose and called the girls to attention.

'I just wanted you all to know how much it means to me that you've come this weekend. We've all got such busy lives and hardly a scrap of time for ourselves, so the fact that you've all arranged baby-sitters, put off spending time with husbands and partners for the weekend just to be here means a tremendous amount to me. And, well, I think you're all amazing!'

A tearful Helen sat down while the girls all applauded, Yaz joking that secretly they had only come for the pampering, and as they raised a glass for yet another toast the waiter arrived to inform them that their table was ready.

'I know we've got lovely treatments and everything

booked for the weekend,' said Yaz, as the girls finished off their drinks and gathered their things, 'but do you think it's wrong for me to be looking forward to this meal most? I'm tingling with excitement at the prospect of a nice meal that I didn't cook!'

Herded by Yaz, the party made their way into a large modern dining room where various tables of diners were already eating. One of the waiting staff checked their reservation and showed them to their table, which Yaz noticed immediately was too small.

'I think there must have been a mistake. This is a table for six.'

The waiter nodded, returned to his station to pick up the reservation book and then consulted it in front of her.

'You are?'

'Mrs Collins.'

'And the number in your party is?'

'Eight.'

The waiter turned the book sideways to show Yaz what number was written down next to her name. There was no doubt about it. It was a six.

'But that can't be right! Yes, initially it was only going to be six tonight but then about three weeks ago I called and changed the number of guests to eight. Whoever took the call must have forgotten to change the booking.'

The waiter smiled apologetically. 'I'm so sorry about this Mrs Collins but I'm afraid I can only go with what's down in the book.'

Yaz looked as if she might explode. 'Okay, fine, can you at least find us another table?'

'I am afraid I can't do that madam as we are fully booked this evening.'

Helen stepped in. 'Okay, so we can't have another table. How about if we all squeeze up a bit? Do you think you could get in another couple of chairs and two extra settings?'

The waiter offered what Helen hoped would be his last conciliatory smile. 'I'm afraid, madam, that's not The Manor's dining policy. Might I suggest that you divide your group into two sittings?'

This suggestion was the final straw for Yaz. She glared at him and barked loudly enough to grab the attention of half the room: 'What a stupid idea! We're on a hen weekend, not a school trip! We're not going to eat in two sittings, we're going to eat all together at a table for eight because I don't care what's in that book of yours, that's what I asked for!'

Helen quickly put her arm around Yaz. 'Look, I'm really sorry. As you can see my friend's quite upset by all this. We'll just do the two sitting thing, okay?'

'No, we will not!' yelled Yaz. 'You all think that I've cocked up somehow, well I didn't! I booked a table for eight!'

'It's fine, babe, honestly,' said Helen quickly, 'No one blames you for anything.'

'But that's not the point!' snapped Yaz, 'The point is that I called and altered the booking three whole weeks ago and they told me there would be no problem and

lo and behold there is one! It's just so typical! You do everything to have things planned out and through no fault of your own it all falls apart! I'm absolutely bloody sick of it!'

Yaz was always forceful but this was far from being her normal behaviour. Helen drew her aside. 'Listen, let's go outside and take a breather for five minutes.'

Yaz didn't reply. She pushed past the waiter and stormed out leaving Helen and at least half the dining room wondering what in the world was going on.

5.

Helen exchanged glances with the rest of the girls. There was something about the way Dee, Lorna and Kerry avoided her gaze that indicated they had more than an inkling of what was really going on.

'Okay, which one of you is going to tell me?'

Dee reluctantly met Helen's gaze. 'She made us promise not to say anything.'

'About what exactly? Has something happened?'

Dee's face fell and she bit her lip.

'She's fine and I'm sure you would have been the first person she told had the circumstances been different.'

'What circumstances?'

'The wedding. You getting married.'

'What's that got to do with her storming off like that?'

'Simon's moved out.'

Helen couldn't believe what she was hearing. 'No! When?'

'Three weeks ago.'

'Are you sure?'

Dee nodded. 'She told us all a few days ago but swore us to secrecy.'

'But that doesn't make any sense. Only this morning

she was telling me this long and involved story about how disorganised he was today getting his stuff together to pick up Phil. Why would she make that up?'

'Maybe she wanted to protect you,' said Lorna. 'Maybe she didn't want you worrying about her on what's supposed to be your special weekend.'

Helen's mouth felt dry and she wanted to sit down. 'Is he seeing someone else?'

Kerry shrugged. 'We don't know. She wouldn't give specifics. She talked about it like it was a trial separation so I'm guessing there's still hope.'

'A trial separation? Why would they do that? They're happy. I know they are. I've got to go and find her. I've got to find out exactly what's been going on.' She looked over at Lorna. 'I'm probably going to be a while and I'd hate for you girls to just be sitting around all night. Can you make sure that everyone gets fed and if there are any more problems . . . I don't know . . . order room service and get them to put it on my bill.'

Leaving them to smooth things over with the waiter Helen rushed out of the dining room and frantically scanned the lobby. Hazarding a guess Yaz might have gone for a cigarette she made her way outside and finally caught sight of her friend heading along the path to the river. Helen called out at the top of her voice drawing the attention of a number of people sitting out on the terrace but she didn't care what they thought of her. All she cared about was Yaz.

'You okay?' asked Helen when she finally caught up with her friend.

Without acknowledging her question Yaz gazed up at a flock of Canada geese flying overhead. 'This place really is amazing isn't it?' she said. 'How great would it be to wake up every morning and see this from your bedroom window?'

Helen put her arms around Yaz and held her tightly. 'It's perfect. You were so right when you chose here.'

Arm in arm they began walking along the river's edge and then out to the sun-bleached jetty where they stood watching the dying embers of the day's light dancing on the water's surface.

'The girls told you then,' said Yaz. She pulled out a lighter and a pack of Silk Cut, lit one up and took a long, deep pull on it then exhaled, sending a plume of smoke up into the air.

Helen nodded. 'Don't be mad at them. I practically had to drag it out of them.'

'I was going to tell you,' said Yaz, ' . . . it was just . . . I don't know . . . I really wanted this weekened to be special. I didn't want anything to spoil it. The last thing I wanted was to turn a weekend that was supposed to be all about you into a weekend that was all about me. I just wanted you to be happy.'

'And I will be. You've already done such a fantastic job that it will be one of the best weekends of my life. But I really wish you hadn't kept this from me. We're friends. We take the good with the bad. That's how it works.'

'You're right and how I ever thought I'd keep it from you for the whole weekend is anybody's business. I

51

suppose I thought if I crossed my fingers and tried to keep a lid on it everything would be okay.'

Helen smiled. 'And how's that plan working out?'

Yaz's weak smile faded to nothing. 'You must have been mortified to see me go off like that. And in front of all your friends.'

'Don't even think about it. They'll all be fine with it. I promise.' She hesitated unsure whether to say more. 'Did you see it coming?'

Yaz began to cry. 'I had no idea,' she sobbed. 'It just came out of nowhere.'

Helen felt awful for making her relive the moment but now Yaz had confessed, the dam seemed to burst.

'I'd just finished putting the boys to bed when he came in and asked if he could have a quick word downstairs. I could see something wasn't right so we went into the kitchen and he just came out with it – he wasn't sure he wanted to be married any more – those were his exact words. It was horrible Helen, really horrible. And all the time he was talking I kept thinking to myself, "Please let me wake up and this just be a dream." '

Through her tears Yaz continued to pour her heart out. Simon had gone to live in the empty flat of one of his work colleagues who had just moved in with his girlfriend and had yet to get around to renting it out. They hadn't told the kids, so every morning he'd come over to help get them ready and every evening he'd come over to help tuck them into bed.

Helen was stunned. It didn't sound like the Simon

she knew. She wondered if Phil knew and had been keeping it a secret all this time. The thought made her stomach tighten and she squeezed her eyes shut until the sensation faded.

The very idea that Yaz and Simon had separated unsettled her greatly. While they were hardly anyone's idea of a perfect couple (Helen had lost count of the number of times she had watched Yaz mercilessly bully Simon in order to get her own way or observed Simon flip from normal to sullen over the smallest comment from Yaz) Helen had always felt that they worked. Somehow Yaz's volatility cancelled out Simon's own, leaving behind two reasonably decent people who loved each other a great deal even if they didn't always show it. To know that it was all at risk for something as intangible as one half of the unit needing 'space' upset her world view.

'So all of that stuff you said to me this morning . . . ?'

'Lies.'

Helen found it impossible to hide her surprise. Before this moment she would have described Yaz the worst liar she had ever met.

'I know,' said Yaz as if reading her thoughts, 'it's funny how good you get at lying once you've run out of options.'

The buzz of conversation and laughter alerted the friends that they were no longer alone – lured by the beauty of the river a number of the hotel's guests were on their way down to the water's edge. Helen looked at Yaz and sighed.

'Do you want to go somewhere else?'

'No, I'm fine, really I am. Let's just try and get the evening back to where it was.'

The first sign that the evening might not be the washout Yaz had feared came as they arrived at the restaurant and spotted the girls sitting at a table for eight.

Delighted on Yaz's behalf, Helen quizzed the girls as to how this had come about.

'Yaz was right,' Kerry explained handing them each a glass of champagne. 'She had booked a table for eight. After you guys left Dee made a bit of a fuss and asked to speak to the manager and he double-checked the booking. Turns out the girl who took Yaz's call made a mistake and rather than amending the old booking she'd simply made a new one and made things worse by writing down Yaz's name as Mrs Cole so there was a whole table for eight sitting empty which was ours anyway. He was massively apologetic, promised to halve the bill for the evening and chucked in two bottles of Moët for our trouble!' Kerry raised her glass. 'I know we've gone a bit mad for the toasting tonight but who cares! Here's to Yaz, always right even when they try to tell her she's wrong!'

A Thai prawn noodle starter and mouthwatering steak main later, Helen was sitting in front of an empty coffee cup laughing as Lorna wheeled out the story of the time she and Dez had met David Bowie at Heathrow Airport and was so completely and utterly star-struck when he agreed to sign an autograph that she passed out, cracked her head on the floor and knocked herself

unconscious. The girls loved Lorna's story, even those like Helen who had heard it before, and had it not been for Dee's suggestion that they all retire to the Silver Lounge for another drink, the conversation would no doubt have turned to other embarrassing celebrity encounters.

'Absolutely,' enthused Ros, 'I've been dying to sample some of those lovely cocktails you all had earlier.'

The other late arrivals, Heather and Carla, nodded in unison and en masse the girls went straight to the Silver Lounge where they commandeered a corner of the now bustling bar. The waiter distributed drinks menus, which they all studied – apart from Kerry, who seemed preoccupied.

'What's up?' asked Helen noticing her young friend's distraction.

'Look over there,' said Kerry pointing as subtly as she could to a tall, handsome man in a dark suit and tie who stood talking with a group of men who had their backs to her.

Helen was none the wiser. 'Who is he?'

Some of the other girls looked up to see what was monopolising their friends' attention.

'Is that who I think it is?' asked Lorna.

'Depends on who you think it is,' said Helen. 'I have no idea.'

'I don't know his name or anything,' said Kerry. 'But I'm pretty sure he's that Man United player. What's he doing here?'

'Same as us, probably,' said Helen. 'Having a weekend

away with his mates. Which means that the last thing he'll want is a group of women on a hen weekend gawping at him.'

Kerry wasn't convinced. 'Have you actually looked at him? He's absolutely beautiful.'

'And you're engaged!'

'And I wouldn't do anything! You know that but . . .' Kerry emitted what was intended to be a wistful sigh but which came out much closer to the low groan of a pervert. As one the entire table burst into peals of laughter.

Kerry was mortified. 'He heard you lot laughing and he looked over! I've got no chance with him now!'

Chuckling, Dee reached into her purse and slapped down ten pounds on the table. 'I'll give you a tenner if you talk to him.'

Lorna shook her head in mock dismay. 'Dee, don't be so cruel. Can't you see the girl's not up to it!'

'Kerry, ignore them, they're just jealous that you're still young and pretty not old and wizened like the rest of us!' defended Helen. 'Don't stoop to their level!'

Kerry contemplated the note on the table. 'What would I have to say?'

'Are you really going to do it?' screamed Dee in delight.

'I'll give you twenty pounds not to,' said Helen fearing the only way this escapade could end was badly.

'Like it's about the money!' chided Dee. 'She'd do it for free, that one!'

'You'll get us chucked out! And what if he's here with his girlfriend? She'll have your eyes out!'

'I'm only saying hello!' protested Kerry. 'There's no harm in that is there? I don't know . . . I was thinking maybe I might tell him that my Dan's a huge fan!'

Lorna cackled. 'Is that before or after you slip him your room number?'

Peering through her fingers Helen watched in horror as Kerry smoothed down her skirt and sashayed towards the footballer, her stomach tightening with her friend's every step. At the last moment Kerry lost her nerve and comically spun around one hundred and eighty degrees before the footballer had even noticed her.

Howling with laughter as Kerry returned to her seat, the girls all congratulated her bravery and even Dee declared that Kerry deserved the money.

Relieved that things hadn't got too out of hand, Helen called the waiter over to take their order and excused herself to use the loo, making sure to take the route furthest away from the footballer and his friends.

Emerging some moments later with freshly reapplied lipstick and hands that smelt of expensive moisturiser, Helen was about to head back to the bar when she was suddenly struck with the need to hear the voice of her fiancé. As anticipated, this thing with Simon and Yaz had disturbed her and she wanted Phil's reassurance that what had happened to their friends wouldn't happen to them too.

Helen searched her bag for her phone but then recalled her earlier decision to leave it in the bedroom in the spirit of freedom. She reckoned she had plenty

of time to make a quick call and return to her friends before they sent out a search party and in a matter of minutes was breathlessly pushing her key card into her bedroom door.

Picking up her phone from the bedside table she called up Phil's number to the main screen and wondered if she was doing the right thing. He was supposed to be on a boys' weekend. What if he was annoyed that she was disturbing him or, even worse, think that she was checking up on him? She decided it would be okay as long as she told him why she had rung before he could say a word. If ever there was a justification for her call, the break-up of their friends' marriage fitted the bill. She pressed the call button and waited. There wasn't even a ringing tone. Instead, after a series of indeterminate clicks, she was directed to his voicemail.

Unsettled, she tried again but the same thing happened. Setting down the phone on the bed next to her she gave herself a good talking to as she began to worry. There were a million and one reasons why Phil's phone might have been switched off and none of them had any bearing on their relationship. He was no doubt in a pub or a club with the rest of the boys and had deliberately left his phone behind so he could concentrate on having a good time much like she had planned to do. She told herself she would see him soon enough anyway. She made one last attempt and this time she left a message: 'Hey you, it's just me saying a quick hello. Arrived safely, the hotel is amazing, and the

girls are all here now and we're having a lot of fun. Obviously I'm not looking to cramp your style in front of the boys but I thought you might like to know that I love you madly! No need to ring me back, okay? Love you, bye.' Satisfied that she had done the right thing, she returned her phone to the bedside table and made her way downstairs to the lobby.

In the bar it was as though she had stepped into another world. The music that had previously been little more than aural wallpaper was now loud enough to be a feature in itself and that, combined with the buzz of a hundred different conversations, gave the room a whole different atmosphere.

Keen to avoid the footballer and his friends, Helen kept her head down as she passed where they had been standing and as she wove her way back to the girls Yaz looked up and waved. She raised her hand to wave back but felt a tap on her shoulder. She turned around to see a face, which – even though she hadn't encountered it in person for what felt like a lifetime – was instantly recognisable.

6.

In her professional life, Helen dealt exceptionally well with the unexpected. There was the time she was producing the breakfast show in Sheffield and the presenter, Jamie Toddington, fainted live on air in the middle of a phone interview with an MP who was trying to justify the closure of a local hospital. Before the MP had even become aware of the problem Helen had dropped her bowl of muesli, raced from her position at the control board to check that Jamie was still breathing, cued a traffic report and ran down to security requesting the assistance of someone with first aid training, while simultaneously placating the MP who was hanging on a second line wondering what was going on.

On another occasion working an afternoon shift during one of her early stints as a presenter, her producer had somehow failed to notice that the two main guests, a couple of former soap star heart-throb actors promoting a new production of *Waiting For Godot* at the local arts theatre, had turned up so drunk that they couldn't form a coherent sentence, unless it was to ask Helen if she had a boyfriend and to make

crude sexual allusions. Helen had kicked both the actors out of her studio, called up the theatre press officer live on air to complain about their behaviour and then filled the remaining twenty-five minutes of the show getting listeners (a heady mix of retired ladies and mums gearing up for their second round of the school run) to nominate their top British actors most unlike the two reprobates who had contaminated her studio. As she passed over to the news desk and faded out her mic, she was besieged by co-workers congratulating her on a job well done.

In fact throughout her career both as producer and presenter she had not only managed to turn negatives into positives, but also to disguise the fact there'd even been a problem at all. That's how good Helen was at dealing with the unexpected. But professional Helen and private Helen were two very different creatures.

'You look like you might need to sit down.'

Helen stared at Aiden Reid, her former fiancé, the nation's most popular radio DJ and the only man to have broken her heart, with a look of utter disbelief. As is often the case with the least deserving, the intervening years had been kind to Aiden and though the ageing process had begun to take its toll around his eyes and around the temples, he was, Helen noted with some bitterness, even more handsome now than he had been when they were together.

Helen exhaled. She wanted this to be over. She wanted this to be over right now.

Mike Gayle

'My friends and I are just about to leave.'

Aiden grinned. 'And hello to you too. I'm sure you don't care what I think but you look great.'

'You're right,' said Helen pointedly, 'I don't care.'

'Don't be like that,' pleaded Aiden, 'I didn't come over to fight. I just wanted to say hello, that's all. I couldn't believe it when I saw you just now. Even though I could only see the back of you I knew straight away who it was. What are you doing here?'

'I'm here for a friend's hen weekend.'

Aiden laughed.

'What's so funny?'

'You'll never believe this but I'm actually here on a mate's stag weekend. What are the chances of that? The two of us here at the same time celebrating two different sets of impending nuptials.'

'Coincidences happen,' said Helen. 'It's not exactly what you'd call newsworthy, is it?'

'Maybe not,' replied Aiden. 'It's just that . . . I don't know . . . it's taken me by surprise seeing you here like this. And I'm guessing by the way you reacted that it took you a little by surprise too.'

Helen had no interest in confirming his suspicions. 'Who is it getting married?'

'Karl Peters.'

'The Five Live guy?'

Aiden nodded. 'Getting hitched to Ally Fallon. Really nice girl. She used to do a Saturday-morning kids' thing back in the day. Now she's mostly in radio.'

'I think I might have caught her show once but she

was so awful I had to switch her off. Karl though, I like him a lot, he's good. Very sharp, very strong, always on the ball.'

'And what about me?' Aiden stared at her keenly. 'I know it's not exactly your thing but you must have listened in at least once. If only out of curiosity.'

Helen shook her head even though this wasn't true. She had heard Aiden's Sony Award-winning show many times and although it verged on being self-indulgent rubbish at times, it was, for the most part, some of the best radio she had heard.

'You've never even listened once?'

'I hear the ratings are good though.'

'Through the roof.'

'You must be pleased.'

'More like ecstatic.' Grinning, he waved over Helen's shoulder.

'I take it those are the hens?'

Helen nodded and glanced over Aiden's shoulder at a group of men watching their every move. She recognised Karl Peters, the footballer that Kerry fancied, a couple of well-known TV actors and an Irish stand-up comedian. It was sickening; being famous was like belonging to an exclusive club where everybody knew each other.

'And I take it those are the stags?'

'Just a few of them. Do you want to come over and meet them? They don't bite.'

Helen could think of nothing she would rather do less. 'No, I'm good thanks. Like I said, we're supposed

to be going soon so they're probably keen to make a move.'

'Yes, of course,' said Aiden. 'I mustn't keep you. It's been really good seeing you after all these years. You look . . . well, you look amazing. And I . . . I really do hope you have a great weekend.'

Although Helen wasn't a great believer in modern miracles, as she returned to the girls a small part of her naïvely hoped that her encounter with one of the country's biggest TV and radio stars might pass without comment. But within milliseconds of taking her seat her friends disabused her of this notion by collectively emitting an ear-piercing shriek of excitement.

'That's Aiden Reid you were just talking to!' shrieked Kerry. 'Aiden "off the radio!" Reid! I love him. He's just so funny and sparky. How do you know him, you dark horse? He's a bit of a ladies' man isn't he? Should a woman in your position be fraternising with such tabloid fodder?'

'I saw him in the paper the other day falling out of some private members' club in London with that young model that everyone's always going on about,' Dee chipped in, 'you know, the one who's always changing her hair colour?'

'Oh and let's not forget when he was half naked on the front cover of *Cosmo* last month,' added Ros. 'We had it up on the door of our office before HR made us take it down because they said it was creating an "inappropriate work environment".'

'I used to work with him,' said Helen. 'That's it. End of story.'

'End of story?' laughed Lorna, 'how can that be the end of the story when I'm only just finding out that sitting under my nose all this time has been the perfect person to introduce me to my future husband! He's gorgeous! We could have got hitched and had babies if you'd done the decent thing when I first met you and given me his phone number. What's he doing here?'

'He's with some friends for a stag do.'

'Who's the stag?'

'Karl Peters . . .'

'Karl Peters! That's the one!' interrupted Kerry. 'So who else is there? Any more famous types?'

'Listen,' said Yaz, exchanging glances with Helen, 'can't you leave the poor woman alone. She's just bumped into a bloke she used to work with who happens to be famous. Let's move on.'

'But we don't want to move on,' protested Lorna. 'Helen knows a celebrity! A genuine celebrity, not just someone who had a walk-on part in *Casualty*. We can't move on until we've had all the gory details. What's he really like?'

'He's fine,' said Helen charitably, 'we just don't get along that's all. Can we talk about something else?'

Lorna wouldn't let it go. 'What did he do to make you not like him? He always seems lovely on his show.'

'Put it this way,' said Helen, 'we didn't see eye to eye on certain issues and that, I'm afraid is all I have to say on the matter.'

The reason Helen's friends were unaware of her connection with Aiden Reid was simple: she had never

65

told them. As Aiden's career had gone from strength to strength it had become clear to her that being the ex-fiancée of a celebrity was a burden in itself. She refused to allow herself to become just another paragraph in his biography and if keeping that part of her life secret from her friends as well as the tabloid press was the price to be paid in order to remain her own person then it was a price well worth paying.

In an effort to change the subject Yaz began telling the girls about the plans for the following morning but she had barely started when she was interrupted by one of the waiters.

'Excuse me, madam,' he began, 'Apologies for disturbing you, I hope you're all enjoying your evening. It's been brought to my attention that you're part of Mr Reid's party and as such the management of The Manor would like to invite you to be our guests for the rest of the evening in the Gold Lounge. If you'd like to follow me, I'll take you through.'

'You'd like to do what?' asked Helen.

'Invite you to the Gold Lounge, madam.'

'And that is what exactly?'

'A private function room that we reserve for special guests.'

The girls all looked at Helen in astonishment.

'He means celebrities!' gushed Kerry. 'He wants us to go to a special room with a bunch of celebrities!'

Helen felt an oncoming migraine hover overhead. 'Are you sure you've got the right table?'

'You are Ms Helen Richards aren't you?'

'I am,' said Helen nodding, 'but I'm definitely not part of Mr Reid's party and my friends and I are quite happy where we are, thank you very much.' She stood up to search for Aiden but the corner where he and his friends had been standing was empty.

'So, you would like me to inform Mr Reid that you won't be joining him?'

Helen felt a wave of indignation. Who did Aiden think he was that he could just snap his fingers and have her follow him about like that! She wasn't impressed by his money or his celebrity friends and she wanted him to know it. 'I'll tell you what I'd like,' spat Helen. 'I'd like you to tell Mr Reid that he can shove his special room right up his—' She stopped short and drew a deep calming breath like the ones she did in yoga class and held it until she felt less angry. 'Please, thank Mr Reid for his very kind offer but we're fine as we are.'

The waiter nodded and walked away, leaving Helen to face the questioning gaze of her friends. She downed what remained of her drink in a few long gulps. She wanted to go back to being happily drunk or retire to her room with a hot chocolate and one of the half dozen complimentary glossy magazines that resided there.

'Look,' she said finally, 'I know you all think it's mean but I really, really, really don't want to spend any time with him.'

'Of course,' said Kerry, 'but couldn't we just—?'

'No,' said Helen sharply. 'We can't *just* anything.'

Kerry looked equal parts embarrassed and annoyed. Helen immediately felt bad and apologised.

'It's fine,' said Kerry. 'You're right. He's probably not even half as nice as he is on the radio. They never are, are they?'

Helen felt even worse. She looked at the rest of the girls, who were all trying to avoid eye contact. If her ambition had been to kill the celebratory mood of the evening then she had quite clearly succeeded.

She looked to Yaz for advice. Yaz gave her a cheery wink, and addressed the girls. 'Look, radio star with celebrity friends or not it's not right that we let a bloke ruin our evening. We were having a cracking time before he turned up and I don't see why it shouldn't carry on. My suggestion is that we order a couple of bottles of wine and decamp to my room or Helen's and carry on the evening there.'

The girls began collecting their things together while Yaz called over the waiter to settle the bill. Helen stared into the middle distance feeling guilty. All her friends wanted was a bit of a laugh, something that they could tell their friends at work or the mums at the school gates about on Monday morning. With the possible exception of Ros, who had briefly worked for a women's magazine, their lives had never intersected with the world which Aiden inhabited. And while from her albeit limited knowledge she knew it to be a shallow, fickle world lacking in substance she also knew it was kind of fun too.

'Listen,' she said calling the girls to attention, 'I'm sorry. I've been a right whiney cow about all this and I've got no right to be. Give me a minute and I'll have

you mixing with the great and the good before you know it.'

The delight on her friends' faces was enough to convince Helen that she had done the right thing. She went in search of the waiter, Yaz close at her heels. The horror on Yaz's face reassured her there was at least one person who understood what a big deal this was.

'What do you think he's up to?'

'I've no idea.'

'How was he when you spoke to him?'

'Fine. Chatty. Which was as well because I was too freaked out to say much of anything.'

'And you're sure you want to do this?'

'As long as you promise not to leave me alone with him.'

'Of course.'

'I mean it, Yaz, not for a second. I don't care if you're in mid-conversation with one of his footballer mates or the head of the BBC, do not leave me alone with him.'

'I promise, he won't get anywhere near you.'

'And I don't want him knowing why we're here, either.'

'Fine.'

'And I don't want any of the girls talking about me to him or any of his friends. Not where I live, not what I'm doing, who I'm with or even what I had for dinner tonight.'

Yaz gave Helen's hand a reassuring squeeze. 'Maybe we shouldn't be doing this if you still feel this way. I

was just thinking we'd drink his champagne, flirt with his mates and have a bit of a laugh but the last thing I want is for you to get upset.'

'I'll be fine,' replied Helen, 'Promise. Drinking his champagne, flirting with his mates and having a laugh sounds perfect. That's the least he can do after everything he put me through.'

Helen found the waiter and informed him that she had changed her mind.

'This is going to be amazing,' said Carla on Helen's return. 'What am I going to say if they ask me what I do for a living? I can't tell them I'm a social worker!'

Lorna chuckled. 'Tell them you're a glamour model, that's what I'm going to do if I get anywhere near that Aiden fella!' She hoisted her ample bosom in comedic fashion to the delight of her friends.

The waiter led them towards the rear of the bar, where there was a gold painted door where a female member of staff dressed in the hotel's grey uniform stood holding a clipboard. The waiter gave her a discreet nod and she stepped aside.

Helen ushered the rest of the girls through the doorway but at the last moment tapped Yaz on the shoulder.

'I can't do this,' said Helen.

'I thought you were fine,' replied Yaz.

'So did I but . . . but . . .'

'But what?'

'I've just got a bad feeling about it. Like . . . I don't know . . . I just don't want to be in the same room as him.'

'Then I won't go either,' replied Yaz. 'We'll nip back to my room and get drunk on the mini-bar.'

'You have to,' said Helen. 'The girls will need keeping an eye on. Just tell them I had a headache or something. They'll be having too good a time to care.'

'And what will you do?'

'Have an early night,' said Helen. 'But don't think for a minute that I won't want to hear every last juicy detail in the morning.'

Saturday

7.

Helen had never been a huge fan of the Saturday-morning lie-in. Most weekends she was out of bed, throwing on her gym kit and halfway out of the door to the local fitness centre by half past seven at the latest. Any longer lying in bed and she would have felt like she was stewing in her own filth just for the sake of it. So it was something of a surprise when she opened her eyes that Saturday morning, fumbled blindly in the darkness of her room for her phone and discovered from its digital display that not only had she managed to sleep past her usual wake-up time but was even in danger of missing the prearranged nine o'clock breakfast rendezvous with the rest of the girls, which was bound to go down about as well as her early disappearance the night before.

Helen was not sure what to make of the evening's events. It all felt like some elaborate dream from which she had been unable to wake herself. First the bombshell about Simon and Yaz separating, then bumping into Aiden, it was almost as if her subconscious mind was doing everything it could to unsettle her as she prepared to be married. The only

problem was her subconscious had nothing to do with it. This was reality, bad luck, and even worse timing.

No one was more surprised by the strength of her reaction to Aiden than Helen herself. It had been such a long time since they had been together that she had long since ceased to consider the man on the pages of the *Sun*'s Bizarre column as anything other than a stranger and the idea that they had once been very much in love seemed unreal.

Still, there was no doubting the emotional veracity of her reaction towards him. This man, this stranger, whom she had succeeded in telling herself she could barely even recall, had turned her world upside down. First, by re-entering her life and second, by exposing her to an unwelcome truth: after all these years he still had the power to upset her.

It wasn't fair. Aiden meant nothing to her, she was sure. How many times as she skimmed the daily newspapers for her show had she come across reports of Aiden in the tabloids and not felt a thing? How many times had she heard his disembodied voice promoting some new car insurance product or cat food on TV and dismissed his rude interjection into her life without a second thought? He meant nothing to her. Absolutely nothing. And yet seeing him in the flesh at the same hotel changed everything. No longer an easily dismissed abstraction from the past, he instead became a living, breathing reminder of one of the unhappiest periods of her life, a time when she

had been prepared to hold back nothing from someone whom she believed she could trust completely and who had thrown it all – the love, the trust, the devotion – back in her face.

At the time Helen had wanted revenge, for Aiden to endure first-hand the torment that she had lived through as she cried herself to sleep night after night. But as time progressed and her desire to heal overcame her craving for justice, she finally reached the point where she knew the only way for her to move forward was to let go of the past – and that included all feelings of hatred towards Aiden. So she let go. Or at least she thought she had.

But did her reaction to Aiden the night before mean that she hadn't quite left him behind? Did the surge of anger and the flood of adrenalin she had felt as she beheld the face that she had once loved mean that she had been in denial all this time? She thought about Phil's: *You know as well as I do that this is all about him. It always has been and it always will be.* Had Phil been able to see the truth when she had been blind? The idea made her shudder. Whatever the answers to these many questions, she needed to stay away from Aiden and talk to Phil as soon as possible.

She dialled Phil's number and again the call went straight through to his voicemail. She opened her mouth to leave a message but the words wouldn't come and after a number of moments listening to the silence that she was supposed to be filling she ended the call.

He was fine, she reassured herself. The most likely scenario was that his battery was dead and he had forgotten his charger. Half convinced by her reasoning she tried to recall if Phil had told her the name of the hotel they were staying at but nothing sprang to mind. She'd asked several times and he'd replied that it was 'all in hand' – whatever that meant. She wondered if Simon had told Yaz where he'd be, but given her friend's recent news she could never ask the question.

She told herself to remain calm and turned on the bedside light. She was immediately cheered by the sight of the illuminated room as its luxury reminded her that she was supposed to be having a good time. With this in mind she climbed out of bed, made her way to the bathroom and turned on the shower. The rainfall showerhead burst into life forcing out sizzling jets of steaming water on to the zinc floor beneath. Helen shed her pyjamas, laid them on the ornate bench at the side of the shower and strode into the revitalising waterfall. Some fifteen minutes later, having been pummelled by the pounding water, Helen re-emerged feeling like she was ready to take on the day ahead.

With her hair done, make-up on and having spent longer than was strictly necessary working out what to wear to breakfast, Helen had tidied her room so as not to totally disgust the chambermaid when there was a sharp knock at the door. She cursed herself for not having woken up earlier, dashed into the bathroom to pick up yesterday's knickers from the floor, tossed them under the duvet and opened the door.

'Yaz,' she said breathing a huge sigh of relief. 'Come in.'

'Who were you expecting?'

'Long story.' Helen fished out her underwear from beneath the duvet and tucked it into the bottom of her case. 'I just wish I'd got up earlier that's all. Sleep well?'

'For what felt like the ten minutes I was there, yes.'

Yaz sat down on the edge of the bed, cupping her head in her hands, while Helen opened a bottle of water, poured some into a glass and handed it to her friend.

'I take it that it was a bit of a rough one then?'

' "Rough" would have been a welcome mercy,' said Yaz. 'I have nothing but admiration for your decision to go to bed early last night. Honestly, if it wasn't for the fact I'm looking forward to a day of pure, unadulterated relaxation rather than sitting at home screaming at the kids to stop killing each other I'd be feeling pretty sorry for myself.'

'But you had fun?'

Yaz nodded wearily and between sips of water said: 'Best. Time. Ever.'

'So what happened then?'

'Obviously the girls were really sorry that you didn't come but I think they all sensed why and for a little while we all felt out of our depth. But then Aiden came over and introduced himself and his friends and from then we didn't look back. Honestly, it was like a walk through the pages of *Heat* magazine. The girls and I

would be talking to one famous guy and another would appear out of nowhere and offer to top up my champagne glass.'

Helen winced. The thought of her friends being plied with alcohol by a group of Aiden's friends on the first night of their stag weekend made her feel queasy. 'They were on their best behaviour, weren't they?'

Yaz cackled and Helen felt glad to have her old friend back. 'Sadly they were all absolute gents. Even that Irish comedian fella – who we all had down as a bit of a letch. In fact all he did was show us pictures of his kids on his phone. It was a great night though, Helen, you should have come. All we did was laugh, knock back champagne and listen to their absolutely outrageous stories about other celebrities.'

'And Aiden?' Helen hated herself for asking the question but she knew it had to be done.

'Do you really want to know?'

'No, you're right,' said Helen quickly. 'I don't.'

Yaz tried to read her friend's mind. 'He was fine,' she said. 'He did ask after you, and I don't think he was taken in by your headache story but I can't fault him as a host. He looked after us well, kept us entertained and didn't ask about you at all.'

'Nothing?'

Yaz shook her head. 'Only why you weren't there.'

'Good,' said Helen even though she was sure it didn't all add up. 'Then let's go and get some breakfast. I'm starving.'

Helen could barely keep a straight face as she

and Yaz entered the restaurant and spotted the girls at the rear of the room looking like they were at death's door.

'You know I love you lot dearly,' said Helen as she sat down at the table, 'and it pains me to tell you this, but you look terrible!'

'Just sit down and stop bellowing, Richards,' wailed Lorna, who had been resting her head on her folded arms. 'Some of us are hurting inside.'

Helen squeezed into the banquette seating next to Lorna and Dee and then stroked Lorna's head mockingly. 'Awwww, did someone have a few too many shandies last night?'

Lorna groaned and pushed Helen's hand away. 'This is your revenge isn't it for that time I made you go clubbing last summer.'

'Oh, yes, indeed,' grinned Helen, 'you're the reason I haven't been able to go anywhere near a vodka gimlet for the last year without immediately feeing nauseous. How does it feel now, my friend?'

'You do know that I hate you, don't you?'

'Well if I didn't,' said Helen kissing the top of her friend's head, 'I certainly do now.'

Breakfast for the majority was brief as might be expected with such a high concentration of hangovers, and mainly consisted of black coffee, roughly three quarters of the fresh fruit that had been laid out on the buffet and wholemeal toast all round. But despite the low moans alternating with various pledges to never touch the demon drink again, Helen could see that her

81

friends were secretly rather pleased that they still had what it took to party like nineteen-year-olds.

The girls' account of the night before pretty much mirrored Yaz's. Aiden had been sweet, his celebrity friends entertaining and the evening so far removed from their everyday lives as to make it an anecdote they would be dining out on for a long while. None of them, even in passing, mentioned Aiden asking questions about Helen.

'Are you sure?' asked Helen as she and Kerry picked at a bowl of blueberries. 'Not a single question about me?'

Kerry raised an eyebrow. 'You sound almost disappointed. Are you sure there was never anything between you? I can easily imagine you being his type.'

'And what's that supposed to mean?'

'You know. Beautiful and feisty. Those girls that he's always falling out of nightclubs with, they'd be no challenge. But someone like you, someone he'd have to work hard to impress, oh, you'd be right up his street.'

Helen laughed. 'I think someone's watched one too many Sandra Bullock movies!'

'So why the interest in what he talked about last night?'

'Because.'

'Is that all I'm getting? Now you're really starting to worry me. You don't fancy him do you?'

'No, of course not.'

'Then what?'

'Look,' sighed Helen. 'Back when I knew him he did some pretty awful things to a friend of mine that I find

it hard to forgive him for. If he's being nice to me, it's only because he's trying to get to her, the person he knew all that time ago, and well, I know for a fact that she's not interested so I'd prefer it if we all keep him at arm's length. Is that okay?'

Kerry nodded. 'Of course. I had no idea he was like that. He seems like such a nice bloke.'

'They always do,' said Helen, 'in the beginning at least.'

Helen plucked another blueberry from the bowl, coating her teeth with its sweet, gooey flesh, while much to her relief Kerry was drawn into a discussion Dee was having with Lorna about the best place to buy MAC make-up in Nottingham. Helen wished that she had never brought up the subject of Aiden; it was telling how in the space of a few moments she had already amplified Kelly's innocent comment far beyond its worth. The madness from which she was trying to protect herself was already leaking out into the real world and if she wasn't careful more would follow.

Yaz stood up and called for everyone's attention. 'You should have received emails confirming what treatments you're booked in for during the weekend and when but I've got copies for anyone who hasn't brought theirs along. The first session is a group mani-pedi at eleven on the dot but for those who need a detox beforehand – naming no names – some of us are heading to the steam room in ten minutes so if you do want to come along grab your things, and we'll all head down to the spa together.'

Relieved to have someone taking charge the girls

began making their way back to their rooms, slowing down only to congratulate Yaz on being so organised and to tell Helen what a good time they were having.

'How right they are,' said Helen as the last of her friends disappeared. 'This weekend is amazing. I honestly don't think anything could—'

'What is it?' asked Yaz as Helen stopped abruptly. 'It's not lover boy and his mates again is it?'

'No,' sighed Helen as every iota of positive energy she possessed drained from her. 'You know how it is when you're having such a great time that you totally forget about the fact that you invited your scheming bitch-faced sister-in-law on your hen weekend until the moment she arrives? Well that's what.'

8.

There were very few people whom Helen actively
disliked. In fact if she had to name them individually
(with the exception of Aiden Reid) only three people
would spring to mind. The first was Chantelle Roberts
who made the list because from the day Helen met her
at Edgehill infant school until the day she left to go to
a nearby private school Chantelle made it her mission
to make Helen's life a living hell with a subtle but none
the less destructive cycle of constant befriending and
defriending. On any given day the six-year-old Helen
would turn up to school expecting to spend her break
time playing 'In the witch's den', only to discover that
for some reason known only to Chantelle, Helen had
fallen out of favour and would have to spend break
walking around the playground looking up at the sky
so that no one could see she was crying.

The second person on her list was Morwenna Kavell,
who was Helen's boss for six months when she worked
at Cardiff FM. Helen never knew exactly what it was
that this woman hadn't liked about her (although she
speculated about it frequently) but it seemed to be
more than enough to turn someone who on the surface

seemed both reasonable and professional, into a scheming psycho who devoted every waking moment during the time that they worked together to finding new and inventive ways of making Helen's life unbearable.

The third and final person was the regional sales director of a Milton Keynes based communications solutions firm, a mistress in the ancient art of one-up-manship and a total cow who happened to be related to the man Helen loved. Worse, she was currently making her way across the restaurant towards them.

'Caitlin,' said Helen kissing her sister-in-law-to-be on the cheek. She stood back to take in Caitlin's immaculately groomed form and felt instantly depressed. 'How are you? How was the journey?'

'An absolute nightmare. Best part of an hour sitting on the M1 just past Leicester. Nearly gave up and turned back! It would've been a shame of course, after all this place isn't cheap, but as it happens I'm off to a new country spa hotel just outside Buckinghamshire in a few weeks that by all reports should knock the spots off this place. Still, here I am, always doing the right thing!'

'Well I'm glad you did,' lied Helen, resisting the temptation to throttle Caitlin. 'The weekend wouldn't have been the same without you.'

Caitlin flashed her best professional smile, the one Helen felt sure she used whenever closing a business deal. 'You say the sweetest things.' She held out her hand to Yaz and although she couldn't be sure Helen

thought she detected an extra glint of spitefulness in Caitlin's eye. 'And Yaz, how are you? Long time no see.'

'Yes,' said Yaz. 'It has been a long time. Been keeping well?'

'Can't complain,' replied Caitlin, carefully. 'You? How are those adorable kids of yours? Still running you ragged? I don't know how you do it. I can't see me ever having kids. They're a guaranteed route to a ruined figure.'

Yaz's face fell as it dawned on her that she had just been Caitlined. Helen was confused; normally Caitlin saved her catty remarks for Helen alone but for some reason she appeared to want to drag Yaz into this too. Realising she had milliseconds to stop Yaz slapping her sister-in-law-to-be into next week Helen quickly jumped into the fray and changed the subject.

'We're all going down to the sauna in a minute,' she said quickly. 'If you hurry up and get changed you can join us.'

Caitlin raised a eyebrow. 'It always takes me forever to unpack so I doubt I'll make it. Otherwise what time should I meet you for the first treatment?'

'Eleven o'clock, in the spa.'

'Great,' said Caitlin. She flashed Helen and Yaz another of her business smiles and then with one swish of her ponytail she clip-clopped out of the restaurant leaving the speechless friends wondering what had just hit them.

'I always knew she was a bitch,' said Yaz, 'but that woman takes bitchdom to a whole new level! She's like a super-turbo-charged-bitch-faced bitch.'

Helen nodded in agreement. 'And . . . might I add, a right royal pain in the arse too.'

'You have my deepest sympathies becoming family with a woman like that. My deepest sympathies indeed.'

In the beginning Helen had rationalised Caitlin's dislike as simple loyalty to her close friend Beth, whom Phil had dated for two years. Caitlin regularly hung out with Phil and Beth and so when Phil called time on the relationship it spelled not only the end of the couple but also for Caitlin spending time with her brother whom she idolised. Seemingly convinced that Phil and Beth were in the throes of getting back together, Caitlin had extended a somewhat frosty reception when Phil had invited her to meet Helen for the first time. Phil had picked up on his sister's hostility but had excused it in that lazy way all men excuse the behaviour of women they like: 'She's not being bitchy,' he explained, 'she just doesn't know you that's all. Give her time and she'll soon warm up.'

The second time was some six months later when Phil decided it was time to introduce Helen to his mum and stepdad and so organised a Sunday afternoon barbecue for his entire family. Helen had hoped that relations between them would improve over time but in fact they became worse. While never openly hostile, Caitlin focused on one-upping Helen whenever the opportunity arose. If Helen told a story about a great weekend, Caitlin would tell a story about an even better one. If Helen bought a new dress and wore it out to dinner, Caitlin made sure to let everyone know how

new her own dress was and how expensive it had been. Whatever Helen did that was good, Caitlin had always done better. And because it wasn't open hostility Phil didn't see it. 'Honestly babe,' he told her as they cleared away after the barbecue when after much deliberation she had finally brought the subject up, 'you're just being paranoid. So what if she's a bit boastful? If she winds you up that much just ignore her.'

Helen tried to take Phil's advice and although months went by without the two of them needing to exchange a word, what with Christmas, Easter and various family birthdays there were other times when there was literally no escaping Caitlin. And although it would be natural to assume that over nine years, two family bereavements, and the handing over of countless tastefully selected and perfectly wrapped birthday and Christmas presents (presents that had quite clearly not been bought or wrapped by Phil), that hostilities would have ceased, this was not the case. Instead they continued to bubble under the surface waiting for the opportunity to erupt.

Inviting Caitlin to the hen weekend was Helen's final olive branch to Caitlin for the sake of the man she loved and if she refused to accept it after this weekend, or at the latest after the wedding, she resolved to stop making the effort and cut Caitlin out of her life for good.

Helen was up in her room frantically stuffing one of the hotel's tastefully designed straw tote bags with

everything she needed for the morning when her phone rang.

'It's me,' said Yaz urgently. 'Listen I don't want to panic you, but we might not have thought this whole thing with Caitlin through properly.'

Helen hadn't got a clue what Yaz was talking about.

'Think about it. We've just invited her to meet downstairs in the lobby haven't we? Now I know she said she probably won't come but what if she does and gets there before we do, introduces herself and the girls start telling her about what an amazing time they all had hanging out with Aiden? I don't know whether you'd planned to tell Phil about bumping into your ex or not but if she gets to the girls before we do I guarantee you won't need to worry about how to break the news to him.'

Yaz was right. This was exactly the kind of thing Caitlin would leap on. Grabbing her bag, Helen snatched up her key card and ran out of the room slamming the door behind her. Racing along the corridor at top speed she passed the lift and took the stairs, then pelted down several steps at a time.

Her heart pounding as if it was trying to escape her chest, Helen sprinted to reception to meet the girls.

'I need to tell you something,' gasped Helen thankful that there was no sign of Caitlin. 'Is everyone here?'

'All except Yaz,' said Kerry.

'Look,' said Helen quickly, 'it's like this: for reasons that I don't want to go into I need to ask you all a massive favour. Whatever you do don't—'

Helen stopped abruptly as Yaz arrived frantically waving her hands.

'What?'

'Nothing,' said Yaz still waving her arms. 'I'm just thinking that you probably need to stop talking . . . now.'

Realising something was up Helen was horrified to see Caitlin standing behind her. In that instant Helen saw she had two options: she could allow herself to fall apart as she had done when she bumped into Aiden or professional Helen could get on with the business of being unflappable.

'Caitlin,' said Helen calmly, 'great you've decided to join us. I was just getting the girls together to explain that they shouldn't . . . drink too much.'

Caitlin looked confused. 'Isn't that sort of the idea of hen weekends?'

Clearly in agreement the others looked on perplexed.

'I'm just saying that—' An idea occurred to her and she pointed to Caitlin. 'Where are my manners? Everybody, this is Phil's sister, Caitlin, everybody this is Caitlin.'

It wasn't exactly the most subtle of ways of getting her point across to her friends that they should keep their mouths shut about the events of the night before, but from the raised eyebrows and silent gasps that spread amongst the girls like a Mexican wave the message had clearly been received. But just to make sure that there weren't any little slip-ups as everyone introduced themselves to Caitlin,

Helen whispered to Yaz to brief everyone individually about what was and what wasn't out of bounds to talk about with the evil one.

The girls made their way out of reception and along the outside path to the Spa. It was a beautiful cloudless morning, the perfect summer barbecue day and even though it was only mid-morning there was no doubt it was going to be a scorcher.

The area around the spa had been landscaped so that it was only once visitors descended the limestone stairs that the spa could be seen at all. Once there the girls knew they were in for a treat. The front entrance looked like a partially buried glass dome jutting out of the slope and as the girls marvelled at its architectural elegance the more confident they became that a building like this wasn't going to be staffed by bored teens fresh out of beauty school.

Signing in, they made their way to the changing rooms where they hurriedly undressed and within a matter of minutes they were settled in the steam room and getting down to the main business of the day: conversation.

'So Helen,' began Ros, 'How are all the wedding plans going? I bet you had it all sewn up months ago. You've always been the most organised person I know.'

'Oh, you know how it is,' said Helen, quickly. She wiped her sweat-laden brow with her towel. 'Even when you're organised, with something this big there are always things to do.'

As those who had experience began to exchange tales of their own wedding organisational nightmares, Helen reflected on Ros's comment. It was true that she was highly organised; there was no way she could do her current job as a presenter and have fulfilled her role as a producer successfully without being organised, and yet she had somehow neglected to bring that same degree of organisational control to bear on what was supposed to be one of the most important days of her life. It wasn't just that she had left the booking of the venue, the hiring of the caterers and the sorting out of the honeymoon to Phil (she argued that as he was his own boss he had more free time to do these things), it was that with less than a week to go she still hadn't decided on a dress.

Since the first of her university friends began to get married Helen had had an image in her head of the perfect wedding dress so when Aiden had proposed, she set to work on making the dream become a reality by gathering together pictures ripped from magazines along with brief sketches of her own. Once she was satisfied that she had all the inspiration she needed she went to see the woman who had designed Yaz's cousin's gown which she had admired some months before.

The designer had seemed to understand what Helen wanted straight away and had shown her some beautiful swatches of material, which Helen knew would be perfect. Several fittings later and there it was: the fantasy dress of her dreams, a more beautiful reality

Mike Gayle

than she'd ever expected: a floor length strapless ivory satin sheath dress exquisitely embroidered with antique beads and trimmed with vintage ribbon.

Gazing at her reflection in the mirror at the final fitting Helen felt every inch the princess that she had hoped to be. She had left the dressmaker's nearly a thousand pounds poorer but with a joy in her heart she would have gladly paid ten times more to possess.

When she called off the wedding, the dress was the one aspect of the cancelled day that she wouldn't allow anyone else to deal with, torn as she was between keeping it and giving it away. In the end, having bagged it up and driven to the other side of the city with the intention of donating it to a charity shop, she just couldn't do it. As selfish as it was she couldn't bear the thought of another woman walking down the aisle in her dream dress and she took the bag from the boot of the car, crossed over to the car park of a nearby pub and with tears streaming down her face threw the dress into an industrial waste container and walked away.

'Are you having any, Helen?'

Helen stared blankly at Heather. She hadn't got a clue what was being asked of her.

'You're a million miles away,' teased Heather. 'It must be all this steam! I was just asking are you having wedding favours on the table? I went to a wedding last summer and the couple were real green freaks and had put several packets of seeds on every table for people to take away and plant so as to offset the carbon footprint of the wedding!'

94

Helen was panic-stricken. 'I hadn't even thought about it.'

Heather looked mortified. 'Sorry, babe! I didn't mean to wind you up into a frenzy. It must be the full-time mum in me: I don't feel normal unless I'm armed with a sixteen-page to-do list! Just step out of this circle of madness, I say, and do your own thing!'

Helen smiled weakly. Party favours were the least of her problems. At this rate she would be getting married in a tracksuit and slippers. She and Yaz had been looking at dresses for months now, starting with a wedding fair at the NEC in Birmingham and branching out to every bridal shop within a thirty-mile radius of Nottingham. And while there had been many hideous creations amongst the dresses she had seen (one in particular, a huge hideous pink meringue that could easily have been the star of its own TV documentary entitled *My biggest gypsy wedding*), there had also been plenty of tasteful and elegant dresses with which she had fallen in love. A cream taffeta dress in a bridal shop in Hucknall and another that could have been plucked straight from the set of a sumptuous Merchant Ivory production to name but two. And yet whenever the shop assistant asked if she would like to come back for a second fitting her response was always: 'I do really like it but I'm going to carry on looking just that little while longer.' And to anyone who asked what her dress was like (a question aimed at her on an almost daily basis) her reply was the same: 'Beautiful. But I'm not saying anything as I don't want to spoil the surprise.'

Helen knew it was madness to leave it this late and that even if she were to walk into a wedding dress shop first thing on Monday morning and choose the first dress, no matter how hideous, that she laid eyes on there was every chance that – this being July – they would be so overwhelmed with orders that even if she offered to pay them double they might not be able to get any alterations done by the Saturday morning. And what kind of bride doesn't have a dress a week before her wedding day?

9.

It was approaching midday and the first beauty treatment of the day was complete. The girls stood in a circle in the changing rooms admiring the results of their joint manicure and pedicure.

'What's yours called again?' asked Yaz, looking down at Helen's feet.

'Boutique Trash,' said Helen.

'So that's pink then,' said Yaz.

'Looks like it,' said Helen. She looked over at Lorna's toes. 'I like yours Lorna. What's that one?'

'Burnt Sunrise,' said Lorna.

'So that's dark orange then,' said Yaz.

'I hate my feet,' said Dee.

They all inspected Dee's feet. 'Don't say that,' said Helen. 'You've got great feet.'

'No,' said Dee. 'My ex used to say I'd got Hobbit feet and he had a point. Just call me Bilbo Baggins.'

'I know you were married to him and everything,' said Helen, 'but your ex was more than a bit of an idiot. Your feet are beautiful and don't let anyone tell you otherwise.'

'I wish I had feet like Caitlin's,' said Dee, 'Just look at them. They're perfect.'

97

Mike Gayle

Everyone looked at Caitlin's feet. Much as Helen loathed her, even she had to agree that in the world of feet Caitlin's were right up there with those of Natalie Portman, Jennifer Anniston and Halle Berry.

'She's right,' chipped in Ros, 'They are gorgeous. That colour really suits you too.'

'Thank you girls,' said Caitlin beaming, 'it's weird but whenever I'm out in my strappy sandals I get loads of compliments about them.'

Helen smiled inwardly at the thought of people queuing in nightclubs just to get a glimpse of her sister-in-law-to-be's feet.

'I think we've all got great feet,' said Helen diplomatically, in a bid to move the conversation on. 'And we should definitely give them an airing when we go out tonight. Who's up for it?' Helen counted up the hands. The vote was unanimous.

'Toes out for the lads it is!' laughed Carla who had been single so long that she feared it might become permanent. 'I've got a good feeling that Gunmetal Rose is going to be my lucky colour!'

Fully dressed, the girls made their way out of the spa with the conversation focused evenly between what they fancied for lunch and how long they would need to get ready to go out to dinner that evening. Helen herself was happy that for a few moments at least she wasn't thinking about wedding dresses and was content to listen to the others but as they headed to the restaurant her heart stopped. Aiden and two of his friends were coming towards them.

From her position at the back of the group Helen could see from the body language of her friends that they were unsure how to react. Most of them simply chose to ignore Aiden and his friends while others, never having had to blank a complete stranger with whom they had spent half the night drinking, offered an embarrassed half wave that Helen hoped had gone unseen by Caitlin.

But Aiden had seen Helen and fully intended to try and talk to her.

'What are you going to do?' asked Yaz, quickly. 'Do you want me to go over and tell him you can't speak?'

Helen shook her head. 'No, you carry on to the restaurant. Tell the girls I'll be along in a minute but don't wait and whatever you do don't let Caitlin out of your sight.'

Helen's breathing deepened involuntarily as she began to walk towards Aiden who was stood standing in the middle of the grass. She wondered whether he was going to make her walk all the way over to him but then he began to walk towards her.

'Morning,' said Aiden as they met halfway.

'Morning.'

'Just been to the spa?'

Helen nodded. 'We all had our nails done.' She dangled her newly manicured hands in the air as if he needed proof.

'Nice,' he replied studying them. 'You won't believe this but I had manicures for a while. Back in the early days I was doing a cable show, my agent clocked how

filthy my nails were and so she set up regular appointments for the eight weeks I was doing the show and then billed the cable company.'

'And did you enjoy them?'

Aiden shrugged. 'Not enough to carry on. It's too much of a detail thing. Us blokes are too big-picture orientated to think whizzing into town to have some bird do our nails and make small talk is worth the effort.'

Helen laughed. 'It's hard to know what to do first: marvel at the ease with which you can insult half the population with your simplistic worldview or ask a follow up question about what this so-called "big-picture" is that you'd rather be doing than appear on TV looking like you spend your spare time rooting through rubbish bins.'

'What can I say?' asked Aiden. 'I'm a guy. We don't sweat the small stuff.' He shifted his weight uneasily. Helen could feel a question coming.

'Did your friends enjoy last night?'

'Yes, thanks. Obviously some of them were a little worse for wear this morning, but they were pretty unanimous about having had a good time. Thanks for that, it was really good of you.'

'It was nothing. They're a great bunch of girls and the lads really enjoyed being around them but I can't say that you weren't missed.'

Helen blushed. 'Thank you. And I apologise. It's just that it had been an incredibly long day and I was shattered. I guarantee you, I'd have been no fun at all.'

Aiden nodded as though he understood but Helen

didn't think for a moment that he believed a single word she had said.

'I know this is awkward for you,' he began, 'and well . . . it's awkward for me too. But isn't it weird that of all the places we could be this weekend we're both here? Maybe this is a good opportunity for us to clear the air.'

'You're not trying to tell me that you, world renowned sceptic Aiden Reid, believe in something as airy-fairy as fate? Next thing you'll be telling me that you Cosmic Ordered this whole thing up.'

Aiden laughed. 'Look, all I'm saying is that we're here and the chances of that were pretty slim. So why not make the most of it?'

'And do what?'

'Give me half an hour of your time.'

Helen sighed. Had she walked a bit faster she could have avoided this whole sorry saga. 'Fine,' she said. 'But make it ten minutes.'

Aiden began walking purposefully though it soon became apparent that he wasn't sure where he was going.

'What exactly are you looking for?' asked Helen as they reached the far edge of the hotel.

'I'll know it when I see it.'

'Some things never change.'

'What's that supposed to mean?'

'I'm just thinking about the summer you were supposed to be best man for your friend Mike's wedding in Darlington. Only we didn't get there until—'

101

'—the whole thing was over!'

'And all because you absolutely refused to ask for directions to the church.'

Aiden chuckled. 'Mike was so annoyed about having to get his granddad to do the honours that he didn't speak to me for months. I can't believe you're still going on about that.'

'What can I say?' replied Helen. 'Some things are too amusing to forget.'

They continued down a tree-lined path that eventually reached a slow running stream. There were a number of smart-looking modern loungers and wooden benches scattered around under the trees but it was quiet and empty.

'I read about this spot in the brochure,' said Helen. 'I'd planned to come down here at some point and read my book.'

'See,' said Aiden. 'And there was you thinking I didn't know where I was going. That's the genius of me: appearing haphazard but actually in total control.'

Helen didn't comment, knowing full well that any attempt at a retort would only stoke his ego further. It was lovely though. Peaceful. Serene. It made her feel disconnected from the rest of the world. Like she was stepping out of place and time.

'So how's Karl getting on? Are you making sure he's having a good weekend?'

'It's hard to tell. We could have bought him a Ferrari and had a naked Scarlett Johansson pop out of a cake to hand him the keys and I swear if it happened the

week before the new RAJARs were due out he still wouldn't raise a smile. He's one of life's worriers.'

'Not like you. You've *never* worried about audience figures.'

'That was the old me,' said Aiden picking up on Helen's sarcasm. 'The new me is a nervous wreck. Anyway, how are the ratings for your show?'

'Pretty solid.'

'Now that you can listen to local radio on the internet I do catch your show from time to time. It's good stuff.'

'Thanks, but it's hardly the groundbreaking arena of rock 'n' roll breakfast is it?'

'Which is why it's harder. I couldn't do afternoons to save my life. In the morning everything's fresh. I'm breaking news stories and waking up the audience to a brand new day. By the time your show starts the new has become the old and the audience are already thinking about what they've got to do tomorrow, there's literally nothing to work with. That's why you're doing such a great job making a solid show against the odds. I swear if they put you on breakfast you'd slay me.'

Helen sat down on the nearest bench and looked at the stream where a group of ducks were congregating amongst the reeds. Aiden sat down next to her.

'I'm getting married next weekend,' said Helen.

Aiden was silent. A sparrow landed on the branch of a silver birch and after a moment checking its surroundings flew to the headrest of one of the sun loungers and surveyed them keenly.

'I thought you said—'

'I lied,' she said quickly.

'Because?'

'Because you don't have any right to know about me.'

Aiden nodded. The sparrow flew to the ground a few yards away from their feet, pecked at a clump of moss and then with what looked like some kind of beetle in its beak flew back to the silver birch.

'Is he a good man? I know that's kind of a stupid question given that you're marrying him, but you know what I mean. Is he everything you're looking for?'

Helen shook her head. 'I'm not going to do this.'

'Do what?'

'Take part in whatever's going on in your head.'

'Then why are you here?'

Helen stood up and began walking back up the path towards the hotel.

'Listen,' called Aiden. 'Stop. I'm sorry, okay? I was bang out of order.' Helen continued to the top of the hill from where she could see the hotel. She heard Aiden running up the path behind her. 'Look, stop,' he said as he finally caught up with her. 'Don't let's leave things like this. I'm sorry, okay? It was a stupid thing to say. Your news just took me by surprise that's all.'

'And why should that be?' asked Helen. 'It was no big surprise to me when you got married.'

'And look how that ended.'

'Do you want me to feel sorry for you?'

'No,' said Aiden, 'but I do want you to know that you're the reason it didn't work.'

Before Helen could muster a response she spotted Caitlin walking towards her. The same disconcerting sensation that had come over her on seeing Aiden the night before was back, this time with twice the force. Her dismay showed on her face.

'What's wrong?'

'That's my fiancé's sister coming this way. She doesn't like me and she's never needed an excuse to do a bit of stirring.'

'Does she know that we used to be together?'

Helen shook her head. 'My fiancé knows but it's not exactly the kind of thing you advertise to your future in-laws.'

'Then what are you worried about?'

'I don't know,' snapped Helen. 'She'll find a way to twist things and make this into something it's not. That's what she does. It's like her superpower'

'Leave it to me,' said Aiden. 'Just keep making out like we're having a casual chat and I'll do the rest.'

While not exactly enamoured of the idea of leaving anything in Aiden's hands, Helen didn't exactly have a choice other than to beg Caitlin for mercy and so she allowed Aiden to ramble on about how nice the weather was while every now and again making inane weather-based observations of her own until Caitlin was within earshot.

' . . . well I'd really like you to give it some consideration,' said Aiden loudly, 'but obviously I need someone quickly so the sooner you can make a decision the better.' He stopped and looked directly at

Caitlin, which Helen assumed was her cue to turn around.

'Caitlin,' said Helen brightly. 'What are you doing here? Aren't you meant to be having lunch?'

'I was about to say the same to you. One minute you were there, the next you'd disappeared and no one seemed to know where you were, so I thought I'd come out and make sure you were okay.'

Aiden held out his hand. 'My fault entirely. The name's Aiden. Aiden Reid.'

'Hi,' said Caitlin coolly, 'pleased to me you. So how do you know Helen?'

'We used to work together a long, long time ago.'

'Really? What a coincidence, the two of you being here at the same time.'

'I'm actually here for a friend's stag weekend – you might have heard of him, Karl Peters?'

Caitlin's eyes widened. 'You mean Karl Peters off the TV? Then . . . you . . . you can't be! You're not *the* Aiden Reid are you?'

'I am indeed,' replied Aiden.

It was obvious to Helen that Caitlin had known exactly who Aiden was the moment she laid eyes on him. And equally obvious that Caitlin wasn't the slightest intimidated by his fame. Caitlin had simply chosen to appear star struck because she thought it would flatter his ego.

'Helen Richards, I can't believe you!' said Caitlin. 'All these years and you've never once mentioned that you used to work with Aiden Reid. I'd be bragging about it to everyone I met.'

It was, thought Helen, possibly one of the finest acting performances she had ever seen. Caitlin was positively oozing faux naïve charm and had she not seen first-hand what her sister-in-law-to-be was capable of, even she might have fallen for it.

'I was just bending her ear about my show,' continued Aiden, 'and Helen made such perceptive comments that I think that she'd be right for my production team. I need someone good at the top and Helen could be it.'

Caitlin turned her gaze to Helen. 'Are you going to take it?'

'I said I'd think about it.'

'Right,' said Aiden, 'I'm supposed to be playing golf with the boys so I'd better get off but hopefully I'll bump into you guys later. See you soon?'

'Yes,' replied Helen, searching Aiden's face for meaning. 'I guess you will.'

10.

Before Helen could spend even a fraction of a second contemplating the complexities of this conversation Caitlin interrupted her, seemingly fired up by her encounter with a celebrity.

'I can't believe I've just met Aiden Reid!' she squealed in an uncharacteristic fashion. 'And he's such a nice guy too. Did you really used to work with him?'

Helen wished Caitlin would drop her act, but she had to be careful not to rile Caitlin so much that she took it upon herself to start asking questions of Phil.

'For a couple of years yes,' said Helen. 'He was a nice enough guy when I knew him.'

'But you don't like him now?'

'I don't know him now. It's been a long time since I've had anything to do with him.'

'But he seems lovely. And him offering you a job, well you must be thrilled. I'm sure it would be much better being a small fish in a big pond, especially working with someone of Aiden's calibre. You should definitely take it. Think how glamorous it would feel after having spent so long entertaining the kind of

people who usually listen to your show – no offence, obviously – but you know what I mean.'

'None taken,' said Helen wearily. 'I'll bear it in mind.' Helen hoped that this would be the end of the conversation and that they might travel the last few hundred yards to the restaurant in a comfortable silence but it wasn't to be.

'He's not still married is he?'

'I don't know,' lied Helen. 'I don't make a habit of keeping up to date with the love lives of people I used to work with.'

Caitlin didn't get the joke. 'Still, he's different isn't he? I mean he's a proper celebrity. Who was he married to again? I can see her face and her name is on the tip of my tongue. It's Sara something . . . or Sonya . . .'

Helen felt like screaming. 'Sanne. Her name was Sanne.'

'That's the one!' exclaimed Caitlin. 'Sanne! She was in that girl band wasn't she? They had that updated Dusty Springfield cover? Very beautiful as I remember. Absolutely stunning in fact. I'm guessing you don't know why they split up?'

'No idea.'

Caitlin wouldn't let it go. 'I'd call my friend Beth and ask her because she's practically got a PhD in celebrity gossip but she's on holiday in Bahrain at the moment.'

'That's a shame,' said Helen drily as they finally reached the restaurant. 'Maybe you should call her anyway. It seems an awful waste to have that much knowledge and miss out on the chance to use it.'

Helen made a beeline for her friends hoping to get rid of Caitlin as soon as was humanly possible but unfortunately now that Caitlin had Aiden on her mind it was apparent that she was reluctant to be offloaded.

'You'll never guess who Helen and I just bumped into,' said Caitlin excitedly as Helen closed her eyes and concentrated all her latent psychic abilities on persuading the earth to open up and swallow her whole. 'Aiden Reid.'

Revealing hitherto unknown amateur dramatic skills the girls sounded totally convincing in their shock and surprise. Helen opened her eyes and as she did so she caught Yaz's gaze and her friend mouthed a silent 'Sorry' across the table.

Caitlin gave the table a blow-by-blow account of the conversation documenting everything from the exact colour of his eyes through to the precise tone of his voice when he'd said goodbye.

'You almost sound like you've got a bit of a crush on him,' teased Kerry.

'I think he quite fancied me actually,' said Caitlin without a moment of self-awareness, 'but he's not really my type.'

Helen stood up. She'd had enough and didn't care who knew it.

'Of course!' said Caitlin, 'you must be starving and here's me yakking on. I don't normally eat much at lunchtime beyond a bit of fruit so I don't really miss it, but I can imagine if you like your food, going without could really make you cranky.'

Too mentally exhausted to rise to the bait Helen headed to the buffet table and picked up a plate. As she tried to choose between a large dish of vegetable lasagne and the beef goulash next to it, Caitlin's 'if you like your food' comment echoed around her head and she put the plate down.

'I'm so pleased you did that,' said Caitlin behind her. 'Carbs at lunchtime are a real no-no and, well, don't forget we all want you to fit into that dress next Saturday!'

The last time Helen had punched someone she had been eight and the person she had hit had been her older cousin Sam. For reasons known only to himself while visiting from Southampton with his family, Sam had spent an entire morning teasing her, only to act surprised when she finally blew her top as he scribbled on her drawing of a castle. Helen lashed out with her right fist and connected perfectly with his nose, shocking herself so much by the act of violence and its effect (within seconds Sam's T-shirt was covered in blood) that she had never hit anyone since. As she looked into Caitlin's eyes and saw all the spite there she felt that same anger. Instead of making a fist, however Helen picked up a serving spoon, poked it fiercely into the lasagne, took out a huge scoop and then gave herself a scoop of the goulash *and* the chicken korma next to it, just daring Caitlin to say a word.

When Helen finally pushed away her plate (with half the food she had loaded on it still looking back at her),

some of the girls had disappeared to get ready for the spa's trademark full-body detox – a ninety-minute beauty session involving dry skin brushing, the application of several different types of poultices and a head-to-toe seaweed mask. Helen's was happening in a short while and she was feeling both excited and apprehensive. The apprehension was due to the disclaimer at the bottom of the brochure: 'Please note that the full-body detox may cause some clients to feel overwhelmingly emotional. For this reason please refrain from drinking alcohol, remain hydrated and take time to decompress before and after attending your treatment.' What with her weekend so far, Helen was afraid she would start foaming at the mouth the minute she walked into the therapy room.

With Caitlin less than two feet away, deep in conversation with Ros and Dee about the intricacies of Aiden's love life, there had been no opportunity for Helen to talk to Yaz privately, so when Yaz stood up Helen took this as her cue to make her escape.

'Listen,' said Yaz, as they stood by the French doors that led to the rear patio, 'I'm really sorry about dropping you in it earlier, but that is one sly cow you've got for a sister-in-law. I had my eye on her virtually the entire time as we came in to lunch and then there was a bit of confusion about what order the treatments were happening and by the time I'd sorted that out she'd gone. I thought about going after her but I was afraid of making things worse.'

'It's fine, really,' said Helen. 'Actually it was Aiden

who bailed me out in the end. He made up some story about wanting to hire me as a producer for his breakfast show but I think Caitlin was too busy flirting to notice how flaky it all sounded.'

'She was flirting with Aiden?'

'Uncontrollably. I've never seen her like it. Phil's always saying that because she's so pretty she tends to give most blokes short shrift. She normally goes for guys with good looks and money, investment banker types and she even makes them work pretty hard. But you should have seen her with Aiden: she was practically all over him from the minute he said hello.'

Yaz laughed. 'Not that I know him but I'm guessing she's not exactly Aiden's type.'

Helen shrugged. 'You'd hope not, but nothing would surprise me with those two.'

'So what did he want?'

Helen rolled her eyes. Where to begin with that one? 'Do you know what? I really have no idea. He was insistent that we went for a walk and took me to this really pretty spot down by a stream and started rambling on about how great it was to see me, how he thought my show was good. Then I finally plucked up the courage to tell him that this is actually my hen weekend and he seemed to go a bit weird.'

'Weird how?'

'Well, put it this way, the last thing he said to me before her royal highness turned up was that the reason he split up with his ex-wife was because of me.'

'Because of you? But that doesn't even make sense!

You hadn't even seen him since you two split up!' Helen looked guilty. Yaz was incredulous. 'Are you saying that you'd seen him before today?'

'It was just the once, I swear,' said Helen. 'About five years ago he contacted me out of the blue basically begging to meet up.'

'So you said yes? Are you mad?'

'I must have been,' sighed Helen, 'because when I look back the whole thing was more like a dream than reality. We met, we talked, he apologised for the way things ended and then we went our separate ways. It was all over in under an hour. I remember thinking to myself, "Did this really happen?" '

'And you never told Phil?'

'What would have been the point? I knew I wasn't going to get back with him.'

'So why did you see him?'

'Because I wanted to show him that he hadn't crushed me. I wanted him to know that I'd moved on.' She laughed bitterly. 'Maybe that's what he wanted too because less than a week later his girlfriend was in all the papers showing off her engagement ring.'

'And now he's blaming you for the marriage not working out because, what, he was still in love with you?'

'I don't know. None of it makes sense.'

Yaz considered the situation for a moment and was ready to dispense her advice: 'Seems to me that you've got two choices,' she began: 'one, you can spend the rest of the weekend driving yourself crazy trying to

work it out or two: go and ask him. You can't just leave it like that, H, you know you can't.'

'I'm not so sure,' said Helen. 'How would I even bring the subject up and more to the point, do I really want to know?'

'So you're just going to leave it?'

Helen shrugged. 'For now I'm just going to do everything I can not to think about it.'

A combination of Yaz immediately having to dash off for her full-body detox, the lure of the outdoors thanks to the strength of the summer sun, and Helen's head beginning to ache meant that for the time that she had left before her beauty appointment she did nothing other than grab her things from her room and lie on one of the loungers flicking through a copy of *Harper's Bazaar*.

She looked at her watch. It was time to go. She grabbed her tote bag and headed across the grass to the Spa.

At the spa reception Helen was handed a clipboard with a form covering everything from her health to her current state of mind. Normally Helen hated filling out forms but as this was more like a quiz in a women's magazine than a tax return she filled it in with gusto.

A few moments later a troupe of young, white-uniformed girls arrived at reception and called out the name of their individual clients. Helen's was a pretty auburn-haired girl who introduced herself as Roisin whom Helen warmed to straight away.

The lights in the treatment room were dimmed, a tall

scented candle was burning on one of the white marbled surfaces and 'new age whale music' was coming from a slim-line iPod speaker. Roisin handed Helen a robe and promised to return once Helen had undressed.

'Right, let's have a look at your details,' she said picking up the clipboard. Her accent was strong and northern. Preston or possibly Stockport, thought Helen, definitely not Manchester.

Roisin sat down opposite Helen, double-checked her form and then set it down on a side table.

'Right,' she began, 'now we can get on with the business of getting you detoxed!' She looked into Helen's eyes. 'So that I can tailor the treatment to your exact needs I need a little bit more information. First off: how would you like to feel at the end of this session: energised or relaxed?'

'Relaxed,' said Helen quickly.

'I could tell!' joked Roisin and then she put her hand to her mouth. 'I'm sorry. I shouldn't have said that.'

'Don't be daft,' said Helen. 'You're fine. I'm not surprised I look stressed. I *am* stressed.'

'Oh no,' said the girl, 'you don't looked stressed. Well, no more than any of the other ladies who come here. I could tell . . . well I could tell from your *aura*.'

'My aura?'

'I'm in training to be the spa's reiki specialist and the minute I saw you in reception your aura just jumped out at me.'

116

Helen frowned. 'That doesn't sound good.'

'It's not, to be honest. It's very negative. But don't worry, there are oils we can use to cleanse it.'

'You're saying my aura needs cleansing? What's wrong with it? I haven't damaged it, have I?'

'It's hard to say,' replied Roisin. 'People usually get a negative aura when they're at a crossroads and don't know which way to go. When I left college at eighteen and didn't know whether to go into hairdressing or carry on with beauty therapy, I went to a reiki healer and they said the same about my aura.'

'And they fixed it?'

'It took a few sessions but yeah, it was okay in the end.'

Helen felt her stomach flip over. She didn't believe in any of this stuff. In her time on the radio she'd interviewed countless healers, exorcists, white witches, new age practitioners and clairvoyants and was always underwhelmed by how transparent their schemes were. And yet this girl seemed genuine, and as Helen reflected on her lack of a wedding dress, she began to wonder whether there might be something in it after all.

11.

'Right,' said Roisin as a comatose Helen lay face up on the therapy table naked but for her paper knickers and a long, thick white blanket-sized towel. 'I'm just going to step outside so that you can put on your dressing gown and then I'll take you to the post treatment room where you can have a lie down if you like before taking a shower.'

Helen stirred. This couldn't be right surely? An hour and a half couldn't have gone by just like that? The last thing she recalled was the girl applying a deep cleansing nutrient mask to her face. She reached up to feel if it was still there but there was nothing but the silky smoothness of her own skin. She opened an eye, tilted her head to look at the girl and with a not inconsiderable amount of panic in her voice said: 'It's not really over is it?'

'It is, I'm afraid. A lot of clients find that time really flies when they have this treatment. That's what happens when you're totally relaxed. Anyway, there's a glass of water on the counter and remember to sit up slowly.'

Sitting upright Helen recalled her troubled aura.

'How's my . . . you know?' she asked, a waggle of her eyebrows completing her sentence. 'Does it still look troubled?'

Roisin smiled. 'It's looking better, definitely. The oils I used took away quite a lot of the negative energy that was surrounding you but there's only so much you can do in one session. You need to look after yourself and try and relax more.'

'That's easier said than done,' sighed Helen.

'I know, but I guarantee you'll feel the benefit.'

As Roisin left the room Helen wondered whether she could justify booking herself another ninety-minute session straight away. She couldn't remember the last time she felt this good: her skin was smooth and supple, her muscles totally relaxed and her brain felt like someone had scooped it out and given it a warm bath before putting it back in place. What's more, she felt sure that whatever the problem with her aura had been before the therapy, Roisin had definitely dealt with it.

Gradually edging herself off the table, she wobbled enough to make her lean back against the table for support. It was the oddest feeling: her legs were weak but her body felt lighter than air. Slowly the strength returned to her limbs and as she began to get dressed she promised that no matter what the expense or inconvenience, the ninety-minute full-body detox would become a permanent fixture in her life.

Once Helen was robed Roisin led her down the corridor and through a side door into a darkened room

fragrant with designer scented candles. There were several low beds (all empty) and each had its own table laden with bottled water and a small bowl of dried fruit and nuts.

'Feel free to stay as long as you like,' said Roisin. 'If you need anything or find yourself feeling light-headed just press the buzzer at the side of the bed.'

'Thank you,' said Helen sincerely. 'And I really mean that: thank you.'

'I'm just glad to have been able to help,' said Roisin reaching for the door handle. 'Enjoy the rest of your stay. And try and stay stress free.'

Helen looked down at the bed with its clean white sheets that looked so inviting. Feeling this relaxed, if she sat down to collect her thoughts she would fall deeply and embarrassingly asleep and so steeling herself she collected a set of towels from a table in the corner and made her way back to the changing rooms.

Showered and dressed but with her hair still wet, Helen made her way back towards the spa reception with a view to getting back to her room and squeezing in as much sleep as humanly possible before she would need to get ready for the evening ahead.

As she reached the spa reception she saw Yaz sitting in one of the comfortable chairs with her nose deep in a glossy magazine.

'Hello you,' said Helen. 'What are you doing here?'

'Killing time while I waited for you. Wasn't it amazing?'

'Incredible. Like nothing I've ever experienced.'

'Did you cry?'

Helen shook her head. 'Did you?'

'Just a bit but it was hard to tell whether that was the therapy or the fact that it was there bubbling under the surface waiting to come out anyway.'

The two women stepped outside into the late afternoon sun and both instinctively drew a deep breath and exhaled. Helen looked at Yaz.

'Are you okay?'

Yaz nodded and wiped her eyes. 'I'm fine, honestly.'

'You know you can talk about everything that's going on, don't you? Just because we're on this weekend doesn't mean you have to be the entertainment.'

'I know and thanks for saying that. But I'm okay. Just having a bit of a wobble, that's all. I probably shouldn't have done but I tried calling Simon earlier, just to say hello, and maybe see if we could talk for a while but the call went straight to voicemail.'

'The same happened to me when I tried Phil. I'm guessing their hotel has got really bad reception.'

'Or they don't want to be contacted.'

'Look, there's no point in speculating, is there?'

'I suppose not.'

Helen's heart sank as she looked up and saw Caitlin coming towards them.

'Oh great, just what I need to undo an hour and a half of ultimate relaxation.'

'Is it too late to pretend we haven't seen her?'

'Yes,' said Helen. 'Far too late.'

'Hi guys,' said Caitlin brightly. 'I'm so pleased I've

bumped into you because you'll never guess what just happened.'

'Why don't you surprise us?' said Helen wearily.

'Okay,' said Caitlin, 'it's like this. I was on my way for a swim before my treatment when who should be coming back from the golf course but Aiden Reid! We got chatting and to cut a long story short I invited him to dinner tonight and he's agreed. Isn't that amazing? Aiden Reid is coming to dinner with us!'

Helen held her breath as the familiar and unwelcome muscular tension and the headache returned. 'You did what?'

'I invited him to dinner. It's not a big deal is it? I was sure you wouldn't mind.'

Yaz stepped in. 'The thing is Caitlin, this whole weekend was meant to be a women-only thing, a chance for us all to relax, have a bit of a laugh and give Helen a good send off. If Aiden comes along tonight . . . I don't know . . . I just feel that it would change the atmosphere.'

'He's just one man,' said Caitlin rolling her eyes. 'I don't see what the big deal is. I doubt that he'd talk to any of the other girls anyway.'

Yaz's eyes narrowed. 'Meaning?'

'Oh, you know, Aiden's Aiden isn't he? No offence but given the lifestyle he's used to he won't be interested in a bunch of mums fawning over him all evening. I promise, I'll totally keep him under control.'

'But you're completely missing the—'

Helen interrupted. 'Leave it, Yaz, Caitlin's right. It's not that big a deal.'

'But—'

'It's fine,' said Helen firmly.

Yaz still wouldn't let it go. 'Are you absolutely sure?'

'Yes,' said Helen. 'I am.'

'Oh, that's absolutely brilliant,' said Caitlin kissing Helen's cheek. Helen couldn't believe it. Caitlin actually looked like she was almost grateful. 'Are you absolutely sure?'

'I've no doubts at all.'

'And you're not just saying that?'

Helen crossed her heart with the palm of her hand. 'Scout's honour.'

'You really are amazing do you know that?' beamed Caitlin. 'And I promise I'll make sure that he doesn't dominate the evening. I really think this could be the beginning of something good. Who knows, this time next year we could all be back here for my hen do.'

'I can't believe that just happened,' said Yaz as they stood watching Caitlin trotting down to the spa.

'If it was happening to anyone but me I might have actually found it funny.'

'How can she not have picked up on the fact that you don't want him around?'

'She picked it up all right,' sighed Helen. 'She just didn't care.'

'So why did you give in like that?'

Helen shrugged. 'I guess I'm just tired of fighting her.'

Frustrated and as angry with herself as she was with Caitlin, Helen suggested that she and Yaz have a drink

on the terrace. They took a seat and ordered two gin and tonics.

'Do you know what?' said Helen as the waiter disappeared, 'I'm forever telling off listeners when they call in saying they hate this and they hate that because hate's a pretty strong term that shouldn't be used lightly but right now I do actually hate Caitlin. I know that sounds harsh but apart from the fact that she popped out of the same womb as Phil she has got no redeeming features whatsoever.'

'Do you think she really just bumped into Aiden or has she been stalking him the whole time?'

'Stalking. Definitely. Probably stalking while downloading a document to her BlackBerry entitled: "How to hold your own when talking about golf" to give herself some conversational starters.'

'And that stuff about: "this time next year we could be here for my hen weekend!" I could've slapped her silly when she said that. Do you actually think she's serious?'

Helen shrugged. 'She's a pretty unstoppable force when she gets going and it's not like she isn't easy on the eye. I can't imagine Aiden really wanted to come to dinner though. Why would he go to all the effort of trying to talk to me if his intention was simply to wind me up?'

'Any more clues why he blames you for him and his wife splitting up?'

'I don't know,' said Helen, 'and I'm not sure I care. Anyway it doesn't matter whether or not he comes out tonight because I won't be there.'

'What do you mean?'

'Just that. I'm not coming. I'll be fine, Yaz. Tell the girls I've got some sort of bug and I want to get an early night in the hope of being better by the morning. They won't doubt it if you tell it right.'

'We can't go without you. It's your weekend. Why not just tell Caitlin that you've changed your mind about Aiden tagging along?'

'And have her looking daggers at me all night or worse still trying to work out why I'm so dead set against her getting together with him? No thanks. I might have to come clean Monday but right now I haven't got the energy. No, she can do what she likes. I don't care any more.'

'Then I'll stay too,' said Yaz. 'I won't enjoy the evening if I have to picture you crying into your soup. The others can go, we'll stay and maybe treat ourselves to a few items off the à la carte menu. How does that sound?'

'If you don't go none of them will and I'll feel obliged to entertain them all evening which is frankly the last thing I need.'

The waiter arrived with their drinks and the two friends fell into an uneasy silence. A young couple (clearly very much in love and celebrating an anniversary) sat down at the table next to them. The man reached across for the woman's hand and her whole being lit up. Helen could see that Yaz was thinking the same thing: how wonderful that stage of a relationship was and why did those feelings all too quickly fade.

Helen took a sip of her drink. 'I'm going back to my room.'

'Are you sure about later?'

'One hundred per cent.'

'The girls will be devastated.'

Helen smiled. 'They'll be fine, if you keep them distracted.'

The two women hugged.

'You take care okay?' said Yaz. 'And if you need anything, just call me.'

Reaching her room, Helen lay down on the bed and closed her eyes. It felt good to be out of the sun for a while and the cool of her air-conditioned room seemed to take away the residual anger that she had felt towards Caitlin. Now she was able to pity her, as she would any human being so full of resentment they couldn't see the good in anyone.

Helen took out her phone and switched it on. There was a text from her boss asking if she was having a good time and another from a phone company offering a new phone deal but still nothing from Phil. Although rationally she knew better than to read anything into this continuing lack of communication, she couldn't help but conclude that whatever else he was doing at this particular moment, he wasn't thinking about her and in this post-detox emotional state this almost reduced her to tears.

The only way forward was to distract herself. She switched on the TV and started flicking around the channels and was relieved when she came across the

film *All About Eve*, easily her favourite Barbara Stanwyck movie. Drawing the curtains, she made herself a cup of tea and climbed underneath her duvet to watch the film and there she remained for the best part of an hour until there was a knock at the door.

Helen's first instinct was to ignore it, but when the knocking persisted she opted to answer it on the off chance it was an emergency.

Helen grabbed a towelling dressing gown from the bathroom door and was still tying the belt around her waist as she looked through the peephole and saw not just one face but many looking back at her. It was the girls.

'I tried to tell them you were ill,' explained Yaz plaintively as they flooded into Helen's room. 'But I don't think they bought it.'

'Listen girls,' said Helen sitting on the bed as they all surrounded her. 'Don't think this show of solidarity isn't appreciated, but as I said to Yaz earlier, I'm not interested in battling with Caitlin. She's a mean, hard-hearted cow who needs taking down a peg or two but that doesn't mean that I have to be the person to do it.'

'All that's fine,' said Heather, 'but why does she get to spoil your hen weekend just because she's Phil's sister?'

'Heather's right,' chipped in Ros. 'We came here for *you* this weekend. There's no way Caitlin should be dictating proceedings.'

'I know it's not ideal,' began Helen but so many of

the girls added their voices to the protest that she couldn't be heard.

'The fact of the matter is this,' said Heather, 'we'd rather stay in our rooms and not go out at all than go out without you.'

Helen looked to Yaz for some support but Yaz shook her head. 'Don't look at me,' she said grinning. 'I'm with them. I don't want to go to some posh restaurant without you. It wouldn't be the same.'

Helen surrendered. If she had been feeling despair an hour earlier, then this was the complete opposite. All these old friends, all their good will, it really meant something. There was no way she could turn them down.

'Okay, okay, I'll go' she said grinning. 'But if that scrawny cow so much as looks at me funny I can't guarantee that I won't smack her one.'

'Don't worry,' said Yaz, 'if she does anything wrong you'll have to join the queue to get to her.'

12.

Helen knocked on the door to Yaz's room so that they could go down to reception together. Although the prospect of the evening ahead filled her with dread, little of it was due to Caitlin. Yes, Caitlin would be her usual mean-spirited self but it was Aiden's presence that truly set her on edge. No good would come of him sharing whatever was on his mind and while her natural curiosity was piqued she determined to override it. Her mission tonight was simple: avoid Aiden.

Yaz looked amazing in a black top with chiffon sleeves and black trousers and Helen told her so.

'You look great too,' she said, admiring Helen's outfit. Helen had been uncertain about diverting from her usual smart trousers and top combo in favour of a dove grey soft drape dress teamed with strappy heels. It was, she was aware, more of a sexy look than was her usual and this had been exactly why she had bought it to wear for the meal tonight, knowing that surrounded by her closest friends, she wouldn't have to feel self-conscious. But Caitlin inviting Aiden to the meal had changed everything. Now Helen was veering between defiance that she had every right to dress the

way she wanted, to anxiety that her choice of clothing would send out the wrong signals. Decades of feminism and the supportive comments of her friend eventually won over. 'Phil is the luckiest man in the world getting to come home to you every day.'

The moment she heard Phil's name Helen's stomach tightened into a ball. Much as she resented this neediness that seemed to have bubbled up from the depths of her subconscious, she really did wish that he had called her back. His lack of communication was yet another issue for her already overstretched emotional resources.

The two women made their way over to the meeting place over loud applause from the rest of the girls, much to the hotel staff's amusement. There was no sign of Catlin yet and so seizing the opportunity Helen called over one of the porters, handed him her camera and asked him to take a photo of them. As the flash went off Helen knew even without seeing the evidence that what had been captured was a proper Kodak moment: all of her oldest, closest friends gathered together in one spot ready to have a good time. A rare thing and something to be treasured.

The girls were all still cackling and making outrageous comments to the porter as Caitlin emerged from the lift.

'What did I miss?'

'Nothing,' replied Helen quickly. 'We were just messing about, that's all. You look great.'

Caitlin smiled but there was no compliment in return.

She glanced around the lobby clearly looking for signs of Aiden but didn't say as much to Helen.

'What time are the cabs booked for?'

'About now,' said Helen.

Caitlin nodded. 'Right, we'll I'm just going to check my make-up. I'll be back in a minute.'

Helen was tempted to herd the girls into a cab the moment she was gone but before Caitlin had taken a step Aiden appeared at the top of the stairs. He was wearing a black suit and tie matched with a white shirt that instantly recalled Phil's Reservoir Dog outfit. Helen swallowed hard. It was as if the universe was doing all it could do to tip her over the edge.

'I'm not late, am I?'

'No,' said Helen. 'You're right on time.'

He kissed her on the cheek. His skin felt soft and his aftershave smelt light and citrusy. She closed her eyes and breathed deeply. She determined never to get that close to him again.

Caitlin moved expectantly into his orbit and Aiden kissed her too. Helen glanced at her watch. How was she ever going to get through this night when it already felt like it had gone on too long?

Aiden smiled. 'Are you sure you're okay with me coming tonight?' he asked. 'I'm sure these things are usually girls only but Caitlin here was very insistent.'

'Of course,' said Helen graciously. 'The more the merrier. Although shouldn't you be out with your friends?'

'I said I'd catch up with them later. Things never really get going with that lot until the early hours.'

Helen looked at her watch again and peered outside. There were two limousines parked outside but no sign of the taxis Yaz had ordered. 'I'd better go and check on the cabs,' said Helen. 'It looks like they're running a bit late.'

' 'Fraid not, fella,' said Aiden. 'They're not coming.'

'And you'd know this because?'

'I sorted those bad boys out front by way of an early wedding present instead.'

Shocked, Helen stepped forward to take another look at the limousines. With their blacked-out windows they were the kinds of cars celebrities emerged from looking radiant at red carpet events. This was so typical of Aiden. Big gestures had always been his thing.

'It's very kind of you,' she said. 'But it's too much, Aiden. We'll be fine as we are.'

'Too late,' he replied. 'They're paid for and you've got them for the night.'

'You'll have to forgive my sister-in-law,' said Caitlin sidling closer to Aiden. 'She's just not used to the high life. They are fantastic, and it's a lovely gesture. Of course we'll take them.'

'Plus,' said Aiden guiltily, 'I've already cancelled your other cars so I'm afraid you're stuck with them.'

Helen sighed. She hadn't even left the hotel and already the evening was turning weird. Why was Aiden trying so hard with her? Was it guilt or was there something more?

'What's going on?' asked Yaz. 'Everything okay?'

Helen gestured to the limousines. 'Grab your stuff, girls. Looks like we've just been upgraded.'

Helen had been desperate to visit their destination for the evening, the Michelin starred restaurant La Salle de Classe ever since she had read rave reviews of its opening in several Sunday newspapers at the beginning of the year. Around her birthday she had hinted to Phil that he should take her there but despite many lovely gifts and surprises from her fiancé (although she had to admit the La Perla underwear he had bought that was two sizes too small had gone down like a lead balloon) the big day had come and gone without the requisite visit. So when Yaz had asked for ideas about restaurants for the second night of the hen weekend Helen got out her laptop, typed the name and its address into Google Maps. Once she was sure that the journey was doable in a taxi, she gave the details to Yaz with orders to book it straight away.

The journey to the restaurant was suspiciously incident free although it hadn't gone unnoticed by Helen that when she, together with Lorna and Kerry, had climbed into the first car, Aiden had climbed in straight afterwards quickly followed by Caitlin. For most of the journey Caitlin locked Aiden into her conversational orbit leaving Helen to chat with her friends while exchanging increasingly excited texts with the second car following behind. Every once in a while Aiden attempted to break free of Caitlin and join

Helen's conversation, but even his extensive verbal skills were no match for Caitlin, and with a surgical skill that betrayed her borderline sociopathic tendencies she made sure that the conversation came back to her and only ever had two participants.

It was just after eight o'clock as the limos pulled up in front of the large plate glass windows of their destination.

'What's this place like?' asked Aiden peering into the packed restaurant. 'Anyone eaten here before?'

'I think it's new for all of us,' replied Helen. 'But I for one can't wait to get inside.'

The décor of La Salle de Classe was as high end as its food and as she waited to be seated Helen fell in lust with so many of the fixtures and fittings that had she possessed a screwdriver and a much larger handbag some of the items she coveted would have quickly been liberated.

As the maître d' arrived to show them to their table Yaz took control of the seating plan. Helen as guest of honour was at the head of the table with Yaz on one side and Heather on the other, whilst Aiden and Caitlin were tucked at the opposite end as far away from Helen as possible. Carla, Ros and Heather set the tone for the rest of the evening by ordering champagne to toast the bride to be.

The meal was stunning and Helen found herself enthusing about the beetroot and caramel sauce on her wild sea bass long after the waiter had handed out the dessert menus.

The girls had done such a good job of keeping her wine glass topped up and entertaining her with stories from the past that she had barely taken any notice of Caitlin and while Aiden had once or twice tried to attract her attention, she had so far managed to avoid making eye contact. As the waiter cleared away the dessert plates and took coffee orders she began to feel that she was home and dry.

It was at this point that her plans started to unravel. Some of the girls began talking about the next stage of the evening, given that it was only half past ten, and a consensus began to form that the only fitting conclusion to the evening would involve going on somewhere else. Helen tried to hint that she wanted to go back to the hotel but the girls were so emboldened by alcohol that the idea assumed a life of its own with suggestions ranging from heading to the nearest wine bar through to going clubbing in Buxton's one and only nightclub. In the end a compromise was struck; they would go clubbing but not in Buxton and after half an hour of Aiden making various calls to people in the know, they got back in the limousines and made the fifty-minute trip to a Manchester club where he had got them on the guest list.

Helen knew all she had to do to put a stop to this madness was play the 'It's my party card' and the girls would fall into line. She didn't want to go clubbing at all and certainly not in Manchester with her ex-boyfriend and her borderline insane future sister-in-law. But her friends were having such a good time that she found

herself saying feebly, 'Okay, if we aren't back too late.' Before she could change her mind, a club hits CD was on the sound system and a bottle of champagne from the car's drinks cabinet was being popped open.

By the time the limousines pulled up in front of Koko's, on the south side of Manchester city centre, a combination of the champagne and the long car journey had left Helen feeling slightly nauseous and she couldn't wait to get out of the car. The fresh summer air cleared her head and as she saw just how excited her friends were she resolved to enjoy herself after all.

According to Aiden, Koko's was Manchester's most exclusive club and the number one destination for the city's beautiful people. Helen cared less about Manchester's beautiful people than she did about whether or not she would be able to dance to the music. It had been a long while since she had enjoyed a good dance and even longer since she had been out clubbing and the last thing she wanted was to have this sterling opportunity frustrated by a DJ playing anonymous dance music.

Reassured that the DJ was one of the country's best they all followed Aiden past the door staff and straight to the club's VIP section where three bottles of champagne were waiting on ice.

'Was this your doing again?' asked Helen as they all sat down.

Aiden shrugged nonchalantly. 'My only concern this evening, my lady, is that you have a good time.'

Before Helen could respond Caitlin appeared at Aiden's side and dragged him over to Heather and Ros under the pretext that they were desperate to hear more of his celebrity stories.

Aiden flashed Helen a look of apology that she felt obliged to acknowledge. Even Helen could see that whatever her future sister-in-law's attractions, he was paying too high a price for the privilege.

Helen rounded up those of her friends that were up for a dance and led them to the dance floor just as the DJ played a track that seemed to be so well known that the whole room erupted. Helen had never heard it before, but with her friends by her side and the champagne flowing through her veins she didn't care. Tonight was her hen night and she was going to have a good time no matter what.

'I know it's all been a bit mad,' slurred Yaz, knocking back the last of the drink in her hand and lighting up a cigarette as they stood looking out across the city on the club's outside terrace after a solid hour on the dance floor, 'but you have to admit it's been an absolutely amazing night. Beats my Blackpool bash hands down!'

Helen kissed her intoxicated friend's glowing cheek. 'I don't remember you complaining too much.'

'You know what I mean,' said Yaz. 'It's been brilliant hasn't it?'

Helen nodded. 'It's like we're all twenty-one again! Last week I would've put good money on us all being in bed by now. It's fantastic.'

137

'And Caitlin's not ruining it for you?'

Helen plucked Yaz's cigarette from her hand and took a deep drag. 'She's good,' replied Helen, savouring the smoke in her lungs before exhaling, 'but not that good.' She handed the cigarette back to Yaz. 'I'm just grateful that you talked me into coming. It would have been awful if tonight hadn't happened just because of her.' She hugged Yaz. 'You, my lady, are easily the best friend a girl could have. Someone should clone you so that everyone can have one.'

Yaz laughed and then shivered. 'It's colder than you think,' she said rubbing her bare arms. She took one last drag on her cigarette and stubbed it out. 'I'm going back inside. Coming? I'm gasping for a drink.'

'Are you sure you haven't had enough? You've been knocking it back since we got here. Why don't you give it a rest?'

'What for? So I can spend the rest of the night thinking about what Simon's up to in Amsterdam? No thank you very much! I'll take being clattered over being sober, clattered is good, sober is just too much of a ball ache.'

Helen watched as Yaz turned and headed unsteadily down the stairs to the club. She thought about trying to talk her around but with everything going on in her own life, she thought Yaz had made a good point.

Helen turned her attention to the illuminated cityscape behind her. She loved imagining the lives behind the lights, lives she would never know, people she would never meet. It was like a visual representation of her job as a DJ.

Helen was lost in thought when she heard footsteps and turned around to see a young man standing in front of her. He looked to be in his twenties, tall and handsome and, judging from the surreptitious glances of some of the girls out on the terrace clearly something of a catch.

'Hope you don't mind me talking to you,' he said. 'You look miles away.'

'Got a few things on my mind,' said Helen.

He raised an eyebrow cheekily. 'Anything I can help with?'

Helen laughed. 'I doubt it.'

He held out his hand. 'The name's Paul but my mates call me Biz. Couldn't help but notice you on the dance floor earlier. You have one amazing body. Can I buy you a drink?'

'That's very kind of you . . . er, Biz . . . but apart from you being way too young for me . . . I'm actually getting married next weekend. So thanks but no thanks.'

'Well tell him from me he's one lucky guy.'

Helen smiled. 'They'll be the first words from my lips.'

He nodded, and gave Helen a wink. 'Knocked back by the pretty lady, you know you've broken my heart don't you?'

'You'll heal.'

He laughed. 'I probably will as well.' He offered a wave of his hand. 'You take it easy and have a good wedding, yeah?'

Grinning, Helen returned her gaze to the Manchester

streets. Chatted up by a hot young guy in a trendy nightclub! The girls were going to love this story.

She picked out a minicab snaking its way through the late-night traffic and tried to imagine who was in there and where they might be going. That was the key to being a good local DJ, being interested in people and their stories. It was true what Aiden had said about her ability to make something out of nothing. It was a skill that not everyone possessed.

Shivering slightly she rubbed her arms and was considering heading back inside when she saw the familiar figure of Aiden outlined against the night sky. Although she could barely see his face she knew he was looking at her. Every instinct told her to walk away but she didn't move.

13.

'Have you been out here long?'

'A little while,' said Helen. A group of young girls were pointing in Aiden's direction and sniggering, clearly having recognised him. 'Where's Caitlin?'

Aiden shrugged. 'She went off to powder her nose or whatever. It's cold out here. You must be freezing.'

'It's not that bad,' shrugged Helen, 'but I was going inside anyway. I'll leave you to have your cigarette in peace.'

Aiden held out a hand to stop her. 'I don't smoke,' he said. 'I told you the day my gran died I'd never smoke another cigarette and I haven't.'

Helen was flooded with shame. Aiden's gran had died of lung cancer in the third year they were together and losing her had affected him deeply.

'That's good,' she said. 'I'm glad you stuck to it.'

It was clear Aiden had other things on his mind.

'I came out here to find you,' he said as if daring her to challenge his assertion.

Helen didn't speak. Engagement in conversation was tantamount to encouraging him and that was the last thing she wanted to do.

'I'm out here because you've been avoiding me all night and I think I know why,' he continued.

Helen could no longer remain silent. 'Well, since we're here,' she said coldly, 'why don't you enlighten me?'

Taken aback by the sharpness in her voice Aiden held her gaze. 'I don't get it, why are you being so hostile? This can't be about your sister-in-law surely?'

Helen flushed with anger. 'Can you even hear yourself? You really think that nine years after you cheated on me I'm going to get upset because you're sniffing around that wannabe wag? Get over yourself! She could be moving into your penthouse and having your kids and I still wouldn't care. I can't think of two people who deserve each more.'

Aiden put his hands in the air in an effort to placate her. 'Helen, please, just calm down for a second! I'm not interested in Caitlin. I thought you would have guessed that straight away. The only reason I accepted her invitation to come out tonight was because I knew it would be the only way that we'd ever get a chance to talk.'

'About what exactly?'

It was Aiden's turn to be indignant. 'Oh come on, don't play games, Helen. When I told you why Sanne and I split up I could see in your eyes that you wanted to know the reason why, but were scared to ask.'

'Well, if that was all so bloody obvious what are you even doing here? It's my hen weekend, Aiden! This time next weekend I'll have promised to be with the man I

love for the rest of my life. Is this some kind of joke? A game where you waltz back into my life just because a very long time ago, we used to mean something to each other? I don't want to know why you split up with your wife. It has nothing to do with me.'

'You know that's not true. When you read about the divorce in the papers it must have been no surprise to you. Because you know the truth.'

'That you're a lying, cheating womaniser? I'm pretty sure everyone knows that truth.'

'Come on, Helen, you know me better than that. Why do you think I begged you to meet up all that time ago? Why do you think I got engaged? Why do you think it didn't work out with Sanne? It was all because I needed to prove to myself that I wasn't still in love with you.'

Helen shook her head in disbelief. 'That's such a lie! You didn't love me. You never loved me. If you did you would never have hurt me like that.'

'I just wasn't ready for that life.'

'Meaning once you'd hit the big time you didn't need a girlfriend!'

'It was never like that!'

'It was exactly like that! I chose you over my career and you knew that you would never be brave enough to do the same. That's why you cheated and that's why you're here because you've finally realised what I, and more than likely your ex-wife, have known all along. You're an emotional coward. You always have been and you always will be.'

'Fine,' snapped Aiden. 'Rage at me all you like, but it won't change a thing. I know you still have feelings for me. I know you still care. I know because my feelings for you haven't changed. The moment I laid eyes on you last night at the hotel it was like the last decade hadn't happened. Above all I know because I saw the doubt in your eyes when you told me you were getting married. You might think you love this guy and that might be enough to push you through but you'll never feel about him the way you felt about me. Never in a million years.'

Helen felt a surge of anger. She wanted to scream, she wanted to shout, she wanted to let out all the rage his arrogance and presumption had stirred up. But more than anything she wanted for him not to be right.

Pushing past him she ran across the terrace and back through the huge double doors into a wave of heat and sound that threatened to drown her. For a few moments she was lost in a sea of unfamiliarity, but as she slowly gathered her wits things began to make sense and once she spotted the tops of the bright red doors through which they had arrived, she headed for the exit.

The club was more packed than it had been. On the far side of the dance floor she could just about make out Carla and Ros although Caitlin and Yaz were nowhere to be seen. Helen began weaving her way around the edge of the dance floor but as she did so the DJ played yet another song that everyone in the club seemed to know and everyone flooded to the centre of the room taking Helen with them.

She almost lost her footing but quickly regained her balance and snaked in between dancing couples and groups of friends towards her destination. Every two inches gained seemed at the expense of one in the wrong direction as she struggled against the rising tide of happy clubbers. Finally she managed to break through when a group of girls dancing frenetically in front of her fell over. In the resulting commotion a few lads who had seen what had happened began holding people back and seizing her moment she dodged her way around them. She could almost see the edge of the dance floor when she felt someone grab her wrist. She turned around to see the young guy that had spoken to her earlier on the terrace. Grinning inanely he motioned that she should join him and his friends but Helen simply shook her head, wrenched her wrist free of his grip and continued on towards the exit.

There was one final obstacle to overcome before she reached the doors. A line of men, poseurs every last one of them, stood, drinks in hand eyeing up the talent. Helen bowed her head and barged right through them refusing to respond to or even acknowledge their comments as she did so. All that mattered was getting out. All that mattered was being somewhere safe.

As the large double doors closed behind her, muting the music, she stopped running so as not to attract the attention of the door staff. She left the club and scanned the street for any sign of the limousines that had brought them. There were lines of minicabs touting

145

for business, but the limos were nowhere to be seen. Just as she was wondering whether she had enough money in her purse to cover the minicab fare if she could find one that would take her back to Ashbourne she heard Aiden's voice calling after her. She had slowed down too soon. Too exhausted to run any more she stopped and turned around.

Aiden walked towards her, encircled her in his arms and held her tightly to his chest. Overcome with emotion, Helen couldn't hold in her feelings any longer and as tears began to flow down her cheeks she looked up and melted into his kiss.

As they drew apart, Helen buried her face in his chest as if trying to block out the world and everything in it. She felt drained and longed to give in to the fatigue but a commotion outside the club demanded her attention.

'Looks like they're throwing out some trouble-makers,' said Aiden.

Helen shook her head. Even amongst the uproar she could pinpoint the voice of her best friend. 'It's Yaz, she's in trouble. She needs me.'

Helen ran back up to the door of the nightclub to find Yaz being manhandled by two of the door staff.

'What's going on?'

'What's it to you, love?' asked the taller of the pair.

Aiden stepped forward. 'Listen guys, this is a close friend of mine. Is there anything I could do to help sort out the problem?'

'She was being abusive to the bar staff, Mr Reid, and she made the whole thing worse by taking a swing at one

146

of them. At this establishment we have a zero tolerance policy towards violence directed at staff members.'

'I just wanted a drink and the bastards wouldn't serve me,' slurred Yaz, attempting to wrench her arms from the door staff's grip.

Helen and Aiden exchanged wary glances. 'She's just split up with her husband,' explained Helen. 'I knew she was drinking a lot but I never guessed she was this bad.'

Aiden nodded and stepped towards the more talkative of the two doormen. 'Listen guys, you haven't called the police have you?'

'Not yet. We were just deciding what to do.'

'How about this,' said Aiden, 'you let her go and I promise that she'll never come here again. What's the name of the person she took a swing at?'

'Dave.'

'Right, well first thing in the morning you get Dave to give me a ring on this number,' Aiden scribbled his number down on a piece of paper and handed it to the man, 'and I'll make sure he's looked after. That means coming down to London, dropping into the show and putting him and a mate up in a nice hotel. What do you say?'

The two exchanged glances and the taller one replied. 'Okay, Mr Reid, but only because it's you. You do need to get her out of here pronto though.'

The door staff let Yaz go and she ran to Helen and started to cry.

Aiden pulled out his phone and made a call to the

limousine driver. 'He's just around the corner,' said Aiden. 'They'll be here in a minute. You get the rest of the girls together and we'll head back to Ashbourne.'

Helen tried Carla and then Heather but both times it went straight through to voicemail. She then tried Dee's number and breathed a huge sigh of relief when after three rings she picked up.

'Where are you?' asked Dee yelling over the din of the music. 'No one's seen you for ages.'

'I'm outside,' said Helen. 'Can you do me a favour? Just get the girls together as quickly as you can and then come out. We've got to go.'

The limousines arrived and Helen and Yaz climbed inside while Aiden waited for the rest of the group. They were there within a few minutes and he explained as tactfully as he could that something had happened and they needed to go. They all nodded and headed in the direction of the rear limousine but Caitlin, who was one of the last to emerge from the club, refused to move from his side.

'Where have you been?' she asked clinging on to his arm. 'I've been looking for you everywhere.'

'Look,' said Aiden, 'can you just get into the car?'

'What's going on?'

'Nothing's going on. Just go please.'

Obviously the worse for wear Caitlin bent down, looked into the limousine and locked eyes on Helen. 'Is this about her? Is something going on between you two?'

'Nothing's going on,' said Aiden. 'Just get into the other car will you.'

'Fine,' said Caitlin. 'But only if you come with me.'

Aiden shook his head. 'That's not going to happen.'

Caitlin's eyes narrowed. 'There is something going on. I can see it. I'm not stupid.'

'You can think whatever you like, Caitlin,' said Aiden. 'But it's probably worth pointing out that you're mistaken if you think anyone actually cares. And while it's up to you if you want to stand here talking to thin air all night, when I get into this car and tell the driver and his mate to go they will do exactly that even if it means leaving you stranded.'

Visibly shocked, Caitlin backed away from the limousine as Aiden got in, slamming the door behind him. Worried that she was about to leave her future sister-in-law marooned in a black sequined minidress in the middle of Manchester, Helen was relieved to see Caitlin disappearing into the second limousine.

The journey back to Ashbourne took place in silence with Yaz asleep on Helen's shoulder and Helen holding on tight to Aiden's arm the whole way. Every once in a while it would cross Helen's mind that she should clarify the situation in which she found herself, but she couldn't find the right words. It was too much of a task to choose the first one when she had an entire book's worth she wanted to say.

Arriving back at The Manor a little after half past three, Helen gave a little speech to the girls to the

effect that everything was okay and it would all be explained in the morning, and they headed up to their rooms. Caitlin didn't look at Helen the entire time and was the first to leave the moment she was done. Helen didn't care. All she needed was sleep.

She helped Aiden take Yaz upstairs to her room.

'This is where we say good night,' said Helen. 'I can't leave Yaz on her own in this state.'

'Are you sure?'

Helen nodded.

Aiden moved to kiss her but Helen turned her face away.

'You'd better go,' she said.

'I'll see you in the morning.'

Aiden closed the door behind him, leaving her alone with a comatose Yaz.

Struggling with the dead weight of her semi-conscious friend, Helen tucked Yaz beneath the covers and, kissing her lightly on the forehead she sat down on the edge of the bed, put her head in her hands and wept.

Sunday

14.

Helen awoke with a start to hear the occupants of a nearby room having a loud conversation about the meal they had enjoyed the night before right outside her bedroom door.

She had returned to her own room in the early hours, leaving Yaz snoring soundly, and sat up until daybreak going over the events of the night, before crashing headlong into an exhausted sleep.

Reluctant to begin what she knew was going to be a difficult day she considered going back to sleep but then she looked at her watch. They were due to meet for breakfast at ten thirty and while she was sure that the majority of her friends were already regretting the decision, she at least ought to be there.

Checking her phone Helen noted the absence of any disappointment on seeing a blank screen but chose not to dwell on it. Setting the phone back on the bedside table she took a deep breath and reminded herself to take this day one moment at a time.

As she stood in the shower an image of her kissing Aiden flashed into her head and as she shuddered and pushed it out of her mind, it was replaced by the image

of her clutching on to Aiden's arm in the back of the car on the journey back to the hotel. It was as though her subconscious was determined to review the events of the previous night even if her conscious mind was desperate to forget them.

Emerging from the shower, Helen switched on the TV to distract her while she dressed and put on her make-up. She wanted to go down to breakfast with Yaz and would miss her altogether if she didn't hurry up. Even though her hair was still damp she picked up her bag and keys, locked her door and made her way to Yaz's room on the floor below. She was about to knock when the door opened.

'Helen,' said Yaz guiltily, 'I thought you'd still be in bed.'

Helen looked down at the suitcase next to Yaz. 'What are you doing? You weren't planning on leaving were you?'

'Don't make a big deal out of it, okay?' sighed Yaz, 'I just have to go, that's all.'

'Without saying anything?'

'I was going to leave my car keys at reception and get a cab to the nearest train station.'

'But why? Not because of last night surely?'

'Of course because of last night! I made such an idiot of myself. I don't know what everyone must think of me.'

'They won't think anything.' Helen herded Yaz back into her room and closed the door. 'Please don't go.'

'But I need to. I've had enough of pretending my life's not falling apart when it so obviously is.'

'Fine,' said Helen. 'Then stop pretending. Everyone will understand. I know you're going through a lot at the moment. I understand that it must feel like it's all too much but that's why I want you to stay. I want to help.' She took Yaz's hand. 'You don't have to go through this alone. Whatever help you need, whenever you need it, it's yours.'

'But I've embarrassed myself. What was I doing drinking so much?'

'Oh, come on, babe, don't you think we've all been there? They'll be fine, I promise. And anyway, if we're talking about monumental cock-ups, your episode will be more than eclipsed by what happened to me: I've really messed up Yaz, I've messed up big time.'

'How?'

'I kissed him.'

'You did what? Why? How?'

Helen shook her head. 'I really don't know.'

Urged on by Yaz Helen told her everything that had happened with Aiden.

'So do you really still have feelings for him?'

Helen shrugged. The idea was too horrible to contemplate. 'I don't know. But I do know that I have had doubts about the wedding . . . about Phil . . . about everything . . . I haven't even bought my wedding dress!'

Yaz put her arms around Helen. 'And there was me worrying because I got lathered and took a swing at a barman!'

'So, we're agreed then,' said Helen raising half a smile. 'I am a total mess?'

'You're no such thing,' chided Yaz. 'Yes, you're in a difficult place but I know you Helen Richards – you'll find your way out.' Yaz tucked a stray strand of Helen's hair behind her ear. 'We're a right pair, aren't we? It's a wonder we can get out of bed in the mornings.'

'But we will be okay, won't we?' asked Helen.

'Of course we will,' said Yaz confidently. 'And if we're not, then at least we've got each other.' She stood up, checked her make-up in the mirror and looked back at Helen. 'You hungry?'

'I could murder a black coffee and toast.'

'Good,' said Yaz. 'Then let's go get breakfast.'

As Helen approached the girls' table it was obvious what they had been talking about. But she had given them a lot to discuss. All that mattered was that they were nice to Yaz and didn't ask too many difficult questions.

Thankfully, the girls were the very picture of discretion, making room for Helen and Yaz at the table, enquiring about how well they had slept but making no mention of the night before.

Helen poured them both coffee and checked out the girls' breakfasts. Although a few had opted for an English breakfast, most were tucking into a bowl of fruit, which made Helen think that her earlier decision to stick to toast had been a little rash. Mentioning as much to Yaz they headed to the bounteously laden breakfast buffet table.

Helen's spoon was hovering over a heaped serving bowl of raspberries and blueberries when she spotted

Aiden sitting with his friends sitting on the far side of the restaurant.

Holding her gaze he got up and walked towards her.

'I didn't expect you to be up so early,' she said.

Aiden smiled. 'The lads want to get a good game in before we have to head off. Plus they were already mad at me for missing last night so I had to come down. How are you feeling?'

'Like someone ran over my skull with a lorry. You?'

'I'm okay. My hangovers tend to hit me about midday so not long to wait now. How's your friend?'

'Fragile.'

'But okay?'

'She'll be fine.'

'And has Caitlin said anything to you yet? I was pretty rude to her last night.'

'She had it coming. I'm guessing she's having breakfast in her room.'

'Have you eaten yet?'

Helen shook her head. 'You?'

'Just coffee. Why don't we get some food?'

Helen carried on filling her bowl with fruit while he helped himself to the constituent parts of an English breakfast.

They stood for a moment alternating glances between their respective tables. She could tell Aiden wanted her to sit with him but was wary of what signals such an action might send out, she was planning to return to her friends when he took her elbow and walked her over to an empty table.

As if struck dumb by the weight of so many eyes resting on them, they ate in silence for a few minutes until Aiden spoke: 'You know you can't go through with the wedding, don't you?'

'Let's not do this.'

'Do what? Not talk about the most important thing in our lives right now?'

Helen nodded. 'I can't.'

'I'm not saying run off with me. I'm not saying please leave him. All I'm saying is what you already know: you can't go through with this wedding.'

'You want me to call it off?'

'Not for my benefit. I'm trying to put the way I feel about you to one side. Right now I'm talking to you like a friend and no friend worth the job description would tell you that going through with this wedding would be the right move.'

Helen pushed her bowl away, glad to dispense with the pantomime of pretending she had any kind of appetite.

'I can't do that to him.'

'Of course you think you can't,' said Aiden. 'But that doesn't change the facts. You have to tell him the truth and you have to do it sooner rather than later.'

'It will kill him.'

'I'm not saying it'll be easy. But do you really have any option?'

'I wish I'd never seen you this weekend. I wish I'd just stayed home and locked all the doors.'

'You think that would have saved you?'

Helen thought about the wedding dress that she hadn't bought and bit her lip. 'Why does everything always have to be so complicated? Why couldn't Phil and I have just been happy as we were?'

'It's just the way life is, isn't it? Some get from A to B via the easy route and people like you and me . . . well we just take a little bit longer to get to where we're going.'

Helen stood up. 'I have to go.'

'What time are you off?'

'Some time after lunch.'

'We should talk again before you leave.' Aiden reached out and touched her arm. 'Are you okay?'

'No,' said Helen flatly, 'I'm not.' She made her way back to her friends and took a seat. In a transparent effort not to appear nosey the girls carried on with their conversation as if nothing had happened. Only Yaz acknowledged its significance with a brief meaningful glance.

The girls were discussing the third and final treatment of the weekend: Helen's wedding-day beauty preparation, a one-hour session in which the spa's top beautician and hair stylist offered Helen hair and make-up suggestions for the Big Day while the rest of them sat around and sipped glasses of complimentary champagne, ate handmade Belgian chocolates and bolstered her spirits. It was the girls' gift to Helen, the best way they could think of to see her off into her new life as a married woman. The more they talked about it, the more nauseous Helen felt.

'Are you okay?' asked Ros. 'You don't look very well.'

'I don't think I am,' said Helen. 'I think I might go for a lie-down before the treatment.'

Ros offered to take her back up to her room, but before she could even get to her feet Yaz was at her side holding her by the arm.

'It's no problem,' said Yaz quickly, 'I'll take her up.'

Helen could tell Ros knew that something was up but thankfully she made no comment. They arranged to meet at the spa later and made their way out of the restaurant.

'What happened? What did Aiden say?' asked Yaz the moment they were out of sight.

'Nothing I didn't already know. Everything's a mess, Yaz. Everything. How am I supposed to go through with that treatment feeling the way I do?'

'How do you feel? I'm not sure I know.'

'That's just it, that's how I feel: unsure. It would be so much easier if I could just blame all this on Aiden. It would be so much more straightforward. But the truth is, I was unsure before I even got here. I've been unsure since Phil brought this whole marriage thing up . . . Let's talk in my room,' said Helen, 'maybe if I tell you everything that happened again, we might be able to find a way out of this hole I've dug for myself.'

As they passed reception, there, at the desk, quite clearly checking out, was Caitlin.

Helen was hardly in the right frame of mind to deal with her sister-in-law and yet to leave Caitlin to her own devices would be to invite all manner of problems. She

was probably contemplating contacting Phil to tell him everything that she knew if she hadn't done so already.

'I've got to speak to her,' said Helen as they reached the lift. 'Just wait here, and then I'll be straight back.'

She hadn't the slightest idea what she was going to say to Caitlin but she had to try.

The moment Caitlin finished checking out Helen walked over to meet her.

'We need to talk.'

'I've got nothing to say to you.'

'Please, this is really important.'

Caitlin turned away pulling her suitcase behind her. Helen followed her through the main doors to the steps outside. It was another bright and summery day, the sun was so strong that it felt as though she had stepped out of a black and white film into a Technicolor one.

'Caitlin, please!'

Caitlin continued down the steps so Helen ran ahead of her and stood in her path.

'Please, I'm begging you! Just stop!'

Caitlin went around her across the gravel towards the car park.

Angry with herself as much as she was with Caitlin, Helen called out after her: 'You go if it makes you feel better. You hated me from day one and you hate me now and that's never going to change.'

Caitlin turned around.

'I don't know what my brother ever saw in you.'

'Is that what this is about? That Phil made a decision without consulting you?'

Mike Gayle

'And a great job he's made of it!'

'What do you mean by that?'

'You know exactly what I mean,' spat Caitlin.

'And this is how you want this to end?'

Caitlin's eyes narrowed. 'You haven't seen the half of it.'

'Meaning?'

'Whatever you want it to mean. I'm done with you.'

'No,' said Helen, '*I'm* done with *you*. After nine years of putting up with your crap I'm going to give you a present that will make your day: the wedding's off. You win Caitlin. Phil is all yours! I hope the two of you are well and truly happy together.'

15.

Helen had no idea where she was going. Nothing
mattered any more now she'd announced her decision.
Leaving Caitlin open-mouthed on the driveway Helen
headed back towards the hotel reception, before
realising she couldn't face even Yaz, worse still, Aiden.
So she headed towards the river mainly because it was
the biggest thing on the horizon.

But reaching the river meant crossing the terrace
and it seemed as though half the guests had come out
to enjoy mid-morning refreshments. Helen ducked
through an open French door that led to one of the
lounges. She quickly composed herself and was about
to go back outside when she saw some of Aiden's
friends walking past the window and had to pretend to
browse the bookshelf until they had gone.

Heading out of the lounge, Helen remembered the
riverside space where she and Aiden had sat talking
the day before. That was where she wanted to be. That
was where she could be alone.

It was just as quiet as she remembered. The only
sounds were the birds in the trees and the river flowing
by, and within just a few moments of her sitting down

163

the hot angry tears she had been holding back since her encounter with Caitlin finally burst through the dam that she had so painstakingly erected.

It was over. The nine years of loving and being loved by the one man in her life who had never done her wrong had come to a horrible conclusion, and the blame was all hers.

During her time with Phil, Helen's continuing fear had been that things would fall apart just as they had with Aiden. Despite trusting Phil implicitly, she couldn't stop worrying that he would meet someone else and end the relationship. In the many scenarios that populated her mind when at her most fragile it was never Phil who pursued these women but the women who pursued Phil. She imagined him out with his friends or at work and a woman who was more attractive or more understanding or who made him feel like his true self appeared in his life and would change everything.

There had even been times when Helen had found herself taking an irrational dislike to women Phil introduced her to who perfectly embodied her phantom nemesis. It didn't matter whether they were married or expressed less than zero interest in Phil while in her presence, if they fitted the bill and she could imagine Phil being happy with them then they were a threat. On rare occasions the jealousy would spiral out of control to such an extent that she would lock herself in the bathroom in the middle of the night frantically checking his text messages for evidence to lend weight to her theory. There was never anything of the kind. On the

contrary: there was only evidence of his enduring love. Texts sent while he was away for work telling her that he loved her, jokey ones sent while she was on air telling her how sexy she sounded, thoughtful ones attempting to lift her spirits when he knew she was in for a bad day.

Helen felt shame when she remembered these moments and the shame was made so much worse by the fact that after all this anxiety and worry, she had been the betrayer rather than the betrayed.

She took her phone from her bag and looked at the screen. Still no sign of communication from Phil. If he had called, would it have made any difference to how the weekend had unfolded? Surely it would only have delayed the inevitable. Even so, she wished that she had heard from him. Hearing his voice would offer her some of the comfort she so desperately craved. Soon all that would change. Phil would hear about the events of the weekend and the next time she heard his voice it would be filled with hurt and anger. She longed to hear that voice filled with laughter and kindness one last time. She wished she had savoured those moments from the past, kept them safe for future reference. Instead, she had taken them for granted and now it was too late for anything other than regret.

Determined to bring her life back under control Helen made plans for the future. She would tell Phil about her misguided feelings for Aiden face to face and then move out. There were plenty of people she could stay with in the short term while she hunted for

a place to rent and in the longer term she was convinced that if she cashed in her savings she would have enough for a deposit on a small place of her own.

Next she would call off the wedding. It would be too horrible and cruel to leave this to Phil. No, it would be her responsibility to contact all the guests and hers alone. A fitting punishment if ever there was one.

She would let Phil take the two-week-long honeymoon to Mauritius that had been one of the things he had organised so that he could have some time away. And depending on how much money she could lay her hands on, she would book herself a break somewhere warm where she could be alone to lick her wounds.

The only thing that Helen couldn't think about was Aiden. It was too soon and her feelings were too raw. She reminded herself that he wasn't the cause of this mess, merely a symptom and as such outside the circle of things that really mattered.

As Helen looked up through the leaf canopy above her head and felt the intense warmth of the sunlight on her face she felt grateful for the soothing silence. The real world felt a very long way off, too far away to harm her.

She heard a noise and looked up to see Yaz coming down the hill towards her.

'Finally,' said Yaz. 'You okay?'

'I'm fine,' said Helen. 'I'm sorry for being such a drama queen. Have you been looking for me for long?'

Yaz shook her head. 'When I came outside and there was no sign of you I went to the car park and there was

Caitlin loading her things into her boot looking for all the world like she'd been crying. I tried to ask what had gone on but she just snapped at me to speak to you and drove off. What happened?'

'I told her I was calling off the wedding.'

'But you didn't mean it surely?'

'I meant every word. Phil deserves better.'

'But there's no need for that. Maybe she won't tell him what happened.'

'She'll tell him all right and take great pleasure in doing so.'

'Well, that doesn't necessarily mean that Phil will want to call it off too. He really does love you, you know. You only have to see the two of you together. He won't give up on nine years just because you got cold feet.'

'I betrayed him.'

'You were confused.'

'Would you be so understanding if I were a man?'

'I'd say it no matter who you were.'

'I'm not sure I'd be so forgiving. Trust is everything to me.'

'But even the people we trust make mistakes.'

Helen shook her head. 'I don't think there's a way back from this. Some things are too bad, too awful to warrant forgiveness.'

'You're too hard on yourself.'

'That's just the thing. I don't think I'm being hard enough.' Helen closed her eyes. 'I think I might actually have feelings for him.'

Yaz could scarcely hide her shock. 'For Aiden?'

Helen nodded. 'You see? That's why I can't marry Phil.'

'I don't understand. When did this happen?'

'Maybe I've always felt this way on some level and just been too scared to admit it.'

'This is just your nerves talking,' said Yaz firmly. 'You've got cold feet about the wedding and Aiden has made it worse. I know you love Phil, and he feels the same way. You have to have faith in him, Helen, you have to have faith in yourself too, but more than that you have to have faith that love is enough.' Yaz put an arm around Helen. 'I promise you this whole mess will get sorted out somehow, just wait and see.'

With the late morning sun already high in the sky the two friends headed back to the hotel with the intention of checking out. Reaching the far edge of the hotel they gazed across the grounds taking in the full glory of their surroundings.

'We should come back here one day and do this whole thing properly,' said Helen solemnly as a flock of geese passed by overhead. 'No weddings, separations, sisters-in-law or anything else that might rain on our parade. Just me, you, and a weekend of high-end luxury.'

'I'll book it first thing, Monday,' said Yaz, 'but for now I think we should concentrate on just getting through today.'

It was twenty minutes to midday by the time Helen reached her room and surveyed all the work that

needed to be done in order to check out on time. At the beginning of the weekend she had been scrupulous about packing dirty clothes away as she used them and generally keeping things organised and tidy but as time passed, her standards had dropped and her room looked like a bomb had hit it. There were dresses and tops spread over armchairs, underwear and swimwear on the floor and the entire contents of her make-up bag spread across the mirrored vanity table.

She opened her case, now largely empty, and made a start with the wardrobe, scooping all the items she had so carefully hung up there and unceremoniously dumping them inside before turning her attention to the floor. Within a few minutes she'd managed to cram more of her belongings in the case than there were scattered around the room but then she remembered the bathroom.

It took the best part of ten very frantic minutes to get everything done and as Helen stood surveying the room one last time she felt a pang of disappointment that this haven would no longer be hers. Soon the cleaners would come, strip down the bed and Hoover, sweep and dust away every trace of her existence ready for the next guest. Wishing the new occupants of the room better luck than she had enjoyed, Helen picked up her keys, left the room and closed the door behind her.

Most of the girls were already queuing up, wheelie suitcases and all, at reception. She joined the back of

the queue behind an older guy who resembled an off duty rock star and his considerably younger significant other.

She wondered whether Aiden and his friends had checked out yet or whether, given their VIP status they had to check out at all, and were instead enjoying an early lunch or squeezing in a last-minute massage. Things were different if you had money. You could spare yourself the things that troubled the lives of mere mortals.

'Did you manage to bag all the toiletries?'

It was Yaz.

'All of them,' she nodded. 'You?'

'I couldn't fit in the conditioner or the moisturiser. I'm gutted.'

'Don't worry,' said Helen. 'I'll treat you for Christmas.'

'Any sign of you know who?'

Helen shook her head. 'I was just thinking about him actually.'

'In a good way or a bad?'

Helen sighed. 'Pretty neutral, considering.'

More members of staff arrived to help at reception and soon the queue had been dealt with and there was only Helen and Yaz left to check out.

Helen handed over her key and closed her eyes in anticipation of the bill. She began totting up some of the goods she had availed herself of that had seemed so reasonable at the time: several bottles of water at six pounds a go, numerous bottles of champagne, the twenty-pounds-per-bottle massage oil and the

thirty-six-pounds-per-tub skin cream that she had asked the beauty therapist to add to her bill. She shuddered at all that wasted money and how long it would take to pay off her next overdraft.

She looked apprehensively at the receptionist.

'How much is it?'

The receptionist looked confused. 'Nothing. Your bill has already been settled.'

'There must be some mistake, I haven't—'

The receptionist looked concerned. 'Is there a problem? Mr Reid assured us that he had spoken to you about this.'

'Oh right,' said Helen quickly. 'It just slipped my mind. When did he sort this out?'

'About an hour ago.'

'Has he checked out?'

'I'm afraid I'm not authorised to give out that information.'

'Of course, I understand. I'll catch up with him later.'

She was surrounded by the rest of the girls.

'So come on then,' said Kerry, 'what was the damage? If it was anything like mine I bet it was a real killer! How they can charge sixteen pounds for a glorified tuna sandwich and keep a straight face is a complete mystery to me.'

'You should have seen mine,' added Lorna. 'When the bloke at reception handed it to me I nearly had a stroke. I said I'd only come for a weekend stay, not to buy the bloody place! Ian is going to do his nut when he sees the next Visa bill. Still, it's got to be a better

use of our hard earned than flying out to Belgium for the weekend to watch motor racing in the rain.'

'So come on then,' said Kerry. 'How much was it?'

'More than I can afford,' said Helen. 'Much more.' She looked at Kerry. 'Could you do me a favour? Could you get all the girls together in the Silver Lounge? I think it's about time I explained what's been going on.'

16.

'So it's really, well and truly all off?'

Helen nodded. The sense of relief now that everyone knew was overwhelming.

'You poor thing,' said Carla giving her a hug. 'You've been completely put through the wringer.'

'I'm fine,' said Helen. 'Or at least I will be.'

'It is the right thing to do though,' said Heather. 'When I was younger and I broke off my engagement with Louis, it broke my heart at the time but it was absolutely the right thing to do. If I hadn't I'd never have met Wes, or had my lovely babies.'

Ros nodded in agreement. 'I know I'm not exactly the right person to be handing out advice given that I'm in the middle of a divorce but the only real crime would be to go through with it out of a sense of misplaced guilt. Of course it's sad, for you and for Phil but in the long term he'll appreciate you were looking out for him as much as you were yourself.'

'Thanks,' said Helen. 'I really appreciate all of your support. But the reason I gathered you all here is because I wanted you all to know that well . . . this whole weekend was supposed to be about us having a

good time and being really close when in fact I was doing everything I could to keep secrets from you.'

'It was a difficult situation,' said Heather. 'Anyway, most of us had guessed something was up and we knew you'd tell us when the time was right.'

Helen smiled. 'Bang goes my future with MI5. Anyway, despite everything, it has been amazing catching up with all of you and when the dust settles we should definitely put our heads together and come up with a good excuse for doing this again.'

'You're making it sound like you're off this very second.'

Helen looked guilty. 'That's because I am. I've got a lot of thinking to do before Phil gets back this evening so I thought it best to go now. I'll get a cab to the station, get a connection to Derby and then on to Nottingham.'

'You'll do no such thing,' protested Yaz and the others nodded in agreement.

'If you go,' said Ros, 'we all go.'

'Don't girls, please. The last thing I want is to ruin this weekend more than I already have.'

'Ruin the weekend?' laughed Dee. 'You have got to be kidding! A top hotel, relaxing beauty treatments, a Michelin-starred restaurant topped off with dancing until the early hours in Manchester! I'd pay twice the money for just half the fun.'

'She's right,' said Ros. 'I haven't laughed so much in ages. I wouldn't have missed it for the world. And while I know you're not putting it to the vote I don't think

you should go home early either. We've still got lunch to look forward to, use of the spa and the swimming pool and while I understand that the bridal treatment we booked might not be appropriate right now, I'm sure they'd swap it for something else you'd enjoy. Just because the wedding isn't happening doesn't mean you don't need to treat yourself well.'

'You're not going to take no for an answer are you?' asked Helen wryly.

'Of course not,' replied Carla, 'we're sitting in paradise! This time last week I was being threatened with a broken beer bottle by a tattooed methadone addict who didn't like the fact that I was making her kids go to school! Frankly I'd handcuff myself to you for the rest of the afternoon if it meant we got to stay here an hour longer.'

'Fine,' said Helen, grateful to be surrounded by so many friends. 'I'll stay. I'd only sit at home and brood. So what now? The choice is up to you guys.'

'Let's check out the thermal pool that we passed on the way to the sauna,' said Ros. 'It's just a tiny covered pool with a bunch of lights stuck in the ceiling but it might be good for a laugh.'

'Or we could go back to the sauna,' said Ros, 'but we should use the plunge pool instead of chickening out like we did last time.'

'I felt the water,' laughed Yaz. 'It was bloody freezing!'

'We should do them all,' suggested Carla, 'and then this afternoon make out like we're posh nobs and hijack the croquet lawn and order afternoon tea. By

the time we leave I want to really feel like we've exhausted everything on offer! I don't want to go back to north London! It's a ming hole compared to this!'

'So it's agreed,' chuckled Helen, 'thermal pool, followed by the sauna, followed by plunge pool, insert lunch somewhere in amongst the proceedings but make sure to leave enough time for croquet and cucumber sandwiches! I can already see they're going to have to call security to—'

Helen stopped abruptly.

'What's up?' asked Yaz. Caitlin was staring intently at them. 'I thought she'd left. What does she want now?'

'I'm not sure,' said Helen, 'but at a guess I'd say: round two.'

The Cross Keys was an old, stone-built, ivy-covered pub, the kind perfect for whiling away a lazy afternoon partaking of a traditional pint and Sunday lunch. Sadly, Helen wasn't there to while away an afternoon but rather to participate in her second confrontation of the day with Caitlin.

Caitlin bought the drinks (a mineral water for herself and a half of cider for Helen) and they made their way out to the beer garden which was heavily populated with locals enjoying the afternoon sunshine. There were no free seats so they followed the path down to the river and sat down on a wall overlooking the water.

Neither woman had said more than a handful of words since they had climbed into Caitlin's convertible,

and as Helen took a sip from her glass she wondered if they were going to talk at all.

'What made you come back?' she finally asked, placing her glass down on the wall.

Caitlin shrugged. 'I felt bad. Truth is I have been a bit of a bitch to you from day one and you did nothing to deserve it. It wasn't fair. I never gave you a chance.' Helen felt dizzy hearing these words as though at any moment she might wake up and find herself in bed with a fever. 'The thing is,' continued Caitlin, 'I love my brother, Helen, I really do and he thinks the absolute world of you so I should have tried harder. I suppose what I'm trying to say is that I really wish you'd reconsider what you said today . . . I know there's nothing going on with you and Aiden and I should have known better than to have suggested otherwise . . . please don't call off the wedding. It would kill Phil if you did.'

'Is that what you're scared of? Phil blaming you if I call off the wedding?'

Caitlin shook her head. 'It doesn't matter why, does it? All that matters is not breaking my brother's heart. I'm begging you, Helen, don't call it off. Let's just put this whole thing behind us. We can do that, can't we?'

'I can't think of anything I'd like more, but it's just not going to be possible.'

'Because of me?'

'No,' said Helen. 'Because of me.'

'But Phil adores you.'

177

'I know,' said Helen. 'But I'm not sure it's enough.'

Caitlin looked bewildered. 'I know girls who would kill to have a guy like Phil in their lives.'

'So do I,' replied Helen. 'He's amazing. A truly wonderful man.'

'But?'

'I know you can never be one hundred per cent sure. I know that nearly all of life is a gamble. But the odds of us not working out feel too high.'

'It's just last-minute nerves.' It was ironic to hear Caitlin echoing Yaz. 'Have you tried talking to him?' she added cautiously.

'No,' Helen wondered if the stress in Caitlin's voice meant that she already had. 'His phone's been off every time I called. Have you managed to reach him?'

'I didn't try,' said Caitlin a little too quickly. 'It's not really my place is it?'

The words: 'Well, that's never stopped you before,' sprang to mind but Helen kept them to herself.

'So what now?'

'I go back to Nottingham and break the news to Phil when he gets home.'

'He'll be devastated.'

'He'll need all the support you can offer.'

'And there's no way around this?'

'None that I can see.'

'My mum was so looking forward to it.'

'So was mine. She'll be heartbroken.'

Caitlin stood up, defeated. 'I should get you back

178

before your friends call the police and tell them I've kidnapped you. I'm sorry this hasn't worked out.'

'Thanks,' said Helen. 'I appreciate that.'

It was a little after one by the time Caitlin dropped Helen off in The Manor's main car park. A number of people were loading up expensive looking cars with expensive looking luggage but there was no sign of Aiden and his friends.

'Are you sure you won't come and say goodbye to the rest of the girls?' asked Helen. 'They'll be sorry not to see you off.'

Caitlin smiled. 'I think we both know that's not really true.'

The two women embraced awkwardly before Caitlin climbed back into her car. Helen stood rooted to the spot as she reflected on everything she and Caitlin had been through. Would this be the last time they would meet? For better or worse Caitlin had been a part of her life for a long time and for her to disappear felt wrong. The thought that this might also be true for her and Phil made Helen's blood run cold.

Caitlin wound down her window and leaned out. 'Helen?'

'Yes?'

'Could you do me a favour?'

'Of course, what?'

'Tell Yaz, I'm sorry.'

'What for?'

Caitlin didn't reply.

She exited the car park and disappeared through the hotel gates. Helen rolled Caitlin's mysterious non-message to Yaz around in her head. What had she meant? Sorry for spoiling the weekend that Yaz had organised or something more? Shivering in spite of the full glare of the afternoon sun, Helen turned to face the hotel but she had taken no more than a few steps when she spotted Aiden.

'I've been looking for you everywhere.'

'I've only just got back.'

'I saw. A showdown with Caitlin?' Helen nodded. 'Are you okay? She hasn't told her brother about us has she?'

'She says not.'

'And you believe her?'

Helen nodded. 'I'm too terrified not to.'

'You don't look terrified.'

'I prefer to keep my worrying on the inside.' Helen wanted a hug and to be told everything was going to be all right, and yet the thought that it might come from Aiden unnerved her.

'I thought you'd be gone by now,' she said blinking away the tiredness in her eyes.

'We're all packed and ready,' replied Aiden. 'I just talked the lads into giving me an extra half an hour to look for you. It's cost me a two-hundred-quid bottle of cognac but it was worth it just to see your face again.' He gently grazed his hand against Helen's cheek. She recoiled.

'I told you this morning. I can't do this.'

'Can't do what exactly? I didn't dream last night, did I? We did kiss.'

'And I regret it.'

'That's the guilt talking, not you.'

'This is so easy for you, isn't it? You really think that a week before my wedding I'm going to leave the man I've lived with for nine years and jump straight into your arms.'

'No,' snapped Aiden, 'I think you'd rather just sit around making yourself feel bad for no reason first.'

'I thought you were being patient and understanding.'

'I was,' replied Aiden. 'I am. It's just that for the first time in a long while I know exactly what I want and it's frustrating that I can't have it.'

'You sound like a petulant schoolboy. Am I just another "thing" that you've got it into your head to desire?'

'It's not like that and you know it. I want you, Helen, I want you in my life right now. I know it's my fault that we spilt up. I know if I'd have done the right thing back when it really mattered we wouldn't be standing here having this ridiculous conversation. That's part of the reason I'm so keen. I'm just desperate to make things right.'

Helen's head was ready to explode. 'This is all too much!'

'I know,' said Aiden. 'And this is me trying to be restrained. Only you can make me like this, no one else.'

'Not even your ex-wife?'

'Not even my ex-wife.' He reached out for her hand. 'I'm trying to show you how committed I am to making a go of things. I know this is my last chance to prove I'm serious. This isn't just me playing at being romantic. This is me laying everything on the line. If you want me to give up my show I'll hand in my notice live on air tomorrow morning. If you want me to move out of London I'll be on the first train to Nottingham. Whatever it is you want you've got it.'

'How about time?'

A flash of exasperation flashed across Aiden's face. 'You really know how to kill a grand gesture.'

'It's what I need though.'

'The resignation didn't float your boat?'

Helen shook her head.

'Fine, if time's what you want then it's yours. But know this: I'll be thinking about you every moment of every day until you call me.' He stepped forward ready to kiss her but Helen pulled away. 'I can't.'

'Maybe not,' murmured Aiden, 'but one day soon you will.'

17.

The girls were having tea at a table around the corner from the terrace. They were all wearing sunglasses and laughing at something Ros was saying. The moment they spotted Helen however the laughter stopped.

'I wish you wouldn't stop enjoying yourselves the second you see me. A girl could get paranoid.'

'How did it go?' asked Yaz. 'Did she pull a knife on you?'

'She was fine,' sighed Helen. 'We went to a pub down the road. Had a drink and a chat. The whole thing was actually quite civilised, she even asked me to pass on her apologies to you. It's certainly a weight off my mind.'

'So you two have made up?'

'I wouldn't go that far. It would be more accurate to say that if I was still marrying Phi, Caitlin and I would have chosen to turn over a new leaf. But as we're not, the point is sort of academic, although I am relieved to have the number of people in the world who hate my guts down to zero.'

'But the Phil situation remains the same?'

Helen nodded. 'She said she hadn't called him but

who knows? I'm not even sure it makes a difference now the wedding's off.'

The girls fell into an uneasy silence, looking to Yaz for guidance.

'We were thinking that we'd go in to lunch now if you're hungry.'

'I'm ravenous.'

'Good,' said Yaz. 'Then let's do it.'

Sick of being the sole topic of conversation Helen made sure to focus on what the girls had been up to as they made their way over to the restaurant. While they regaled her with tales of plunge pools, high-pitched screaming and stern reprimands from spa attendants ,she succeeded in tucking her problems out of sight and enjoying the weekend for what it was meant to be.

They were disappointed to discover that all the tables on the terrace were taken but just then a group sitting outside left and with the best part of a dozen women simultaneously pleading to be given the table once it was cleared the waiter didn't stand a chance of refusing.

Seated in the sunshine, with a huge plate of prawn and avocado salad in front of her and a final bottle of champagne on its way to the table Helen felt her spirits lift but as she opened her mouth to take her first forkful of food she heard her phone vibrate as it received a text message.

She tried to ignore it, reasoning that there was no spam text worth delaying food as good as that on her plate for, but after a moment she automatically reached for her phone.

She looked at the screen. She didn't recognise the number and yet for reasons she couldn't begin to pinpoint she was convinced that she knew who the text was from.

'Are you okay?' asked Yaz topping up Helen's water glass.

Helen waved the glass away. 'I'm fine. It's just . . . it's just . . . it's just that this text . . . well, I think it's from Phil.'

Yaz was confused. 'How do you mean?'

'It's from a number that's not in my phone but I'm absolutely sure it's from Phil.'

Yaz held out her hand. 'Let me take a look.'

Helen handed her phone to Yaz. 'Don't open it.'

'Why not?'

'Because who knows what it says? What if the text is asking if I'm free to talk? I'm the world's worst liar. If I talk to him he'll know right away something's up.'

'But why do you think he needs to talk to you?' asked Lorna. 'If he's anything like my Dez, chances are he's texting to remind you to record the Grand Prix for him. Why don't you just read it and find out?'

Helen shook her head. 'I've just got a bad feeling about it.'

'What?' said Lorna, 'You don't think they've had some kind of accident do you?'

'No, if it was something like that he'd phone and there are no missed calls. I can't explain but the more I think about it the more I don't want to read this text. I'm going to leave it until I've seen him tonight and told him everything.'

'You don't think he already knows, do you?' said Yaz anxiously. 'Caitlin could have been lying about not contacting him.'

'She'd have nothing to gain.'

'In that case,' said Yaz. 'Give me the phone and if it's something you need to know I'll tell you.'

'And have to spend the rest of the day trying not to read meaning into your every action? No thanks.' Helen gave in. 'Okay, I'll read it and deal with the consequences.'

With the whole table watching her intently Helen manoeuvred her thumb into position but it refused to press the button that would reveal the contents of the text.

'I just can't do it,' she said.

Before Helen could voice her opposition Yaz snatched up the phone, opened the text and smiled.

'What?'

'You don't want to know,' teased Yaz.

'Of course I do.'

'It's not bad news.'

'So what does it say?'

Yaz handed the phone back to Helen and as her eyes locked on the screen she wanted to smile and cry at the same time.

Ros leaned in to take a peek. 'What does it say?'

Helen wiped her eyes. 'It says: "I love you Spoonface." ' With bated breath her friends waited for an explanation. 'It's the pet name Phil gave me years ago.'

Yaz laughed. 'We gathered that. Why Spoonface?'

Helen shrugged. 'He made it up and it stuck. He only ever calls me it when I'm sad or moody or worried. It's his way of relieving the tension.'

'And what's your pet name for him?'

'I've never felt like he's needed anything other than Phil,' said Helen quietly

'Why does everything have to be so difficult?' she said eventually. 'Why can't things be straightforward?' How desperately she had wanted to receive some form of communication from Phil and now that she had, it just made things worse.

'What should I do? Reply or leave it?'

Yaz spoke first. 'Leave it. He won't think anything of it.'

'But I always reply. What if he calls?'

'Just ignore it. There could be a million and one reasons why you didn't take the call.'

Helen wasn't convinced. 'I should call him.'

'And say what?'

'I don't know.'

'But you said yourself that you're the world's worst liar.'

'Then I'd better improve,' said Helen snatching up the phone once again, 'because right now I've not got much choice.'

Clutching her phone, Helen headed across the terrace towards one of the benches overlooking the river.

The afternoon sun was fierce and Helen felt her

187

brow dampen with perspiration. A middle-aged couple stood watching their two young children skimming stones across the surface of the water. Helen envied them. She wished she could be enjoying the pleasant surroundings and the beautiful weather without a care in the world instead of having to make a telephone call which could completely wreck everything she held dear.

She called up Phil's number and was ready to press down on the call button when the phone rang. She checked the screen.

'Hi, Mum, everything okay?'

'I'm fine, sweetie. I've just finished washing up and thought I'd call you before I go and have a sit in the garden. Are you having a nice weekend?'

'Yes, it's great. The weather's beautiful.'

'And how have those treatment things been?'

'Wonderful. Really relaxing.'

'Are you okay? You don't sound like your usual self.'

'I'm fine,' said Helen quickly. 'Just a bit tired. We had a late night and I still haven't recovered.'

'You shouldn't be having late nights this close to the wedding. Not if you want to look your best for next Saturday. The week before I married your father I was in bed for nine o'clock every night.'

'And every day you were up at six for your morning constitutional.'

'Left out of Granny's house, all the way along Spencer Street, right again at Larch Crescent, all the way along Radcliffe Street and back home in time to make

Granddad's morning brew. Did me the world of good. You should try it.'

Helen laughed. 'I'll add it to my list, Mum.'

'Anyway, the reason I'm phoning is that I've had a call from your cousin Joe to say that he and his girlfriend can't make it because she fractured her ankle and he's got to look after her. I told him he should come on his own because there was no point in you and Phil losing the money on two meals but he wouldn't hear of it. Anyway, I mentioned it to your auntie Sue and it turns out that her Andrew who said that he couldn't come actually can. I told her that it would be too late in the day to be getting new place cards but Sue insisted that he wouldn't mind. Is that okay with you?'

'Of course.'

'Good. I'll call Sue now and let her know. Love you sweetheart.'

Helen had a million things she wanted to say. Everything from how she still wanted her dad to walk her down the aisle through to being sorry for never quite being the ordinary daughter with the ordinary job that she knew deep down her mum wanted her to be.

'Mum?'

'Yes?'

'Nothing.'

'Are you sure?'

'Yes,' replied Helen. 'I'm sure.' She rung off.

The urge to call Phil had gone. Her mum had saved her and while it had raised problems of its own that

she would have to face during the coming week, for now at least she felt strangely calm.

Feeling more buoyant now, Helen returned to the table.

'How did it go?' asked Yaz.

'I didn't make the call. Chickened out and took a call from my mum instead. You'll be pleased to know however that my cousin Andrew and his girlfriend are coming to the wedding that isn't happening in lieu of my cousin Joe and his girlfriend.' Helen sat down. 'This is really going to be a kick in the teeth for Mum when she finds out it's not happening.'

'You'd be surprised,' said Yaz. 'I thought my mum would give me a hard time about Simon and me separating but she didn't say a word. She just listened and gave me a hug afterwards. And if I know your mum she'll be the same. That's the thing about mums: whatever you do, whatever you say, at the end of it they are always on your side.'

Helen sat down and looked at the food on her plate but only managed a mouthful before pushing it aside.

'I know it sounds mad but part of me wishes that I hadn't booked this week off work. I can't think of a better way of coping than by having a show to do. When I'm at work nothing else matters and I'm in complete control. It's just real life where I struggle to cope.'

Yaz grinned. 'You know what you need to lift your spirits? Chocolate, more champagne and a group threading session.'

'Is that what you swapped the wedding makeover thing for?'

'Yeah, when I called the spa the girl started reeling off what else we could have for the same money and the second she mentioned threading I was like, 'let me stop you there'.

Helen raised her hand to her eyebrows. 'I'm booked in at a place in town to have mine done on Thursday.'

'Well now you can cancel it and put the money towards something more useful like that last-minute holiday you'll be needing.'

Helen sighed. 'I thought about that, too, but what would be the point? Being away from home would make me miss Phil more, not less. At least if I'm here I can see friends, visit my parents or go flat-hunting.'

'You do what you've got to do,' said Yaz, 'but at least you'll be doing it with professionally shaped eyebrows.'

It was twenty-five past two when they walked, for the final time, into the spa reception. While the rest of the girls took a seat Helen and Yaz made their way over to the desk to book in.

'Hi,' said Yaz, 'we're the two-fifteen group threading session. Sorry we're a bit late, but we've had a complete nightmare of a day.'

The girl smiled. 'That's fine. Can I just take your name?'

'Mrs Collins, Yasmin.'

The receptionist looked at her computer screen. 'I'm afraid I don't have anything in that name.'

Yaz and Helen exchanged puzzled glances.

'Okay, how about Helen Richards?'

The receptionist glanced again. 'Got it,' she said triumphantly. 'Helen Richards, 2.30 p.m., wedding preparation hair and make-up session.'

'Actually,' said Yaz firmly, as she wondered whether there was no booking this hotel could get right, 'it's a group threading session. We were booked in for the other thing but I called this morning and was told that it would be no problem to swap it.'

'I'm afraid there's no record of that.'

'Great,' said Yaz. 'Well can we cancel it now and do the threading thing instead?'

'The beauticians who do hair and make-up are specially booked in. You could cancel the session but I'm afraid you'd lose the fee. What would you like to do?'

'Looks like we've got no choice,' said Helen grinning at her friend. 'So I say let's pimp this bride!'

18.

When Yaz had initially sold the idea of the wedding makeover to Helen she had promised it would be a 'bit of a laugh', which Helen took to mean that the chances of her emerging with hair like a drag queen and make-up like Coco the Clown were high. Helen had sat at enough department store counters having make-up consultations and, in her younger days, had her hair cut by a sufficient number of student hairstylists to know that there were few mistakes that couldn't be rectified by a quick wash and blow dry or half a pack of Johnson's baby wipes. But in all her years of haircuts and makeovers nothing had prepared her for what she saw when after the best part of an hour of being prodded and poked, the older of the two stylists, a tall woman with red hair, announced to the room, 'I think we're done,' and held up a mirror.

'What do you think?'

Helen couldn't think of a response. Her mind had gone blank. Fortunately Yaz was on standby. 'You. Look. Amazing!'

Helen took in her reflected image as the rest of the girls chipped in with enthusiastic comments of their

own while they took pictures with their phones. Helen tried to identify a flaw that she could point out for her friends to laugh at, but there were none to be found. These two women, skilled in the dark arts of blow-drying and make-up had performed a miracle, transforming taking an exhausted Helen into a dewy skinned ingénue. Her hair, her skin, her eyes, her lips, everything was exactly the way that she had always wanted to look but never managed to achieve.

'I don't know what to say. It doesn't even look like me.'

'Oh please!' said the younger stylist, a dark-haired girl with deep brown eyes. She looked over at Yaz. 'Is she always like this?'

Yaz nodded sombrely. 'Always.'

'There's just no pleasing some people.' She looked over Helen's shoulder and smiled. 'For the record: you looked amazing before we started. All we did was cross a few T's and dot a few I's. That fiancé of yours is a lucky man.'

It was a harmless comment given the context and wouldn't have affected Helen had the makeover been the disaster she had been expecting, but with it being so remarkable, it served as another painful reminder of the mess in which she found herself and tears threatened.

Embarrassed to be behaving like some hormonal teenager, Helen led them out to reception where they handed in their luggage tickets to the concierge and prepared to leave the hotel for the last time.

194

'My house is going to look a real dump in comparison to this place,' joked Yaz as they walked towards the car park. 'Twenty-four hours from now I'll be knee-deep in the ironing basket and this will seem like nothing more than a very good dream. A taste of honey really is a dangerous thing.' She covered her mouth in horror. 'I didn't mean you . . . I meant—'

'It's fine,' said Helen, 'and you're right. For people like me it's about as dangerous as it gets.'

They said their goodbyes and headed off to the various vehicles that had brought them to their destination. Helen, Yaz, Lorna, Dee and Kerry, reluctant to be the first to leave, waved the rest of the girls off before loading their own luggage into the back of Yaz's people carrier.

As Yaz started up the engine and changed CDs Helen looked over to the spot in the car park where just a few hours earlier Aiden had said all those amazing things. Never had she felt so conflicted.

'I just want to do the right thing,' said Helen aloud. 'Do the right thing and know that it's the right thing.'

'Well if you find out how to do that,' said Yaz turning down the music, 'make sure to bottle it and we can go into business flogging the stuff to mugs like you and me.'

It was five o'clock as Yaz pulled up in front of Helen's house having already dropped off the others at Kerry's. Helen looked up at her home, a late Edwardian four-bedroom terrace in the centre of West Bridgford, with

a mixture of trepidation and delight as she recalled the first time she and Phil had visited the house with the local estate agent. It had been part of a deceased estate and if she had been under any illusion about why it had been on the market for so long and priced so reasonably, all had become clear the moment they smelled the musty air, saw the vile woodchip wallpaper painted a sickly shade of orange and peered along the hallway into the kitchen where a pigeon was sitting on top of a disassembled moped.

Helen had hoped it would improve, that some quirky detail or original feature would capture her imagination and make her fall in love with the unlovable but there had been no such moment. The house was dark, dank and depressing and even though it was some sixty thousand pounds cheaper than similar sized houses in the road Helen felt that, even if they could get the price down by another ten thousand pounds as they had discussed, it would still be overpriced for what it would require to turn it around.

Phil had wanted it though. Leaving the house grinning like an idiot at all the potential he could see, he was talking about loft conversions and full-length kitchen extensions and knocking out walls and adding RSJs. Helen had tried desperately to share his vision, but no, she just couldn't see what he was seeing.

In the end Phil had left the decision in her hands. Yes, he loved the house but if she couldn't imagine them living in it then they would simply rent for a little while longer and carry on searching until they

found something that spoke to both of them with equal clarity.

Torn between trusting her own judgement and wanting to please Phil, she had struggled for over a week with the decision and only when they received a call from the estate agent to say that the vendor had received an offer from another couple did Helen finally make up her mind. That same afternoon they made an offer, which was accepted.

Over the months that followed as the guts of the house were ripped apart by builders and reassembled with the help of architects, Phil would often ask her what had changed her mind and Helen would always tell him that she didn't know, she just had a feeling.

Helen began unloading her luggage wishing that the same feeling would return. All she wanted was to be sure. To be convinced that a day wouldn't come when she wished she had chosen a different path.

'Are you going to be okay?' asked Yaz as they hugged goodbye.

'Never mind me,' said Helen. 'It's you I'm worried about. If you need anything this week, promise you'll call, okay?'

'Only if you promise to do the same.'

Helen stood on the pavement waving as Yaz pulled away before making her way along the front path to the door. As she reached in her pocket for her keys she heard her next-door neighbours' front door open.

197

'Afternoon, Helen,' said Mrs O'Brien cheerfully. 'Lovely weather we're having isn't it? How was your weekend away? Was it what you were expecting?'

Helen smiled. 'Not really, Mary. It wasn't what I was expecting at all.'

Stepping over the threshold Helen picked up the post from the floor. Most of it was junk mail or flyers from local takeaways. Tucking it under her arm she reached for the control panel of the burglar alarm, entered the code and then slipped off her flip-flops, walking barefoot through the kitchen to the fridge. She poured herself a glass of mineral water then sat down on one of the stools at the kitchen counter and began sorting through the mail.

There was little to get excited about: a couple of bills, a form from the tax office and a remittance statement from her agent for some voiceover work she had done in London a few months earlier.

Seeing the remittance statement started Helen off on a train of work-related thought: the meeting with her accountant that she needed to arrange, the task of getting her website updated and a million and one other things that she had been putting off until the wedding was out of the way.

She picked up a Biro and then, scanning the counter for something to write on, a notepad lying next to the microwave. She was about to begin scribbling down the mother of all to-do lists when she looked down at the pad and saw what was written there:

I, Philip Michael Hudson, choose you, Helen Leah Richards. I choose you to laugh with, I choose you to cry with. I choose to make my home with you. I choose to stand by you shoulder to shoulder against whatever obstacles come our way. I choose to comfort you when you are low. I choose to celebrate with you all of your successes. I choose to make you warm when you are cold. I choose to love you 'til I die. (And when I'm gone I'll choose to love you still.) I choose to be your confidant and lover. I choose to be your friend. Your buddy. I choose to make you smile. I choose you first above all others. I choose to share all I have and all I'll ever be because you make me what I am. But most of all I choose you, dear Helen, to be my wife, my life, my all. And I'll choose you to the end.

The sun had long since disappeared as Helen arrived at East Midlands airport and made her way towards Car Park 6. Leaving her car in the nearest free spot Helen walked to the bus stop for the transfer pickup along with a couple in their twenties and a young family with a small baby.

The bus to the terminal arrived and as Helen boarded she checked her watch for the third time in as many minutes. Phil's plane was due to have landed fifteen minutes earlier and while there was no way he could get through customs in so short a time, the longer the

transfer took the greater the chance of them missing each other would be.

Instead of proceeding straight to the terminal as Helen had hoped, the driver visited each of the five car parks in between picking up passengers and by the time they were making their approach to the terminal Helen was close to tears.

Racing to the front of the bus before it had stopped Helen ignored the driver's pleas for her to take a seat and practically flew from the bus when he finally opened the doors.

Entering the main departure lounge Helen looked up at the information screens frantically searching the arrivals board and soon found what she was looking for. Phil's flight from Amsterdam had been delayed by twenty minutes, so although he had landed there was a strong chance that he was still coming through customs.

Helen ran full pelt along the station concourse collecting curious looks from everyone she passed. She didn't care what all these strangers thought of her, she barely even registered them. All she cared about was seeing Phil and telling him how much she wanted them to stay together.

At the arrivals gate Helen came to a halt and waited, scanning the crowds for any sign of Phil and his friends. Just as she was about to give up all hope the doors opened and passengers began to emerge.

Helen ran over to the first person through, an elderly man with the air of a retired academic.

'Excuse me,' she asked. 'Which flight were you on?

I'm trying to find a friend who was on the Amsterdam flight. Was that yours by any chance?'

The man nodded. As Helen scanned the rest of the passengers her mind flipped back to that moment in the kitchen when she had opened up the notepad and saw Phil's vows written in his unmistakable scrawl. Helen had never felt so loved, so cherished, every word was perfect, every sentence a hymn to the life they had shared. Phil loved her. He really loved her, he always had and he always would. No one else could ever make her feel what she felt at this moment and now she wanted nothing more than to spend the rest of her life loving him in return.

Did Phil need to know what had happened during the weekend? Helen could see no justification at all for sharing her doubt. If there were a burden in keeping her secret then it would be borne by her alone. But for now, having overcome the greatest odds to reach this moment of absolute clarity, the story of how she had got there was nobody's concern but her own.